Mandy Nicholas
Jun 1992

EXCHANGE OF DOVES

KENNETH ROYCE

EXCHANGE OF DOVES

Hodder & Stoughton

LONDON SYDNEY AUCKLAND TORONTO

British Library Cataloguing in Publication Data

Royce, Kenneth, *1920–*
    Exchange of doves.
    Rn: Kenneth Royce Candley   I. Title
    823'.914 [F]

    ISBN 0-340-51343-8

Published by Hodder and Stoughton,
a division of Hodder and Stoughton Limited,
Mill Road, Dunton Green, Sevenoaks, Kent TN13 2YA.
Editorial Office: 47 Bedford Square, London WCIB 3DP.

Photoset by Rowland Phototypesetting Limited,
Bury St Edmunds, Suffolk
Printed in Great Britain by
St Edmundsbury Press Limited,
Bury St Edmunds, Suffolk

For
STELLA

1

The sign flickered and Towler thought it would go out. Even when the lights steadied he could only just make out the name of the hotel: The Florida. In a temperature of three below zero it was difficult to take the weak, intermittent glow in a Paddington back street seriously. The shabbiness of the hotel was almost lost in the darkness, the portico pillars of the entrance hiding their flaking plaster.

The visibility was not good; the street was lined with cars on both sides and it had not been easy to find an unrestricted view from half-way down sub-basement steps across the street. Towler, though frozen, resisted rubbing his hands or stamping his feet. He was trespassing and had no idea who lived in the basement apartment; but the uncomfortable situation was not new to him. Belfast, in February, could be much colder than London.

He kept his gloved hands in his pockets and watched a dog go past the railings close to his face. He drew back as the dog picked up his scent but the animal was too cold to linger. Towler focused across the street. He did not believe Mitwald would come out again; it was past midnight. And, anyway, he doubted the German's importance, but assessment was not his job.

The observation team used a van during the day but it was considered necessary to operate only one-man shifts during the night and nobody at all between 2am and 5am. Towler had his own ideas of why night duty invariably fell on him. He was on trial for this snotty lot of buggers in MI5. He had seen far more dangerous service than any of his new colleagues and perhaps that was part of the trouble; his face did not fit and they did not really want him. Besides, he was an 'other rank'.

Some of them even called him 'Sergeant' to make the point.

A shadow moved behind the glass panes of the hotel door but nobody came out. Someone appeared to stumble and the shadow fell down, disappearing from sight. Towler gripped the railings as a vivid memory returned, triggered by the falling shadow. Taffy had crumpled like that. As Towler lowered him to the ground, the blood turned the ice a sickly pink. Towler had not even heard the shot for there was a good deal of traffic noise coming from close by. Taffy had got one straight through the lung and had it not been for the angle the high velocity round might have passed straight through Towler, too.

Taffy died before Towler could use the radio, and the gurgling and frothing at the mouth was terrible to witness. Towler saw the radio shaking in his hand and his cold fingers fumbled the switch. Losing his best friend was just one more horror in a recent chain of horrors and he knew that his nerve was beginning to go. He was SAS, for Christ's sake, but even the toughest were, in the end, like all others.

He was drained and morose when he returned to quarters some time later, after Taffy's body had been spirited away. His colleagues knew what he suffered and rallied round as only men in action can. Perhaps he had done one tour too many, had been too long at undercover work, and not only in Ireland. The memory was so real that, as he kept an eye on the Hotel Florida, he momentarily lost contact with reality and looked around for the spreading blood patch. He shook his head to dismiss the nightmare and tried to undo the knots in his stomach.

The hotel door was opening and Towler was forced to concentrate as a figure appeared on the steps hunched in a topcoat; it was not Mitwald. Yet there was something familiar about the man's stance, even from this distance. He was dressed as a European but was an Arab. Despite the visibility, Towler was in no doubt. As though to make things easier for him, the man walked slowly down the steps and crossed the street towards him.

Towler eased down another step, his face just above street level. And then he remained absolutely still, wishing he was armed as his unease grew, but the department would not allow that. He was so used to carrying arms, on and off duty, that he felt undressed without a gun. As the Arab reached his side of the street, Towler got as good a look as he could expect in the dark. When he passed by, Towler listened to the fading footsteps until he could no longer hear them.

Towler stood watching his breath rise in vapourised clouds above the street while he considered what to do. His job was to keep an eye on Mitwald, not to dig up old memories. But he had seen that Arab before and he could not recall where. Not in Britain. Nor Europe. The Middle East? He had done a long tour of duty in Oman and a shorter one in Kuwait. He would have to report the sighting.

Soames gazed across the desk, aware that Towler was nervous; he did not make it easy for him. Even when he said 'sit down' it came out as a concession. Towler was no longer among his own kind and it was obvious he missed his weaponry; he kept adjusting his jacket and was sitting slightly forward as if he still carried something lethal in his hip pocket. As he studied him, Soames had to admit to himself that the sergeant looked desperately weary.

Years of undercover work had left its mark on the drawn, lined features. Towler looked tough and self-contained but something had gone from his eyes; they were tired, of course, but they no longer held the certainty and fire they once had. Clearly Towler was physically fit. Not much under six feet, his frame was lean and wiry and gave an impression that it was being recharged even as he sat. It was in the mind that he had suffered. The medical report stated that he needed a long spell of relief from field duty but, as Soames studied the new recruit who had been forced on him by his masters, he could not help but think that Towler, at thirty-four, had already burned himself out.

The middle-aged Soames had an irritating habit of tapping a pencil on his desk; to Towler, trained in total concentration, it was a weakness. Soames was flabby, his face unhealthily pasty. His thinning hair was combed forward to hide the bald patches. His eyes were sharp, though, and penetrating.

'I'm not clear what you are trying to tell me,' Soames said in a slightly supercilious tone. 'You saw this Arab? But you can't positively identify him. So?' The dark eyebrows lifted slightly. Soames' expression was pained, his annoyance conveyed through the ever-tapping pencil.

Towler suddenly wondered what he was doing there. If this was the typical scene it was a miracle the department ever caught a terrorist. 'Could you please stop doing that; it cuts through my thoughts.'

'Doing what?' Soames bridled, not used to this sort of insolence. 'Oh!' He tossed the pencil on to the desk. 'You're touchy, Sergeant. Not a good sign. Tell me about this Arab.' He sat back in his reclining chair, hands clasped, thumbs twiddling.

'I've seen him before. I think he's trouble.'

'A terrorist?'

'Not one who goes around planting bombs or shooting people. I think he's a professional agitator. He operated in the sheikdoms, stirring it up among the Shi'ites. Those small Arab countries live in constant fear of anti-government uprisings; they are so easily stage-managed and the authorities can't compete with the power of their big brothers in countries like Iran, who are always looking for a chance to destabilise pro-Western Arab states.'

'I had no idea,' Soames countered with heavy sarcasm. He reached for the pencil again but thought better of it. 'What's his name?'

'I don't know. He'll have several, none of them his own. Call him Abdul.'

'What do you think he is trying to stir up here?'

'I've no idea.' Towler could feel the doubt from across the desk and in return resented Soames' attitude. 'I'm only reporting what I saw. If you don't want me to, that's O.K. Just say the word and I'll ignore any baddie I come across.' He smiled slightly. 'It's the way I've been trained, you see; to pick 'em out. I thought you did the same here.' He watched Soames' tight-lipped control, then added, 'I shall still put the sighting in my report.' He was pleased with that; Soames could not now ignore the issue.

'So what do you suggest we do?'

'I thought that sort of decision would come from you.' Towler knew that he was getting reckless, but he was being made to feel that he did not belong to 'Five' and he no longer cared. 'Look, this bloke is not here on holiday. He'll be on assignment. And as he operates in the Middle East his presence here needs some explanation.'

Soames nodded; his first sign of agreement. 'All right. You take care of it.'

In his old unit Towler would have been in no doubt as to what that meant but he was not used to the new set of rules, if there were any at all. 'What does that mean?'

Soames was surprised. 'Keep an eye on him.'

'On my own?'

'We can't spare extra men. Not at this stage at any rate. You say you've identified an unlisted Arab whose name you do not know, who hitherto operates only in the Middle East, and about whom you could, in any event, be wrong. Give me something more concrete and I'll action it. Meanwhile I will, of course, take you off the Mitwald surveillance. Just do the best you can.'

There was no way one man could cope with such a surveillance. 'If we check with Hereford we'll probably find they have somebody in the Middle East who can give a positive ID on Abdul.'

Soames was late to grasp what Towler was saying. He stared across the desk without expression and then said slowly, 'Are you saying we should fly someone back from the Middle East to identify this man?'

'It would save a lot of time.'

Soames hesitated. 'Do you think there is going to be an attack on our Royal family?'

Towler could see he would not get anywhere. 'There might be; this guy is an organiser.' He rose. 'I take it that you don't think it important enough, sir?'

Soames was careful how he replied. Towler had a reputation in his own field and had already shown his contempt for Soames' judgment. But here, in the offices of MI5 in Curzon Street, he was nothing. 'Just get me a little more evidence, old boy, before we start using the taxpayers' money fruitlessly.'

It was a ridiculous surveillance but Sam Towler did manage to scrounge a small plain van which he had difficulty in parking every day. He had to get as near to the hotel as possible and that was sometimes not near enough. He quickly discovered that late night was Abdul's favourite time for leaving the hotel which meant that he could remain in the cab rather than crawl through to the uncomfortable rear. It was freezing cold anyway and he kept some blankets in the back and wrapped up warm for the cab.

The daytime vigil was scrappy. No man could keep up observation round the clock, so he had to pick out what he considered the most likely times. Three nights later Abdul left the hotel about the same time Towler had first seen him. Towler climbed from the van.

It was not a night for lingering lovers. The only sound was litter being moved by a light, biting wind. Both men knew how to move silently and coped well with the treacherous ice patches.

Abdul performed the usual moves to shake off a tail. What more confirmation than that should Soames need to convince him that Abdul was on a job? Towler followed, used to all the ruses.

The sudden approach of a car forced Towler to slip between two parked cars and keep his head down. The headlights were dimmed and the car stopped about forty feet away. Abdul climbed in and the car eased forward. It was impossible for Towler to get a clear view of the driver as it went past but he was convinced it was a European.

There was nothing left for Towler to do but traipse back to the van in the increasing cold. As he walked through the empty streets he reasoned he had enough to convince Soames that Abdul was worth watching.

When Abdul checked out the next day, luckily at a time Towler was watching in the van, he booked in at another hotel not more than five hundred yards away. Towler realised that it would be dangerous to use the same van and, at last, a slightly worried Soames reluctantly put on a full surveillance team. Abdul stayed two nights at the new hotel before moving on to yet a third, still in the Paddington area. At that point Soames had to agree he would very much like to know what Abdul was up to.

There were two ways of finding out: keep him under permanent surveillance until something happened, or pull him in and squeeze the truth from him. The latter was a method that saved men and time. Soames had been getting away with a great deal for a long time; it was necessary for the protection of the State against its enemies, so many of them fanatical, and perhaps he was right. He decided to pull Abdul in.

They waited until Abdul went out on one of his jaunts two nights later. Towler was part of the team because he could point the finger at Abdul. It was an operation which must not be seen by outside witnesses; Abdul would simply disappear. So they waited until Abdul was well clear of the hotel, and, on Towler's advice, arranged for a van to approach from the opposite direction much as the car had done which collected the Arab.

Figures came out of the darkness and Abdul was surrounded before he knew what was happening. He was quickly gagged and bundled into the van just as the car came heading towards them. The driver must have seen something of what happened because the car squealed to a halt and the driver brilliantly spun it round, aided by the icy conditions. There was a shattering of glass and a faint screech of metal as the car struck others each side of the road, and then it was away in a plume of exhaust fumes and disappearing tail-lights. By this time the van was also on its way.

How much of Abdul's kidnapping had been seen by the car driver was impossible to judge, but Soames was not pleased about it when told. Abdul was locked away in a comfortable cell in a small mews hideout, referred to by Five as the 'Mayfair Suite'.

There were two cells, luxurious as cells go. A bed, small table and chairs and an en-suite toilet and shower in each. The whole place was geared to surveillance; listening bugs and TV scanners all unobtrusively placed. They might as well have been on open view as the only people likely to be contained in the cells would expect them to be there.

Soames visited Abdul the following morning to find him quite cheerful, as if the Arab knew he would not be detained for long. Soames was now as intrigued as Towler.

Soames entered the cell, the padded door being closed behind him. The Arab had been searched for weapons and knew he was being watched through a peephole in the door and by the scanners. Soames was in no danger. He pulled a chair from under the small table and straddled it, arms along the back. Abdul was sitting on the bed, a slight figure now that his topcoat had been removed; it was warm in the cell. He was clean-shaven, face thin and bony as were his long-fingered hands. His black hair was cut quite short. His clothes were cheap but in good condition and he wore thick-soled boots. He spoke before Soames could ask his first question.

'What name would you like me to give?'

'You seem very sure of yourself. Any name will do; just something to call you by.'

'Then you choose one. I am sure of myself because you have no reason to hold me here and will have to let me go.'

'We probably will let you go. But in what condition depends on you. Meanwhile nobody knows you are here. Think about it.'

'It won't take my friends long to find out. You will then be in trouble for you are holding me illegally.'

'You know who we are?'

'Of course. Who else would be so heavy-handed but your Security Service.'

Soames, not put out by any of this, said sweetly, 'Then we'll have to move fast. Why are you here in London?'

Sam Towler sat with shoeless feet on his bed, his back against the headboard. It was 2am, and a gas fire threw warmth and fumes into the room. His bedsitter had a small kitchen-diner attached and he had his own shower-room and toilet; a luxury in this part of Kilburn. But the Security Service wanted him to have reasonable privacy so long as he worked for them, and they had been forced to help. There was no way he could afford an apartment like this on his army pay.

Towler was not enjoying what he was doing. Life had been turning sour before Taffy Williams was killed by an IRA bullet. It had nothing to do with disillusion. He still fervently believed in what he had been doing. He had enjoyed the finest mates in the world, men he knew would always protect his back. Yet he had not protected Taffy's back so well that night in Belfast. There was no point in going over the reasons; he knew them all. He did not have to make excuses to himself or anyone else.

Perhaps he was getting beyond the demands made upon him. They had been going on for so long.

To a man who had served so honourably and well, the mere danger of losing his nerve was almost impossible to face. Perhaps the doctors were right, he simply needed a rest. But that did not tie in with farming him out to MI5, with whom he had worked closely at times in Ulster. But they were different in London; they were not under guerilla warfare conditions. They seemed to him to be a coterie to which he did not belong.

He was not married although there was one girl he would very much have liked to marry. But she was a Catholic in Armagh and her brother had been up to his eyeballs in IRA activity before he was shot dead by the SAS. The sister had been the one who spirited the weapons away, so that the cry that her brother was unarmed at the time could be relayed through the world press. Towler knew she had done it but kept silent. From that moment he held the potential romance at a distance. It was not easy to do but he knew there could be no hope for either of them with the pressures that would follow.

Perhaps that had been the start of a gradual wearing down of his nerves? He would maintain that he had put the incident, and the dreams of love, well behind him, but could he ever know for certain? It was a part of his life that he kept to himself; he never told the doctors.

His life had now changed in a way he neither liked nor really understood. To switch off from being on a daily knife-edge affected him more than the constant pressures of fear. He could cope with being in danger but now all he had to do was surveillance and report to plum-in-the-mouth Civil Service types like Soames. He realised that there was much more to the plumping and balding Soames than that but no real attempt had been made to make him feel welcome at Curzon Street. It seemed that the department did not take too kindly to those they saw as the death-and-glory boys; the field operators would be seen to be more in line with MI6 than Five.

It might all be in his mind but Towler did not think so for he felt too uncomfortable in his new job. Maybe it was just *him* they disliked. Perhaps he was too blunt for them for he had never been one for bullshit. And maybe he was beginning to feel just a little too sorry for himself. He faced that one head on; it was just another form of danger. The answer to that was that he would rather return to Ulster than stay with Five. Any day.

Towler began to undress, throwing his clothes untidily on to a chair. For years he had folded his clothes neatly, and his blankets the next morning. But it was an immediate give-away when undercover; he had learned how to be untidy. Once in bed, loneliness took over. He heard the gas fire hissing; he had forgotten to turn it off. For an awful, uncaring moment he no longer cared whether it was on or off or even if the flame went out and the gas continued. He felt at rock bottom. He missed his mates and was out of his element. And he had had far too much time to think about the girl who could only remain a dream.

Late the next day Soames summoned Towler to his office. He was just a shade less hostile and even softened his voice as he bade Towler to sit down. The old leather chairs were like club chairs, a comparison not lost on Towler. The pencil tapping started as Soames reasserted his authority and said, 'Are you absolutely certain you can't give me any more information about Abdul?'

So they had got nothing from him. 'I think the Omanis were watching him. Like all these things, there was an overlap and I saw him now and again and always in a crowd. But he wasn't my pigeon. A wired mug shot to Oman might sort it out. Or Hereford should have someone who can identify him.'

'Yes, well I'm not too keen for it to be known that he is here. You say he's an agitator?'

'So far as I know. But he wouldn't be over here for that; there are enough of them here already.'

'And you're satisfied that he's not an assassin of any kind?'

'He wasn't then. But I'm going back a bit. I gather he hasn't said too much. Do you want me to try him?'

Soames almost shuddered. 'We have skilled men working on him but it takes time.' He gave a nod of dismissal. 'I just wondered if you could produce a little more.'

2

Kate Parker was a striking girl. She was tall and walked like the model she had once briefly been. In her late twenties, she had long, pale gold hair, good bone structure, and soft hazel eyes which surveyed life with faint amusement. Her career so far had been varied: modelling, a little acting and TV advertising, and at present she ran a health club in which she held half the financial stake. She was a good advertisement for her profession.

The health club was positioned behind the BBC Television studios at Shepherd's Bush and was not the easiest place to find. But its reputation was growing with an increasing clientele, many of whom were in the entertainment business and came to keep in trim. Kate and her partner Suzie Trent, another small-time actress, took alternate classes.

This particular night was no different from most others except that Kate had stayed on after everyone else had gone, to bring the books up-to-date. The figures were pleasing and she was in a good mood. The club was above a greengrocer's who owned the premises, but both girls believed they would soon be able to afford a better place. She locked up and went down the stairs beside the shop and locked the narrow street door. The shop itself had been closed for several hours but behind it was a small yard with a garage. The yard itself was often crowded with empty crates but there was enough space for the girls to keep their cars.

Kate went round the back dangling her car keys and cursing the cold. It was so dark she produced a pencil torch to pick her way through the crates, but she had no time to switch the torch on. There was a sudden, excruciating pain on the back of her head, and she collapsed among a pile of rotting cabbage

17

leaves. Two young Arabs lifted her up and carried her towards her car using her keys to open the doors.

She was laid in the back quite gently but one of the men leaned across the seat to bind and gag her. He then shifted her position and climbed in beside her. The other one drove, crushing a crate in his haste. By the time she came to they were clear of London and on the M40 to Oxford and Wales.

The Right Honourable James Dawson, Home Secretary in Her Majesty's Government, was in the House of Commons to attend a debate on the continuing increase in crime, when he received a note. The debate had yet to start, and, intrigued and just a shade concerned, he went to the Central lobby where the white-gloved Badge Messenger directed a moderately well dressed young man towards him. Dawson took the man to be an Arab; certainly Middle Eastern.

Dawson was polite and led the way to one of the curved, padded benches on full view to anyone in the lobby. He glanced at the note and then at the young nervous stranger by his side. 'I'm afraid I can't give you much time, Mr Arani. I'm soon due in the chamber. Now what do you know of Kate Parker? Are you a friend?'

'At the moment, sir, I most assuredly am. Otherwise she would be dead.'

Dawson stiffened. He quickly gazed around him. The hall was loosely crowded and there was the comforting presence of police. The security check was only yards away. Acidly he said, 'You'd better explain yourself'. He noticed that the young man was agitated, his fingers intertwining.

Arani coughed. The stiff-backed, grey-haired Cabinet Minister could be a forbidding figure. He knew him to be generally quietly spoken but he had also heard he could be formidable; it seemed like that now. But he knew what to say and stuck to it. 'At the moment she is alive and well but that will change if we do not receive your help.'

Dawson quickly gazed over to the nearest policeman and half rose.

'If anything happens to me she will be killed at once,' added Arani.

Dawson sat down slowly. This was ridiculous. He was surrounded by security yet this seemingly innocuous young man was threatening him in the very heart of the mother of parliaments, on open view. He had only to shout, for help to come. He did not. Instead he took a new interest in the Arab and could see nothing to suggest he might be a cold-blooded killer. 'What do you want?'

'Your Security Service is holding a man in an illegal prison in Mayfair. You must know of this place; or perhaps you prefer not to. We want that man set free and Miss Parker will be released unharmed.'

The Arab was well educated, spoke good English and it occurred to Dawson that he might be one of the many Arab students in Britain. No doubt one of his own departments had sanctioned his entry into the country.

'So you've kidnapped her?' It was a fatuous question but Dawson had to know the truth or whether this was a gigantic bluff.

'We collected her after she left her health club last night. We expect you to check, of course, but there's little time.'

'Who is this man you say we have?'

'Who he is does not matter. He was picked up in Paddington while out walking. He is not important but we want him back at once. We must have this agreed by tomorrow.'

Dawson was beginning to cut through his confusion and, yes, fear. Whoever he was dealing with was not short of nerve, and if they did not get their way it endorsed their intention. Just the same he must have time to check.

'You understand that our policy is not to deal with terrorists. An exchange could not be sanctioned.' Dawson was scared by his own words.

'Normally this is so. But this is not an ordinary exchange. Your Prime Minister will not know that MI5 have our man. You yourself are not yet sure. It will all be done quietly without fuss and nobody but ourselves will ever know. We want no publicity from this. That is important to us.' Arani smiled. 'An exchange of doves, Minister. No one will get hurt.'

Dawson was gazing at Arani thinking he was out of his mind. How could this be happening in the Central lobby of the

House of Commons under the noses of so many witnesses? It was crazy. But he had been taken by surprise and the whole business was so preposterous that it had to be true.

'You say nobody but ourselves will know. But if the Security Service have him, then they already know. I'm in a difficult position.'

'So are they. They are holding him illegally.' Arani rose. 'I will contact you tomorrow evening. I will ring you at home. It won't matter if you have your phone tapped for I shall use a call box. But you would be foolish if you decided to call in your police force.'

Without another word, Arani walked towards the main exit. And the man who was overlord of all the police forces in Britain, who could have called up all the help he needed, sat still on the padded bench, pale and shaken and indecisive. But he would do nothing that might hurt Kate.

The debate had seemed the longest of his life and Dawson believed he had given his worst performance. In fact he was far too professional to let himself down and nobody noticed his growing distress as he dealt with the demanding questions of the Opposition. It was late evening before he got away and as he sat in his car to be driven from the Palace of Westminster, it was one time when he could have done without the police bodyguard sitting beside the chauffeur. He had once been Secretary for Northern Ireland and a bodyguard was a permanent feature of his life.

He was tempted to use the car phone. Instead he instructed the driver to take him to an address in one of the charming little mews tucked away behind Park Lane. As he mounted the steps of the house his bodyguard stood by the car below trying not to look cold. Dawson ran his fingers down the tenants panel and pressed the appropriate bell. 'James Dawson,' he announced into the box. The front door release immediately buzzed and he entered the discreetly lit hall.

Nigel Prescott was waiting at the elevator when it stopped on the top floor and Dawson stepped out. The two men shook hands as Prescott led the way to his apartment.

'An unexpected pleasure, Minister.'

'I should have telephoned, Bluie, but this is rather private. Is Celia in?'

As Prescott led the way into a magnificent drawing-room, tastefully furnished and set off by soft, shot-silk drapes at the large windows, he knew that Dawson was indicating that what he had to say was not for his wife Celia's ears. 'Gone to the ballet with some friends. She'll be sorry she missed you.' Professional lies tripped out smoothly as a daily ration; Prescott was Deputy Director of the Security Service.

Once they had brandy balloons cupped in their hands and were seated on opposite sofas, Prescott said, 'It must be important for you to come unannounced. As you know I'm often late back.' And then with sudden concern, 'Have you eaten, Minister?'

'I'm not hungry. And this is not a formal meeting, Bluie; do be yourself. Cheers.' Dawson needed the spirit but was well aware that he was drinking on an empty stomach and must keep his wits about him. The man opposite him was big and turning to fat. He had a full head of dark hair, mysteriously not turning grey, and the brown eyes were ever-watchful, even when smiling as now. He was a powerful figure in every way and the vibrancy of the man was tangible.

Dawson quickly gazed around him while he considered how to start. Prescott's salary would not cover the expensive tastes so well displayed about the room; he had a large private income, having inherited a family fortune. He was called Bluie because of his Oxford days when he had played rugby football for the university. As Dawson gazed back at the open scrutiny from his host he knew that Prescott was aware that anything concerning State security should be raised with Sir Malcolm Read, Director of MI5, and not his chief deputy.

Prescott dropped the small talk as a direct invitation to Dawson to get on with it. He could see that the Minister was close to floundering and that was most unlike him. He even detected a trace of fear and the reluctance to voice it was obvious. So he just waited, embarrassing Dawson into making some kind of statement. He could not recall seeing this kind of uncertainty in the grey-haired, almost military figure, sitting opposite him; it rang a faint note of alarm.

Dawson's fingers tightened round the bowl of his glass. 'I

have a personal problem. Kate Parker has been kidnapped by Arabs and will only be released when your boys release an Arab they picked up in Paddington.'

That was direct enough. 'Whom are we holding?'

'I've no idea. No names were mentioned. I'm not even sure when it happened but would guess during the last few days. I'm told you are holding him somewhere in Mayfair.' Dawson knew exactly where but thought it best not to give that impression.

Prescott conceded the legitimacy of the evasion. 'I'm unaware that we have this man. I'd be surprised if we have.'

'But you will check?'

'Of course.' Prescott put his goblet down. 'Will you excuse me while I make a telephone call from my study? I keep the scrambler in my desk drawer.'

Dawson watched him leave the room. Prescott moved quietly for a big man and Dawson noticed a faint limp of which he had not previously been aware; perhaps caused by an old rugby injury or simply the extreme weather. He was considering irrelevancies – his mind was so numb he did not really know how to cope. But he had kept calm, at least outwardly, and had at last related his problem to someone he hoped might help.

Prescott returned, giving Dawson a nod as he sat down. 'Well, you're right. We are holding an unknown Arab. How exactly did you get this information?'

Dawson told him and Prescott found it difficult not to grin. 'You've got to hand it to him. Right on the doorstep. They wouldn't do that unless they were extremely worried.'

'No.'

'How would they know about Kate Parker?'

'That was my question to you. Clearly you know about her.'

'It's my job to know. But this couldn't be something they've just learned; it had to be on file for them to action it so quickly.'

'It's an open secret. It's dreadful that they should use her like this. Will you help?'

'Arrange an exchange?'

'Of course arrange an exchange.'

'The PM wouldn't stand for it.'

'The PM would never know.'

22

Prescott raised heavy brows. 'I don't think either of us believes that. Frankly, I don't believe in exchanges either.'

'I'm asking as a personal favour, Bluie.'

'Why me? Why not Sir Malcolm?'

Dawson took a thoughtful sip of his drink. 'There's nothing I can offer him, and anyway, he's due to retire in six months. I'm unlikely to lose my job in that time. I can help you fill the gap.'

A bribe. But not an unpleasant one. Prescott smiled. 'It's a very dangerous favour you are asking of me. If it goes wrong you might lose your appointment but, after a while, you'd be back in the Cabinet in some other post. If I go I'll go for good.'

'You're far too valuable.'

Prescott was tempted but slowly shook his head.

Dawson said, 'You do realise I can't agree to your holding this man in this way. There would be hell to pay if that got out.'

'We can hold him under the Anti-Terrorist Act, as you well know.'

'But you are not, are you? He's not in a police cell where your form would be cramped. You have him where you can use your little ways to make him talk. And I'll bet that you didn't get Special Branch to pull him in to make it all nice and official. Don't be difficult with me, Bluie. I'm ready to risk my office for this.'

'Seemingly, mine too.' The exchange had suddenly sharpened. Prescott was seeing the tougher side of Dawson.

'Don't be absurd. Anyway you're the last person anyone would believe to be agreeable to an exchange. I can't stand by and let her die like this. I love this girl. I'll do anything for her.'

'More than for your own family?'

Dawson winced and almost lost his temper. But he needed this man's help. 'Certainly as much. Perhaps more. I don't expect you to understand.'

'I had to know just how much you are emotionally involved.'

'Now you know.'

Prescott was uncomfortable and, seeing this, Dawson added, 'What on earth can you possibly do with him? You can't force confessions from him because you know that I know he's there.

Charge him? You'd have done that already if there was real evidence against him. Execute him? Let him go?'

Prescott was aware that Abdul was being held illegally and so far had shown no inclination to talk; it can take a long time to break down such a man. Sooner or later they must make charges, have him quietly assassinated, or deport him. Prescott liked the Minister and knew that his own department was on very thin ice. Especially now. 'I don't like it but I'll see what can be done.'

Dawson was relieved and showed it. 'This isn't your average terrorist deal. There are no demands for the mass release of prisoners, safe transit or money. For whatever reason, they want no more publicity than we do.'

It was a point that worried Prescott a good deal. It made him wonder again, just who was Abdul? 'I'll set it in motion.'

On instructions from Prescott, Soames reluctantly left his home to go to the 'Mayfair Suite' that same evening. He did not know why Abdul was to be released and he was not too concerned, for the Arab was becoming an embarrassment. He turned out that night because these matters were never so simple as just letting someone walk out of the front door; there had to be a degree of disorientation to make the prisoner bewildered and unsure. And, anyway, Prescott had told him an exchange was involved, which considerably intrigued him.

On arrival at the 'Suite' he spent a few minutes trying to persuade Abdul to talk and got no further than before. Eventually he said, 'All right, you win. We intend to release you back to your friends tomorrow. An exchange will be arranged; nothing of note.' Abdul remained stony-faced; up to the last he was giving nothing away. There was a moment, just as Soames left the cell, when he believed Abdul was about to speak, but it was too late and he locked the door behind him.

When Soames returned to the 'Mayfair Suite', early the next morning, he went straight to Abdul's cell. He looked through the spy hole, stood there for some moments in thought, and then turned to stand with his back to the door. He broke his reverie and suddenly strode quickly towards the staff room. He waited a moment before quietly opening the door.

Jerry Cutter, the Duty Officer, was seated in one of the

24

armchairs facing the battery of television monitors with his head lolling forward on his chest. He was asleep, an open magazine still propped on his knees. Soames scanned the monitors before stepping across the room to switch off the main control. The screens went blank and Cutter began to wake up, the magazine slipping through his legs to the floor.

'Must have dozed off.' Cutter struggled to rouse himself barely able to see the hazy figure of Soames but fully aware of who was there. As he climbed unsteadily to his feet he expected a blasting from his chief. And then he noticed that the screens had gone dead. Fully awake now he gazed at Soames.

'You're lucky,' said Soames mildly. 'Abdul no longer matters. Go home and catch up on the rest of your sleep.'

This was not like Soames at all but Cutter did not argue; he had literally been caught napping. 'Sorry about that, sir. Not like me at all. What's to happen to him?'

'We'll let him go. By the way, who was on duty before you?'

'The new fellow. Towler.'

Soames nodded as if expecting the answer. It was increasingly clear to Cutter that Soames wanted him to leave at once. As he left he thought it was strange that Soames was there so early in the morning, particularly as he did not appear too well.

3

After his late-night duty Sam Towler was tired and surprised to be called in so early in the morning.

Soames came straight to the point as he passed a list of names across the desk; they were all Middle Eastern, mainly Arab. There were eight of them. 'I want you to check with the registry that those people are all where they are reported to be. I want it done today. I would also like to know whether or not they are living alone, have girlfriends, or whatever. You can get mug shots from the registry. It's urgent.'

Towler studied the list in detail.

'Don't think you are being used as a dogsbody, Sergeant. This is much more important than watching Abdul or Mitwald. I am relying on you entirely.'

In spite of Soames' reassurance Towler still felt like an odd-job man. As he looked across the desk he realised that Soames did not look at all well. The pasty face was paler, and was moist along the hair line. And he was not playing with his pencil. Whatever bugged him had disrupted Soames' routine; he simply was not himself.

'Are you all right?' Towler had great difficulty in calling Soames, 'sir', so did so infrequently.

Soames looked up. It was doubtful if he actually saw Towler just then. 'Quite all right, thank you. Do get on with the job.'

Towler left the room thinking Soames was ill. He glanced at the sheet in his hand and ran down the stairs to the main computer-room.

'God Almighty, what an unholy mess!'

Soames had hardly entered the top-floor office before Prescott shot out the words.

Soames crossed the floor; it was still only 10.30 in the morning but he felt as if he had already worked a full day and would rather go home. He sat down in the usual chair, unheeding of Prescott's mood; he was suddenly beyond caring but knew that Prescott would not allow that attitude to persist.

'You'd better explain.'

'I can't. It's incomprehensible.'

'What about the Duty Officer?'

'No problem.'

Prescott glared. 'I hope your judgment is better on that appraisal than the last. A young woman is likely to be killed because of this.' Prescott gazed acidly at his subordinate. 'They won't let her die pleasantly. She'll suffer.'

'Who is she?'

Prescott let the question go. 'My own head is on the block. You'd better find a solution, quickly.'

Soames was inwardly fuming. Prescott could burble about an exchange but what was he hiding? Who had he intended to get back? He sensed something of enormous importance. It had all started out as nothing, simply picking up what he considered to be a small-time Arab agitator. He should not have listened to that damned sergeant in the first place; he did not belong in the Security Service; he should have been off-loaded on to Special Branch. Prescott was waiting for his reply; he was going to be the scapegoat. 'You still want this exchange to go through?'

'The girl is not expendable.'

Soames stirred uncomfortably; 'About Abdul . . .'

'I think it better you don't mention that name again,' Prescott cut in.

'We'll have to find someone else. A ringer.'

Prescott turned sideways in his swivel chair. In profile he was even more forbidding, a huge threatening outline. 'You don't think they'd notice?'

Soames fidgeted. 'Not if it took place in the dark.'

'Once they had him back they would know.'

Soames found new strength. 'It really depends on how important the return of this hostage is. If her return is imperative then *someone* will have to be expendable. We'll have to make it look like somebody else's job. It could turn out to be complicated.'

'As complicated as trying to explain to those concerned why we failed to prevent the ghastly murder of an innocent young woman? If this gets out we'll be crucified. If the press gets so much as a smell of it there'll be questions asked in parliament. And can you imagine what the Civil Rights lobby will make of it? Nobody will believe what happened. Nobody will want to believe.' Prescott rubbed his temple. 'How long will it take to find someone?'

'A day or two. Once we have one singled out . . .'

'I asked how long, not the damned detail; that's your problem.' Prescott held up a restraining hand as Soames was about to reply. 'Get this straight. I want nothing coming back to us. Nothing. Even as we stand, we're in trouble.'

'A delay will have to be arranged.'

'I'll deal with that.' Prescott glowered. 'If you think you have problems you should have what I've now got to handle. I must have an operational date as soon as you're ready; forty-eight hours at most. Anything longer will be too late.' Prescott swivelled round to face Soames squarely. He could not shy from the grave position they were in. He himself was keeping the information from the Head of the Service, Sir Malcolm Read, and that alone could lose him his job. But he was committed to the Home Secretary.

Prescott sat quite still, unnerving Soames by saying nothing for some time. Eventually he said, 'Why don't you like this SAS sergeant you've taken on?'

Soames found that question more easy to answer. 'He was forced on to us. I thought you had played a part, sir.'

'Not me. I believe the PM heard about him, and was sympathetic to his plight; probably had a word with the Director. Towler's only here for a trial period. It's up to you as to whether he finally makes the grade. Is that all you've got against him?'

Soames was careful, wondering whether Prescott was cunningly trying to show him the way. 'I don't think he's the right type. He should have gone somewhere like Special Branch. He's too used to the gun for us.'

'Why don't you come out with what's on your mind?'

Why was Prescott pushing the matter? 'I just don't think he belongs. His style is not ours. I concede he has had a very rough time in Ulster, and in that context has done valuable work. But he's battle-weary. And I think his nerve has gone. I think he's seen one corpse too many. He's not in good mental shape; he seems to have too much on his mind. I also think, and I hope this is not taken the wrong way, that he'd be happier in the Sergeants' Mess than with us. I am sure, if he himself was asked, that would be his answer.'

'What's his family background?'

'He was an adopted child. His real parents are unknown. His legal parents both died in a car crash some twelve years ago when he was already in the army. I think they left him some money.'

'Not a happy background?'

'I understand he had a great regard for his adoptive parents but their deaths could account for why he drove himself so hard later on.'

'A loner?'

'He operated alone a good deal; of necessity in that job. And the sort of team-work he used was not the same as ours. The approach of the two services is entirely different.'

Prescott wondered if Soames' bigotry had got in the way of his judgment. 'Not officer material, then?'

Soames saw the trap. 'I'm in no position to judge; I was not his CO. Is this important, sir?'

Prescott dropped his gaze for a second. 'That's up to you, Soames. You've got to use all the facilities you have available, and you've precious little time.'

They met outside the National Gallery and stood on the top step under the enormous pillared canopy. An almost deserted Trafalgar Square lay before them, the pigeons scratching for food. The fountains had been switched off due to the freeze-up and the empty ponds appeared forlorn. Apart for the traffic travelling endlessly round the Square, coming up from Whitehall and Northumberland Avenue, or being flanked by the exodus from the Strand, the scene was a tableau of near misery. People hurried to get into buses or taxis or anywhere where there was a little warmth. Overlording it all, an impervious Nelson stood on his column against heavy snow-filled, grey skies.

The two men turned into the gallery. Prescott, huge in a topcoat, and limping very slightly, said to the slighter, hatless figure of Dawson, 'There's been a small complication. Nothing serious, but it will hold things up for a day or two.'

Dawson was uncomfortable, already aware that he had been recognised by gallery visitors. 'I don't like it. What do I tell them?'

They gazed at a bearded face above a splendid ruff, both too preoccupied to care who it was the canvas portrayed. 'When are you expecting contact?'

'Probably this evening. He said I would be telephoned at home. You haven't answered my question, Bluie.'

'Simply tell them that the deal is on, but for reasons beyond your control it will take a few days to set up. They should understand that. Do you want a bug on your phone?'

'*No!*' And then more quietly, 'He said he would be using a call box. Anyway he won't stay on long enough for a trace.' Dawson shrugged. 'I don't like the idea of a delay. What's happened?'

'Nothing. But we have to arrange a time and a place and it needs some planning. We don't want anyone to be seen or caught. When he phones, just tell him.'

Dawson nodded unhappily. 'I must get back. We're acting like a couple of spies meeting like this.'

Prescott laughed. 'It's better than meeting in your office or mine. I'll advise you the moment we're ready. And please don't worry. Everything will be fine.'

It was late evening by the time Towler had finished checking on the eight people on his list. They all lived in London but were quite scattered so that he had travelled a lot in the Ford Escort allotted to him from 'Transport'. They were all young, many were Iranian and all were Moslems. Some of them were students at the LSE.

He had a meal in a café off the Strand before returning to Curzon Street. He agreed with the security which demanded that all reports be made out on the premises. Anyway he did not like working at home, and when he finally arrived there the loneliness set in as always. He no longer had mates to talk to and the dream of a love affair that could never be was even more remote here. He felt not only shut off, but shut out.

It was too late to go to a cinema so he went to bed early. His telephone rang at 2.30 in the morning telling him to meet Soames at the office straightaway.

James Dawson received a telephone call about the same time as Sam Towler went to bed. He had been agitated all evening, a fact not lost on his pleasantly featured, fair-haired wife. They had eaten late and she could not help but notice that he played with his food and ate little. Sandra Dawson was a good cook and was irritated by his sudden loss of appetite.

'What's on your mind, darling?' She had to repeat the question to draw the answer that all was well. Quite obviously it was anything but. She was puzzled. His job produced immense problems, of course, but he seldom brought them into the house. She sensed, without knowing why, that his present preoccupation had nothing to do with his job. 'Is it anything you want to talk about, Jimbo?'

'I'm sorry,' he said across the dining-table. 'You know me too well. It's one of those niggling security problems I can't really discuss. I'm waiting for a telephone call about it and it's late.'

He helped her put the crockery in the dishwasher and switched it on. Their two children were both grown-up and leading their own lives; Jenny was married and expecting her first baby and Tony had a job in banking in America. They caught the BBC news half-way through and the telephone rang just before it finished.

'I'll take it in the study,' Dawson said quickly.

He made sure he closed the study door behind him and rushed for the telephone. 'Dawson.'

'Are we in business?'

The accent was far more noticeable over the telephone. 'Of course, but . . .'

'Then we'll exchange tomorrow night. Listen carefully . . .'

'Tomorrow night is impossible,' Dawson cut in desperately. 'There are complications. We must have a day or two to prepare.'

'Prepare what? Why are you stalling? Tomorrow night, or it will be too late.'

'I'm not in control of the detail. There is no funny business.' Dawson was already beginning to wonder whether, in fact, there might be. Was Prescott up to something? He was so concerned with Kate's plight that it had not occurred to him before. There would be hell to pay if he was. 'Can you ring at this time tomorrow when I might have more news for you? Believe me, nothing has changed. Or give me a number to contact.'

'Don't be stupid. I will pass your message on. They won't like it. There can be no reason why the exchange should not be done tomorrow night. This is highly suspicious.'

'You have the girl, for God's sake. Use your head. I can't afford to take risks.'

'I'll be in touch. If I'm not, then forget the girl.'

Dawson shouted out but his caller had hung up. He put down the telephone, his hand shaking. He should have known better than to expect a reasonable attitude. Prescott had been too plausible. He considered phoning him there and then, but was too worried and confused. He needed time to think things out. And he must calm down and try to act normally before returning to Sandra in the drawing-room. He edged round his desk in a daze.

Kate Parker had remembered very little about the journey. Her head was very close to the floor of the car and her first recollection was the dust irritating her nostrils and the tremendous pain at the back of her head. She heaved at the rough motion and because of the awkward way she was positioned.

She did not know what had happened but gradually realised she was in a fast-moving car and was being kept out of sight. She knew she had been hit hard on the head because of the pain but she could not remember the blow. It was difficult to think things through like this. She had obviously been kidnapped and at first struggled in panic thinking she had been taken by a sex maniac.

Kate slowly concluded that whoever had taken her must surely have a different motive. There were at least two men, for there was one sitting beside her on the rear seat and there must be at least one in the front. She was bound hand and foot but, so far as she could tell, had not been physically harmed apart from the terrible blow on the head. It was a miracle that she could think at all.

When she tried to struggle up she was forced down again and the unnatural position began to distress her more than the pain. She passed out again and when she recovered found that her position had been slightly changed. She was on the floor of the car, wedged between the front and rear seats. Her head was now upright although she could see nothing.

She felt a leg near her head and she said with a groan, 'Did you have to blindfold me as well?'

Nobody answered. She tried to shift her position and the leg moved away. From then on she drifted. The journey seemed endless and it was clear that nobody intended to communicate with her. Why were they doing this?

They reached hilly country and the roads curved more noticeably. She had no idea where they were, nor for how long they had been travelling. She was increasingly afraid, finding the absence of talk ominous and difficult to bear. She must have drifted again, for the next thing she knew they had stopped and there was something strange about the utter silence. They were obviously somewhere right out in the country. Even in the overheated car there was a fresher smell. They dragged her out and carried her into a building. She felt the intense cold at once.

She could hear two men. They spoke in a strange, guttural language which might be Arabic. She was pushed up some bare wooden stairs and the place was freezing cold. She was bundled into a room, thrown on to a bed and one of her wrists was manacled to the metal bed head after they had untied her bonds. Her blindfold was removed and she could just make out the shapes of the men. She thought they were hooded but it made no difference because the light was so poor.

She found she could sit on the edge of the bed and even move half-way to the pale gap of the door. Someone pushed a bucket towards her. Oh, God, she thought, just the basic needs.

*　　*　　*

Before they left the room, she pleaded with them to tell her why they had brought her here but they merely stared back through the holed stocking masks. Then she pleaded for some heat before she froze to death and one of the men brought her some blankets and tossed them on the bed. They left, locking the door behind them, and she wrapped the blankets around her in an attempt to stop shivering. She was alone in a dark room in a strange place and she had no idea why.

Daylight crept through ill-fitting shutters with many draughts of ice-cold air. Her teeth were chattering; it had been far too cold to lie on the bed. She had sat up all night with the blankets clutched round her, periodically calling out for some heat in the room. Kate knew she could not last long like this.

At 9.30 they brought her some coffee and she clung to the mug as if it was a hot-water bottle. Her teeth still chattered and this seemed to worry one of the hooded men who left the room and returned with a bucket of coal; his colleague brought in some logs. They lit a fire in the old cast-iron grate and later brought her an egg sandwich. They stood in the open doorway and watched her eat ravenously.

'You feel better now?'

It was the first time they had shown concern and she thought they were suddenly worried about her condition. The English was spoken with a thick accent.

'I won't last another night like that,' she gasped. 'Can't you bloody well see I'm freezing to death?'

'The fire will soon warm the room.'

'Why have you brought me here?'

Her question was a signal for them to leave. They locked the door she could not reach and she did not see them again until late that evening. They brought her coffee and a ready-cooked moussaka which was already turning cold. They brought up more coal and logs and she had a better night than the previous one, but her sleep was intermittent and she had far too much time to think of what might finally happen.

The next morning they brought her cold cereal and hot tea. Their attitude was not unfriendly but they always wore masks and never stayed long.

It was about 10.30 that night when they returned. She had

34

been dozing. The diminishing fire threw a confusion of light and shadow into the room. There were three men now and she sensed a change of mood, something much more menacing. The third man was somehow different, stockier and powerful and clearly in charge; all were hooded. She backed away as they advanced, suddenly much more afraid.

They grabbed her and forced her flat on the bed and she thought they were going to rape her as they separated her legs. She stared up at the man who was holding her by the shoulders but her silent pleading was lost as he averted his gaze. She felt the other two pulling her legs apart and she struggled and shouted but they held her squirming body with some difficulty. When she was temporarily exhausted by the struggle she felt an excruciating pain in her foot that made her scream out in stark terror. The pain was so intense that she fainted with the shrill scream still on her lips.

If the roads were icy by day they were treacherous at night. Towler drove carefully but was well used to the conditions. It was the first time he had put in an appearance in the dead of night and he had a little trouble at the front desk with an over-zealous custodian. When that was solved, he went up in the elevator to Soames' office.

Soames was almost friendly and looked as if he himself had just got out of bed. There was a pot of hot coffee on his desk and two mugs which he filled, and said, 'There's no cream, but help yourself to sugar.'

Towler took the cup gratefully. 'Something urgent?'

Soames was studying Towler's report about the eight Moslems. 'Good work. Nice job.'

Towler was surprised and then suspicious. He did not really trust Soames. 'It was done in a hurry. I would have liked more time.'

Soames tapped the stapled papers. 'No, this is all right; enough for what we want, anyway.' He looked up. 'Three of these men seem to be living alone. There are no ties indicated in this country?'

'Their parents are in their homelands. I think that's the case for all but one. Like most students, they find digs where they can, although different nationalities are inclined to gang up in certain areas. That's not always possible, so some are quite scattered. They have meeting places, though.'

Soames nodded, then leaned back and eyed Towler shrewdly. 'I have a job for you to do, and one much more in your line.'

Towler gazed across the desk at the man he did not particularly like but who, he had to recognise, must know his job or he would not be sitting there. But he felt on edge for some reason; he doubted that Soames really understood his line and he waited for Soames to explain.

'I must stress that what I am about to tell you must stay between these walls. You really must understand that.'

'Are you doubtful about my security clearance?' Towler was quite angry. 'Men's lives have depended on my silence. And my complete, unquestioned loyalty.' Soames was back to form, reflected Towler, just when he thought he had seen a glimpse of someone different.

'I don't doubt that, Sergeant. But in this, more than lives are at stake. I was merely stressing the importance and am not challenging your credentials. A young girl has been kidnapped by Arabs and they will kill her if we don't arrange an exchange. I want you to be the escort on that exchange.'

'That's in my line; an escort for a kidnap exchange?'

'There's more to it than that and your undoubted qualifications will be of immense use. The point is the Arabs who have this girl think we have one of their men. It's difficult to understand why. They don't accept our word that we are not holding him. We in turn can't understand why they think we have him.'

'Maybe it's Abdul.'

'We let Abdul go. We got nowhere with him. The man we want is on the list you checked. Yasser Azmin.'

'Surely they must know he's still around. He's at the LSE.'

'He hasn't put in an appearance there for over a week.'

'But he's still at the address shown on the registry. I checked.'

'Did you actually see him?'

'No. But I checked with neighbours. A girl identified his mug shot.'

'Then she must be helping him. How many of the eight did you actually see?'

'Only three. You can't expect them to be on tap when you want them. My local checks were thorough, though.'

'I'm sure they were. But when somebody decides to opt out, it takes more time than I gave you to do the job in depth. That is no criticism. We want you to bring him in.'

'When?'

'Tomorrow evening. Take him to the Mayfair Suite.'

'Tomorrow evening? Did I have to be pulled out at this time of night?'

'It was good enough for me. There are plans to make. You'll need a police identity card and you'd better draw a pistol from the armoury. We can't afford mistakes.'

'Why should I need a pistol?'

'In case he resists arrest. He is, after all, a dedicated supporter of the extremist faction of the PLO. But we certainly don't want you to harm him.'

'Where will the exchange take place?'

'We don't yet know but you will stay with the prisoner until it's all over.'

'Wouldn't it be easier to tell whoever has the girl where Yasser Azmin is?'

Soames laughed. 'Really, Sergeant. Any denial of holding him at this stage merely convinces them more that we not only have him but don't want to let him go. We just give them what they want. There is also the fact that we genuinely don't know where he is. But we've been tipped off that he'll be returning to his digs tomorrow evening to get some things and see his girl. It is a rather stupid and dangerous thing for him to do but these things happen. Perhaps he knows that they think we have him and feels safe.'

Towler was intrigued by this premise. There was no doubt that terrorists did do stupid things at times and made tragic mistakes by sheer incompetence. But was Azmin a terrorist or just a wayward student? He saw it as no big deal.

Dawson was going frantic trying to raise Prescott the next morning but the big man was not available even to the most urgent messages from his own ultimate overlord, the Home Secretary. It was fortunate that he was not needed in the House that day because, by the afternoon, he still could make no contact with the MI5 Deputy Director.

He wanted to avoid personally going to Curzon Street but he saw no alternative. He was about to leave the Home Office when his secretary brought in a small parcel. She smiled as he gazed at it suspiciously. It was addressed to him and heavily marked 'Personal and confidential', otherwise his secretary would have opened it.

'It was hand-delivered by a messenger service. It's quite all right. It's been under a scan. No bomb.' She was still smiling as she left his office and closed the door behind her.

Dawson cut the string and fumbled with the brown paper covering. He was impatient to get away and tore at the sello-taped lid of the small cardboard box inside. He finally ripped the lid off and was immediately sick. He was still heaving as he groped for a handkerchief. A small toe, hacked off at the still bloodied joint, lay on a wad of stained cotton wool. A typewritten note stated 'First Instalment'. The pink painted toenail warned him who it had belonged to, but he knew anyway. He turned away and was sick again, his mind screaming.

4

Prescott was not at Curzon Street and his secretary did not know where he was nor when he would be back; would the Home Secretary like to see Sir Malcolm? The last thing Dawson wanted was to see the Director who, he hoped, knew nothing of what was happening.

Prescott's absence would not normally have mattered; there was always someone else who could act for him. But this was the one occasion when Dawson could not put his trust in anyone else. He was already trapped by his own conspiracy and was suffering deep pangs of frustration. That Prescott was obviously keeping out of his way was ominous and there was absolutely nothing he could do but wait and hope and pray, and try to control his mounting fear.

He tried to make light of it to Prescott's secretary who would already be wondering why the Home Secretary had called in person when he would normally summon whomever he needed to see, including Sir Malcolm.

Dawson went back to the Home Office and busied himself. When it was time to leave he dreaded going home to face his wife. Sandra would see straight away that there was something wrong; she had already. When he reached home at about 7.30 he let himself in and his wife called out, 'Nigel Prescott phoned. He said would you phone him at home.'

Dawson somehow refrained from rushing to his study and even called out to Sandra to pour him a whisky. He closed the study door hoping that she would not bring the drink in to him. He telephoned Prescott and tried to control his anger as he came on the line. 'Where on earth have you been?'

'Working flat out on your behalf, Minister. I think we've

got somewhere. We should be able to do something tomorrow night.'

'*Should* be able? I've got to give an answer, damn it. There's been a horrible development.'

'I decided against it in view of the private nature of the issue. It would be better to have no record of events. What development?'

Dawson's free hand went to his pocket. It was dreadful carrying around an amputated toe but he did not know what to do with it, and in any event had intended to show it to Prescott. He managed to get the words out but kept his voice low. 'Someone delivered one of her toes to me at my office this afternoon. It was terrible. My secretary might have opened it.' The very thought of it still sickened him.

There was a long silence before Prescott said, 'Are you sure it's one of hers?'

'For God's sake what does it matter? It belonged to someone. Certainly a woman. And it was . . .' Dawson had great difficulty getting the word out, 'fresh.'

'Was there any kind of message?'

Dawson's anger increased as Prescott showed no sign of sympathy. 'Typed on a piece of paper was the message, "First Instalment".'

'Let me have it. And the toe. We'll get some private forensic done on them. If they ring tonight tell them that tomorrow will be O.K. We must be sure of the detail.'

'When do you want these items? I can't keep them.'

'Wrap them up well and I'll send a messenger round.'

Just talking about it unnerved Dawson, but at least he had at last made contact with Prescott. He pulled himself together and left the room to face his wife.

Towler cased the area during the afternoon. Yasser Azmin rented a bedsitter in a long Victorian terrace in Islington. He had waited patiently for a slot to park his car as near to Azmin's place as possible and had decided to take his man while still on the streets. He waited until late afternoon when it was almost dark and the street lights were dull.

It was a situation he knew well and had operated too often. He found his spot behind a line of cars and waited, not even a shadow in the darkness. People came and went but nobody dallied in the cold. Azmin finally came round the corner at about 5.30. He had his girlfriend with him.

Towler waited to see how it would develop. The couple reached the steps leading up to the apartments where Azmin lived. They stood for a short while, talking and shivering. Then they parted, Azmin mounting the steps as the girl continued on. Towler noted the house he turned into as he raced behind the line of cars, cursing the ice under his feet, and then broke through a gap and chased Azmin up the steps.

Azmin was just about to open the front door when Towler reached him. 'Excuse me. Can I have a word?'

Azmin turned. It was very dark on the steps and at first all he could see was the mist of Towler's breath. But the voice had sounded friendly.

Towler already had his false warrant card in his hand and showed it as he stood beside Azmin on the steps. 'Yasser Azmin? I'm Detective Sergeant Henry. There are a few questions we would like to ask you. Nothing too serious but it would be better done at the station. I have the car over there.'

Azmin could barely see the identity card but did not query Towler's authority. 'What about?'

'The usual crap. Routine. It won't take long. Shall we go?'

'It would be warmer in my room.'

'I'm sure it would. But we can give you coffee at the station and I can drive you back. Take about an hour.' He hoped Azmin would comply; he did not want to use the gun.

'O.K. But it's bloody annoying. You people are always on to us. What am I supposed to have done this time?' His English was colloquial but the accent tortuous.

Towler waited until they were in his car before replying. The engine was cold and he had some trouble starting, but at last it fired and then they had to wait while he sprayed the windscreen with de-icing fluid. When at last they pulled away he said, 'There's been some trouble outside the Egyptian Embassy. Arab students ranting about something or other. That wouldn't have mattered but someone fired a shot and shattered a window. So students get rounded up mostly to show the Egyptians that we're doing something about it. If you're not involved you'll be home in no time.'

But as Towler concentrated on the driving conditions part of his mind was on the casual way Azmin had been returning to his apartment while he was supposed to be on the run from his enemies. He wondered if Soames had got it right; Azmin had appeared as if he was returning home like any other time. Towler wondered if he had been fed lies just as he had now fed them to Azmin.

The only time he had to use his gun was when they drew up in the mews outside the Mayfair Suite. Azmin had become increasingly suspicious about the journey and Towler had dealt with their strange route by more lies, but the mews was the last straw for Azmin. But by then it was too late, and the sight of Towler's Browning convinced him not to flee.

There were two Duty-Officer cubicles with a shower room and toilet in between. The cubicles were small but comfortable though it could not be missed that the two prisoner cells were both larger and, in some ways, better equipped. There was also a close-circuit television-room with six small monitors on a shelf which relayed whatever was happening in the cells, and two speakers which could relay any sound coming from prisoners. At the far end of the room was a flat-screened television set to offset possible boredom for the Duty Officers. The whole place was compact and well thought out.

Towler was quietly amused by the setup. Whatever else they might complain of, prisoners could not claim discomfort. He turned up the amplifier for Azmin's cell and viewed the monitors. Azmin was sitting on the low bed, head between hands, and gazing at the blank wall opposite.

Towler lifted one of the microphones by the television set. He flicked the switch. 'You'll be out in no time. Don't worry.' He saw Azmin gazing round the cell, trying to locate the source of the sound. He felt for him to some extent; he did not like seeing anyone caged.

Towler watched television for a while, his Browning in a waistband holster. He did not know what Soames was up to. He felt like a baby-sitter and so far did not really understand what he was supposed to be doing. Perhaps he would have been happier if he trusted Soames more.

Trust was a word which meant a good deal to Towler. He

had trusted the officers who gave him orders because they were hand-picked, knew what they were doing and took the same risks. And *they* trusted him; they knew he would do the job or go down trying. This was a commodity he had not yet found in his present job. There had to be trust, of course. Somewhere. But he had yet to find it. Perhaps they were simply testing him. Well, they had nothing to worry about.

He had been instructed that Azmin did not warrant all-night vigil, unlike Abdul while he was here. Before turning in he checked the quantities of video and sound tapes and then slept better than for many a night.

Dawson rang Bluie Prescott at eleven o'clock that night. 'They've contacted me again. They say . . .'

'Wait. Hold it there, Minister. Have you a pen handy? Then please hang up and ring me back on the number I'm about to give you. It will be safer. I'm sure you won't leave the number lying around.'

When they were reconnected Dawson said, 'It's almost in Wales. Up Hereford way.'

'That's cheeky of them. Maybe it's a way of cocking a snook at us. I hope they've considered the weather. It's bad enough down here but up there it will be far worse. I take it they think that cars can get through?'

'I raised it myself. Tomorrow evening.'

'Let's have the detail.'

When he had finished talking to Dawson, Prescott called Soames and told him to meet him at Curzon Street.

'Did you have a good night?' Towler asked Azmin amiably.

'You should know; check on your tapes.'

Towler grinned, finding the situation slightly amusing. 'We're going to do a swop. You for somebody else. You'll be free by late evening.' He was leaning back against the closed door of the cell having taken Azmin some breakfast. He had left his gun in his cubicle to take temptation away from his captive.

Azmin sat on the bed weighing his chances against Towler but there was something about the sergeant's all-too-casual stance which warned him not to try. If he wanted confirmation of that decision he found it in eyes that stared back at him quietly, willing him to start something.

'Swop? That's ridiculous. I'm of no value. I'm just a student.'

'Sure. I've seen some of the outside video clips with you on them. I don't know whether you've reached the trigger-squeezing stage but you're right in there, Yasser. Someone, somewhere, tells you what to do and when. Anyway, you should be pleased.'

Azmin was about to rise when he realised Towler might misinterpret the move so he stayed on the edge of the bed. 'I'm still not worth an exchange with anyone. You've got the wrong man.'

Towler smiled. 'If we listen to that line we've never had the right one.' He winked in a friendly way. 'Have your kit packed by three this afternoon.'

Azmin almost flung his plate at him and Towler left the cell quietly laughing. Back in his own cubicle he again wondered why he had received no relief from duty. Certainly he had everything he needed but surely it was common practice to do only so many hours on duty at a time if only to remain on top of the job? His instructions had come from Soames over a scrambler, early that morning. He was as isolated as the prisoner.

'They've insisted on a one-man escort but you will have a driver,' Soames explained. 'It's unusual but they clearly don't trust us.' He shrugged. 'It's a small enough deal, anyway. I personally cannot see the importance of Azmin. As far as I'm concerned the exchange is hardly worth the trouble. But there it is.'

Soames and Towler were drinking coffee while they vaguely watched the monitors. It was midday and pleasantly warm in the 'suite', the air-conditioning was good but there were no windows and the effect could be claustrophobic.

Towler was more than happy to be a single escort provided the efficiency of the work was not affected. He could see no problems. The job seemed to be simple enough.

'Well, it should be better than standing in basements watching the Hotel Florida sign on the blink.'

'Quite. Here's a sectional map. The driver will take this

turn-off on the Hereford road about six miles north of Ross-on-Wye. The turn-off is not ideal but I'm advised that it's passable, partially protected by the hills and high ground either side of it. There should be no need to use chains but that's up to him. You travel exactly 3.4 miles west and stop. It's hilly, open country.'

'I remember it well,' Towler remarked. He was thinking of the arduous early training he had done with the SAS at Hereford. It would be a good place for an exchange for there was nothing there, particularly in this weather. 'Is there a turn-round point?'

'That's exactly why this spot has been chosen. At the point you stop there's a natural lay-by where it levels out away from the road. At 8pm a car should approach, stop about fifty yards away, flash its headlights twice and you will respond once. Both drivers will keep their headlights on. Get out with Azmin but don't walk more than twenty paces with him; just enough to make sure he's on his way. You will then let him continue alone only when you see the girl coming towards you. Don't make contact with the other side. They seem to be sensitive about possible recognition.'

'Do you trust them?'

Soames shrugged the question off. 'You will be armed. Any funny business and get Azmin back. Shoot him if necessary. Keep a gun on him until the girl has reached you. Don't make them nervous; she must make it on her own to where you will be waiting. Your driver will stay in the car with the engine running ready to whip you both away. He'll drive you back home and will then take the girl on.'

'So you don't want me to know where she goes?'

'The driver won't know either; he will merely drop her off for her friends to collect. Our job will be over. Any questions?'

'I'd like to keep Azmin handcuffed the whole way.'

'That's up to you. The car will be round at 3pm. That will give the driver time for a break *en route* if anyone feels the need.'

Soames suddenly looked tired and nervous. Towler knew that, in spite of detailed planning, arrangements could still go wrong, delays could occur, accidents and hold-ups causing time loss. Yet to leave too early would mean hanging around

45

filling in time in the freezing cold. It would be a long drive but there should be plenty of time and the driver would be good; they always were. No doubt ex-police traffic cops.

Meanwhile, all Towler had to do was to occupy himself.

Towler was on the rear seat with Azmin. They had cleared London and he had admired the skill with which the driver, who answered to Ted, squeezed them through the mounting traffic until they were on the M40 heading for Oxford and Wales. Azmin was silent next to Towler. His wrists were handcuffed in front of him so that his hands were on his lap and discomfort was minimal. Disposable plastic cuffs had been used to cut down the weight.

Azmin seemed not to appreciate the concern for him; he constantly complained that he should not be captive in the first place and did not want to be part of any exchange. He became increasingly agitated as the journey progressed until he began to distract Ted from his driving. Towler cut it short by threatening Azmin with the butt of his Browning if he did not keep quiet.

Eventually they were in open country and the traffic was sparse enough to use full beams which cut clearly through the crisp air. They could hear the crackle of ice under the wheels but Ted kept the speed within the limits he knew the car could cope on treacherous roads.

They made one stop on the hard shoulder of the motorway at Azmin's repeated insistence and Towler made sure he was kept out of sight of passing motorists after they climbed out. Back on the road Towler could not fail to notice Azmin's increasing reluctance to complete the journey. Perhaps his prisoner understood as little as he did and was becoming scared of the unknown. In the proximity of the closed car it was disturbing.

Once they left the motorway and slipped on to the minor roads Ted reduced speed. They picked up a good deal of traffic on the approaches to Ross, but the splendour of the snow-bound town and countryside was lost on them as they neared the exchange point.

Ted's timing was impeccable. He reached the turn-off with little over half an hour left to cover the 3.4 miles to the exchange area. He dimmed his lights, reducing speed on the empty road, and they began to climb. He stopped a mile short and dowsed the lights. It was suddenly extremely dark. Towler lowered his window and ice cold air caught him in the back of the throat. 'Switch off,' he said to Ted.

It was quiet. Not a sound. Eerie and empty all around them. With the engine off, the heater died and, with the window still open, the temperature dropped sharply. Towler glanced at his luminous watch, his bated breath almost obscuring his view. Fifteen minutes in hand and a mile to go. They might as well do it. There was nothing ahead of them. 'Let's go,' he said, and Ted switched on and eased the car forward.

They were barely moving and alertness in the car mounted. The high beams exaggerated every minute undulation on the road and the snow ridges at the sides formed a shallow canyon, shedding a ghostly glow beyond which was total blackness. Suddenly this unimportant little affair took on a significance they all felt and as a result nobody spoke. They craned forward for sight of another car but there was nothing on the road, not even a foraging animal.

Ted dipped his beams to see if he could see any lights beyond them but there was nothing. He braked slowly and drew into the natural lay-by that suddenly came to view. He swung the wheel slowly so that they were on half-turn and ready for a quick escape. He kept the lights dimmed. They had five minutes to go.

The five minutes passed and the three men, in their separate ways, began to get nervous. Four beams flashed out slightly above them, blinding from the darkness. Then again. Ted flashed back.

Towler drew his Browning and handed Azmin the key to the handcuffs. 'No funny business, Yasser. Just follow me.' He opened the door and backed out, his gaze never leaving Azmin. 'Just follow me.' It was ridiculous to feel so worked up about so simple a matter yet he was on edge and wary. He gave Azmin room to step out, and said, 'Your problems are over, sonny. Your mates will probably drive you back to London.' He did not believe what he was saying but was trying to calm Azmin down.

It was like a film set, the glare of lights blinding and the

47

stretch of road the illuminated stage. The ice sparkled in the two sets of beams, and at any other time the strange beauty combining nature and artificial lighting would have been worth watching. As it was the biting air was full of suspicion and uncertainty.

Towler kept his eyes on Azmin who was screwing his own against the glare. It was impossible to see anything beyond the beams. 'Let's start,' said Towler and stepped slightly behind Azmin, his Browning levelled at him. He counted the paces and stopped after ten because he could still see nothing ahead but the terrible glare which intensified as they drew nearer. 'O.K.' They moved forward again and Towler sensed that Azmin would opt out if he could, but there was nowhere to run. After another ten paces he told Azmin to stop again.

Towler could still see nothing, nor could he hear anything. He did not care for being spotlighted like this, it was contrary to all his covert training. Then he saw a fuzzed image, wide and unnatural, wavering at the edges as the headlights facing him formed an ethereal aura around the shape. He suddenly realised that it looked unnatural because there were two people close together who appeared as one.

The shape froze and then split into two and one of them came on alone, darkening into a wavering outline. It must be the girl but she seemed to have a strange way of walking as if she was injured.

'On your way, Yasser. I'll be aiming at your back all the time, so don't chicken out. You'll be O.K.'

Towler watched Azmin walk away from him, shoulders slumped in unhappy resignation and wished that he himself could escape from the light. After a short while his gaze switched to the girl and he could now see much more clearly that she was limping badly. His inclination was to go forward to help her but he remembered his instructions and held his ground.

The girl and Azmin drew level, then Azmin began to become indistinct and the girl more definable. She was in pain. Towler watched as he saw her struggling. Another shape was coming forward to meet Azmin and Towler suddenly thought, to hell with it, the girl needs help. He ran forward as a sub-machine-gun

48

burst out on his right flank and he felt the swish of air behind his back.

His immediate instinct was to throw himself flat, but he noticed that the girl had stopped and was gazing about in bewilderment and fear. Towler raced on towards her. Beyond her more firing broke out and he saw Azmin and another man collapse to the ground just as he reached the girl. He threw himself at her and they both went down heavily. As they hit the ground he held her tight and rolled towards the edge of the road until they hit the snow-banked verge.

'We must get over that bank,' Towler called to her. The light was a curse. Bursts of fire still thundered out like artillery in the still air, but the shots seemed to be going over their heads. Then one set of car lights went out and Towler bawled, 'Over. Now.' He helped the girl rise but virtually threw her over the bank and dived after her. As he landed and rolled it suddenly became very dark and he realised that the position of Ted's lights had changed.

The girl was stunned when Towler reached her. Remembering her limp he said, 'Hold on tight and for Christ's sake trust me. We're far from out of this.' He grabbed her closely again and they rolled down a steep slope gathering snow like a stone, but it gave them protection. When they reached the bottom, Towler picked up the sound of a car and then saw headlights going away from them. The car that was supposed to have picked up Azmin was racing away and by the sound of gunfire someone was trying to stop it.

And then he heard Ted's car and saw his lights flash over the leaden sky as he swung round and headed back. Shots followed him but he was not hit and it seemed to Towler that both cars were escaping in opposite directions. Whoever had the guns were either lousy shots or the conditions were too bad to operate in. Yet the gunmen had been good enough to cut down Azmin and the man who had gone forward to help him.

He was still holding the girl tight and she seemed to be in shock. He released her gradually but had no comfort to offer her.

'They'll have seen us. We've got to get away from here bloody fast.'

49

5

The silence was more unnerving than the firing. Towler was satisfied about the rough direction of the shots but had no idea where the danger might come from now. As he helped the girl up he was worried about the time they were losing. There had been two gunmen and he knew just how quickly they could move when they had to. Only part of their target had been destroyed; they would try to complete the job.

'What's wrong with your foot?' He was holding her upright and her breath was rising on the air close to his face.

'They cut off one of my toes.'

'Oh, Christ. Can you manage if I support you?'

'Will they come after us?'

'They'll be on their way. We must move.' Towler gazed around but where they were standing, in a shallow valley, there was little in the way of cover. They were exposed and the endless snow formed its own kind of illumination.

She started to shake the snow off and he stopped her at once.

'Leave it on. Camouflage. So we'll get wet and cold but it's better than being dead. Come on.'

He forced her to climb up the opposite slope when it would have been easier for her to go just above the snow drifts of the valley floor. He pushed, pulled and harried her until they reached the ridge and then he made her cling to him again and they rolled like a barrel down the other side. There were more trees here, more cover. He knew they were leaving a rough trail but that was impossible to avoid and it would not be so easy to follow at night with such an overcast sky.

When he helped her up she had to pause for a while and was obviously in pain. But he was anxious to get on and she was aware of it.

'What the hell's happening?' she burst out.

He put an arm around her. 'My name is Sam Towler and I was sent to get you back. That's what I intend to do.'

She positioned herself so that he supported her on her injured side. 'You haven't answered me,' she said as they waded through the snow.

'I don't know what's happening either. I'm still trying to work it out.' He helped her along, unwilling to show much sympathy knowing that they were moving too slowly. But beneath his rough attitude he felt deeply for the girl; who the hell would want to cut off one of her toes? It was sick; or desperate; or a warning to someone. 'We're heading north,' he said while he tried to get her to go faster. 'There must be another intersection somewhere. We need a telephone.'

Movement warmed them but the deep snow slowed them down. The girl's limp was worsening. 'Keep going,' Towler urged. 'If you break down I'll give you a fireman's lift. O.K.?' He would have done it before but the snow was so deep the extra weight would have made it more difficult to get on. As it was they were both saturated up to their knees and he hoped that the severe cold would have a numbing effect on her foot.

Eventually she had to stop. She leaned against a tree while he held her up and even in the bad light he could see that her face was drawn with pain and was almost as white as the snow clinging to her clothes. He had been so preoccupied with escape that he had not really noticed what she was wearing but he could now see that she was not clothed for the present conditions. The plain skirt would normally be warm and so too would the loose, patterned pullover, but she had no topcoat and he hastily removed his and slipped her arms through the sleeves.

'I'm sorry,' he said. 'I should have noticed before but those bastards are still out there somewhere.' He remembered that he had slipped the Browning into one of his topcoat pockets and he pulled it out and placed it into his waistband.

It was difficult to define her features in the poor light but he could see that she was young. He carefully lifted her injured foot. The low-heeled shoe had been cut so that she could get her bandaged foot in, and it was a wonder that it had stayed on; the leather was soggy which was perhaps as well.

51

'Trust me,' he said and promptly bent to heave her over his shoulder and slip his arm between her legs to grasp her wrist.

To avoid the worst of the snow he had to climb higher up the slope and it was hard going. He was just below the ridge when he picked up a sound. He stopped at once, carefully lowering the girl to the ground and placing her against a tree so that she was hidden from the valley floor. He warned her to keep quiet. He eased his way down to a tree just below her position and drew his Browning.

Someone was pushing their way through the drifts below. Two dark forms came slowly into view and they were carrying sub-machine-guns at the ready. The first man, just a dark blur against the dull white, stopped and then slung his gun over his shoulder. He peered around until his colleague joined him. It would have been easy for Towler to pick them both off; they were in range and stationary. Later he was to believe that it might have been better for both he and the girl if he had done. But just then he thought that the sound of the shots would carry round the hills and warn any others who might be out there searching for them.

He heard them whispering but not what they were saying. What disturbed him, though, was the conviction that they were speaking in English. The two men were obviously unde-cided and had reached a point where they needed to reappraise. Finally they started to climb the opposite rise, going away from Towler who watched until they disappeared. Even then, he waited on the off-chance of their return. By the time he reached the girl again she was shivering violently and he guessed that shock had added to the problems of the extreme cold.

After trying to restore her circulation, Towler carried her up towards the ridge from which they had originally rolled down. After a while he had no idea of time or motion. His legs simply kept going under their own motivation and the weight round his shoulders grew heavier, yet he reached a point when he knew that, if he lowered the girl to rest, he would not be able to pick her up again. He lost sight of direction and became aware that the girl had shown no sign of life for some time. There was nothing he could do but stumble on as long as he could. The moment he stopped was the moment they would start to perish.

He crossed an almost hidden farm track and had actually gone beyond it before its importance registered. He went back and picked up the signs of wheel ruts beneath the snow. Fortunately it had been recently used and earth patches showed through here and there. Instinct dictated direction and he staggered on until he saw lights ahead.

It was perhaps the most dangerous period, for someone might be waiting for them. The last part of the journey was the worst; it always was. He staggered through the corroded iron gates and managed to reach the front door of the old farmhouse and to raise the heavy knocker. He slipped the girl off his shoulders and made sure his gun was handy, although his numbed hand could barely feel it. It seemed an eternity before someone came and he almost passed out, aware only of a woman's soft Welsh voice calling back into the house for help from someone called Barry.

Towler remembered tucking his gun away quickly and clinging to his senses just sufficiently not to pass out. It was a close thing. The girl, on the other hand, had been unconscious for some time. Friendly hands pulled her in and placed her in front of a roaring kitchen fire.

A man's voice, it must have been Barry, said that he must phone for an ambulance, but Towler managed to stop him, insisting that there was no need and that it would be wicked to bring an ambulance out in these conditions when they could cope without one. All they needed was warmth and a hot drink. He could raise a friend if there was a phone available. He was not sure of the truth of that but he must try. Towler did not want anyone to know where they were until he had sorted out what the dangers actually were and from whom.

Later, when they had thawed out and the girl had come to, her tights and shoes drying in front of the fire, Towler told his hosts – a wiry, balding, middle-aged sheep farmer named Jones, and his hard-working wife – that he had taken the wrong turning and that the car had broken down; without the heater functioning they either had to get out and walk or die from cold in the car. They had seen nothing else on the road.

While the girl resisted the entreaties of Mary Jones to change the dressing on her foot, Towler found the telephone in the large hall and was left alone to make his call. His hands started to tremble the moment he picked up the phone and he had to sink on to a chair. He had not felt like this since he had tried to resuscitate the dead body of his mate Taffy. He thanked God that he was alone just then.

He glanced towards the kitchen door hoping that nobody would come out. After a while he steadied himself and rang a Hereford number. 'I want to speak to CSM Chandler. Tell him it's Sergeant Towler. Sam Towler. And tell him it's urgent.' Now he was actioning something again he felt better. It was still the right side of midnight and he prayed that Chandler was there. He was left holding on for so long that he began to forage for alternative plans.

'Sam? Sam Towler? You bastard. Where've you been?'

It was so different from listening to Soames' fruity voice, it was like returning home. Towler did not have to worry about a reaction the other end of the line, for there was a man, barely older than himself, who had taught him most of what he knew and had made him suffer in the process; a man he highly respected and above all, trusted.

'I'm in trouble, Sergeant-Major.' Even though they had later become friends, only during off-duty moments had Towler found himself able to call Chandler, Jack; it was another way of showing respect and discipline. 'I'm on a job and holed up in a farmhouse with a girl who is part of the deal. There are a couple of trigger-happies roaming the hills looking for us with SMGs. We need pulling out and taking to the nearest rail station. We're not many miles from you.' Towler gave directions.

Chandler said, 'Where's your back-up?'

'Out there trying to kill us.'

'Jesus. Sounds like you've been set up. Are we your nearest help?'

'Nearest, and as things stand, the only one I trust.'

'Gotcha. Are you O.K. for a while?'

'We're being looked after very well. I don't think the enemy will be too fussy who they shoot if they find us here, though. I am armed.'

'I'll be stepping out of line so it will take a little time for me to get this cleared but I won't take a no. I've got to get wheels but I'll be there. I'd better bring a couple of men with me. It's

54

time some of the buggers were woken up.' Chandler checked the position of the farm again and hung up. Towler went back to the others in the big, warm kitchen.

'Help's on the way,' he said as they all turned towards him. 'It might take a little time, though, if you can put up with us.'

'Stay as long as you like, lad. Don't worry about us.' Barry Jones smiled. 'How far have your friends got to come?'

Towler hesitated. 'From Hereford.'

Jones nodded wisely and glanced at his wife as if to say 'I told you so'. 'That will account for your gun then? Good luck, lad. Whatever you're on, we're right behind you.'

Towler noticed the girl's quick glance at him. Perhaps she had not realised he was armed and he was annoyed that he had been careless enough to allow the Joneses to see the gun. He sat down opposite the girl across the big kitchen table. He needed to talk to her and he could see that she felt the same.

Jones said, 'You two won't mind being left alone for a bit? Mary and I have things to do. We'll be upstairs if you want us; just give a shout.'

Towler knew that they were simply getting out of the way and he was grateful. When they had gone he moved nearer to the girl, pulling up a chair beside her where it was closer to the fire.

'You've recovered quickly,' he observed.

'I was frozen through. They've been marvellous, those two, and they haven't asked one embarrassing question.' She gazed at Towler warily. 'I didn't know you were armed.'

'I didn't hide it from you; you were too far gone to notice. I don't even know who I've stuck my neck out for.' He could now see that she was very attractive and finely built, but she had suffered and her eyes were screwed with pain. Her foot obviously needed attention.

'You mean you don't know my name?' She could not believe it.

'You were just an anonymous exchange.'

'Kate Parker.'

'Is there something about you that I should know? I mean, you were kidnapped and did rate an exchange.'

'It's all a mystery to me. I run a health club with a friend. I was coshed on the way to my car. I don't know why; I wish to God I did.'

'I can't help you. I just do what I'm told.'

'Yes, but who tells you? Who's rescued me? I think you said you are Sam Turner?'

'Towler. Sam's enough. A Government department has rescued you, but it was one big cock-up, wasn't it? The other exchange is probably dead, and the man who went to meet him. I think you were meant to die. Perhaps me, too. And out there somewhere, two guys with SMGs are still searching for us to finish the job.'

'SMGs?'

'Sub-machine-guns. You can't throw any light on any of this?'

Kate placed her hands round the still warm teapot. 'None at all. It's terrifying. I think they must believe I'm somebody else. Otherwise it makes no sense.'

'Why did they cut your toe off?'

She shuddered and it was some time before she replied. 'I don't know that either. At first they were indifferent to me. The first night with them I thought I'd die of cold. Then they became a little friendlier and brought me food and drink. And then the third night their whole attitude changed and they held me down while one of them . . .' She broke off at the horror of recollection.

'Who were they?'

'They wore stocking masks, but I think they were Arabs.'

'That makes sense as it was an Arab I was exchanging for you.'

'But on that third night there was another man, also masked but he was not like them. He spoke Arabic but hesitantly and with what sounded like, well, an American accent. He was the one who took my toe off.'

Towler could hear the Joneses moving about upstairs but suddenly he thought he heard something else. It was too early for Jack Chandler. 'Keep talking,' he whispered and rose to walk over to the window keeping his shadow off the old-fashioned blind.

'I fainted. I think they used a bolt-cutter. It was well into the night before I came round. They had swathed me in blankets against shock and I discovered that the amputation had been dressed. I haven't had the nerve to look at the damage but it hurts like mad.'

Towler slipped a finger behind the edge of the blind and peered out through the narrowest of cracks. It was difficult with the kitchen lights behind him but he could hear nothing now. 'Go on.'

'That's all. I was in so much pain and discomfort that I lost track. All I know is that this morning one of them came in to tell me that I was being exchanged for someone else, that I would be home before midnight. I asked no questions because those I'd asked previously had been studiously ignored. During the evening I was brought to the rendezvous.'

Towler still stood by the window. 'Where's your coat?'

'It's in my car. They used my car to drive up here. I've no idea what they've done with it. I'll have to report it to the police.'

'Don't do that. Not yet, anyway.'

'Why? I want it back.'

'I doubt that it'll be found. We want to know much more about what's going on before anyone else is brought into it.'

He backed away from the window carefully until he was alongside her.

'Is there something wrong?' she asked shakily.

'We've been shot at and we're hiding out and you ask that.'

'I mean now. You are acting most strangely.'

Her voice was upper-class, he thought; she spoke beautifully without affectation. 'I thought I heard something. It was probably an animal. The problem is that if they're waiting out there, they won't wait for ever. If we put the lights out, we encourage them to come in and they'll do it through different doors. If we leave the lights on, as time passes, it might convince them that we're here. Farmers go to bed early, and rise early.'

Towler pulled out his gun and laid it on the table. 'Now you know that I have it, it might as well be handy. We're out of the cold, Kate, but nothing else has changed.'

After a while the temperature dropped and Towler topped up the fire. Chandler was taking his time and Towler had the strong feeling that he and Kate were running out of it. He put his finger to his lips. Someone was trying to lift the old-fashioned window. He picked up his gun and circled the table towards the door to the hall. If they were trying the windows, the doors had already been tried.

He went out into the hall. The telephone stood on a small period reproduction table and he wondered if he should ring Hereford again. There was no sound from upstairs and he guessed that the Joneses were probably getting a little sleep while they could. He returned to the living-room where Kate had her injured foot up on a chair.

She looked anxiously at him. 'Are they here?'

'I'm not sure. I wish my friends would pitch up.'

The sound of a vehicle came as a distant buzz. Towler went out into the hall again and headlights flashed across the glass panels in the door. It had to be Chandler. It must be. The vehicle pulled up outside and the lights remained on and the engine ticked over like a clock. The crash of the door-knocker sent loud echoes through the house and the Joneses appeared on the upper landing.

Towler was trying to hide his gun so as not to alarm them but he had no intention of opening the door without it. He stood back, reached out and pulled the heavy latch. The door swung open away from him and a voice rasped out, 'Are you there, Sam?'

It was recognition of the voice that made Towler respond. He whispered loudly, 'There are prowlers out there. Dowse your lights.'

Chandler sprang away from the door and almost immediately the vehicle lights went out.

Towler switched off the hall light and called up the stairs. 'We're off. We can't thank you enough. Lock your door after we've gone.' He went back into the living-room and helped Kate into the darkened hall. They came up beside the open front door and Towler knew that Chandler would be crouched close to it and would have deployed his men. 'We're ready.'

'O.K.,' Chandler's crisp voice answered. 'A carrier is straight ahead. Get in the back and keep down. You'll be covered.'

Towler and Kate crawled forward and once outside Towler reached up to pull the door without actually closing it. 'Now,' he said, placing an arm around Kate. They ran for the dark shape of the personnel carrier and he helped her climb in and then followed. Moments later two battle-clad figures, with woollen hats pulled low, clambered in after them; both were armed and they immediately took up defensive positions.

The carrier moved away almost immediately. As Towler peered from the back he saw a vague shape emerge from behind a tree but, before he could give a warning, one of the men beside him sent off a short burst to send snow spray into the path of the man who scuttled for cover and stayed there. The Heckler and Koch was almost noiseless and the result uncanny as the snow spat up in a straight line.

From then on the journey was rough but uneventful. The three men exchanged banter but nobody asked questions. Kate crouched in one corner, fearful and grateful at the same time. Three days ago she had entered a world completely foreign to her, something she had sometimes read about happening to other people. She was scared and her foot hurt abominably.

Chandler had fixed up accommodation for them in a small hotel just outside Hereford knowing that there would be no trains that night. It was a double-room and the best he could do. As his action so far had received only the tacit consent of his Commanding Officer, there was nothing more he could do for them. Towler and the girl were on their own again but at least out of the immediate firing line. There were unqualified thanks and delight at two old warriors meeting again, if only briefly, then the trio was gone.

The room was small and cold and the bed was double. 'Don't worry,' Towler assured. 'Sleeping rough is nothing new to me. I'll take the floor.'

Kate was shivering again but he thought it was part shock at what had happened to her.

'You want me to take a look at your foot?' he asked. 'You don't want to get it infected.'

'I'd rather wait for a doctor. Anyway, we have no fresh dressing.'

There was a small shower-room and he went in while she undressed. She called out and when he returned she was in bed, pale and vulnerable. She had tidied herself up as best she could for neither of them had toiletries with them. Her pale hair formed a frame against the white pillow. 'You're beautiful,' he said with the same affection he would give to some new form of weaponry; it was an appreciation rather than an emotional statement. 'You must be fit to endure what you've been through. Do you mind if we talk for a bit?'

'I'm tired out, but I'm afraid to sleep in case those men come back.'

He removed his shoes. 'They're unlikely to try anything here. The farm was different, they could have knocked off the lot of us. But there are too many people here; it's all too chancy.' He sat on the dressing-table stool and faced her from the foot of the bed. 'There has to be something about you that warrants the exchange, if not what followed.'

'Don't you think I've been harassed enough without you starting?'

He glanced over to the door to make sure he had locked it. He felt tired out too, but why had it all turned into a sitting-duck shoot? 'I'm not harassing you but we won't know what to do unless we get some sense out of it. Someone rated Yasser Azmin as a fair exchange for you. Now Azmin can't have been the small fry I thought he was or none of this would have happened. And neither can you. Have you a sugar-daddy who's high up the ladder? Someone really important?'

She pulled the clothes up tight under her chin and glared at him. 'I find that offensive.'

'That's not an answer, Kate.'

'No I damn well haven't.' She hesitated a fraction and then frowned. 'I don't know why I was kidnapped. I'm worth nothing to anybody. I have no money, no parents and no current boyfriends. It was all a terrible mistake.' Suddenly she pleaded with him, 'For God's sake, Sam, think about it. I run a health club and I've lost a toe. I'll be out of action for some time which means my partner will have to carry the can until I'm ready again. She must be worried sick about my not turning up. She might have gone to the police. It would be a natural thing to do. It's been a nightmare these last few days. Don't you think I've been racking my brains, too?'

Towler was not convinced. 'If she did go to the police there's been no press or TV mention. Missing young ladies are high priority news these days.' He thought she might be holding something back. 'Kate, when we leave here we're back to square one. Apart from any other need to get rid of us, we've witnessed at least two murders. They won't leave us alone. If you think of something you must let me know.'

'But you won't go to the police, will you?'

He detected something in the way she said it; she was no longer sure herself. 'O.K.,' he said, 'if you feel like that we'd better ring them.'

'*No!*' The word shot out before she could stop it. She pulled herself further up the pillows so that she could see him better, keeping the blankets above her naked shoulders. 'Perhaps you were right the first time.'

He did not ask her why she had changed her mind and he let her off the hook for she was now confused by her own vehement rejection of his bluff. 'My reason was simple,' he said. 'I'm operating for a Government Department. Either security is lax or we were set up. If it was a setup there must be a reason; the police won't find out anything because they'll be told to leave it alone, or at best be misled. It could be another agency who have their own reasons for wanting us out of the way. The answer lies with you and Azmin. Either one, or the other, or both, are of much more importance than it appears. Help me, Kate, you might hold the key.'

He felt sorry for her; so far as he knew she had asked for none of this. 'Just bear in mind that in a few hours we have to step out of here, and we wouldn't have been too difficult to follow. Is it worth your life to make the effort? Someone wants you dead and, if I'm in the way, I go with you.'

'What's happened to the girl?' Prescott's tone was blistering.

Soames was almost beyond caring. He had done what he could; everything had been well planned. If the sergeant had obeyed instructions and stood his ground instead of hurrying forward to help the girl, everything would have been fine. That small difference had destroyed everything. 'These things do happen,' he replied mildly. 'It is impossible to predict somebody's reaction at a given moment. Clearly the girl is with Towler. He probably thinks he saved her when in fact she should never have been in danger.'

'With the show you put on he probably did save her.' Prescott waved a hand apologetically and shifted his huge frame in his chair as if he was never quite comfortable. 'I've got to account for all this to someone I'd rather avoid. It is a cock-up, let's face it; one after the other. So what happens now?'

'I've increased the team up there. We must get the girl and get rid of Towler.'

Prescott clasped his hands on the desk and gazed at Soames who steeled himself against an act he had seen before. 'Are you saying that it was part of your plan to *kill* the sergeant? You never told me that before. Are you crazy, Soames?'

You damned hypocrite, reflected Soames; you knew bloody well and now you're detaching yourself. You shit. 'How else could I manage it? You instructed me that the return of the girl was imperative. As the Arabs holding the girl would not have been fooled for more than two seconds that Azmin was not their man, they all had to be taken out, and to make it look authentic the sergeant had to go with them. We made it appear like a Mossad job. Only the girl was to survive.'

'I had no idea that you had something so drastic in mind. This is far worse than I realised.'

Soames struck back. 'Right. Then I'll cancel all orders to find and destroy Towler. At least it's not too late for that.'

It had developed into a game of survival between them and both were expert. Prescott countered, 'Yes, it is too late. You sent your men after Towler, and, if he didn't know before, he certainly knows now that he's a target. You've left yourself with no alternative but to finish the job.' Prescott sat back thoughtfully. 'We have to hope to God that the PM never finds out about any of this. The SAS are the pet heroes. And I gather that they came in on this unfortunate act.'

'Towler must have contacted old friends at Hereford who pulled him out of the farmhouse and fired on my men as they left. Fortunately nobody was hit.'

'Then they weren't aiming at them,' Prescott commented drily. He shook his head slowly. 'I just don't like the idea of getting rid of Towler. Had I known that was your intention, I would have stopped you. It's a dangerous game to play.'

'And what would you have suggested instead?' Soames retorted recklessly. 'His loyalty was not to us. He didn't like us and certainly not me. He's a misfit. Why would he go to ground if he did not suspect something? He has not reported in which is highly indicative of the way his mind is working. He has to go once we have the girl. Nothing has changed.'

'It's changed all right. The police have found two dead bodies, both Arabs, and an abandoned Uzi SMG which must have been part of your strategy to mislead. The escape of the sergeant has made all the difference. Regrettably, I have to agree with you. You've placed us in a position of no return. Find and destroy. And you'd better do it quickly and a damned sight more efficiently than hitherto.'

Soames rose but before he left the office, said, 'The local police have been told that Special Branch are taking over the murder investigation, with their help, of course. It's a move that enables us to use and to confuse the locals at the same time.'

With a cushion under his head and his topcoat over him, Towler slept restlessly on the floor. He woke early, and showered and dressed before Kate was awake. His clothes and shoes were still damp but that, too, was nothing new.

He slipped out of the room, locking it after him, and went down to the kitchen to take back some breakfast. He woke Kate and she came to in a panic. He calmed her down and as she sat up the bedclothes slipped down. She pulled them up, embarrassed because he was standing there with the tray and showed no reaction. She thought he must be either indifferent to the female form, or had tremendous self-control. She could not decide which.

'I'm going out,' he said as she took the tray. 'I'll lock the door behind me; that way I'll know you can't open it to strangers.'

She began to panic again. She had met him for the first time only last evening and under the strangest and most dangerous of conditions, yet already the thought of his absence frightened her. He had got them through a very nasty time and had some useful friends. She did not want to be left alone so soon. 'Can't we go together?'

'I'm going into Hereford to rent a car. It's a little distance and you'd find it difficult to cope.' He saw she was about to protest again and he added frankly, 'O.K.? You'd slow me right down. I won't be long.'

'I thought we were going by train?'

'They'll be watching the station. A car leaves the route optional.' He turned at the door. Just the faintest smile moved his lips. 'Do you always look this great in the morning?'

'Only when I'm shot at the night before! Please don't be long.'

He went out the back way through the kitchens having already made friends with the small, early-morning shift. It was snowing slightly but that was in his favour. The hotel held no more than forty-five guests, and lay back at the end of a gravel drive on a 'B' road about three miles from the town. He cut straight across country from the rear of the hotel. He waded through snow drifts and his clothes were soaked again, but on this route there was no way anyone could follow without him knowing.

It was just after 8am and the light was grey in spite of the snow, visibility was poor but good enough for what he wanted. His directional sense was in-built and he just kept going, occasionally checking his rear. He kept away from trees and copses and stayed on open ground. It was the sound of slow-moving traffic that warned him he was nearing town and ten minutes later he was on the streets of Hereford.

He located a car-hire and taxi company but had to wait for it to open, so he found a café where he had breakfast. He sat with his back to the wall of the small room and watched the comings and goings, exchanging the odd greeting. The coffee machine steamed away on the counter and clouded the windows. Nothing seemed real anymore.

His life had changed overnight. This was not Belfast nor Oman with their obvious extremes of warfare and climate. He was well versed in undercover work but what had now happened to him was totally different. He could not envisage a situation in either of those countries where his mates set out to destroy him, and his present situation had that terrible smell about it. He could be wrong. He had to find out. And if he did he would settle the issue before they settled him. It was another kind of war but in this one he no longer knew his friends.

He used a credit card to hire a Ford Granada and drove slowly back to the hotel. He stopped at the front entrance of the hotel and left the car where it could be seen from the lobby. He went upstairs and knocked on the bedroom door.

'Who is it?'

'Sam,' he called back and unlocked the door.

Kate was standing just inside the tiny shower-room but, when she saw him, came out quickly, still limping badly. She had dressed. 'Did you get a car?'

'I used plastic; I've not much money on me.' He locked the door behind him.

'I don't know what they did with my handbag so I've no money at all. I'm sorry. Are we leaving now?'

'If you're ready. I'll settle the bill on the way out but don't leave my side.'

'No, sir.'

He stared at her in surprise. 'Did I sound like that?'

'Not really. But you don't offer me choice or leave me in any doubt. Perhaps it's just as well.'

He helped her along, preferring the stairs to the small lift in spite of her disability. In the lobby she saw the Granada outside and said, 'If that's ours I'll get in while you pay the bill.'

'Stay where you are.'

His tone forbade argument and frightened her. She was left with the feeling that in spite of daylight it was all starting again when in fact it had never stopped.

Outside he said to her, 'Don't get in until I say so.' Without warning he lay flat in the snow and rolled to peer under the car, taking his time. He climbed to his feet and opened the bonnet to check the engine. 'O.K.,' he said, 'you can get in.'

When they were side-by-side in the car she said, 'You were looking for bombs. Would they go to that extreme?'

As they moved off he smiled at her naïveté. 'A bomb, a bullet? What's the difference? It was just a routine check; the day you miss it is the day you shouldn't have.'

'You're scaring me.'

'I hope so. It will make you keep your wits about you. I'm SAS, well, once removed now which is why I've told you. There will always be a ready excuse for blowing us up. Whoever is after us will only have to blame the IRA. The sooner you part from me, the sooner you'll be safer. Where am I to take you?'

'Where would you have taken me if the exchange had gone through?'

'That was the driver's job so I've no idea. You must have friends you can stay with. And you really must get to a doctor.'

'Can I make a phone call on the way back? I'll then know what best to do?'

Towler was taking the 'B' road to join the main road at Hereford before heading south and it gave him better opportunity to make sense out of what he saw in his mirror. 'I don't want you isolated in a call box. We'll see how it goes. What happens to you once we part worries me. But if you're with good friends or family for a while it will help. Once you've left me I won't be able to stop you ringing the police; it'll be up to you. They might provide protection.'

She glanced at him. 'I won't feel safe without you, Sam.'

'You might be in far more danger with me. Don't look now but we have a tail.'

6

Matt Steiner drove over the route Towler had taken for the exchange but in the opposite direction. He was a powerfully built New Yorker who really needed more than his middle-height frame to carry his weight. Beneath the trilby hat was a full head of dark wavy hair which poked out at the sides like wings. His features were strong, even severe, and the lips of the wide mouth were thin. His eyes were uncompromising, steady and hard, and at times there was a suggestion of cruelty about him. He was on his own in the car and he drove slowly because of the conditions and because he did not want to miss anything.

In this weather it was far from being a busy road but some of the curious suddenly found that coming this way to work was really no great hardship. The morning news had announced two murders which had taken place on the route.

Steiner saw the police cars in the distance, and, in daylight, he thought that this was too open a place for an exchange of prisoners. He could now see that there were too many folds and steep undulations in the terrain which offered cover for the ambush which had taken place. But he had not been expecting an ambush.

There were police signs up well in advance of the scene, and cones for the motorist to follow a narrow channel along an already fairly narrow road. He slowed down dutifully, the blue police flashers penetrating the dull grey morning light and reflecting on the roadside snow banks. As he reached the scene he could see where his two men had been gunned down and the long wavering tapes fluttered and swayed in the freezing breeze. It was cold, but he had known New York to be just as bad, and crossing East River on a day like this in a strong wind had never been his idea of fun. The police waved him down and he lowered his window, gasping as the air cut at his nicotine-coated throat. He poked his head out as he stopped. 'What's the matter? Someone crashed?' He guessed his rich Brooklyn accent might draw attention and it did.

A young policeman came over. 'You can get through, sir. Bit of a squeeze but there's room. You want me to guide you?'

'Hell, no. What's going on here?'

'Two men were murdered last night. Arabs, it seems.' The young policeman was trying to lose himself in his greatcoat and was clapping his gloved hands together.

'No kidding? Arabs? Out here?'

'As unusual as Americans, sir,' smiled the policeman. 'There's a car coming up behind you, you'd better move on.'

'Sure. Were they blown up, or something?'

'Shot. You're holding up the car behind, sir.'

Steiner revved his engine; he started to move very slowly. 'Any idea who did it?'

The policeman shook his head and glanced pointedly towards the car behind Steiner. 'No idea, sir.'

'Where would they take guys like that? What do you do with them?'

'Probably take them to the Hereford General for a postmortem.' The policeman was suspicious of the question and his expression changed.

Steiner moved forward a fraction more. He grinned widely. 'Used to be a cop myself,' he explained. 'I guess things don't seem much different here.' He moved off, picking his way along the line of cones while he took in what he could.

Clear of the police he started to look for a turn-off so that he could go back without using the same road. His expression tightened as he drove on. He was inwardly seething. He had expected no trouble over the exchange and it had taken him by surprise which in itself was annoying; it was seldom he was caught with his pants down. But what worried him most was that only his escort had been gunned down; what had happened to the other one? He must discover who he was and then find him and squeeze his head for some answers.

As Steiner made his way back to the outskirts of Hereford he considered the possibility of an outside agency; there were quite a few who would have wanted to kill Rashid Khayar, but,

68

if that was so, then there had been a leak and it was not from his end. He groped for his cigarettes on the shelf, tapped one out from the open-ended soft pack and lit it. His expression was brooding and hiding an anger which grew. Someone would pay heavily for the loss of Rashid.

As soon as Dawson received Prescott's telephone message he knew it meant trouble. Kate Parker should have been released the previous evening and he had spent a sleepless night which he tried to hide from his wife. He had received no news at all and his late phone calls to Prescott had not managed to raise him; Prescott always disappeared from reach when matters went wrong.

Fixing a venue was becoming increasingly difficult. If he saw Prescott too often at his office or at the House of Commons or at Prescott's own office, it would not be missed by Sir Malcolm Read. Consequently he had to wait until opportunity presented itself to both men and these long interludes did nothing for his nerves. The Right Honourable James Dawson found it abominable to be reduced to clandestine meetings, made a mockery by the discreet presence of his bodyguard. But there was nothing he could do.

Prescott was good at it and they met by 'accident' at a bar off Whitehall. It might have been unnatural, in the circumstances, if Dawson had not offered Prescott a drink and they were early enough to find a table.

'Cheers,' smiled Dawson as he raised his whisky. 'Just what the hell is going on?'

Prescott was amiable and ostensibly relaxed. 'The girl got away all right. But we don't know where she is. Not at this particular moment. She's alive so far as we know.'

Dawson was compelled to control himself, but it was difficult. The pub was crowding up with MPs among the customers; some gave him a nod of greeting. 'Was the exchange done or not?'

'In a way, Minister.' It was impossible to gauge from Prescott's tone that anything was wrong at all. 'There was an ambush. Evidently someone wanted our hostage very dead and made sure that happened. Two men were killed and we've arranged for Special Branch to handle the matter. Miss Parker was in no danger but her escort thought otherwise and went to earth with her. We have men on the job to trace them and to bring them back.'

Dawson was shaken and confused, but sure he was not hearing the whole story. 'How the blazes can you possibly know she was in no danger? Don't fence with me, Bluie.'

'The driver who took our escort up to collect her saw it all happen. He was quite convinced that the firing was only directed at our hostage and the man who came to collect him. Our own man apparently panicked and whipped the girl away in the dark.'

'He would, wouldn't he? He wouldn't hang around to ask if the shots were meant for him or Kate.' Dawson was still holding his empty glass and trying to look as if nothing was happening when part of him was falling apart. 'Presumably the driver didn't hang around either?'

Prescott had yet to touch his drink, a measure of his control. 'It was impossible for him to follow and, anyway, he wouldn't have stood a chance against the wiles of an ex-SAS sergeant. We'll find her. She's out there somewhere. In a way, the sergeant did a good job.'

'Evidently the only one who did. I suppose these were the two murders on the Welsh border mentioned on the early bulletins. This is terrible news.'

'Not at all. Miss Parker has been rescued. We simply have to make contact. Attempts to trace her are well advanced.' Prescott glanced at the clock above the bar. 'I'd better go.' He drained his drink irritatingly slowly as Dawson watched. 'I will keep you informed, Minister. Perhaps I can work out a simple telephone code so that I can contact you at home.' Prescott rose, nodded politely and left Dawson staring stonily into space wondering how he could cope with a constantly changing situation which seemed to make no progress at all. He knew that Prescott was covering up something and that there would come a time soon, unless Kate appeared, when he would have to have a thundering big row with him. He hoped that it would not come to that.

They drove for two hours without stopping. Towler had taken a long, circuitous route and had cut down to cross the Severn

Bridge and join the M4 the other side of the river and by-pass Bristol. The motorway had been kept clear of snow and only the white fields on both sides of the carriageway gave indication of conditions. But the pulsing speed limitation signs were up and he did not exceed them. The motorway was far from busy and the traffic well spaced out.

'Are they still with us?' Kate asked once again, weary of being told not to turn round.

'Of course. They'll stay with us.'

'They can't do much on a motorway, can they?'

'They know that. They'll be patient.'

'Maybe they just want to know where we're going.'

'Maybe. It makes no difference to what they finally intend to do.'

After a while Towler asked, 'How's your foot bearing up?'

'I think it's about to fall off.'

'Feel like something hot to drink? There's a service station five miles on.'

She looked at him suspiciously. 'I thought we weren't going to stop for anything.'

He quickly smiled at her. 'I've changed my mind. Just keep close to me all the time. Don't detach yourself.'

'Even in the "Ladies"?'

'I'll be waiting right outside.'

She turned in her seat, partly to ease her foot and partly to study him a little. His gaze rarely left the road even when talking. She had noticed before that he could produce intense concentration, a single-mindedness that sometimes made her feel he was unaware of her. And then he would say something that showed he had her very much in mind and could be considerate.

In view of all that had happened during their short association she had complete confidence in what he did and she was not looking forward to being left alone; he was her protection and she felt safe with him. His expression was grim at the moment but she had seen it more relaxed and then he portrayed a completely different person. His training must have been exceedingly tough; he was a survivor and while with him she enjoyed that same confidence.

He had suffered, too. She could see it about his eyes which,

71

during unguarded moments, reflected pain. And yet, in spite of his solid image, she noticed that there was a slight tremor in his hands on the steering-wheel, almost as though he had been drinking heavily. And the hands sometimes clasped and unclasped again as if to release tension.

'Have you seen enough?' he asked without turning.

'I've been trying to weigh you up,' she said pleasantly.

'I know you have. You won't get far, I've been trying it for years.'

'Why are your hands trembling?'

His only visible reaction was to grip the wheel tighter. 'It's a judder from the wheel. Comes up from the road surface and through a too sensitive steering-column.'

This she knew to be untrue but made no further comment. Instead she asked, 'Are you married?'

'It wouldn't be much of a life for a wife. I've never come close to it.'

'So you've never loved anyone?'

'That's not what I said. You're on dangerous ground, Kate.'

'I'm sorry. I hope she didn't hurt you too much. You're one of the nice guys.'

He shot her the briefest of glances. 'You don't know me. Don't mistake a Ford Granada for a white charger. I'm just doing a job.'

'Thank you,' she retorted. 'You know how to make a girl feel wanted.'

He smiled thinly and put his left indicator up. 'We're here.'

Towler swung on to the service road and after a short while checked in his rear-view mirror. There were a surprising number of cars parked but still plenty of room. He chose a slot as near to the restaurant entrance as he could. He remained seated until he had located the parking slot of the following Nissan and then climbed out and came round to the nearside to help Kate out. They were both stiff and their clothes damp.

He held her arm on the way to the double doors. 'You'd better go to the Ladies first.' They found the toilets and he waited outside while she limped in. He saw the two men who had been following and they studiously ignored him. One went into the Gents and the other stayed outside not too far from Towler.

'Good morning,' called Towler.

The heavily coated man chose not to hear him and Towler smiled. There were a number of people moving around and the two men were never isolated. Kate eventually came out and Towler guided her towards the restaurant.

'What about you?' she asked.

'I can wait,' he replied and they went to the end of the short queue for the self-service. When they had their trays laden with hot soup and crusty bread he led the way to a central table so that there were people all around them.

'Look without moving your head,' Towler instructed. 'To the left of me, three tables away, are two men who are looking everywhere but here. One is hefty with a dark coat and woollen cap over blond hair. The other is a supercilious looking bastard, slim, with his coat thrown back over his shoulders as if he thinks he's a bloody film actor.'

'Are they the two who are following us?'

'That's them. Now I'm going to leave you alone here for a while. They won't try anything, there are too many people around and we're too centrally placed, but, if they do, just start screaming the place down. O.K.?'

Kate was clearly nervous; she did not like the idea of being left alone with killers nearby. She said, 'Don't be long.'

'The chances are that one of them will follow me out. As long as one of us is here they won't go for the car.'

'How do you know they haven't phoned for extra help?'

'They've had no time to phone; they're afraid we might suddenly split.' The truth was probably something different, thought Towler. They wanted the job finished and were waiting for the right moment. He pushed back his chair. 'I'll be back in a moment,' he said and headed for the doors.

Towler sensed the man behind him and in the reflection of the glass doors saw it was the 'actor'. He made his way to the toilets, entered a cubicle, and when he left it a little later, surreptitiously wedged the door with toilet paper. He saw the 'actor' washing his hands at a row of sinks and noticed that there were two other men at the urinal, their backs turned to him.

Towler walked behind the 'actor' and knew he was being watched in the mirror over the sink. He went past him, keeping an eye on the two men. He stopped at a sink near the 'actor' and turned on the taps. The two men at the urinal went to the sinks in turn, washed briefly and both went round the corner where the hand-driers were. Towler slipped a wet hand inside his jacket just as the 'actor' said in a rich fruity whisper, 'Don't try it old boy, or I'll blow your bloody guts out.'

Towler turned his head to see the 'actor' still bent over the sink but across his body a silenced automatic pointed steadily at him. The supercilious face was smiling vindictively. He moved towards Towler, aware that he had to finish quickly before anyone else came in.

Towler had deliberately kept one hand in the sink and, as the 'actor' stepped towards him, he scooped a handful of hot water into the self-satisfied face. As the gunman spluttered, Towler continued the momentum of his hand to catch the man side-handed in the windpipe and, with his other hand, struck him hard in the crotch. As the 'actor' doubled up, Towler grabbed the gun hand, bent back the wrist, and broke the trigger finger in the guard to pull the gun free. He then smashed the barrel of the gun on the base of the head.

Towler held the 'actor' up by his collar and dragged him into the cubicle he had used. He lifted the man on to the seat and closed the door as he left. By the time he reached the end by the hand-driers, one man was still there, the hum of the machine having helped cover what little noise Towler had made. As Towler left he held the door open for another man to enter.

He went out to the car park and located the Nissan the two men had used. He waited until there was nobody near and then used the silenced gun to put a bullet in all four tyres.

Towler returned to Kate who was waiting nervously for him, and said, 'We're off'.

They walked slowly to the car and even then he examined underneath and inside the engine hood. There could be no let up. They climbed in and Towler watched the antics of the man with the dark, heavy coat as he ran over to the Nissan. The car was out of action and his colleague had vanished. The last Towler saw of him was running back towards the restaurant.

'Where's he going?' asked Kate fearfully.

'He'll be going to a phone. We'll get off the motorway at the next junction.' He swung the car out of the service road.

'But what's happened to the other man?' Kate asked nervously.

Towler hesitated; 'He had tummy trouble.'

Kate glanced at Towler pointedly. She sat back, worried and scared. She knew that she had survived because of the efforts of the sometimes uncommunicative man sitting next to her. She was dreading leaving him.

Ali Jahila approached the hospital tentatively. When he entered the reception area nobody took notice of him but he found the generally subdued atmosphere intimidating as if the staff were waiting for him to make a mistake. He was not happy about what he was doing, but he had been told to do it by the aggressive American, Steiner, and was being very well paid. He was in his mid-twenties and was wrapped up in an old topcoat with a frayed bottom and wore a balaclava with the bottom rolled up above the ears. He approached the counter nervously.

A middle-aged receptionist, noticing his reticence, tried to put him at ease. Although he had rehearsed what to say he faltered before blurting out, 'The two shot men you have here; is it possible to see them?'

The receptionist stared in surprise. 'But they are dead. Is there some special reason you want to see them?' She was looking around for someone to help her and signalled a trainee.

'I think one of them might be my brother.'

'Oh, dear.' She turned to the fresh-faced trainee. 'Tell whoever's in charge of the two DOAs brought in this morning that this young man thinks one might be his brother.' She knew the message would go straight to the detective on duty. 'Have a seat over there, sir. It shouldn't take long.'

Jahila crossed over to a long bench but did not sit down. He knew what was happening and tried to concentrate on the sum he was getting for the job. He strolled nervously up and down.

The tall, fair-haired young man who came down the corridor towards him had 'copper' written all over him; so far as Jahila was concerned they were the same the world over no matter the differences of dress.

The policeman introduced himself as Detective Constable Byron and flashed a warrant card. He took Jahila to a quiet part of the vestibule and said, 'I understand that you think one of the men brought in this morning might be your brother, sir?'

'It's possible. I will know for sure if I see them.'

'And what's your name?'

'Mohammed El Saide. I am a student at Birmingham University.'

'You're a foreign national, sir?'

'Yes. I'm Iranian.'

'Have you your passport with you, sir?'

'I don't carry it about.'

'And what makes you think that one of the two on the slab – the deceased – might be your brother?'

'I hope he is not, but my brother has been missing for several days now. And he is a wild one.'

'Have you reported him missing to the local police?'

Jahila was feeling more comfortable with every lie. He laughed drily. 'Why? He is always going missing. It is nothing new.'

'And the university puts up with it?'

'He's not at university; he's on a tourist visa. May I have a look to put my mind to rest one way or the other? If he is one of them I shall have to telephone my parents in Iran. I only want to check.'

DC Byron nodded briefly. 'All right. You'd better let me have your name again, and your address. I'll then take you through. By the way how did you know they were here?'

'A policeman at the scene of the murders told me.'

'Right. Come with me.'

They walked side-by-side, the detective noticing the increasing nervousness of the Iranian. There was a uniformed policeman outside a door through which Byron took him. Shrouds covered the two bodies layed out on separate examination slabs. Two white-coated men were conversing in one corner and another man, who looked like a senior detective,

76

gazed with a mixture of curiosity and suspicion as Jahila entered. Byron stood with his back to the door.

Jahila stood awkwardly as the well-built older man introduced himself as Detective Superintendent Grimswell and asked Jahila to relate again what he had already told his subordinate.

Jahila tried to vary the manner of the telling so that it looked less rehearsed but there was something about Grimswell that made him wary as if he was no ordinary policeman. It was difficult to define the difference but he was left with the feeling that the man was not local and that the association between Byron and Grimswell was not entirely natural, as if they had not met before.

When Jahila had finished Grimswell turned to Byron. 'You got his details?'

'Yes, sir.'

'O.K. Pull the first sheet back.' Grimswell wanted to stand aside to watch closely Jahila's reaction.

Jahila gazed at a face he did not know nor had expected to recognise. This part could not be rehearsed and he was aware of Grimswell's acute scrutiny. How was he supposed to react as he gazed down at the dead man? He was appalled, of course, death stared him in the face and a last expression of pain seemed to have locked on the twisted features to set hard in rigor mortis. Perhaps it was all in his mind.

'Well?'

Jahila did not hear at first and then he heard the voice again, this time more accusing.

'How long does it take you to decide whether or not it's your brother.'

'I'm sorry.' Jahila shook his head slowly. 'It was the shock of seeing someone like that. No, it's not Hassan.'

The sheet was pulled back over the head and Grimswell gave a faint nod to Byron who flipped back the second sheet.

Jahila knew that he had to hurry this time but if he were to follow Steiner's instructions fully, it was not easy to do. He took as long as he dared and could feel the suspicion oozing from Grimswell. He stepped back. 'No,' he said shakily. 'It is not him.'

'Neither of them?'

'No. I'm sorry.'

'Sorry? I thought you'd be pleased that your brother is not one of them.'

Jahila simply wanted to get out now. 'No, I'm sorry for wasting your time. I am relieved that my brother is not here.' He turned towards the door. 'I feel sick.'

'Take him to the loo, and check his name and address again,' Grimswell instructed Byron. He would have preferred to hold Jahila in custody for a while but it was difficult under the circumstances. He was not satisfied about the Iranian. As the two men were leaving he called out, 'Would you mind waiting a few minutes at reception Mr El Saide? I'll join you there.' He smiled, which changed his features completely. 'You might just possibly be able to help us.'

But later when Grimswell and Byron went to reception Jahila had gone and, later still, when his address was checked, it was found to be false. Neither fact surprised Grimswell and he instructed the local police to follow it up.

7

They telephoned in turn from a call box in the bustling market town of Newbury in Berkshire, just off the M4. Towler had parked the car round the back of the High Street in Tesco's car park. He did not know whom Kate was phoning although he knew she would have told him had he asked. In a way he did not want to know, for once she was in the hands of friends the responsibility was no longer his. But he knew he would worry about her and in this respect he would have liked a number at which he could contact her.

When Kate had finished her call Towler rang Soames at Curzon Street. He was put through immediately.

'What the hell's been happening? And where the hell are you?' Soames burst out but Towler could hear his relief.

'You know bloody well what's been happening, and where I am doesn't matter.' Towler replied acidly. 'We were set up. They nearly got the girl.'

'Who set you up?' Soames sounded anguished.

'I didn't get time to ask them,' snapped Towler. 'So you tell me.'

'I can't discuss this over an open line, for God's sake. Hang up and come in. We'll try to make some sense of it. Is the girl safe?'

'I'm not coming in until I'm satisfied. You discuss this now or not at all. The girl's O.K. but she was butchered; she had a toe amputated with bolt-cutters. I'm dropping her off with friends.'

Soames was startled by the news of the toe; he wondered if Prescott had known. 'Which friends?'

'You'll have to ask her and she doesn't want anybody else to know. Like me, she doesn't trust a soul right now. I'm just letting you know we're all right.'

'Stop being childish and report in. This has to be discussed and we must find out who's behind it.'

'Who do you think's behind it?'

'Don't be absurd. I can't discuss that now. We're breaking every security rule in the book by talking as we are.'

'Please yourself, Soames. Personally, I'm beginning to think you're behind it. If you're not, then you have a leak. I'm not coming in until I'm satisfied.'

'We think it was Mossad. This is crazy. If you won't come in then let's meet out in the open somewhere?'

'If it was Mossad they spoke bloody good English . . . just like us. Where?'

'Is the Embankment open enough for you in the middle of winter?'

Towler felt the pangs of betrayal. He thought for a while. 'Opposite the rear entrance to Embankment Underground Station. 3pm tomorrow.'

'What on earth is wrong with you? This is urgent. Why not today?'

Towler hung up. He had an uneasy feeling but accepted that it had been necessary to contact Soames if he was to understand anything that was going on. Before phoning he had changed some notes in the nearest bank so that he could amply feed the box for a long call. He turned to Kate who was leaning against a wall close by and was watching him impatiently. He noticed how she was lifting her injured foot off the gound and he signalled that he would not be much longer. After checking directory enquiries he dialled another number and a woman answered in a North American accent.

'May I speak to Lewis, please?'

'Who wants him?' The voice was warm but slightly slurred.

At least he was there. 'Tell him we met in Northern Ireland last year.'

Towler heard voices over the wire and they became raised with annoyance before a man said, 'Lewis Quinn.'

'Lew, it's Sam. You probably don't remember me. The Grafton pub bombing. I was in uniform at the time, a sergeant. We stood there side-by-side viewing the result of the carnage.

We met later a couple of times and had a drink or two.'

'Sure I remember you. In those circumstances could I ever forget? I never got your surname, though. And when we had a chance meeting some time later you weren't in uniform and tried to avoid me. It's O.K., I'm not dumb enough not to know why.' Quinn's voice had warmed considerably, his New Yorker's accent getting more pronounced. 'What can I do for you?'

'I need to talk to you. I'll be in London this afternoon. Is it possible to meet?'

'Sure. You can come here. You know the address?'

'I've still got your card.'

'Fine. Say, evening at six? Drink time.'

'I'll be there. And thanks.'

Towler helped Kate back to the car aware that they drew attention by their general state and the fact that Towler needed a shave. As he pulled out of the car park and headed back towards the M4 they were silent for quite a long time. Soon they would be separating and the realisation subdued them. They had known each other for less than a day but into that time a lifetime of danger had been crammed and the trust of each other, which had at first been forced upon them, now came naturally. They had formed a bond and it was about to be broken.

'It's like knowing someone for ever,' Kate said as they reached the approaches to London.

Towler smiled. 'That's a fact.'

'Can I have your phone number?'

He laughed. 'Shouldn't I be asking that?'

'You should but you're not going to, are you?'

He was grinning wrily now. 'I don't know where I'll be. I'm not going back to my pad to be picked off. There are a few things I must investigate. You should be going somewhere where you'll be difficult to find.'

'You sure they're still after us?'

'You know bloody well they are. They won't give up but I must find out why. I can't give you personal protection; I shall be too busy and, anyway, by splitting I can draw them away from you.' He concentrated on the road and did not shift his gaze as he added, 'It's not satisfactory for either of us. Discuss what's happened with your friends and take it from there.'

'But you still don't recommend going to the police?'

He shook his head slowly. 'Normally I would say yes, it's the obvious thing to do. But they will refer the whole thing to higher authority and you will have given away your location. I'm not sure whether someone set us up, Kate, or if someone leaked the exchange to other interested parties. For the time being I think you should just keep your head down.'

'Until when?'

He grinned nervously. 'O.K. I'd rather not have it in case someone tries to knock it out of me, but you'd better give me a number through which I can raise you, but not the number where you'll actually be staying. Don't contact your partner yet. Let her carry the can for a while.'

Kate felt happier. 'You'd better stop at the next bank or Post Office; I've no pen or paper.'

Towler nodded briefly. He was by no means happy with the arrangement; he would prefer not to know, but he reluctantly accepted her point.

Matt Steiner looked out across the violent currents of the river at Symonds Yat and watched three canoeists struggling to keep upright. In this weather, he thought; they had to be raving mad, or, more likely, some of the SAS training from nearby Hereford. It was a beautiful, yet stark, scene. The snow climbed the opposite banks to the high ground, expensive villas snowed in and cut off. Beside him Jahila shivered in his old topcoat. The café behind them was closed until reasonable conditions returned and it was lonely on the road.

'Did we have to meet here?' Jahila complained. 'I had to get a taxi.'

'No. But it's cold wherever we go so what's the difference? It's beautiful here. Now describe the stiffs again.'

Jahila groaned. 'I've told you; I can't change the detail by going over it.'

'I want to know just how observant you were. You might come up with something you've forgotten.'

Jahila went through it once more, dredging the depths of memory. When he had finished he added, 'I couldn't stay any longer, the cop was suspicious.'

'You're free, aren't you? Stop beefing. So you reckon that one was no more than in his mid-twenties?' He knew who the other man was for he had sent him as escort.

'That's right. He looked like a student.'

'Like yourself?'

'Yes. There were no scars, birth marks or anything like that. Of course, I only saw the face.'

Steiner pulled out a wad of dollar bills and peeled some off. He knew he was over-paying but he might need Jahila again. 'You did well.' He grinned to show large, spaced teeth. 'Not so difficult was it? You go back to London and get on with whatever you were doing. If I need you again I'll give you a call. I'll drop you off at the station.'

They walked towards the parked car and Steiner was deep in thought and quietly fuming. Whoever the young corpse was it was certainly not Rashid. There had been a double-cross and he had to find out why. The shooting and the killing made no sense. But where was Rashid? Meanwhile the other escort and the girl had escaped and that had to be put right quickly. Bastards.

Towler dropped Kate off in Edwardes Square, off Kensington High Street. She was vague as to where she actually wanted him to stop but the issue was settled by the shortage of parking space; he eventually found a slot near an apartment block.

They sat there for a while, reluctant to part and conscious of a mounting atmosphere, as though a suspicion had grown up between them. Towler looked at her. She had suffered a lot, the strain was clear; and there was a slightly haunted look about her which he had not seen before.

'Are you sure this is near enough to where you want to go?'

'Oh, yes. I can manage from here.'

'Get the foot fixed quickly. Once it's healed O.K. you'll find you'll manage quite easily without a small toe.'

Kate put her hand on the door lever. 'I owe you a lot, Sam. Take care.' She leaned across the seat and gave him a peck on the cheek before opening the door.

'Are you sure you don't want me to help you along?'

'No.' Her tone was sharp, but then she smiled. 'I'll be all right.' She closed the door and stood on the pavement waiting for him to go. It was clear that she would not move until he had.

As she faced him like that, barely able to put her foot to the ground, he could see her anguish more clearly. He gave a little wave, checked his mirror and then pulled out. He drove slowly, watching his mirror all the way; Kate was still standing there and to let him know she was watching, gave him a long wave. By the time he reached the High Street she was still standing there.

The moment he turned the corner he accelerated as fast as the traffic allowed. He re-entered the square further on and raced round the cramped, narrow roads until he was forced to slow down for a taxi. A car pulled out ahead of him and Towler was quick to seize the opportunity. He pulled in, ignored the meter, and ran round the corner to view the spot where Kate had been standing. She was no longer there.

There was hardly anyone on view but he did not move until he was sure that Kate had gone. She could have entered any of the high-bracket terraced houses that lined the square. Or she could have gone into the apartment block. With her injury it was unlikely she had gone far.

Towler was less hurried now, and he continued down to the point where he had left her. He was curious about why she wanted to maintain contact yet did not want him to know where she was going. He turned left into a narrow dead end street which served nothing but the apartments. There were two entrances spaced at each end of the block. He mounted the steps to the first, opened the glass doors and approached the porter's desk at the far end of the lobby.

'I've forgotten the apartment number my girlfriend is visiting.' Towler gave a friendly grin. 'Only just managed to park the car.'

The porter looked up. 'The lady with the limp, sir?' He was eyeing the state of Towler but the girl had been in just as bad a condition. Young people simply did not care these days. '6o6C.'

'Thanks.' Towler moved towards the elevator and stopped mid-way. 'Damn, I've left my keys in the car.' He ran out and slowed to a walk as soon as he was clear of the block. So in the event he had parked quite close to where Kate had wanted to go. He searched for a phone and rang the rental company to tell them where the car could be found and that a Mr Soames at the Curzon Street address would settle all outstanding hire charges and any fines incurred by parking. He walked to the nearest underground station, aware that, in spite of their shared dangers, Kate was holding something back.

'She's back.' The Home Secretary was clearly delighted. 'Thanks, Bluie. I was sure you could do it.'

Prescott straightened his arthritic knee; he was not really comfortable on the chair in Dawson's office. This time the meeting was not clandestine as Prescott was acting as envoy for Sir Malcolm Read on another matter.

'Good. I did tell you it would be all right. Have you seen her?'

'No. But I've spoken to her on the telephone. At the moment she's in a private clinic having her butchered foot sorted out.'

Prescott did not appear to be as happy about events as Dawson. He gazed warily across the desk. He said hesitantly, 'Has she told the police anything?'

'I gather not. She did not say too much over the phone.'

Carefully, Prescott said, 'Would it not be better if you tell her not to contact the police? Place a mysterious hood of security over the whole affair so you don't have to explain too much.'

'I've already done that. There is no need to create a mysterious event; damn it, it exists.'

'What had she to say about Towler?'

'She's sure that he saved her life. I think she's formed an attachment for him. In the circumstances it would be natural enough.'

Prescott shifted again but now the discomfort was mental. He spoke slowly. 'We are not at all sure about Towler. My people think he might be involved in what happened. Saving Miss Parker might have been part of an act. Did she say where he went after dropping her?'

'She doesn't know.' Dawson was still filled with the euphoria of Kate Parker escaping but he picked up the innuendo and was worried by it.

'There, you see. Why hasn't he reported in? My bet is that he won't.'

'What are you trying to say, Bluie?'

'Well, it's quite clear that the man he was supposed to deliver in exchange for Miss Parker is now very dead together with the other escort. Towler escaped but for some strange reason has gone underground. He has confused the issue by ostensibly getting the girl off the hook, but how convenient was his escape? He knows all about the shootings and the killings and we need his report to form an assessment. We simply don't know where he is.'

Dawson put Kate out of his mind for a moment. 'What am I supposed to infer from that?'

'Towler is a wild card. He spent a long time with Abdul, in fact he was the last of our men to be on guard duty with him.'

'So?'

'Minister, Towler was the man who was first suspicious of Abdul. Nobody else knew him.' He paused to make sure he had Dawson's full attention, then continued, 'It's possible that he wanted Abdul pulled in for reasons of his own.' He waved a hand airily. 'Of course this is sheer speculation; the man served in the SAS for years with distinction although the latter part of his career was not up to standard and some thought he had lost his nerve. There may have been another reason.'

'Do I need to know this? If he'd lost his nerve he made a remarkable job of recovering it the last couple of days.'

Prescott did not answer but gazed back dubiously, allowing Dawson to draw the conclusion he wanted the Minister to draw.

'Are you suggesting that he did not act bravely? That he knew what was going to happen and that he would be in no real danger?'

Prescott shrugged heavily. 'We simply don't know. But it is a line of thought. There was shooting, there were deaths, someone was responsible and only a very limited number of people knew that the exchange was to take place. He was one of them and he is the only one we don't really know. His army record, in security terms, is open to question. He was rather foisted on us. And we do like to choose our own people.'

86

Dawson was puzzled. 'Surely this is a matter for you alone? I can't help you.'

'Of course not. I'm only telling you because you are involved in the affair.'

'Involved?' The word was a whiplash.

Prescott backed down uneasily. 'I mean, you are involved with Miss Parker.'

'And that's the beginning and end of my involvement. I'm very grateful for what you have done. I do understand the reason why you can't discuss your suspicions with Sir Malcolm, but don't use me as a surrogate chief. If there's a rotten apple then pluck it out. If you produce conclusive proof and you don't want to raise the dust, then refer to me again and we'll sort something out. The problem, meanwhile, is yours.'

'Yes, of course. I thought you might be interested as Miss Parker almost lost her life. If we come up with anything solid I will, naturally, let you know.' He rose awkwardly, making great play of his knee. When he was upright he said, 'I wonder if you will ask Miss Parker to let you know if Towler tries to contact her again?'

Dawson nodded. 'I can do that.' But he was not happy about it. He said suddenly, 'Is there something about this affair that you are not telling me, Bluie?'

It was too near the mark but Prescott fenced the question off with convincing guile. 'There is probably a good deal about it that I'm not telling you, Minister. But only those parts we do not know ourselves. But as you point out these problems are for us to solve.'

Prescott was satisfied. He had sown the seed but it would need nurturing. The Abdul–Parker exchange was far from over.

8

Lewis Quinn lived in an apartment off the Kilburn High Road on the fringe of Maida Vale. He was on the first floor, what he, as an American, called the second floor, of one of those very big houses that had been converted to apartments. The rooms were delightfully large with big windows that let in the draughts. The street door was always left unlocked because vandals kept filling the keyhole with gum.

When Cathy Quinn opened the apartment door Towler saw an immediate problem. She was slightly drunk. A red-head, she had a once-beautiful face that showed early signs of fast living but was still attractive enough to draw attention. She was well covered in some expensive creation which was somehow suggestive; Towler thought that it would not matter a good deal what she wore, she would always look like that.

'Are you Sam?'

'I am,' he replied, noting that she had made no move to let him in. 'Sam Towler.'

She smiled and he could see a deep-rooted, cynical humour in eyes that could not be ignored. 'You look as if you've been dragged through a hedge,' she said, 'unless it's a new fashion. You'd better come in.'

She barely gave him room to pass and her smile was provocative as he tried not to make contact; a faint smell of liquor vied with an expensive perfume.

'Straight ahead,' she said. 'Lew's on the phone right now but it won't matter. If you prefer, you can wait with me until he's finished.'

Towler stopped in mid-stride and turned to face her. 'Which would you prefer?' he asked coolly. He saw her brief hesitation; she was used to men being afraid of her, or succumbing.

Her smile wavered, unsure now of how far she could go with this grim-faced, good-looking stranger. 'Please yourself,' she retorted. 'I'll be in here if anyone wants me.' She opened a door off the hall and disappeared, slamming it behind her.

Towler smiled; Cathy Quinn was used to getting her way and was unsure how to cope when she could not. Towler crossed to the door she had indicated, knocked, and entered.

Lew Quinn was standing at a battered desk talking into a telephone. He gave Towler a brief, friendly grin, indicated a chair, and continued talking.

Towler gazed around. The walls were covered with press cuttings and cartoons. They were pinned haphazardly and most contained the by-line of Lewis Quinn. There were also photographs of Quinn with various celebrities. The desk was covered in papers held down by a variety of paperweights, and seemed to be in a general mess. Clearly this was very much Quinn's own room.

Quinn himself supported the general scene. Almost black hair was dishevelled and hung in strands over his forehead, and his hungry, intense face seemed to be in need of a shave, but in fact, he never looked different. He wore a T-shirt and jeans; his arms were sinewy and as dark as his face. The smallish room was dull and almost oppressively hot.

Towler removed a pile of newspapers from an old leather swivel-back but did not sit down. He was thinking of how they had first met. Quinn was in Ulster as a stringer for the *New York Times*; he had lost his by-line some time previously in circumstances he never divulged to Towler.

After the trauma of the carnage they had both covered in their respective ways, they had struck up an unlikely friendship. Quinn was an Irish-American and Towler was at first suspicious of his attitude; but the London-based American proved to have a far more realistic grasp of what was happening in the province, and was more fully aware of the real issues rather than the emotional ones, than the vast majority of foreign journalists. He had shown that he knew the score and was no pushover for IRA propagandists. Some of the articles he sent back suffered when editors attempted to appease Irish-American readers strung up by the usual myths.

When Quinn finished his call, he came round the desk and the two men shook hands warmly.

'What can I do for you?' asked Quinn.

'Give me a bed for a couple of nights?'

Towler now lowered himself on to the chair he had cleared while Quinn went back to his desk and groped in one of the drawers.

'You look as if you need a drink,' said Quinn placing two glasses and a bottle of bourbon on the desk. 'After that little bombshell I certainly do.' He did not ask whether Towler wanted water or ice but just pushed a charged glass across the desk. He then sprawled on an ancient but sturdy typist's chair and added, 'It must be serious. Do I get any reasons?'

Towler gazed at his drink and then at Quinn. He felt drained and badly needed sleep. 'You're thinking that we don't know each other all that well and why should I ask you?'

'That's exactly what I'm thinking. Give me what you can.'

Towler grinned. 'That's one of the things I like about you, you cut through the bullshit. You know I can't go too far.' He picked up his drink.

'So far,' said Quinn, reaching for his own glass, 'you've gone no distance at all. By the way, did I ever get to know your surname?'

'That depends on how good a journalist you are. It's Towler. I need your help because I can't go to any long-standing friends and there are few, if any, short acquaintances that I would trust in this way.'

'Thanks, Sam.' Quinn raised his glass in acknowledgment. 'The nicest thing said to me for a long time.' He smiled awkwardly; 'And from a man trained to be suspicious, it is a bonus. Who's after you?'

'I don't know. I'm not even sure they're after me at all; it might be someone else and I happened to be in the way.' Towler slowly shook his head. 'Someone's playing silly buggers. I can't go home and I can't go to anyone I'm known to know.'

'If you did?'

Towler thought carefully before replying. 'I'd be topped.'

'Shit!' Quinn put his feet up on the desk, dislodging some papers; he seemed not to care. 'Are you with the good guys or the bad guys?' The question was serious and he watched Towler closely.

Towler did not reply at all at first. He sat staring at Quinn, then he started to chuckle.

'I didn't realise I'd said something funny.' Quinn remarked.

'I can't answer you,' Towler retorted. 'I don't bloody well know. I think I started out with the good guys.'

'You wouldn't have changed sides so I guess you're saying you are no longer sure about the good guys?'

'You could be right. Have you a connection with the Company? Here in London?'

'If I have I'd be bound by the same rules as you. As a journalist I used to know one or two of the London-based guys.'

'Any you could trust?'

'Some I liked,' Quinn replied cautiously.

'O.K. Any who had a grudge or a contempt of our Security Service?'

Quinn was now all attention, his dark eyes never leaving Towler. 'Which section in particular?'

'Five.'

Quinn removed his feet from the table and leaned forward over the desk. 'MI5? Are you serious?' He answered his own question. 'I see that you are. Certain individuals didn't always see eye to eye but that's normal on both sides. There are operational differences. But a grudge? That would suggest that someone would do something about it.' He thought long and deeply and finally shook his head. 'I don't know anyone like that. To hold contempt for particular people is one thing, and such feelings were returned, but I don't know anyone who would act dumb over it. What's your point?'

'I just wondered if you knew anyone in the Company who might do a bit of probing for me?'

'Hey, Sam, they couldn't take that risk; they're on friendly foreign soil.' And then hesitantly, 'Just how hot are you?'

'Probably hotter than I think I am. I'd know better if I knew what the hell was going on.' Towler gazed at Quinn while he tried to fight off the enervating effect of the too-hot room; coupled with the drink and no sleep, he was having considerable difficulty in keeping awake. 'I've got to tell you something meanwhile, but if I get out of this I'll give you what I can. The lead's been flying about and there has been a follow-up which I managed to stave off. But I need safety and time to sort things out.'

'That would put us in the firing line. And you can't promise me a story?' Quinn was turning his glass round in his strong fingers.

'Does helping me depend on that?'

'You bastard. I'm a newspaper man for chrissake.' Quinn then smiled wrily. 'You know how to aim low, Sam. Just a couple of nights, you say?'

Towler stood up afraid that he might doze off if he did not. 'Look, if this thing breaks a certain way, I'll give you a story. If I'm wrong about it then I won't be able to. But you can help me get at the truth.'

Quinn shrugged. 'So a couple of days is a figure of speech?' He drained his bourbon and put down his glass. 'Are you sure you can trust me?'

'No. But I'm bloody sure there are some I don't want to trust right now. What about your wife?'

Quinn closed his eyes as if to shut out pain. He rose slowly and suddenly his image changed. 'She let you in. She wouldn't have missed the opportunity with a strong fella like you.'

'You don't have to worry about me, Lew.'

'I can accept that. But she enjoys a challenge. Don't kid yourself you're impregnable.'

'I'm trusting you, you trust me. What went wrong?'

Quinn shook his head and reached for the bottle. He turned. 'You want some more?' And, when Towler declined, Quinn half-filled his own glass. He ran a hand over his head then rubbed the back of his neck. 'She'd rather be in New York. She likes visiting London but doesn't like living in it. I can't go back and get a job there, not easily. I blotted my copy-book with one of the press barons a long time ago. So Cathy is making me pay for it. All the time.'

Quinn wandered over to the window and gazed down into the darkened street lightened only by the glow of frozen snow piled to one side of the pavements. 'It's happening right under my goddam nose,' he said bitterly.

'Couldn't she go back?' Towler risked asking.

Quinn crossed the room to switch on a light. 'She has her own money, so I guess she could. Maybe she gets satisfaction from making me pay for what happened. She accepts no restrictions.' Quinn fought with his feelings for a while and Towler did not intrude. Then he picked up his glass, raised it in a silent toast to Towler, and said, 'Before you ask, Sam, old boy, I love her. If I didn't, I'd have kicked her out years ago.'

Towler said uncomfortably, 'I've come at a bad time. Look, forget it, Lew. I'll manage.'

'You look as if you're dropping on your feet. Follow me and we'll sort out the rest later. Meanwhile we'll operate under the banner of transatlantic friendship.'

Matt Steiner arrived at Marylebone Railway Station and queued for a taxi. The train had been late and it was freezing cold but he gave no indication that these problems affected him. He was so solidly built that he would be impossible to miss even in a crowd and his lack of inches only emphasised his build. He was taken to a turning off Addison Road and paid off the cab.

He walked along the strip cleared through the frozen snow and climbed the steps to the entrance of one of the imposing town houses which had stood solidly against any kind of weather for over a hundred and fifty years. Steiner felt an affinity with buildings like these; they were here to stay. He rang the bell and identified himself as a Mr Willis and the door catch was released after a little hesitation. He mounted soft carpeted stairs rather than take the elevator and rang the bell of number 2b on the second floor. He knew he was being checked through the spy hole so stood full-face towards the door.

A bald, brown-skinned, bespectacled, middle-aged man opened the door and bade Steiner enter. The greetings on both sides were affable but restrained as if a slight suspicion of each other might be hidden. Steiner entered a large, expensively furnished room with Middle-Eastern rugs scattered over the polished wood flooring.

'Is this room clean?' asked Steiner as he stood between two massive ottomans. He gazed round almost insolently at the obvious opulence.

Nabih Malouf appeared to be offended before he picked up

the meaning. 'You think my enemies would try to bug my apartment?'

'The British might. You have been known to upset them.'

Malouf laughed lightly. 'That was some time ago and a misundersanding.'

'Was it hell! So it's safe to talk here?'

'If it weren't, I would be dead by now. I do know how to look after my health, Mr Willis. Won't you sit down?' Malouf spoke perfect English with an Oxford accent, though he was born in Palestine.

Steiner made no move to take off his heavy coat. Suddenly he said, 'How would you like to get back at the British, Mr Malouf?'

Towler still had work to do before he was prepared to sleep. Quinn had offered him a small guest room with an en-suite shower at the end of the apartment. He wondered just how much Quinn contributed financially. He was too good a reporter to be ignored even by furious press barons, but he was no longer the respected journalist he had once been, and his income must have nose-dived. But he had kept his journalistic integrity and there was not too much of that around these days.

Towler sat on the edge of the bed wondering how someone with Quinn's moral strength could cope with the flaunting activities of a nymphomaniac wife. Even when the three of them had dined together Cathy had been coquettish with Towler who had simply ignored her when his instincts demanded that he make her look cheap. But he could not do that in front of Quinn who was being more than helpful when he had no need to be. It was an uncomfortable meal and Towler was glad to make his excuses to take a shower.

None of Quinn's clothes fitted Towler, so he went out late at night in the clothes he had arrived in. Quinn had wanted to come but Towler thought it too soon. By a combination of buses and Underground trains he arrived within a hundred yards of the apartment he had been allocated as a temporary measure by Soames. There were few people on the streets and the rows of parked cars appeared to be frozen solid in their parking slots, frost glittering like diamante on the bodywork.

He walked slowly and quietly, turned a corner and continued

94

on. When he reached the next corner he slipped on a patch of ice and almost fell. He crouched where he was and cursed silently. He peered round the corner and then across the road. His own apartment was in the row of houses on the opposite side of the street about half-way down. There were the usual two rows of parked cars, some with covers over them.

Towler had his hands in his topcoat pockets and he wore a tweed cap he had borrowed from Quinn. A sharp, icy wind made his eyes water. He stood as part of the shadows, observing and at the same time wondering what he was going to do about money; he was running short.

He crept along the wall using the parked cars as staging-posts. All the windows were frosted up except where newspapers had been tucked under wipers to protect the glass. It was therefore easy to pick out the car which had comparatively clear windows. The engine was not running so the heater was not on and that meant that someone inside the car was periodically wiping the frost off, probably using a spray.

Towler crawled past the car and several more. The main entrance to the apartments was a little further on. Then he saw the van. He crept up to it to read the logo on the side: R. T. Phillips, Painter and Decorator. As he crouched Towler could see the hole bored through the middle 'O' of the last word. There would be a similar hole on the other side. It would not matter if the windows iced up as there was probably some sort of heater in the body of the van. There would be at least two men inside.

Towler remained crouched below the level of the hole and pulled out an Elastoplast and tore off the strips. He worked his way round to the other side of the van, located the drilled hole, reached up and stuck the plaster over it. As he ran across the street he heard someone swear inside the van. He could not move too fast because of the ice but he kept low, knowing that he would now be on view to the car further down the street. He mounted the short railinged steps leading to the front door of his apartment block and with frozen hands inserted the key. Before he had closed the door he heard running footsteps crossing the street towards him and someone called out, 'It's him. Let's get the bastard.'

9

'I'm sorry I'm so late, my dear. But I couldn't get away from the House until 10.30.' And then as Kate hobbled towards him Dawson added, 'My God, what have they done to you?'

He hurried forward and held her for some time before helping her to a chair where he lifted her bandaged foot on to a low, padded stool. 'Kate, I'm so sorry this should happen to you.' Clearly upset, he sat opposite her and added emotionally, 'I'm surprised they let you out so soon. Are you sure you're all right?'

Kate looked pale against the background of the heavy blue dressing-gown she had borrowed from the modelling friend with whom she was now staying and who was out. 'A bit shattered, very tired, but that's all. The doctor isn't worried. I'm strong, healthy, and will be on both feet in no time. So there, James. There is no need to worry.'

'Of course I'm worried.' Dawson's concern was obvious. He noticed the metal crutches by her chair; 'Can you manage with those awful things?'

'Of course. They're only to take the weight off my foot. I don't really need them.' Her tone changed as she added, 'How did I get caught up in this dreadful business? Was it to get at you?'

'Something like that. But it's all settled now. There's nothing more to worry about.'

'I must be an embarrassment to you. I'm sorry.'

'Embarrassment! My God. You'll never be that, my darling. It's my fault that you've suffered so. It should never have happened. I can't give you the detail but there was a delay in the exchange which must have frightened your captors. Can you tell me anything about them?'

'I never saw their faces. I'm sure they were Arabs and I'm equally sure that the one who took my toe off is American. I haven't told the police about it. Sam didn't want me to and nor do you.'

'Sam? Oh, your escort. My people seem to be worried about him. They think he might be involved.'

'Involved? Of course he was. What do you mean exactly?' Kate pulled her dressing-gown more tightly around her, her face cocooned by the heavy collar.

'I simply don't know. He has disappeared. He should have reported in. Don't you find that strange behaviour?'

'We were *shot* at. Two men were killed. We had a dreadful time. He doesn't trust anybody and I don't blame him. He saved my life, James. He'll do the right thing as he sees it. Has nobody at all heard from him?'

'Not that I know of. I shouldn't be telling you this but as you've suffered so much because of it, it's only fair to say that we think the Israelis are involved. There are strong grounds for this belief. They had to be tipped off by someone and this man Towler might have done it.'

Kate angrily pushed herself upright. 'To get himself shot at?'

'He wasn't hit, was he?'

'But we were both chased through the snow, and at the farm. He took risks for me.'

'It might have been an act. Don't concern yourself with it. We'll find out.' And then irritably, 'It would make it a damned sight easier if he reported in and the whole messy business could be sorted out.' Dawson peered across the room as if he was having difficulty in seeing her. 'Have you formed an attachment for this man?'

Kate answered warily, 'We couldn't have gone through what we did without some feeling. I'm worried for him. He seems to be having a raw deal.'

'Well, if that's all I'm sure that everything will work out.' He rose wearily. 'I'd like to stay longer but I must let you get some rest. One day perhaps, I will be able to explain what happened to get you in to such a dreadful situation.' He smiled with immense affection and crossed to kiss her. 'You look after yourself, my love. I'm on the end of the telephone if you want anything. I'm tempted to give you a police guard.'

'I thought it was all over?'

'Yes, well perhaps not. Do let me know if you hear from this Towler fellow. We must make contact with him.'

'I'm not likely to, but I will if I do. I think you're wrong about him.'

Dawson gave her a long questioning look, blew a kiss and refused to let her see him out. On the way down in the elevator he felt perturbed at Kate's reaction and wondered once again if he was hearing the full story from Prescott. He fervently hoped that she would be unable to make contact with Towler who seemed to invite trouble.

Towler slammed the door and stood behind it where there was a wide space on either side. The hall was large and the stairs ran off it in dog-legs to the three upper floors; there was no lift. He pulled out his gun, took off the safety-catch and waited. The running footsteps were quite clear and he could see vague shadows against the two glass door-panels. An instrument was inserted in the lock and someone was fumbling.

The door was slowly pushed back in Towler's direction but he had made allowances for the swing and was well to one side. The hall light was left off as three men moved forward towards the stairs; they wanted to attract no more attention than he did. They were either familiar with the lay-out or had been briefed. They crossed the hall and maintained their silence as they went up the stairs in single file.

Towler could barely see them but could pick out the softest of movements. When he reasoned that they were on the second dog-leg he crept round the still-open door, stepped outside, closed the door quietly and locked it. He crossed the road at an angle to the van, keeping upright and knowing that, if anyone was still in the car, in the dark he would look like one of the men returning to the van. He came from the rear and yanked open the van door.

The driver almost fell out in surprise and Towler pulled him out and held him against the side of the van with his gun pressed under the chin. He knew he had very little time so pushed the muzzle hard into the man's throat and said, 'Who sent you?'

'Christ, I can't breathe.' It was barely a croak. 'Take the bloody gun away.'

'You won't breathe again, you bastard, if you don't answer. Who?'

'I don't know. It's a contract job. We never know.'

'You lying bastard. Was it Soames?'

'I don't know a Soames. You'd have to ask Harry, he's the one who organises us.'

'Harry's inside the house?' Towler screwed the gun harder expecting the front door across the street to open at any moment. Suddenly there were footsteps coming towards them. Towler did not hesitate, he crashed the gun over the driver's head and held him in position until two girls had passed the other side of the van. When they were clear he dragged the driver into the gutter and lowered him there. He climbed into the van and switched on.

The engine did not fire at once and by the time it did the three men emerged through the door across the street and came racing towards the van. One of them slipped, arms and legs flying. The others jumped round him, somehow maintaining their balance, as Towler drew out. He pushed his gun through the open cab window and fired between the two of them. Both men dived for cover and in that moment he saw that they were armed. The tail of the van swerved as he tried to pick up speed and he felt something crunch on his off-side; it must have been the man who slipped.

In his mirror Towler saw two of the men scramble to their feet but he did not think they would fire so openly. Before he reached the corner he saw the car race up, skidding to a halt as the two men piled in. Towler turned the corner in a four-wheeled skid, and, for a moment, thought he was going to crash into the line of cars on his off-side. There was nothing he could do as he lost control but somehow the tail swung to correct the skid and he gave the briefest touch of brake in order to straighten.

The car came racing round in a wide arc, bounced off one of the parked cars with a screech of torn metal, and veered back to the centre of the street. Towler watched it happen in his mirror and knew that any moment now someone would be phoning for the police. The men behind him must have thought the same for they reduced speed and merely kept him in sight as he drove as fast as he dared.

Towler took another turning, and then another and the headlights behind him remained at a constant distance. He reached a main road and this gave him breathing space. In spite of the atrocious weather the street was busy but speeds were down to a sensible level. At a red traffic-light the car made no attempt to draw up beside him and that told him what he needed to know. They knew he had to stop sometime and they would wait for that moment. The freezing air was blasting through the still-open window which he now closed.

Towler drove steadily and kept to the main streets as one led to another. He checked the fuel gauge; there was no problem there. A police car went past but nobody was crazy enough to exceed the limit in these conditions.

As he drove on, noting the car about three vehicles behind him, he began to believe that the van driver had told him the truth. The cab radio was not sophisticated enough to belong to the 'firm'. The special equipment pack was missing from the door pocket. Also, when he had covered the hole in the side of the van, he could now recall that it had been roughly, and probably recently, drilled. Refinements were missing that would normally be there. So who had contracted the men chasing him?

The traffic dropped off dramatically as he entered the less busy streets. He reduced speed, watching his mirror closely; they were still there. He took a right turn and suddenly the street was empty of everything but parked vehicles. There was just enough space to overtake so he kept a central position to block the car off. He turned again and now he was in a much narrower street with a crossroads at the far end.

As Towler approached the end of the street he suddenly accelerated, roared up to the junction and jammed on his brakes. The van spun in a frightening movement in the middle of the street. For a moment it balanced on its two off-side wheels and then crashed down to block off any on-coming traffic as it finally came to rest side-on to the approaching car.

Towler did not wait for the van to stop rocking; he opened the door on the blind side to the car and jumped out to head for the nearest side-street and to dive down the first basement steps to crouch among the refuse bins. Through the railings he saw the grotesque shadow of the van cast across the street by the blazing headlights of the car as its doors opened and closed and running footsteps came padding towards the junction.

'Which way did he go?'

'Christ knows; we'd better fan out.' The voice was just above Towler's head.

'We can't leave the car like that, someone will send for the fuzz. I'll reverse back. You get the van going, Jim, and then take the left junction, and you take the right on foot, Willie. I'll bring the car round to come up the middle road. Be careful; this guy's no mug.'

The car was reversed back and the shadow of the van shortened and weakened until there was none at all. Footsteps passed above Towler and continued on, hesitating now and then as a flashlight probed doorways and basements.

Towler prepared for a long wait. He had taken the keys from the ignition when he had jumped and it would take Jim a little time before he could start the van without them. The van was eventually manoeuvred out and took the left turn very slowly.

Towler went cautiously up the basement steps. He had not heard Willie for some time, and now at street level he could not see any sign of a flashlight. He could still hear the van but there was no sign of the return of the car. He had to move. It was a gamble; it always was.

Matt Steiner left Nabih Malouf reasonably content. There were always difficulties when two men such as they, with different aims and declared sworn enemies, tried to reach agreement on a common interest. Both were experienced in survival and in pursuing what they believed. But if the media held out no hope of such men combining on any issue which attracted both in the same way, then they lacked realism.

Perversely, too, if such agreement was reached and a common objective followed, neither would cross the other, for to do so would leave future mutual options closed forever. So Steiner was satisfied that, in this particular case, Malouf would do what he could.

It was now 11pm but Steiner was not yet finished for the night. He walked some distance on the emptying streets before finding a cab to take him to the Grosvenor Hotel, where a colleague had a suite under the guise of an American business man. The hotel was like an illuminated oasis at the dark end of Park Lane and Steiner crossed the lobby with the faint feeling of coming home. He had not warned Tony Bellardi that he was calling but there was nothing new in that. It was fifteen minutes to midnight when he knocked on Bellardi's door.

'Jesus, whatever it is, couldn't it wait till tomorrow?' The lanky, dark-eyed Bellardi was still trying to rouse himself, a blue dressing-gown gaping, his narrow face even more gaunt than usual. Steiner had once likened him to Count Dracula, and at that moment the description came close.

'Give me a drink,' Steiner demanded, not the least put out by his friend's objections. 'The usual. It's been quite a day.'

'For me, too.' Bellardi was slowly coming round. He went to a cabinet and poured two stiff whiskies and filled the glasses with cubes from the small ice-box. He handed a drink to Steiner who sat on the edge of the bed, still with his hat and coat on, and drank half the liquor in a gulp.

Bellardi sank on to a chair. 'Well?'

'The guy who was shot was not Rashid Khayar.'

That announcement knocked the sleep from Bellardi in one blow. 'Shit. You sure?'

'Sure enough. We've been scammed. And someone is going to pay for it.'

'Why?' Bellardi watched Steiner, still full of life; the bastard never got tired and he wondered yet once again if he ever slept. 'Why would they do that?'

Steiner shrugged his heavy shoulders. 'I don't know why. Maybe Five know more than we think they do but it still makes no sense. Anyway, just where the hell is Rashid? We can't afford to lose him right now.'

'You'll have to show your hand and ask the straight question.'

'You're not thinking, Tony. I had Dawson bearded in the House of Commons, for chrissake. By an Arab. I cut off the toe of a loved one. I can't show my hand now.'

'You shouldn't have touched the girl; it was a mistake.'

'Was it hell. Don't lose any sleep on her. She was once a teenage acolyte of Vanessa Redgrave and Jane Fonda and that crowd. She's been active enough, and for all I know, still is. Dawson should know better. Anyway it produced the fast result I wanted. But why did they switch?'

'So what do you intend to do between now and dawn?'

Steiner gazed over at his friend and a slow grin softened his craggy features. 'You've no stamina, that's your trouble.'

'But I've a brain. One of us has to have it and you're certainly not showing much. Who did the shooting?'

'If I knew that I'd have some of the other answers. The girl escaped with her escort and I find that suspect. We must find the guy who was with her. And I feel inclined to snatch the girl again.'

'No.' Bellardi crossed his long legs, soft slippers looking incongruous on his big feet. 'No. At least not until we know a little more of what's going on. Maybe we should have been a bit more open about the whole business in the first place?'

'You know damn fine that was impossible. We may just as well have put an ad in the newspapers. I must find that escort to discover what he knows about Rashid. That's the main issue. We must get to Rashid fast before his real enemies do.'

Bellardi yawned, making no attempt to hide it. 'Are you sure it was Rashid who was picked up by Five?'

Steiner gazed scornfully at his colleague. 'What are you talking about? I saw it happen. A minute or two earlier and he'd have been safe in the car. When I checked at that flea-pit of a hotel the next day his account had been settled in cash and the receptionist made like the guy had never stayed there. You think they'd have agreed to an exchange if it wasn't them?' Steiner rose and drained his drink. 'Go back to bed, Tony, your fuse box is scrambled.'

10

Towler walked along the Embankment from the Blackfriars end. It was a long walk but he wanted to give himself space and time to spot anyone planted by Soames. There were not many people about in spite of the fact that it was mid-afternoon and the blocks of offices and the Savoy Hotel on the Charing Cross side were a blaze of lights in the winter gloom.

Even in this bitter weather the Thames still induced people to lean on the parapet to view the grey, powerfully moving currents below them. Across the river the Oxo sign stood out like a warning. Towler suspected each sightseer, at the same time thinking they were too obvious, but Soames would have his men around somewhere. Far behind Towler, a taxi kerb-crawled, keeping pace with him.

Towler positioned himself opposite Embankment Underground Station with his back to the parapet. Below him was the landing-stage where the pleasure boats moored. He turned to lean over the parapet and to check the steps leading down. The place was deserted but he moved further away from the steps. Across the street the station was constantly busy with a frequent exodus of hurrying people. Some used the footbridge close by to brave the crossing of the river against the icily cutting winds. Towler stood there soaking up the scene, trying to miss nothing.

Soames arrived on time, his shapeless body sunk into a pale sheepskin coat and wearing a fur hat, looking like a Russian. He wore ungainly gloves. He crossed the street without checking the lights but the traffic was kind to him as if he knew it would be. He arrived by Towler's side, protesting irritably.

'For God's sake, Sergeant, this is ridiculous. What on earth do you think you're doing? You've been with us five minutes and created mayhem. At this rate I really can't see you staying with us.'

'Neither can I,' Towler agreed drily. 'Your boys had another go at me last night. They're not very good.'

'What on earth are you talking about?' Soames clapped his gloved hands together. His nose was red, his eyes watering.

'A car and a van were waiting for me when I went back to my pad to pick up some things. The men were all armed.'

'Well, it was nothing to do with us, old boy. For God's sake have some sense. Perhaps they were the same thugs you say tried to get you the night of the exchange. I've no idea who they are. The little evidence we have points to Mossad. And what their game is, heaven only knows. They would like to kill every Arab in sight and sometimes do, often on someone else's patch. They really get out of hand at times.'

Soames turned to face Towler who still had his back to the river. 'This really is ludicrous standing here in the freezing cold. Come back to the office with me and let's discuss this sensibly in the warm over a cup of hot coffee.'

Towler noticed Soames' almost imperceptible glance up at the footbridge as he spoke. He did not turn but assumed that direction was cut off, or at best, he would pick up a tail if he went that way. He had expected nothing less. He said, 'The only reason I'm meeting you at all is to try to get some sense into the situation. I don't trust you, Soames. We don't like each other, O.K.? But why set me up? Why try to kill me or the girl or maybe both? Even a shit like you has to have a reason. What the hell have I done or is it something I know, or that my face doesn't fit?'

'It was a mistake to meet like this.' Soames adjusted his hat as if it had slipped. 'You are really off your rocker, Towler. I'm giving you a direct order now to report in or I will have you picked up by the police under a breach of the Official Secrets Act.'

'Balls. You'll never use the police because you've got too much to hide. And your hired help won't get anywhere. But I'll tell you this.' Towler stood over Soames and prodded his chest hard enough to make him step back. 'I'm going to find out what this is about. You must have been desperate to try to pull such a stupid stunt. I'm coming out from under, Soames. I'm going to unscramble you.'

'You poor rambling fellow. You spent too long in Ireland. I'll have you picked up and then, perhaps, we can talk sensibly.'

As Soames turned to cross the street, Towler said, 'Your goons on the bridge won't get me. Nor those tucked just inside the tube station and those towards the Savoy. The car across the street is facing the wrong way. You've got to come and find me, Soames and every time you do you'll be choking a little more on your bloody lies and showing more of your stinking hand.'

Towler scratched his nose and immediately the cab which had been following raced towards him just as Soames stepped off the kerb. Soames jumped back in a flurry as Towler opened the cab door and climbed in. Before closing the door, Towler called out, 'Watch your step, Soames; it can work both ways.'

Towler looked back through the rear window as the cab sped away. The car he had noticed outside the rear of the station was trying to do a U-turn against the run of traffic. Soames was standing still, his gaze on the disappearing taxi, his expression beneath the rim of fur, grim. 'He's making note of the number,' said Towler, 'to check later where we were dropped off.'

At seat level a voice said, 'It won't help him, Sam, we're not going too far in this.' Quinn, who had been keeping himself out of sight, now pulled himself on to the seat. 'You really are a ball of fun. I know that guy we nearly ran down. He's a dangerous bastard and didn't look too pleased with you. Watch your back, he's got a lot of pull.' Quinn twisted round to gaze back with Towler; 'The cops have got the car; it's caused a traffic jam.' He turned to face the front. 'There could be a good story in this after all; you keep strange company. I only hope that I don't have to render a posthumous account of your part in it. Are you sure you know what you're doing, Sam?'

Kate Parker had the apartment to herself for a few days as her friend had a modelling assignment in Canada and had flown off that day. She was combing her hair when the telephone rang. She hobbled into the tiny hall and lifted the receiver.

Before she could speak a voice she would always remember said, 'How's your little piggy?'

'Sam!' She was delighted. 'Hold on. I'm on a mobile, I'll take it back to the drawing-room and talk in comfort.'

'There's no time, Kate. The phone might be tapped and I don't want to give them time for a trace.'

'Tapped? Nobody but my friend knows I'm here.'

'I do. Your friend does. Are you absolutely sure that nobody else knows?'

She hesitated for far too long and Towler said, 'There you are then. Nobody's a lot of people.'

'But why would they want to do a thing like that?'

'There's no time to explain. Can we meet? Tonight?'

Again she hesitated and Towler said quickly, 'Are you expecting someone?'

'Perhaps. I'm not sure. Friends are keeping an eye on me at the moment.'

'I'm a friend. You haven't asked me where I'm staying. Don't you want to know?'

'Yes. No. You're confusing me, Sam. I do want to know but perhaps it's better that I don't. Not yet, anyway.'

'Look, I'll have to ring you back. We'll sort something out.' Towler hung up; he was in a call box on Waterloo Station. He went out to the taxi rank and queued for a cab to return to Quinn's place. Quinn was out when he arrived and Cathy had just come back with some shopping. She was in the kitchen unpacking and Towler offered to help her.

'I'm sorry I'm such a nuisance,' he said. 'I know I'm causing you extra work. As soon as this business is over I'll get out of your hair.'

Cathy smiled provocatively across the central kitchen counter where her bags were propped up. 'You've never been in my hair but that's where I'd like you to be, Sam. Lew would never know; I wouldn't do that to him.'

'Nor would I, Cathy. He's doing me a big favour and you're asking me to stab him in the back.'

'All I'm asking, Honey, is that you do me as big a favour as he's doing you. That would be only fair wouldn't it?'

Towler gazed back at her over the counter and saw how difficult she was to resist; and how she knew it. This was the first time since arriving that they had been completely alone together. 'Why do you do this to him? For Christ's sake, he loves you. Give him a break.'

'I love him, too, Sam. I can't help the way I am. Figure it this way; it's better for him if his friends give me a break rather than a total stranger, wouldn't you say?'

'You're bloody sick, Cathy. Let it be.'

'And you're goddammed old-fashioned. You're too young to be like that. You'll regret not taking the opportunity. I can be fun.'

'You're fun right now, gal. Where do you want these tins?'

'Well, let's have a drink together, then.' She went over to a cupboard where Lew kept his liquor.

'It all leads to the same route to heaven, Cathy. You want it drunk or sober, don't you? You never give up.'

She turned back empty-handed and continued to unpack. 'You're right about that, Sam. I never do.' Her expression was difficult to resist and there had been a point when she had almost won and he believed that she knew it; no, she would not give up.

Prescott gazed at the hand-written letter in Arabic and buzzed the intercom. He was working late which meant that so was his long-serving secretary. When she came in he handed her the letter and said, 'Have we still got the envelope?'

'I'm sure I can dig it up. It's been handled, though.'

'We might get something from it. Take this down to the Middle East Section and get it translated. There should be someone still there, if not get someone back in. It's urgent and I'll hang on until it's ready. How did it arrive?'

'By hand. I'll find out if anyone can remember anything.'

'Good girl.' He had a nasty feeling what the contents might be and was worried before the event. Half an hour later he knew he was right. The letter came back clipped to a typed translation, and read: 'We do not appreciate your treachery. The man who was exchanged for the girl, Kate Parker, was not the man we asked for nor was agreed with you. Produce the right person in twenty-four hours or we will retaliate with something far worse than abducting the girl. We will make contact.'

Prescott rubbed his knee; it was playing up more than usual. Having had a report from Detective Superintendent Grimswell in Hereford, via Special Branch, it was not difficult to understand how the 'ringer' had been uncovered. Prescott was sorry that he had ever given way to the Home Secretary but it had happened and that was that. He summoned Soames to find that he had gone home and derived some pleasure in sending out a call to bring him back. Right now, Soames was not doing too well and Towler was still on the loose.

Prescott gazed at the finely written letter and wondered who the hell had sent it. This was part of the problem; right from the beginning they had had no knowledge of whom they were dealing with. There were so many Arab groups.

As he awaited the arrival of Soames, which might take the best part of an hour, he reflected that whatever slim chance of survival Towler might have had before, he could certainly be allowed none now. It had all gone too far and was out of hand for a number of reasons. It was a mess. A bloody great mess which should never have been allowed to happen.

Towler took Quinn to a local pub; it was safe enough while his general whereabouts were not known and they went early evening before it began to fill up. They took their drinks to a corner table and Towler came straight to the point.

'I need some money. I'm down to my last twenty quid. Can you help me?'

'Haven't you got a cash card? Cheque book? O.K., if someone is keeping an eye on your bank, you don't have to draw from there. You can draw from anywhere.'

'All my personal stuff is at my digs. I tried to get in last night. I knew it would be staked out but I wanted to see what I was up against. There was a van, a car and at least four armed muscle men.' Noting Quinn's questioning look he added, 'My last assignment was not exactly one on which I would carry identification in case something went wrong, which it did. It's normal practice.'

'So you want a loan?' Quinn smiled uncertainly. 'You're staying rent free at my place, and now you want me to fund you? How long have we known each other?'

'Before I pitched up at your place? Five, six hours. A lifetime.'

Quinn laughed. 'You're pushing your luck, Sam. I'm not loaded.'

'I could ask Cathy and she'd probably give it to me. But the price might be too high.'

Quinn sat back, his features tightening. 'That was below the belt, Sam. Has she been at you?'

'In no way you need worry about.' Towler was looking as drained as Quinn. 'I'm sorry,' he said. 'It was under the belt but I can't operate without funds. I have the money but I can't safely get at it. I can give you a written entitlement in case I don't make it. I can even make out a will and we can get it witnessed. But look at me. My clothes are beginning to stink. I need a change and I need cash. I'm having to use taxis because I can't safely hire a car for which I haven't enough money, anyway. I'm asking for the moon from someone I'm only just getting to know, and I'm well aware of it. There'll be no hard feelings if you refuse. You've done more than enough already.'

Quinn twiddled with his glass. 'That's the longest speech I've heard you make.' He looked up. 'If you'd made empty promises about a marvellous story at the end of the rainbow it would be easy to deal with.'

'I'm not going to try to sway you in that way. I do promise you your money back plus interest. I can cover that.'

'What would you do in my place?'

Towler smiled bleakly and carefully considered the question before saying, 'I'd tell me to piss off. There's one other person who might fund me but she could turn out to be a security risk; I can try her.'

Quinn said, 'If you've still got twenty quid you can get another round in. I'll back you as long as I can. But I'm still hoping for a story.' He pushed his empty glass across the table. 'I must be dumb.'

The United States Embassy in Grosvenor Square was officially closed when Steiner arrived. He flashed his ID and went up to the Department of Defense Intelligence Agency offices on the top floor at the rear of the building. It was warm inside after the sub-zero temperatures on the streets but he kept his coat on, though he did remove his hat. He checked some reports in his office then went down the long corridor to one of a few unmarked offices near the end and entered after the most cursory of knocks.

The knock was not one of necessity since he outranked the man inside, nor out of courtesy, but rather one of warning as he was the only man known to knock on a door in the form of a whisper. Joe Lingfield looked up from his desk immediately; the man known as the 'sleeping bear' had arrived. The nickname was not one of affection but a sarcastic reference to Steiner's build and the belief of those who worked with him that he never slept. Where Steiner trod, trouble followed.

Lingfield was young, about mid-thirties, with much of the all-American-boy appearance. He had been with the CIA since graduating from law school and had known no other work. He was bright, astute and knew how to cope with the abrasive manner of Steiner.

Steiner was a Deputy Director of the London Station of the Department of Defense Intelligence Agency, a military organisation which co-ordinated and generally supervised the other Intelligence agencies. In certain quarters these powers were resented and even derided, but the fact remained. Lingfield saw Steiner as a man who resented delegating and lacked administrative ability; a man who acted like a field man rather than a co-ordinator, yet the DIA undoubtedly possessed their own huge network and Steiner chose to see himself as part of it. He could never sit behind a desk for long, much to the annoyance of his own staff and of those whom his department orchestrated. He was not a popular man, but he knew far too much about the Intelligence game for others to attempt to cross him.

Lingfield was well aware that Steiner could not directly interfere with his work, but could go through channels which might eventually result in the same thing, so it was a question of applying common sense to any request he might make. If Steiner rough-rode him he would make him take the formal course which would delay whatever it was Steiner wanted. Lingfield sometimes wondered how Steiner had got his job for he was an anachronism and belonged to the days of the G-Men. Yet those who really knew him had great respect for him, and the results he achieved, if sometimes closing their eyes to his methods.

Steiner could present himself in many forms and had learned the attitudes of Lingfield a long time ago. He smiled broadly and said, 'Hi, Joe. You're working late. Didn't really expect to find you here.'

The younger Lingfield was taken partially off guard. He smiled a welcome before he could stop himself. 'What can I do for you, sir?' It was too late to bite out his tongue.

'I hear you have some useful friends in Five. Maybe you can do me a big favour. There was trouble near Hereford a couple of days ago. Some Arabs got shot up. Nothing to do with us but you'll have heard about it. Do you think you could tap in on your friends to find out who the escort was and where is he now?'

'Escort? What sort of escort?'

Steiner looked surprised. He had closed the door behind him and now stood by the window at the side of Lingfield's desk. 'You don't know? I would have thought a smart young fella like you would have had the size of it. It was an exchange job Five had got itself wrapped up in. Nothing important. Small fry stuff which is maybe why the detail hasn't reached you. Perhaps your minions didn't pass it on. It went wrong and Five's escort went to ground. I'd like to have a word with him.'

Lingfield stared suspiciously at Steiner whose broad back was turned to him at that moment. 'Wouldn't it be easier if you asked them yourself? You have better contacts than I.'

Steiner turned round smiling. He pulled out a cigar. 'Here, have one of these. I lifted some from an illicit haul; have a pal at Scotland Yard.' When Lingfield had reluctantly taken the cigar Steiner went on. 'I don't want to rouse the big brass at Five for all sorts of reasons. I don't want to show we're too interested. Anyway, I'm not really supposed to know about it. It's small enough stuff but I just figure this guy can help me in something. All I want is a low-key approach on the old-boy network. Kid's stuff. I'm asking as a favour to me, Joe.' It would be easier to trace Kate Parker and squeeze the information out of her if she knew anything, but he was afraid she might identify his shape and voice. And that could cause some wild problems.

*　　*　　*

112

Towler caught the Underground to Kensington High Street after leaving Quinn outside the pub off the Kilburn High Road. As he emerged from the station, the cold air caught the back of his throat and he turned up his coat collar. He walked to Edwardes Square, approaching the apartment block with care, head down against the wind. He decided to go right round the square hugging the railings on the inner perimeter with the snow-bound gardens to his right all the way round.

He met nobody on the narrow inner pavement which was still treacherously patched with ice. The High Street, at the head of the square, was a mass of activity as always.

He rounded the gardens once, then turned about to approach the block of apartments from the opposite direction. In the short dead-end where the two entrances were, was a row of cars squeezed in where they were not supposed to be. It was a kind of courtyard with the building on one side and a wall on the other. At the far end was a delivery van and, as it was blocked off, it was reasonable to assume that it would be there for the night.

Towler went behind the row of vehicles and approached the van which had been parked as close to the wall as possible; as it had sliding doors this left very little room between it and the wall. It was a good place for observation and a bad one to be trapped in. Towler wedged himself in and waited, his gaze on the entrance nearer to the square. The second entrance was almost opposite him.

As he gradually became colder it seemed to him that much of his life had been spent in similar situations. Just watching and waiting and knowing that loss of concentration could cause loss of life.

He concentrated on the entrance, glad of the fair visibility for diffused light spread from both doorways in adequate measure and added an illusion of warmth.

He closed his mind to time. He blanked out everything except the comings and goings at the far entrance. There was a spate of activity and then it quietened down again and there was a long gap when nobody at all appeared. He had been there well over an hour before he saw a face he recognised.

A chauffeur-driven car had pulled up to block off the entry into the dead-end and two men climbed out, one, well dressed, carrying a bunch of flowers. Although the man was heavily coated and wore a hat, Towler recognised him as soon as he reached the light. There was nothing surreptitious about his approach and the second man stayed slightly behind him as he walked towards the first entrance.

The man with the flowers went in and the second man stood on the top steps and took a careful look around him. Towler recognised the signs at once. The man on the steps was an armed police bodyguard and the one who had entered was James Dawson, Home Secretary in Her Majesty's Government.

Towler put his gloved hands slowly to his mouth. His breath was rising like steam on the night air and he tried to disperse it. The presence of the Home Secretary could mean anything. Wealthy people lived in these apartments; the politician must have friends all over the place and the visit here was being made openly with chauffeur and bodyguard. And he could be visiting anyone in the building. That was the common sense angle. The gut feeling was different. Which was why, Towler told himself, he was here looking for a missing link.

Dawson reappeared a few minutes later without the flowers, so he must surely have visited a lady. There was a jocular exchange between Dawson and the bodyguard and they were both laughing as they left. The car appeared on cue and drove off as soon as the two men were in it. Towler continued to watch but what he had seen drove out all impression of cold until he eventually tried to move his numbed feet. He stood against the van trying to get some life back into them.

Towler eased his way out from behind the van and trod slowly towards the entrance nearer to the square. From behind the first car he could see the porter reading a newspaper at the small reception counter. He waited over half an hour before the porter left the counter by a side flap and disappeared somewhere at the rear of the lobby.

Towler hurried across the gap, up the steps and beyond the heavy glass doors, ran lightly across the lobby and mounted the stairs. Once he was climbing he felt safe from the porter. From now on he took his time finding the sudden warmth stifling. The elevator whirred while he was still climbing, and the gates clanged somewhere above his head. After a while it descended. He waited until it had passed and continued up.

Once outside Kate's apartment he was uncertain. He rang the bell, felt her watching him, then heard the hurried removal of the door chain as she opened up to embrace him in the open doorway.

'Oh, Sam, it's so good to see you.' She was almost crying. 'You've no idea how cooped up I've been.' She led him by the hand into the drawing-room and hobbled to a drinks cabinet to pour a large scotch. As she handed him his drink she exclaimed. 'You're still in those dreadful clothes. Why haven't you changed?'

'Because my pad's staked out by some of the same gorillas who tried to do us at Hereford.'

They sat on a sofa, side-by-side. Kate made no attempt to hide her delight at seeing him – they clinked glasses in a silent toast and Kate was clearly happy as she drank his health. As Towler sipped his drink his gaze roamed the room until it focused on the bunch of flowers on a small table next to the television set. The paper had been unravelled and the stems spread out, preparatory to putting into the decorative jug beside them. It was clear that Kate had just been about to arrange them in the jug when he arrived.

Towler felt sick. 'How's your toe?' he asked, giving none of his feelings away.

'It's coming on fine, Sam, since it's been treated properly. I'm a prisoner at the moment because I'm not willing to try those damned crutches with all that ice out there. But I have everything I need and my friend who rents this place will be back in a few days so I'll have some company.'

He took her hand loosely in his. 'Don't you have any visitors?'

'Very few. I'm not advertising I'm here.'

'I don't blame you. Any visitors today?' He knew it was clumsy but she seemed not to notice.

'No. Nobody.'

'So who sent you the flowers?'

Kate turned to view them. 'Oh, those. You've got a quick eye.' She smiled. 'But, then you would have, wouldn't you? They were sent much earlier but I've only just got round to arranging them.'

In the uncomfortable silence that followed the lie dropped between them like an unexploded bomb.

11

Kate slowly withdrew her hand from his. 'You don't believe me, do you?'

'No. I saw him arrive with the flowers.'

'Who?'

'Come on, Kate, you're no good at it.'

She rose unsteadily and limped to the table with the flowers. She held up a single bloom. It was a magnificent orchid. 'Where would you get these in this weather except from a hot house? You can identify these? You saw a man arrive with these actual flowers? How long ago?'

'Kate, why don't you come straight out with it? The guy is too well known. You can't cover up a thing like this. It's a wonder the press haven't been on to it a long time ago.'

She smiled bitterly, her joy crushed. 'Longer than you think, Sam. I don't intend to argue. I was over the moon to see you. Now you've left me with nothing else to do but to ask you to leave. I'm sorry.'

Towler rose angrily. 'Jesus, Kate. I nearly got my bloody tail shot off for you. At first I thought it was you they are after. But it's not; it's me. I can't keep on the move for ever and I've run out of friends because they'll be an obvious target. Now what the hell is going on?'

'Nothing's going on.' She seemed about to cry but checked herself and added desperately, 'What right have you to question me like this? Please go.'

He crossed over and gently took her by the shoulders but she shook him off and sat on the arm of the sofa.

'Don't be so bloody stubborn,' he said. 'I'm chasing around with gunmen after me and I think you know part of the reason why. I'm not interested in your bloody affairs but I must know whether he called or not.' He found it strange that he could not even name Dawson as if afraid of being terribly wrong.

'How dare you!' Kate rose, steadying herself on the arm of the sofa. 'How dare you say that. I don't know who or what you're talking about. Now get out.'

'Kate . . .' Towler stepped towards her again.

She backed away and bawled, *'Get out.'*

He stood there gazing at her, then slowly walked towards the door. 'You're protecting the wrong bloke,' he said as he turned the handle. 'If I get my head blown off I hope you remember this little fracas.' He went out and closed the door quietly behind him.

Sigi Grief shook hands with Sir Malcolm Read before lowering himself into the leather chair opposite the Victorian desk, a personal possession of Read's. Read showed restrained pleasure at receiving his guest; the two men had not met for some time.

'You should have given me more notice,' Read said. 'I would have arranged lunch.' Read was an ex-RAF man, unusual for Five. He had retired as an Air Vice-Marshal and many of his present subordinates would say that he never forgot it and still acted as if he were in the Air Force. His manner was usually severe. His grey hair was brushed straight back, his features pinched, and he carried no superfluous weight.

Sigi Grief was quite the opposite: short, overweight, a mass of tight curly hair, a round face and a bubbly nature with very dark eyes invariably twinkling; when they did not it usually meant trouble for someone. He had a tremendous sense of humour but showed little of it at the moment.

'That's kind of you, Sir Malcolm, but I don't think lunch would be appropriate for this occasion.' Even Sigi Grief, well known to and liked by most Western Intelligence Agencies, sensed the impropriety of calling Read, Malcolm. To do so would demand equal ranks and Grief, as high up in Mossad as he might be, did not quite reach the commanding heights of Read.

'So what can we do for you, Sigi?' It was quite all right for a higher rank to be familiar with a subordinate, and it showed a lack of snobbery; Read had been weaned on such premises.

Grief was well aware of Read's imminent retirement. That fact surprised nobody; what did was how he had been appointed in the first place. Grief would much rather see Prescott, who really ran the show, but protocol demanded that he visit the severe-looking man now behind the desk. Grief said, 'We've picked up word that we are being blamed for the shooting of two Arabs near Hereford the other day. I'm here to say that we were not in the least involved.'

'Good. Is that all?'

Grief curbed his impatience. 'Someone wanted to hide behind our war with the Arabs. Someone planted the blame on us and that will now be translated world-wide. We want a retraction.'

'I don't blame you if what you say is true. But what has this to do with us?'

For a moment Grief thought he was dealing with an idiot but whatever Read's failings he was certainly not that. Grief quickly saw that Read did not know what had really happened.

'It would appear that the rumour of our involvement started with your service.'

Read sat bolt upright; integrity was at stake. 'You've been misinformed.'

'I don't think so. Our source is solid.' Grief shrugged, 'I'm not saying it's infallible but on something like this we check most carefully. Of course, like you, we expect our enemies to spread malicious lies but not our friends. I wonder if you would be good enough to check this out? Nigel Prescott might know something about it.'

Read was ruffled; it was not on to be embarrassed by a foreign agency. It suggested that they knew something about his own service which he did not. 'I think you're quite wrong, Sigi, but I'll find out what I can. Will you be in London for a while?'

Grief shivered. 'Not if I can help it. This weather is killing me. I can't wait to get back to Tel Aviv and some sunshine. I'll stay just long enough to clear this up and to find out what's behind it; no more than a couple of days.' Having given Read his deadline he smiled and rose. 'So nice to see you again. You are going to be missed when you retire.'

*   *   *

With Quinn's money Towler bought off-the-peg clothes from the nearest Dunn's. He left the shop clad in his new clothes, carrying the old ones in a plastic bag which he dumped in the first litter bin. He returned to Quinn's apartment to pick up his Browning and two spare ammunition clips each containing twelve rounds. He knew Quinn was out covering an assignment and the moment he heard Cathy splashing around in the bath he left the apartment as fast as he could.

He went to Islington where he had picked up Yasser Azmin. It was late morning and there were plenty of people about. Conditions had not improved. It seemed that the winter had frozen itself in and that thaw was a word which had lost meaning.

He went past the house where he had arrested Azmin, feeling considerable remorse for what had happened to the young Iranian. He was beginning to think that he was a name taken almost from a hat and sent to his execution for reasons unknown. He mounted the steps of the house where he had seen Azmin's girlfriend disappear and hesitated at the top. He did not know her name and it had been dark when he had briefly seen her. He rang a bell to discover that it was disconnected, turned the knob of the front door to find it was not locked, and entered a dark, dingy hall.

There was no name plate; he should have known. He tried a light switch and nothing happened. When he located the light the bulb was missing. He mounted the stairs and the place became progressively gloomy. He knocked on a door on the first landing. A pretty West Indian girl opened up and he asked her if she knew the girlfriend of a Yasser Azmin who lived just down the street. She stared up at him and asked, 'You a copper?'

He produced the warrant card he had used on Azmin. 'I'm not here to nick her. Just want a chat.'

She laughed. 'Push off,' she said and slammed the door in his face. He tried two more flights and received similar treatment. The third call verged on trouble as a West Indian in his vest, in spite of the cold, and with the physique of an all-in wrestler, gave the impression that he would take Towler apart. When Towler gave no ground and their eyes met and held he somehow changed his mind but was no more co-operative than the others. At the top apartment nobody answered. There were no others.

Towler decided to return later that evening. Half-way down the stairs he heard light footsteps coming up and he went back to the top floor. The girl came round the corner of the landing like a heavily wrapped mummy and stopped when she saw him by her door. She was about to turn back when he called out to her.

'I'm a police officer, not a mugger. I'm here about Yasser Azmin.'

She approached cautiously and stopped half-way along the landing.

'Look it's not my fault all the light bulbs have been nicked. I'm not standing in the dark from choice.' He held out his ID.

'What's happened to Yasser?' She was standing her ground, not trusting him. 'I haven't seen him for four days.'

'That was the question I wanted to ask you. Someone reported that he is missing. Do you think we can go inside? Probably half the house are listening to us.'

That was something she could accept but she still advanced cautiously. He moved aside to give her plenty of room as she fumbled in her bag for her key. It was virtually a one-room apartment with a curtained-off portion for the kitchen. It was neat and tidy and there was a prayer mat by the window.

Towler did not sit down; he did not want to stay nor spend more time lying to her than he had to. The girl was upset and clearly worried about the disappearance of her boyfriend and only he knew that she would not be seeing him again. To build up her hopes would be sadistic, yet he could not tell her the truth. He showed his ID again in the better light but she gave it only a cursory glance as she now accepted that he was a policeman.

'When was the last time you saw him?' he asked, despising himself for the question.

'I already told you. I said goodbye to him four nights ago, we were to meet later, and I haven't seen him since. Who reported him missing?'

'It was an anonymous phone call. Usually they come to nothing but from what you say he really is missing. I thought it might have been you.'

She slipped out of her coat and threw it on to a chair. 'No. I should have done.'

'Why didn't you, then?'

'The police aren't liked around here. We think they're racist. I passed the word around, though.' She spoke quite good, but heavily accented, English. Hesitantly she said, 'He's a bit of a girl chaser. I thought he might have pushed off with someone else for a while. But I did intend to go to the police some time tomorrow if he didn't show up by then.' She picked up her coat and hung it in an old-fashioned wardrobe.

'Did he have any enemies you know about?'

'Yasser? A trail of girls who probably all felt like killing him.'

'Real enemies?'

'What sort of real enemies could he have? He's just a straightforward student with a one-way hobby. He has no real enemies. He has a lot of friends, though.'

'What about politics? Iranians usually have strong religious and political views. That creates enemies.'

'Yasser wasn't like that. He'd become very Westernised. He did not express anti- or pro-Khomeini views.' She shrugged. 'I'm tired. Are you going to sit down?'

'I'll be off in a minute. Hasn't the LSE made enquiries about him? I mean, they'd be curious about his absence wouldn't they?'

Her expression suggested she had not thought about it. 'Nobody's been here. But they might not know about me.'

'Have you the key to his place?'

Her eyes flared. 'Why should I have?'

'I take it that's no. So we can't get in?'

'Not without breaking down the door.'

'So he had no strong politics, no enemies, but was fond of women.'

'That sums it up.'

'Then I won't trouble you any more. Thanks for your help. We'll let you know of any development.' He felt sorry for her as he left. She had hidden her true feelings well but they were just beginning to show as he took a last glance back at her. He had been right; Azmin's name had been plucked from a hat and his luck had ended with the girls.

It was not until much later that the girl wondered why a

policeman enquiring about Azmin had not even troubled to check her name, nor how he knew about her.

Lew Quinn met Joe Lingfield in a fashionable bar off Bond Street. The two men had known each other for some time and there had been occasions when Quinn, with his many connections gained by living in England, had been helpful to Lingfield and his colleagues. Their friendship was such that there was no need to beat about the bush. Lingfield was a realist; he did not believe that everything he did was secret work. If it was then he simply said so to Quinn and that was that. But there was much of the quid pro quo about the two men; there were times when they needed each other so the relationship was good.

Lingfield knew better than to ask about Cathy, so her name did not come up between them. They sat on high stools facing a long polished mirror with brass trimmings. The place was comfortably full.

Quinn sipped his Dry Martini and longed for a Whisky but Lingfield had ordered the drinks too soon. 'Do you know anything about that shooting up at Hereford a few days back?'

For once, Lingfield was immediately cautious. How could that incident crop up innocently twice so rapidly? 'No more than I read in the dailies. It was shovelled under the carpet wasn't it? After the first reports there were no more. I did hear that Special Branch had taken it out of the hands of the local police.'

'Doesn't it intrigue you?' asked Quinn.

Lingfield crossed his long legs, finding it awkward against the curving bar. 'I don't see why it should. We'd have been notified if it had been of interest to us. Why do you ask?'

Quinn called for a Scotch, unable to finish the Martini. 'I sense a story there. Anything that's hushed up or has a D-notice slapped on it has to be of interest. I thought you might have an inkling.'

'Probably Mossad knocking off a couple of stray Arabs. Not big enough for us, Lew.' Lingfield gave his friend a long sceptical look. 'Is business so bad?' And then, while Quinn was gulping his whisky, 'Maybe you have something for us on it?'

Quinn shook his head. 'I thought you might do a little digging for me. I could do with a story right now. Do you think you can raise anything from your friends at Five?'

Steiner, and now Quinn, asking a similar favour. 'What about your own contacts with Five?'

Quinn moved as he was jostled from behind. He lowered his voice. 'You're kidding. They know I've done odd jobs for the Company; they wouldn't give me a thing.'

'Is this important to you?'

'I have a feeling that it could be.' Quinn turned to his younger friend and winked. 'Could turn out to be important to you too.'

'O.K., I'll do what I can.' Lingfield was left wondering whether or not he should tell Steiner about Quinn's interest.

Towler contacted the London School of Economics the following morning by telephone from Quinn's untidy office. It took time to find the right person and to trace Azmin's name on the register but eventually he obtained his answer. Azmin had returned to Iran for the funeral of his father who had died suddenly. It was probable he would not return as he might have to carry on his father's business interests.

Did Azmin himself cancel his course? Apparently he had left in such a hurry that someone had done it for him. It was a pity; he was bright.

Towler put down the phone. There had been a thorough cleaning up job. Poor sod; Soames must have known that Azmin was going to be murdered the moment he asked Towler to pick him up. Towler was now sure that he was meant to die too. If he had not stepped forward to help Kate Parker, he would be dead.

He sat down in Quinn's uncomfortable chair and wondered why it had all happened. Something had gone wrong that he did not know about. He kept thinking of Kate and the Home Secretary. He could think of no reason why Dawson should want to have him killed. That he might have a young mistress was nothing new in politics and had increasingly less impact. It kept niggling him as to why Kate should have been kidnapped in the first place; not to be exchanged for someone as inconsequential as Azmin, that was sure. It was difficult thinking about Kate. He wanted to get her off his mind but that was impossible.

He scribbled a note for Quinn stating that he would be away most of the day; it was better than leaving a message with Cathy who was taking every opportunity to get him into bed and was using some disturbing methods which he would not want Quinn to know about. She was also drinking heavily. He made one last phone call before leaving for the West End.

They met in Leicester Square. The gardens were a fairyland of snow and frost and gossamer and the benches were coated in frozen snow.

Towler shook hands with his old colleague, Jock McLean, and they walked side by side around the perimeter, with collars turned up. McLean was shorter and of slighter build than Towler. His dark head was bare and was angled forward aggressively as if looking for the next punch.

'So you're still in?' asked McLean in his Geordie accent. He had been born in Newcastle of Scottish parents.

'Sort of. I'd rather be back, though. In spite of what happened to Taffy. I'm getting over that. It was just the last straw of a long bad period. It's O.K. now. I'm attached to MI5 but they can stick it. I'm in more trouble since I joined them than ever in Yemen or Ireland.'

'You serious?' McLean was laughing, clapping his hands together to get them warm. 'You should have got out like I did. You've been at it too long, Sam. Is that what this is about? You want a job?'

'I couldn't work for you, you mad bastard.'

They both laughed. They were talking as only old comrades can, affectionately insulting.

'So what then? You wouldn't drag me out into this for sod all or to say you've missed me.'

'Someone's trying to knock me off. A second-rate team but enough of them to be successful in due time. I need a pair of eyes to watch my back and to do some surveillance. Can you give me a hand?'

'The short answer is no.' McLean was looking at the ground as if watching for pitfalls but he missed nothing either side of him.

'That's that then.'

124

'Sam, I'm up to my eyeballs in this new security company. We're building it up, just about breaking even, and I'm working round the clock and on the verge of divorce because of it. But in a year or two we'll be rolling in it. I'm meeting you now instead of having a lunch break because you're my old mate and we've been through a few times together. If it wouldn't bugger things up for everybody, I'd help you like a shot. You know that.'

Towler shrugged as they took another corner away from Shaftesbury Avenue. 'I understand. I had to try.'

'Who's after you?'

'Five. Don't ask me why but they've suddenly found me expendable.'

'Shit! You're joking.' McLean was gazing intently at Towler now, anger showing on his dark features. 'They'd do that to you? Are you sure?'

'The one thing I've learned since I joined this lot is that you can never be sure. But they're my best bet. It might turn into something else. The only thing I know with certainty is that someone is gunning for me and they don't intend to give up.'

'Bloody hell. If you're right that closes all your doors. You can't go to the police or through any official channel because all roads will lead back to Curzon Street. Why would they want to do this to you?'

'I don't know. I'm a square peg with them. They don't really want me. My face doesn't fit.' Towler smiled bitterly. 'I'm not suggesting that because of that they'd go to these extremes, that would be stupid. There's something else. They needed a patsy and I came along to fit the bill. That's why I called you.'

'That makes me feel a shit. I've never let you down before but if I drop everything I'll be letting a lot of other people down.'

'It's O.K., Jock. It was a long shot anyway. Don't mess up what you're working for.'

'I want to help, and I could do with the action. How long have I got to think about it?'

'You've done that. Don't go back on it. You'd be a fool. I can manage.'

'Glasshouse,' McLean exclaimed suddenly. 'Glasshouse Willie Jackson. He's around here somewhere.'

'Jacko? I thought he was doing time. You suggesting I should try him? He's a bloody villain.'

'No worse than those you're working for as far as I can see.'

Towler stopped walking, deep in thought. 'He's crazy, Jock. Worse than you and that's saying something.'

'He'd do it for you. He never forgot that you watched his back that time in Armagh. You were treading on water that night.'

Glasshouse Jackson. Jacko. Towler recalled some of it. At first there had been nothing wrong with him, all the guts in the world and totally reliable. Then his younger brother was killed in an air crash and he was never the same after that. Until then, nobody knew he had a brother. Jacko went wild time after time and finally went berserk in a Republican bar and was lucky to come out alive. He served time in a military prison on the mainland, the 'glasshouse', and got his nickname from that. On his release he was sent back to his own regiment; it was a disgrace to be forced out of the SAS in that way. He was so difficult to handle from then on that he was eventually discharged. The last Towler heard of him was that he had turned to crime. This was the man Jock McLean was recommending him to turn to for help.

'I couldn't rely on him,' Towler said reflectively. 'And I couldn't pay him anything.'

'Weren't you going to pay me then?' McLean feigned shock. 'Anyway, from what I hear, he's not short. He's probably into bank jobs.'

They stopped outside the Odeon Cinema. Towler was still thinking it over. 'I'd be mad to use someone like Jacko.'

'If you've got an armed tail you'd be mad not to.'

'Do you know where he is?'

'Not for sure. I haven't kept in touch. I know he used to go to a club off Dean Street called the Hot Pot. It's always being raided but it survives. I'll walk you there. Then I must get back.' McLean slapped Towler on the back. 'It's been bloody marvellous seeing you again, Sam. If I find I can help later on where do I contact you?'

'You can't. I'm on the move.'

'Even from me?'

'Even from you, Jockie. Just in case someone decides you're worth watching.'

Prescott had prepared for the possibility but was still not sure how best to cope with it. A main consideration was that Sir Malcolm Read would not be here by the end of summer. Now February, by the end of August at the latest, Read would have retired. The interim would be a time for strong nerves and for occasionally reminding the Right Honourable James Dawson, MP, of his earlier promise regarding Read's successor. Meanwhile the situation was delicate.

Prescott had been summoned to Read's office and could guess why. He sat in the club chair where most visitors sat and faced the humourless severity of the man across the desk.

'Sigi Grief has been here,' Read said sharply. 'He says that Mossad has been blamed for the shootings in Hereford. Do you know anything about this, Bluie?'

'One of the dailies reported that it might be a Mossad job. I gather an empty magazine belonging to a Uzi SMG was found nearby. The whole business is too small-time for us. Nobody we know was killed; it looked some kind of private war. In view of the fact that the two men killed were Arabs we handed it over to Special Branch. I don't think they've got anywhere except to establish that neither man was of any significance to us. Yes, I suppose it could be a Mossad job.'

'Sigi seems to think that the rumour started from here.'

'As it's in print that's difficult to swallow. Do you mean he flew over just for that?'

'He was already in London. He seems to be certain of his source.'

'He always is but he's not always right. I don't know why he's bothered. We've laid no complaint. Other people use Uzis. If the Arabs had been of some significance I can understand him getting worked up but this is one of those minor affairs with two dead men nobody seems to care about and my guess is that SB will get nowhere with it. There are so many splinter groups around that even we haven't got them all listed.'

Prescott waited to see how Read was taking this and then proffered a faint smile. 'They run a monthly competition downstairs on the number of indexed terrorist groups there are world-wide. Remembering their names can be a problem, too. I wouldn't worry about it, Sir Malcolm. It's difficult to see why Sigi is concerned bearing in mind what Mossad have done on our soil, for which they haven't been blamed.'

'So you think there's nothing in it?'

'Absolutely not. Sigi is being unusually sensitive. This emanated from the press, not us.'

The moment Prescott was back in his own office he summoned Soames. He stretched out his leg beside his desk and waved Soames to a chair as soon as he entered.

'It's time to straighten a few things out. I can understand you setting up Towler to endorse it as an outside job, but that went wrong and Towler is still loose. Now who else is in on this who can do us damage?'

Soames was prepared. 'Towler's driver is an old hand and solid. He witnessed some of the shooting but has no knowledge of the setup. He was told to pull out if there was a problem and this he did. He's been posted to Gibraltar until this is cleared up.'

'And the gunmen?'

'We contracted out. The usual procedure. We've honed down the chain of contact to a fine art. We can get action in twenty-four hours most times. They haven't a clue who hired them, it's done through a top villain who could be jailed for life any time we choose.'

Prescott did not raise the problem of Barry and Mary Jones, the sheep farmers who had helped Towler and Kate Parker, because Soames did not know about them. As soon as the girl told Dawson what had happened he informed Prescott. Prescott had been so nervous about the possibility of the press getting hold of the story that he had personally visited the farm the day he heard about it. He had convinced the Joneses that it had all been part of a realistic SAS hostage exercise that had wandered too far off course. He was immensely apologetic and compensated them extremely generously for the help they had given Towler and the girl and told them to tell nobody. Whatever the SAS did came under the Official Secrets Act and even the police must not know. Yes, Towler and the girl were fine and were grateful for the help they had received.

Prescott had taken the precaution of obtaining a receipt from the two to blank out future problems, but they were kind, simple people who were over the moon with their reward. They remained a possible weak link but one that could be handled.

Prescott said, 'The motive for dealing with Towler has changed. He will now try to find out why he was set up and that he must never discover. This is more urgent than ever.'

Soames agreed. 'I realise that, sir. I think we can get extra help. He has nowhere to run and sooner or later he will show himself. There are some ways in which we can squeeze him out from whichever stone he is under. I've already actioned it. He's tricky but he's pushing himself into an alley from which there is no way out. We'll get him.'

'Of course you will,' Prescott smiled. 'Your future depends on it.'

12

The Hot Pot was a basement club under a film agency and between a wine bar and a strip club, off the south end of Dean Street. 'I gather you're not coming in?' said Towler to Jock McLean.

'It's the time factor, Sam. Hope you find him and, anyway, give me a call if you get really desperate. Good luck, mate.'

They shook hands and Towler descended the stairs towards the smell of a sickly air-freshener. When he reached the bottom he could barely see a thing. There was a door with a hatch and a bruiser's face framed in it like an artist's nightmare. On a board fixed across the base of the hatch was an open book for members to sign in.

If the bruiser receptionist had little going for him visually, there was nothing wrong with his memory. 'You're not a member, squire. You want a temporary membership?'

'I'm trying to locate Willie Jackson. I believe he comes here.'

'Never heard of him.'

'Don't mess around. We're old friends.'

The scarred eyes, victims of many a fight, viewed Towler bleakly. 'You've got "copper" written all over you. Piss off.'

'You're right,' countered Towler producing his false warrant card. 'Now open up and let me in. This is not a raid.'

A door at the side of the hatch was released and Towler went through. Jock was right, he thought, the bruiser was no substitute for Miss World but the interior decor was surprisingly tasteful. The air-conditioning was good and the place relatively free of smoke. Towler went to the crescent-shaped bar along the nearest wall, and flashed his card at the barman whom he could barely distinguish in the subdued pink lighting.

'Don't worry about the ID,' said Towler. 'It seems the only

way to get quick service here. I'm looking for Willie Jackson. We're old mates.'

'Do you see him?'

Towler rested his elbows on the bar and gazed round the collection of tables and the line of fruit machines at the far end. 'No.'

'Then he's not here. He's no longer a member.'

'I'm not surprised if you're a reflection of the rest of the staff. O.K., I'll arrange a raid tonight and every other night for the next two weeks. Let's see how many members you have left after that.'

'You shit.'

'That's better. When is he likely to be here?'

'About now. Not every day but most. Please avoid trouble for the sake of our clientele.'

Towler managed a grin. 'I could almost tag them with the prisons they've served in. I'll have a beer and none of your fancy prices.'

'It's on the house. Don't spill it on the carpet.'

Towler stayed at the bar and Willie Jackson came in ten minutes later and went straight up to Towler to give him a great thump of affection on the back.

'You the copper who's looking for me?' Jackson was grinning widely.

Towler said warmly, 'Hello, Jacko. How's crime?' He noticed his old colleague had put on weight and was smoking a cigar. His clothes were expensive but on the flashy side and he had allowed his dark hair to grow down to his shoulders. The red-striped shirt was silk as was the tie, its knot half-way down the deep chest.

'How do you like it?' asked Jackson opening his jacket to show the red silk lining.

'Different,' replied Towler wondering if he had made a terrible mistake. The length of hair did not matter, short hair was a give-away on operations, but there was little he could see of the original, tough, tremendously fit, granite-faced NCO who could always be relied upon.

Jackson turned to the barman and ordered two large whiskies. He said to Towler, his expression less pleasant, 'You really a copper?'

'Let's go over to that corner table and I'll explain.' As Jackson picked up his drink Towler noticed the crooked little finger which had been broken in training. They walked over to the table as Towler explained, 'Jock McLean said you might be here.'

'Jock? He's gone into security. He should have come in with me. I'm bloody nearly a millionaire. I expect to be one by next month.'

Soames sat despondently at his desk eating sandwiches. He usually lunched at his club, but today he wanted to be alone. He hoped he would receive no callers for the next hour and had locked his door to give the impression of being out. He was worried because he suspected that Prescott had not given him the full story and was covering up for somebody. As Prescott was a man who very much looked after his own interests he must be protecting some part of his personal life or someone very high up the tree. There was really no way Soames could find out unless Prescott confided in him and that was unlikely to happen.

Soames had little conscience about Towler; the man had not really fitted in and he strongly resented personnel being foisted upon him. These things happened from time to time but the important aspect was always to protect the image of the service. Most people had no idea what security was all about but were quite happy to find comfort in its protection.

None of this really worried Soames. What did, was that two days ago he discovered, by accident, that Towler had not handed in his police identity card after bringing in Yasser Azmin. The card should have been returned immediately after the operation. The gun, on the other hand, was a necessary part of the equipment in a prisoner exchange in case matters went wrong, and, anyway, was untraceable. The gun would have added confusion to the Hereford shootings if found on Towler's dead body. That he would have later been identified would not have mattered; he had gone rogue and almost any sort of story could have been spun round him.

The real worry was the police identity card. Soames had not told Prescott about it. It was an administrative blunder; because Towler was to retain the gun it was wrongly assumed that he should also keep the card. Depending on how he used it, this might cause problems; enough to start an enquiry if it was being flashed around.

The ultimate fate of Towler was not in question; his execution would take place one way or another so that people like Prescott, and whoever he was shielding, could sleep at night. But if the ID was found on his dead body, it might cause trouble if the police discovered it first. It must be recovered, unless it could be arranged to appear as if Towler had stolen both the gun and the ID. It was one confounded problem after another. Soames chewed on a sandwich without tasting it, wishing the Towler affair would end quickly so that everyone could get back to normal. None of this mess would have occurred if Towler had not been seconded to the department; it had all stemmed from his sighting Abdul. But it still left the mystery of Abdul himself.

'I'm perfectly all right. Don't worry about me,' insisted Kate Parker. 'I have everything I want here and, anyway, who wants to go out in this weather?'

Dawson gazed across at her as she sat on the arm of the settee, her hair framed against the light from the window behind her. There was something wrong, something troubling her, she was not usually tetchy like this.

'I can't help worrying about you. I feel it's all my fault.' He stared at her from across the room as if distance between them was essential at the moment; but it was distance of the minds, too, and he felt it. This sort of nervous strain had never happened between them before.

'Why?' Kate was holding a stout walking-stick which she used to lever herself up. 'I understand that there are certain things you might not be able to tell me but is there anything you can say that would not breach security? There must be something, James. All I know is what happened from when I was kidnapped. I've gone over and over it, and I really know nothing.'

'Kate, there's nothing I can tell you yet. I'm not sure that I know it all myself. You were used as a leverage to release the poor blighter who was shot. That's as far as it goes and you know that much already.' He spread his hands in a helpless gesture. 'I'm bound to worry about you for God's sake.'

Her expression softened. 'I understand. But don't you think you're spending too much time here? Sandra will notice; it could cause a problem.'

Dawson grimaced. 'It would certainly be a change if she noticed anything at all about me. But you're right, I'll have to cut down my visits. But first I think I should have you moved from here.'

'Why?'

'Just in case. To keep on the move for a bit won't do any harm.'

'I'm staying here. And if it happens to be on your mind, my toe is going to be fine. It's no more than a sore inconvenience. I will not be lame and will be able to walk quite normally as soon as it's properly healed.'

'I can get you an apartment of your own.'

'I've got an apartment of my own and I'm not allowed to go back to it, which means that this business is not yet over. At times it frightens me.'

'Yes, I know. I'm sorry. I think I'll arrange police protection.'

She heard the doubt in his voice. He did not want it; questions would be raised and he would not want to answer them. 'I don't want bloody police protection. What I want is the address of Sam Towler. He is the only one I trust apart from yourself and he's able to give me the kind of protection you seem to think I still need.'

Dawson stirred uncomfortably and could not meet her gaze. 'You must not contact Towler at any cost.'

'He's already been here. And he saw you arrive last night; perhaps tonight, too.' She had not meant to be bitchy but she was getting nowhere and she did not like the anti-Towler attitude, not even from Dawson.

'What? Why didn't you tell me before? You were supposed to let me know if he made contact. Oh, Kate, how could you deceive me like that?'

'I don't know where he is if that's what you think. He just wanted to see how I was getting on. Don't worry, I denied that you had called although he spotted the flowers. But I need to speak to him again; I was rotten to him in protecting you and I can't forgive myself.'

Dawson wiped his brow. 'Thanks for that. But it's a dangerous business. He's not what he seems.'

'Who told you that?' The question was a cutting challenge.

'You have to take my word for it.' Dawson crossed the room to look at the flower arrangement.

'I can't do that.' Kate rose and leaned on the stick. 'You forget I spent some dangerous hours with him and he protected me. Now you suggest he's up to something; well, my word, he had plenty of opportunity. Where is he?'

'I don't know, my dear. And if I did I wouldn't tell you. I asked you before and I ask you again: if you find out where he is, tell me. A good deal could depend on it.'

'Like his life?' Kate's voice had risen.

Dawson bent over the blooms and lightly touched one or two. He was seeing something new in Kate and it disturbed him. 'Don't be ridiculous.'

'They are trying to kill him.'

'He told you that?'

'He told me and I told you before. Why can't you accept it? They're trying to get rid of him and he won't tell me where he is because he can't trust anyone. And that hurts.'

Dawson stared at her as if he did not know her any more. The face was the same, the figure, but something had changed her apart from the trauma of kidnap. 'Kate, you're fantasising. This fellow seems to have affected your reasoning. Why would anyone want to kill him?'

'For the same damned reason that they kidnapped me, amputated my toe, shot two men dead and chased Sam Towler and me through the bloody snow to kill us.' She threw the stick down angrily and supported herself against the settee. 'Can't you see what's under your nose? Or is it that you don't want to face it? Why are you running away from the problem, James? Tell me.'

He could see that she was close to tears, either from anger or concern. 'My God, Katie, that was a bit strong. It's only you I'm worried about.' He moved away from the flower arrangement. 'All right. Let's take your premise . . .'

'It's not a bloody premise. It's a fact, damn you.'

Dawson could not believe his ears. She was under stress, that was it. 'Who's trying to kill him? Tell me that.'

'He doesn't know. The same people who tried the other night. He seems to think it might be his own crowd.'

Dawson paled. His voice shook a little as he said, 'Have you any idea who he works for?'

'I can guess.'

'And you think they want to kill him?'

'*He* seems to.'

Even now, even with Kate, whom he trusted implicitly, Dawson was sufficiently professional to curb what he said. 'Do you realise all that implies? Why on earth would they want to do that?'

'I don't know.' Kate was feeling desperate and reason was weakening her stand. When she spoke like that it all seemed impossible. 'The fact is that somebody is trying to do so and it could be them.'

'I'm sorry he's fed you with this malicious nonsense. Keep asking yourself why they would want to do it. Presumably he gave no reason?'

'No.' When it was argued like this she began to have doubts. Then she thought of Sam and strengthened sufficiently to say, 'Can't you get to the bottom of it, James? For me if for no other reason?'

He came over to hold her. 'For you is sufficient reason, Katie. Leave it to me. Meanwhile take my advice and don't let him come near you until we've cleared it up.' He held her away from him. 'If he would only report in, the whole matter would be cleared up in no time. Just what do you think could be done to him in broad daylight even if you're right? Don't you think that makes his story suspect?'

She did not want to reply. It seemed to her there was nothing logical about any of it.

In a soft, kindly voice he asked, 'How did he know you were here? Isn't that suspect? Why would he want to know?'

'To see me.'

'Yes, but why? Katie, if he can find you, so can other interested parties. Think over my offer. Give me a ring at my office but don't leave it too late and be very careful whom you open the door to.'

When he left and stood by the lift, his expression changed completely, the soft lines being replaced by obvious worry. He was not yet ready to go down to where his bodyguard and chauffeur were waiting. He stood by the shaft listening to the whine of cables and pulleys as the lift moved up and down but never stopping at his floor. The indeterminate progress of the machine reflected his own doubts. The suggestions Kate had made appalled him. They simply could not be true. Slowly his hand rose to ring the bell. And if they were true did he really want to know?

Once outside, with his bodyguard beside him, he took surreptitious stock. Was he being watched at this very moment? And if he were, did he want his bodyguard to know? The armed police officer by his side was a rock of discretion. All the bodyguard team were, for they had to be with the knowledge they picked up. Just how much was he seeing now and saying nothing? Dawson was a disturbed man as he stepped into his car.

Steiner took off his topcoat and threw it over the back of his chair; for him it was tantamount to stripping off. He went straight along to Joe Lingfield's office, gave his almost inaudible tap on the door and went in. Lingfield had his secretary in the room and Steiner took in the scene in a flash. Lingfield was a young, old-fashioned guy who played straight by his wife and his secretary was nowhere near him. It was the sort of pointer Steiner stored for future occasion; where there was some indication of intimacy it could often be useful when he needed information someone did not want to give him.

Lingfield weighed up Steiner's entry and gave a wink to his secretary; they both knew the form. When Steiner stood just inside the door, pointedly looking at the girl, Lingfield gave her a nod and she departed with a disdainful tilt of the head as she passed the stony-faced DIA man.

'She thinks you should spend more time in your own department,' explained Lingfield.

'It's none of her goddammed business,' Steiner replied, flopping into a chair. 'I'm bushed.'

Lingfield did not believe it; Steiner was never bushed. But he might be frustrated and that could be interesting. 'What's your problem?'

'I'm waiting to hear from you. What've you got?'

'You only saw me yesterday.'

Steiner looked surprised. 'How long do you need? You're the whizz kid around here. Maybe it's all bullshit.'

Lingfield gave in; there was no winning against Steiner. 'I didn't pick up too much from Five but there is an interesting twist. An old pal of mine, a journalist who's done work for us, has shown an interest in the Hereford shootings. He doesn't say why except that he feels there might be a story there. He's an experienced man; slipped out of favour from across the pond, but knows his job.'

'What's his name?'

'Lew Quinn. Some years ago he was working on one of the big New York dailies when he screwed his boss's wife. The story goes that she made a play for him and in a drunken spree he obliged her but was not too careful. Influential multi-millionaire press barons don't take kindly to that sort of thing and he deliberately screwed up Quinn in revenge. Quinn lost his job and soon discovered he could not get another. He came to London but even here his old boss has managed to put the boot in.'

'I know of the guy. His wife is a nympho; seems he attracts them. So what's your point?'

Lingfield was sorry he had mentioned it but could not see that it would do Lew Quinn any harm. 'Just thought you should know. All I've got out of Five so far is that they think Mossad might be behind the Hereford job.'

'That's already been suggested in the yellow press. Which is probably where your man picked it up. I asked you about the escort, Joe, not newspaper crap.'

'The escort was an SAS sergeant on loan or approval or something like that. Nobody at Five knows much about him. He's gone to ground and nobody knows why.'

'Did you get a name?'

'Sam Towler. Good solid English name.'

'If he's missing, maybe he's neither good nor solid. Towler. They've no idea at all why he ducked out?'

'None.'

'Which means they have but are acting dumb. O.K. Where does Quinn hang out?'

13

Towler occasionally peered round the corner. The red brick of the MI5 block failed to lift it from the bleakness of the general scene. It was a quarter past five and everybody was in a hurry. Taxis were at a premium and rarely in sight and there were far fewer cars on the streets as the frost started to harden again.

Towler did not know how long he would have to wait and it might turn out to be abortive. He had his coat collar turned up and was wearing a cony-fur hat, not unlike one of Soames', and heavy fur gloves. Whenever he saw someone he recognised come his way, he rolled out of sight until they had passed.

The typists and secretaries were the first to leave in any number and office lights intermittently flicked out, leaving dark hollow patches in the building. It was going to be difficult, he saw that, but he clung to the hope that luck might break his way. One or two of the men he had briefly got to know began to appear, often splitting up once they were clear of the building.

It was almost six o'clock when Jerry Cutter came out with another man Towler did not know; both were carrying document cases. The two stood talking outside for a few minutes and then moved off together. Cutter was tall and his fair hair was uncovered, making an easy target for Towler who slipped round the corner and slowly followed, keeping on the opposite side of the street. He was banking on this being the last place Soames would expect to see him.

Cutter was trained in surveillance and Towler kept further back than he would have liked. They were heading towards Half Moon Street and suddenly crossed to Towler's side of the street. By the time Towler turned the corner, Cutter and his friend were well towards Piccadilly. He closed up a little as they disappeared round the corner.

When he reached the corner Towler could see no sign of them. There were far more people about and it was difficult to see through the constantly moving crowd. He stood on the edge of the street, conscious of standing out, but unable to pick up a trace. Then he saw them still on the north side of Piccadilly and guessed that they were heading for Green Park Station. Again he risked closing up and dived against the nearest wall as they stopped, chatted for a while, and then parted, with Cutter entering the station. Towler ran forward. It was rush hour and the place was packed.

Inside the booking hall Towler gazed around and picked up Cutter in a fast-moving queue to reach a down escalator. Towler bought a top-price ticket and by this time Cutter had long gone from sight. Towler took a chance and went down to the Acton Town and Hounslow platform. He quickly picked out Cutter who had not moved far along and was standing near the edge. Towler hung back against the wall.

Cutter took the first train in, and Towler had difficulty in pushing his way on to the next coach. It was now impossible to keep Cutter in sight and all he could do was to squeeze his way to the doors to see if Cutter had alighted every time the train stopped.

At South Kensington Towler was grateful for Cutter's extra inches and he spotted the fair head above the others as Cutter made his way up to the Circle Line. Towler followed. The station was crowded but the bottleneck of the West End had been broken and it was now comparatively easy to keep Cutter in sight without being too close to him.

The coaches were still crowded with standing room only but Towler managed to get on the same coach as Cutter but much further down. Cutter finally alighted at Bayswater and Towler followed him up and out into the crisp air. He followed Cutter allowing the distance to lengthen as the number of people decreased. It had been a long way round and he wondered if Cutter had deliberately taken evasive action; or perhaps there was a hold-up on the Central Line, which would have been more direct.

Cutter turned into one of the many old streets and Towler lengthened his stride to close the gap again. The hurrying footsteps should not worry Cutter unless he was actually expecting trouble; everyone was hurrying, even Cutter himself. When Towler noticed Cutter slow and start fumbling in his pocket Towler made his move. There were few people evident in this quiet part of Bayswater and Towler sprinted forward.

Cutter did not look round until he was actually turning into one of the gateways and even then he sensed no danger, least of all from Towler whom he barely recognised, even when the Browning was painfully twisting behind his ear.

'For God's sake, man, be careful with that bloody thing.'

The reaction was almost laughable. Towler said, 'Get it into your head that I'm serious, Cutter.'

'About what? Are you going to shoot me here?'

So Cutter had guts. Towler kept his voice down. 'Where's the best place to talk? Inside?'

'My wife's there with my daughter. You'll frighten the life out of them with that thing. Someone will already have seen and will be reporting it to the police even as I speak. Everyone's looking for you anyway.'

'So you'll understand that I'll shoot you if I have to. Let's go further in. This shouldn't take long.'

They went half-way up the slippery concrete path and were in the shadow of the porch when Towler told him to stop and to drop his case. Towler kept slightly behind Cutter and was no longer actually touching him. The move unsettled Cutter, who could not see what was happening.

'Don't turn,' said Towler. 'Put your hands in your pockets and keep them there and face the house.'

'Why don't you just report in and act like the rest of us?'

'Have you any idea what's been happening to me?'

Cutter was silent. He gazed up at the heavy drapes at the front windows of the house and could barely see the light through them. There would be no help from that direction. He considered shouting but was not sure just how desperate Towler was; certainly desperate enough to pick up his trail and to follow him home. Eventually he said, 'I've no idea, dear boy. Do tell me what's going on.'

'Don't shout or try to draw attention for I've nothing to lose by topping you. Soames has a death squad after me. They've already made one or two attempts and sooner or later will get me unless I can find out why they want to do it. You don't know, I suppose?'

'Soames plays everything close to the cuff. But I find what you say impossible to believe.'

'So do I. But it's happening. Remember Abdul?'

'The Arab you spotted? The one we brought in and you and I shared a night shift over?'

'That's the boy. Did anyone ever find out who he is?'

'Not so far as I know. But then Soames did most, if not all, the interrogating himself. Fancies himself at it. Particularly with the uncommunicative ones. You know it really is bloody cold out here, Sam.'

'You'd be colder dead, Jerry. I've nothing against you but I must find out what happened to Abdul. He suddenly disappeared. Tell me about it.'

'Why do you imagine I know any more than you?'

'Because Soames hated my guts; he wouldn't give me the time of day unless it involved a caper. Get on with it.'

'I don't know a thing. You had the midnight to four shift and I took over after that. It's a senseless duty as you know; just to keep someone on tap. All those cameras and lights are simply to put the wind up the prisoner; they achieve very little except rob them of privacy. Few are worried by that. What the hell can they do in a locked cell, for chrissake?'

'What you mean is you went to sleep on duty.'

'Everyone does. There's a bell the prisoners can push if they suddenly break into the need for a confession. Are you saying you didn't kip?'

'That's right. When we're on duty we're on duty. I'm beginning to feel less sorry for you. Go on.'

'There's nothing to say. Soames pitched up about 7.30 in the morning and told me to piss off.'

'Just like that?'

'Almost. He was looking tired and irritable at being up so early but, even so, he told me I need not see out the half hour I had left to do as he was letting Abdul go. I didn't argue; I can't stand the place, always get headaches looking at those damned monitors.'

'Is that it?'

'As far as I'm concerned, yes.'

'Why would he let him go if he got nothing out of him?'

'Why bring him in in the first place? Soames didn't like the idea but you put the seed of doubt in his mind and he acted against his own judgment. His judgment is sound, I might tell you. He may be a pompous ass but he's shrewd and knows his job.'

'He knows his job so well that he released Abdul out of pique and because he is sorry he ever came across me. Bullshit. Think harder. And keep looking to your bloody front. I want more, Cutter. Just remember I now know where you and your family live. Think about it.'

Cutter could not miss Towler's change of tone and he did not take the threat as empty. Towler's desperation came through; so even SAS men got the jitters. Suddenly he was nervous without really knowing why. Something had changed. He thought carefully before saying, 'The day after we were on duty I heard Tony Wilshaw complain that the cleaners had to be rushed down to the Suite.'

'The cleaners? What does that mean?'

'A cleaning-up job. I don't know the details, it's not my department.' Cutter could hear Towler's heavy breathing behind him and was afraid the sergeant was getting out of hand. 'That's all I can tell you.'

'Where does Tony Wilshaw hang out?'

'Don't be ridiculous. I can't tell you that.'

'Yes you can, Jerry. I can make a hospital case of you. On the other hand if you tell me, it's our insurance. It will discourage you from telling Soames that we met because he won't take kindly to it, and there's no way I shall tell him. Make your choice.'

Kate Parker opened the door for Nigel Prescott and watched his large figure limp past her into the living-room. She smiled to herself; he was limping on the opposite side to her. 'We'd better not be seen walking together or we might cause some amusement.'

He lowered himself into one of the heavier chairs and

nodded his agreement. 'There are other reasons, too, why it would be better for us not to be seen together.'

'That sounds ominous.'

'Not ominous, just sensible. It was kind of you to see me at such short notice after my phone call. Would you like me to show you some identification?'

Kate sat opposite him, placing her stick by the side of her chair. 'It's a bit late for that, you're already in.'

Prescott smiled. 'You're obviously level-headed which should make things easier. I really am in the Ministry of Defence as I told you on the phone. And my present interest is to protect the Home Secretary as, I'm sure, so is yours.'

'Does he know you are here?'

Prescott stretched out his painful leg. 'No. He'd probably crucify me if he knew.'

'Then why are you?'

Prescott glanced across the room. 'Could I have a drink? A large whisky, perhaps? I'm sorry to impose on you but I think I need one before I answer that.'

As Kate pushed herself up Prescott hurriedly clambered to his feet and said, 'That was thoughtless of me. Let me pour for us both.'

Kate settled for the same and Prescott brought the drinks over. 'Cheers,' toasted Prescott as he sat down again. He raised the half-filled tumbler of neat whisky and took a long, thoughtful sip. 'I think there is some danger of matters getting out of hand and certain issues need clarification.' He put down his drink on a side table, his head lowered as if he were undecided what to say next.

'The Home Secretary told me about your attitude to Sergeant Towler. While this is very commendable I thought it better if I took you into our confidence; as far as we can.'

Kate seized up, her face stony as it seemed always to become when criticism of Towler was about to start. 'Why on earth should you feel the need? I'm no threat to you.'

'Of course not. But you're tied into a mystery for which, increasingly, we feel that only Towler has the answers.'

'My strong impression from him, Mr Prescott, is that Sam Towler is looking for a few answers himself. Like, who the devil is trying to kill him.'

'That's part of the problem, Kate. I hope I'm old enough to call you that without offending you. So far as I know, nobody is trying to kill him.'

'So what happened to us in Hereford was all a bad dream?'

Prescott could not miss the biting anger. 'Two dead men can hardly be a dream. Of course it happened. What we would like to know is who was behind it.' Prescott rubbed his knee. 'As painful as this may sound to you we are beginning to believe that Towler himself has at least some part in it.'

'Rubbish. He was in the firing line with me.'

'Yet you both came away unhurt. It was very well done. But then his training has been exemplary. He is a highly trained field operator.'

'If he hadn't been we'd both be dead. Are you suggesting that he's a marvellous actor too? In the most unbearable of conditions?'

Prescott shrugged. 'I thought this might be difficult. I understand your feelings. He has created a strong impression on you. But nevertheless we have supporting evidence that he is involved in some way. What we don't know are his motives although we have some ideas.'

'Such as?'

'Ah! Now you are asking me to delve into classified material. I've already gone much further than I should.'

'Why have you, Mr Prescott? What's the point of all this?'

'I want you to be very careful of Towler. Very careful indeed. And if you can find out where he is staying it would be very helpful to all of us if you would let me know.'

'But not so helpful to him? Look, I've already told James that I don't know where he is. In fact I asked James if he would let *me* know if he found out. This really is a wasted visit.'

'No. I've seen for myself how you feel about Towler and that alone is useful. But I can't stress too much that you must keep all this to yourself. If you don't you can do the Home Secretary immeasurable harm. It could ruin him. He did, after all, get himself involved in this messy affair in order to protect your life.'

Kate hesitated and studied the not unkindly face opposite her. Prescott did not come over as a monster and in his way she felt he was trying to help her. 'I know that. I know that

145

only too well. And there is nothing I would do to hurt him.'

'That's very reassuring. That alone was well worth the visit to hear.'

'Is that all you wanted? To be sure I wouldn't harm James? He knows that.'

'Perhaps he is at present unsure. Your co-operation is essential if we are to get anywhere. If the press got an inkling we could be in deep trouble.'

'You mean that my exchange was done under the counter? The PM knows nothing about it? Well, I guessed that much. James has nothing to fear from me so why should he feel unsure?'

'Perhaps I misunderstood him. Perhaps it's your association with Towler that concerns him.'

'So we're back to that again. I have no association with Sam. But if I had, it's none of your damned business.'

'I'm afraid it is, Kate. I'm afraid that any dealings you might have with Towler are our business. Until matters are sorted out. He's a wild card. No matter how discreet you might be, and the rest of us, he could do the Home Secretary untold damage. Whether or not you like it, that's a fact. Perhaps that's his underlying object. For if the Home Secretary falls in these circumstances, so too could the government. The public would never believe that the PM did not know; they would see it as closing a blind eye for a friend. It would also create havoc in our security services.'

'And James knows all this?'

'Of course. He's at the centre of it.'

Kate said carefully, 'I wonder if he knows everything that's going on? Or is he being kept in the dark about classified aspects as well?'

Prescott heaved himself up with a smile. 'That's an uncharitable thought, Kate. We are answerable to him. Our concern is for you both. Your interests are possibly different but we really are obligated to protect you both. It's vital that we do.'

Kate smiled sweetly. 'I'm sure that is right, Mr Prescott. What's beginning to worry me, though, is what else are you trying to protect?'

*　　*　　*

Matt Steiner rang the bell and Cathy Quinn answered the door. Unusually for her, she did not like Steiner on sight. She immediately saw him as a rough, tough, sexless, unfeeling creature with whom she would get nowhere, no matter what she tried. From the moment she looked into his wintry eyes she loathed him and played him at his own game.

'Whatever you have to sell we already have it and don't like it. G'day.'

He put his weight against the door as she tried to close it. 'O.K. So you don't like me. I must be the exception. I'm a friend of your husband's. Is he in?'

'If you're a friend of his then I must tell him to be more careful about his choice. No he's not in.'

'And what about your choice, Honey? Are you so choosey?'

'Who are you?' Her eyes were blazing.

'My name is Matt Steiner and all I want to do is to have a word with your husband. What's your beef?'

'I don't like the look of you. Anyway he's out.' She had not protected Lew like this for years and was surprised how good it felt.

A door slammed somewhere in the apartment and Quinn bawled out, 'For chrissake shut that door, the place is freezing.'

Steiner smiled. 'His brother?'

'The lodger.' Cathy was seething at being let down. 'I'll ask him if he wants to see you.' Before Steiner could move she slammed the door in his face.

Quinn was coming from his room as Cathy approached. 'What's the matter?' he asked.

'There's a creep out there who says he knows you. Name of Matt Steiner. He's compounded granite all the way down. Shall I tell him to butt out?'

He suddenly saw that she was concerned, even protecting him. He raised a hand to her cheek before realising what he was doing. 'Thanks, Honey. The name rings a bell. But I don't think I've ever met him.'

'He looks like the Mafia. Don't see him, he's trouble and cocky with it.'

'I'm a newspaper man, Cath. I have to see the good and the bad.'

'Then do it on the doorstep. Don't let him in.'

Her unrelenting attitude surprised him. 'O.K. Keep the other doors closed or they'll slam.'

Quinn opened the front door and Steiner was standing exactly where Cathy had left him. He had some reservations but not as many as Cathy on seeing Steiner. 'Hi. My wife doesn't trust you and she's right because you said you are my friend. We've never met.'

'I sometimes have that effect on people who don't know me. I did stretch it a bit. I'm a friend of a friend. Joe Lingfield suggested I drop by. I gather you two go back some way.'

Quinn was immediately wary, assuming that Steiner must be in the same line of business as Lingfield. 'So?'

'Can't I come in?'

'My wife's forbidden it. We can talk here. We won't be overheard.'

Steiner shrugged it off. 'A strange way to greet a fellow American in a foreign city.'

'London isn't foreign to me, Steiner. Can we get on with it?'

'Joe said you showed undue interest in the Hereford shootings. I wondered if you could tell me something about it. On a commission basis, of course.'

'Joe didn't say that. I doubt that he suggested you come here either. Just to get rid of you, my interest is a normal journalist's interest. I thought there might be something there.'

'And is there?'

'I don't know. That's why I saw Joe. Why should you be interested?'

'It was a strange business. You never know with these things; there could be something in it for us. You obviously thought so.'

'Only as routine. You've taken a lot of trouble over a nebulous issue.'

Steiner grinned. 'The story of my life. That's why I'm better than the rest of them; they're too busy sitting on their butts. I was hoping you might be able to help.'

'What could I offer a self-confessed genius? And if I had something I'd need it for my own copy. Is that all?'

'Not quite. There's a rumour that a girl and a fella escaped the shooting and have gone to ground. Would you know anything about that?'

'Well, that's something I've learned. Good of you to tell me.'

Steiner's gaze hardened. 'Don't take me for a fool, Quinn. I thought we might have helped each other. From what I hear you could do with a decent story.'

Quinn felt pleased that he had penetrated Steiner's colossal ego. 'From what you've told me, you haven't got one to offer.' As Quinn was about to close the door he saw Towler approach; he must have come up the stairs very quietly.

Steiner saw Quinn's quick change of expression and turned his head to see a tall, rugged looking, quite well dressed man approach along the landing. And he noted the fractional hesitation in Towler's step.

As Steiner turned his head Quinn shot Towler a silent warning and the Londoner gave a brief nod of greeting and continued past the apartment door to mount the next flight of stairs.

'Who's he?' asked Steiner when Towler had passed out of sight.

'Why don't you get a registry of all the occupants? He lives upstairs. I don't think we've anything more to discuss.'

'You're probably right. If you think of anything get through to Joe.'

Steiner walked away and Quinn heard him go lightly down the stairs. Quinn closed the front door and stood behind it. It was a little while before the bell rang. He opened the door and Towler slipped in.

Steiner saw Towler go in. He then went down the stairs as silently as he had come up them after leaving Quinn.

14

'We'll have to use our own men,' Prescott stated flatly.

Soames squirmed on his chair. He started to tap his desk until Prescott glared a thunderous warning and he put the pen down. From the moment Prescott had rung through and had deigned to come to Soames' own office, Soames recognised trouble.

When Soames did not respond sufficiently quickly, Prescott added, 'These people you have hired are simply not doing the job. They might be all right on a sitting target but Towler has made good use of ground and cover. We simply can't continue on this long chain of command. It takes too long and is too damned clumsy.'

Soames lowered his head unhappily. Normally, delegation for this kind of work to outsiders had many advantages. For one, nobody knew the source whatever the speculation. And that was vitally important. Cover-ups were infinitely easier. But Soames did not like the idea of using staff on someone like Towler. There had been past problems with the various A1 departments, used for surveillance, break-ins and sometimes worse, and A6(F) had always been a section to avoid. The last cover-up, and that had not involved an actual assassination, so far as anyone would ever admit, cost the MOD almost half a million sterling. It might be more complicated but was infinitely safer, to contract out.

'If you say we must,' Soames eventually said.

'As matters stand, the delays are dangerous. It should be over and done with by now. And while he's still around there are other complications which, to say the least, are a continuing embarrassment.'

'You couldn't enlighten me on that?' Soames asked hopefully, his pale, plump face moist from stress.

'No, I could not.'

Soames looked up, made a move for his pen, then thought better of it. 'We've made some progress. Towler followed Jerry Cutter to his Bayswater home. Threatened him. Cutter put him on to Tony Wilshaw and we've got a tail on Wilshaw and his place in Bucks is staked out.'

'Cutter? How long has he been with us?'

'Eight years.'

'And he told Towler about Wilshaw?'

'What would you do if you had a Browning pressed against your ear?'

Prescott, uncharacteristically, accepted the rebuke. He knew Soames' position only too well and realised the resentment that had built up which, to Soames, would appear to be a lack of trust from his superior. Soames was a long-serving, capable officer. But there was no way that Prescott could reveal the involvement of Her Majesty's Secretary of State for Home Affairs.

'Perhaps he exonerated himself by contacting you at the first opportunity. So you think Towler will go for Wilshaw?'

'If he's looking for answers he'll have to. We're waiting.'

'You could have told me this before.'

'Nothing's happened yet. There's another thing. Joe Lingfield has been making enquiries about the Hereford affair.'

Prescott stopped rubbing his knee. 'Why would the Company be interested?'

'I don't know. He's been probing quite hard, though. I can't see their interest but there clearly is one. Thought you should know.'

'It brings us back to Towler, doesn't it? It wouldn't do for them to run across him.'

'Why should they try?'

The question hung between them. They eyed each other and their thoughts were not too far apart.

'Could they be in this in some way?' ventured Prescott.

Neither man wanted to answer. It could produce a dimension that was totally unwanted and could make matters far worse than they already were.

'Get Towler, Soames. For God's sake pull your finger out. I don't care how you do it but have him out of the way once and for all before everything gets out of hand.'

When Towler entered the apartment he stood with Quinn, their backs to the front door. There was no way of knowing whether Steiner had made a connection between the two men. On the face of it there was no reason why he should but they both accepted that he had. Quinn had been right when he told Steiner that they had never met, but, as he talked it over with Towler, he recalled that he had certainly heard of him and that what he had heard was not good. Steiner would go through a brick wall to get what he wanted and would not worry about who got hurt on the way.

An hour later Towler was heading north-east on the Metropolitan Line. He watched the white fields roll by as they reached the open countryside of Buckinghamshire. The lines of trees were tinselled with frozen snow and even the strongest boughs bent under the strain. He spotted some blanketed horses nibbling at bundles of hay and the continuing scene had a therapeutic effect until he dozed off. He almost missed his station but managed to scramble out in time at Chalfont and Latimer.

He stood outside the station. To his right the entry road curved away to join the main street pointing to Chorleywood in one direction and Amersham in the other. Around the curve was a collection of parked cars, their windscreens protected by old newspapers, their roofs glittering with frost. He managed to get a cab and was vague about where he actually wanted to go but thought the house was in the general direction of Chalfont St Giles; he would recognise it when he saw it.

The main roads had been cleared some time ago but many of the narrower country roads left much to be desired and, although the snow had been heaped on either side, there were plenty of ice patches and, often, little or no room to pass. He located the house quite early on. It lay well back on a semi-circular drive and was Mock Tudor. As the cab went past Towler wondered how many men Soames had put on.

After a while he told the driver to take him back to the station. From there he rang Quinn who had agreed to be on stand-by, not knowing what was going on but now totally convinced that there was a strong story to be had.

Towler said, 'I'd like to borrow Cathy. I'm at Chalfont and Latimer and the house I want is staked out. I saw two cars pugged away but there'll be more. Would she be willing to come out here? I'll explain it all to her. We can come back together.' Towler lightened his tone; 'She'll be safe with me. I couldn't raise a smile in this weather; it's arctic up here. I've put enough in the slot to hold on.'

After a short while Quinn came back on. 'She said she'll do it for me, particularly if it's to do with spiking Steiner.'

'Then it is to do with Steiner. It's only half an hour from Baker Street.'

Sheikh Ibrahim Nazzal saw James Dawson at the Home Office. Normally Dawson would not have met the Sheikh who had no Saudi Arabian governmental designation, but was a minor member of the Saudi Royal Family and immensely wealthy. Britain had always had a special relationship with the Saudis and did not want to upset her friends in the Middle East. So, although the appointment had been requested at such short notice, he conceded to the meeting.

To Dawson, Nazzal looked the same as any other Arab Sheikh, long flowing robes and a dark beard. They shook hands and faced each other politely across Dawson's desk. Tea was ordered as a matter of courtesy.

The procedure of polite enquiry about Dawson's family was agonising to the Minister who was finding his work slipping behind and concentration more difficult each day.

Nazzal finally got to the point; 'It has come to our notice that a man named Rashid Khayar was arrested by your Security Service and it would seem that you are still holding him. I wonder if you can throw some light on the matter?'

It was all so polite but Dawson knew better than that. He felt numb. It was all happening again. He said, just as politely and with as pleasant a smile, 'The name means nothing to me, Sheikh Nazzal. Is he important to you?'

Nazzal stroked his beard as he pondered the question. 'He means something to the Royals of the Islamic world and almost certainly to the Royals elsewhere, especially Britain. He could also mean something to heads of state in the Western world.'

'You mean he's a threat to them?'

'On the contrary.'

'Could you enlighten me?'

'It would destroy many confidences if I did and could put his life in jeopardy.' Nazzal held up a heavily jewelled hand. 'Don't be insulted by that, Minister. We trust you implicitly, of course. It's those beyond you who we do not know, that must be held in doubt. A precaution, no more.'

'So there is nothing you are prepared to tell us about this man?'

'Only that he is important to us.'

'Who is "us", Sheikh Nazzal?'

Nazzal's smile wavered. 'That's almost as difficult to answer. There are some of us who are trying to improve the Arab image which most people seem to think centres around terrorism of one kind or another. It is not easy to do on a clandestine basis as most of us are well known. To express certain views publicly would be to invite the assassin's bullet. So we work away quietly and hopefully and are making some progress.' Nazzal gathered his robes more tightly about him although it was warm in the office. 'May I say that my older brother remembers you well from your days at Oxford together.'

'Ismail? Played cricket rather well; nice bat, brilliant slip fielder.'

'He still is. I can only say, Minister, that I am sure our interests are the same; we seek stability.'

'Presumably, if we have this man, you want him released?'

'We would be most grateful.'

'If we have him you realise that I would have to be guided by our own security people. They may know something about,' Dawson glanced at his pad, 'Rashid Khayar that you might not.'

'That is always possible. But if that turns out to be the case perhaps you could advise us and of the evidence against him?'

The exchange was so civilised that Dawson failed to understand the tightening in his guts. There was a terrible, underlying threat to this whole business and he did not doubt for one moment that it was all tied up with the original problem.

* * *

Cathy arrived wearing a dark musquash coat, matching hat, and high-heeled boots in which she somehow coped with the ground conditions. The early office leavers, the advance guard of the rush hour, were taken with her striking image. Cathy was turning heads at a time when all people wanted to do was to get home.

She greeted Towler who was waiting for her on the platform, like a long-lost lover. She threw her arms round his neck knowing that he could not make a scene.

When he managed to separate, he led her to the exit and she looped her arm through his, amused by his discomfort. 'I told you I'd get you,' she whispered in his ear as they emerged from the station.

'Listen to me,' he said at last. 'This caper could be dangerous. It's important that you know.'

'I'm the wife of a newspaper man, Sam. I'm doing it for Lew.'

'You could have fooled me. How much has Lew told you?'

'He's left it to you.' She kissed him hard on the cheek. 'He trusts you.'

'You do that again and we'll get a round of applause. Be serious, Cathy. There are men out there waiting to knock me off. You could be in the firing line.'

'But you don't really think so, Honey, or you wouldn't have had me come.'

'I'm beginning to think it's a mistake. Maybe you'd better go back.'

Cathy calmed down and Towler signalled a cab. He gave the address and when they were seated, her arm still looped through his, he explained what he wanted her to do. When he had finished and was sure that she understood, he added, 'I don't know how many men there will be. I don't know whether you'll have a sobering effect on them or whether they won't care if you are in the firing line. I just don't know. All I know is that I'm pretty sure I can't do it without you. But the danger is real. Think of yourself and think of Lew. You have time to opt out.'

She looked at him in the darkness of the rear of the cab and her pretty face was too near for comfort. He thought she was going to kiss him again but suddenly she was surprisingly serious. 'What I'm doing now is better than swigging vodka. Right? Better than whoring around and sending Lew up the wall with worry.'

'Then why do you do it to him?'

Cathy patted Towler's hand. 'It's a long story. He let me down and it ruined our lives.'

'If it was so bad you could have left him.'

'Maybe I wanted him to suffer. Are you coming to bed with me when this is over?'

Towler grinned in the gloom. 'You're getting to know that's a safe invitation. You know I wouldn't let Lew down but it doesn't mean the temptation isn't there. You're a dish, Cathy. I'm getting to like you; don't ruin the friendship.'

Cathy squeezed his hand before withdrawing her arm from his. 'Pins and needles,' she explained and they laughed.

Towler leaned across her. 'This is it. Now do the best you can.'

The cab turned off and crunched over the shingle drive in a slow arc towards the house. Cathy noticed that Towler was suddenly tense. He had so far struck her as an impregnable kind of guy and his sudden nervous alertness unsettled her. It was too late now for second thoughts, the cab was pulling up in front of the house.

There was a light on in the arched porch, a deviation from the basic Tudor style. They climbed out and Cathy started to laugh like a drunk. She caught Towler's arm to save herself from falling just as he was paying off the cabbie. 'Damn your weather, Johnnie, it's never like this in California.'

Towler's reply was lost as the cab drew away and the two stood in the porch with Cathy trying to keep upright as she clung to Towler who rang the bell. A man opened the door after the usual spy-hole inspection. Towler hoped that the concentration would be on Cathy but he had his hat pulled well down and was wearing his new clothes. He did not identify the man but did not think he was facing Tony Wilshaw.

Towler said, 'Is Tony in?'

Cathy swayed, holding tightly on to Towler. 'I guess we should have warned him.' Her American drawl was pronounced.

Both Towler and Cathy had spoken loudly enough for

listening ears but it was clear that the security man was taking no chances. 'He's not home yet. Can you come back later?'

'Come back, you jerk? Who the hell are you? I'm his sister, damn you. Now let us in out of this goddam cold.' Cathy turned angrily to Towler. 'This is a mistake, Honey. I didn't want to come in the first place.'

'You can't go back without seeing him.' Towler turned to the man at the door. 'Are you going to let us in?'

'There's something of a problem at the moment. Stay there while I check with Tony's wife.' He was about to close the door when a woman's voice called from the back of the hall, 'Tony's sister died six years ago and had never been to America in her life.'

'I'm sure you'll let us in anyway.' Towler said, and held the Browning just above his pocket and below the arm Cathy still had linked through his. Cathy did not see the gun but the security man did. They stepped in as the man stepped back into the hall and Towler closed the door behind them with a flick of his heel.

Towler said, 'I don't intend to harm anyone as long as they don't try to harm me. What's your name?'

'Frost. You are being very stupid. The place is surrounded.'

'Oh, I know that. And very tightly; that's how we managed to get through.' He suddenly snapped at Cathy, 'Stop her using the phone.'

As Cathy ran down the hall Towler took stock of Frost. He looked like a villain, and probably was one, but he was fit and searching for half a chance. He was in his late thirties, fair-haired and had agate eyes.

'Take it out by your finger tips and don't be daft about it.'

'You've been lucky, Towler; it'll run out. You won't get away from here.'

Suddenly a woman screamed and then Cathy bawled out, 'You try that again, you cow, and I'll cripple you.' Something crashed to the floor and a bell tinkled.

Towler said, 'Sounds like the phone has had an accident. The gun, Frosty.'

Frost took his gun out from a waist holster and dropped it between them.

'Hands on head and turn round. You know what to do so

157

just get on with it.' Towler ran his free hand over Frost's body, unhooked a radio transmitter from the waistband, picked up the gun, and ushered him into the drawing-room where a dishevelled Cathy, hat missing and hair hanging, stood over a pleasant-looking but bloodied brunette, with a bottle of cognac.

The woman was scared and blood ran down her cheeks where Cathy had scratched her when the two had fought over the telephone which now lay on the floor with its cradle broken. She gazed up at Towler and saw the gun. 'Please don't harm Tony.'

Towler was not willing to reassure her in front of Frost. 'Where is he, Mrs Wilshaw?' Towler threw her a handkerchief to wipe her face.

'He's not home yet.'

'What time do you expect him?'

She glanced fearfully at Frost and Towler added, 'He won't help you. He's too slow and disarmed. In about an hour's time?'

She nodded miserably and began to cry.

Towler turned to Cathy. 'Find the kitchen and something to tie him up with. On your knees, Frost, and then lie flat.'

Frost glared but obeyed and stretched out in the middle of the room with his arms out knowing that would be Towler's next instruction.

Cathy returned with a ball of twine and some scissors and looked to Towler for instructions. Towler said to Frost, 'Put your hands behind your back.' When that had been done he knelt beside Frost in a position where he could keep his eye on Mrs Wilshaw, and placed his gun against Frost's head. 'O.K.,' he said to Cathy. 'Tie his wrists first and then his ankles. Don't cut off his circulation but make bloody sure he can't untie the knots.'

Towler watched Cathy, but kept an eye on Mrs Wilshaw. When Cathy had finished, Towler gagged Frost with a handkerchief. He had already checked that the transmitter was off and now smashed it under his foot. He stepped over Frost whom he left in the centre of the room and said to the frightened Mrs Wilshaw, 'What's your first name?'

'Jane.'

'Who were you going to phone?'

Her lips trembled. 'There's a number on the phone table. I don't know whose it is but was told to use it in an emergency.'

Towler picked up the telephone pad and ripped off the top sheet. It was a London number but not one he recognised; he slipped it in his pocket. He handed Cathy the spare gun and said, 'I'm going round the house. Make sure she stays where she is.'

Cathy took the gun reluctantly and swore softly at him. He had warned her; she had not taken him seriously enough. It was too late now to worry about what she had got herself mixed up in. She stood well away from the prone Frost and aimed the gun at Jane Wilshaw, not at all sure if she would have the nerve to use it. She suddenly wished Lew was with her.

Towler went round the house thoroughly. It was clear from photographs that the Wilshaws had children. Once satisfied that nobody else was in the house he went back downstairs.

Time passed uneasily. There were drinks on a sideboard and Towler noticed Cathy's gaze constantly wandering there. They had got into the house, but the difficult part would be getting out again. He said to Cathy, 'Forget the booze. Time for that later.'

She glared venom at him. Frost's gun lay on her lap and she kept her hands away from it as if loath to touch it. Jane Wilshaw sat huddled on a chair in the corner of the room, back to the heavily draped windows. She kept intertwining her fingers and sobbing periodically.

It was the silence that reached them more than anything else. Towler sat with his gun pointing at Jane Wilshaw to keep her seated. All they could do was to wait and this was particularly difficult for the loquacious Cathy who now had too much time for regret.

Towler got up and crossed to a baby grand piano. There was a framed wedding photograph on top and he noted Wilshaw's features.

The bell rang twenty minutes later. It rang three times; one short, one long and one short. A signal. Towler told Cathy to keep Jane Wilshaw covered, and went into the hall. The porch light was still on to make the spy hole more effective. Towler kept to the side of the wall and approached the door obliquely. He peered through the spy hole and saw a muffled figure with his face turned away.

Towler hesitated. Wilshaw would have a key but might have been warned not to use it so that he would not walk into a trap. He waited, his eye to the hole. The figure was beating his gloved hands and beyond him Towler thought he could now see the vague shape of a car, but the focus was wrong. The figure turned impatiently to press the bell again. It was Wilshaw.

Towler opened the door, standing to one side, and Wilshaw burst in complaining that he had been kept waiting too long. He had taken off his coat and was hanging it on a hall stand before he realised that something was wrong. He turned slowly, saw the gun, took a deep breath, and enquired, 'Towler?'

Towler nodded. 'Your wife is O.K. At the moment. Frosty, or whatever his name is, is resting on the drawing-room carpet. Let me have your car keys.'

'You think I'd drive in this? I came by train.'

'And walked all the way from the station? Don't mess about. I have a friend in there who has Frosty's gun pointing at your wife, and she wants to get home quickly.'

'You wouldn't hurt her, for God's sake? What has Jane done?'

'No more than I have, and look what's happening to me. The keys.'

Wilshaw handed them over and Towler slipped them into his pocket. 'Where's the car?'

Wilshaw hesitated before answering. 'Just outside.' And with resignation, 'A Porsche.'

Towler said, 'We can finish this business right now. It's up to you. All I want to know is what kind of cleaning-up job you did the night Jerry Cutter and I split a night duty down at the Mayfair Suite.'

'You know I can't tell you that. Why do you think my bloody house is surrounded? So that I don't have to tell you. Do you think I like the setup?'

'But this bunch of second-grade pirates haven't done their job properly and here I am. I don't want to start on your wife, she's distressed enough.'

As if on cue Jane Wilshaw called out in a tearful voice, 'Tony, is that you?'

Wilshaw moved towards the drawing-room and Towler stopped him in a tone that froze him on the spot.

'Don't answer and don't move. You can stop all this right now.'

Wilshaw turned to face Towler again. 'You wouldn't touch her, surely?'

'To get an answer, I'd touch anyone who tries to stop me. You know what hard bastards we are; we shoot unarmed people on the streets. Save us all time, Tony. It's a simple enough question.'

It was difficult for Towler to equate Wilshaw with the kind of job he did. The man appeared almost effeminate but he had a family and a pleasant wife so there had to be something to him. His pale eyes were weak yet he had shown little sign of nerves except concern for his wife.

'Was it Jerry Cutter who told you I was there?'

'What does it matter?'

'Because if it was Jerry, I was pulling his leg. I owed him one. That's all there is to it.'

Towler suddenly grabbed Wilshaw and flung him against the wall. A picture crashed down and Jane Wilshaw screamed from the drawing-room and Cathy shouted, 'Sit down or I'll let this thing off.'

Towler shoved the Browning hard under Wilshaw's chin to force his head back. 'Stop stalling, Tony, or it all ends here. Now tell me, you bastard. What happened?'

Wilshaw struggled and Towler back-handed him with the gun and Wilshaw slipped slowly to the ground in a sitting position, one side of his face grazed and bleeding. Towler leaned over him and placed the gun against his forehead. 'Just what the hell have I got to lose?' he ground out. He pulled back the hammer and Wilshaw yelled out:

'O.K., O.K. It was a tidying up job, that's all. One corpse for removal. I don't know who the . . .'

He was interrupted by a frantic ringing of the front-door bell and a crashing of glass from the room adjoining the hall.

Towler swung a fist at Wilshaw as he sat propped against the wall and dashed into the drawing-room to find Cathy standing over Jane Wilshaw with her gun shaking in her hand. 'Leave her and come with me,' bawled Towler, reaching out to take her hand.

Cathy grabbed her hat and ran into the hall where Wilshaw lay slumped, blood trickling on to his shirt collar. Towler quickly locked the door before joining her.

'You've killed him,' cried Cathy in horror, unable to take her gaze from Wilshaw. Someone was still leaning on the door bell but worse than that others were breaking in the front windows and Towler picked up a similar sound from the back. He pressed Cathy against the wall and she stood there, gun hand hanging down, and too scared to say anything more. She looked at Towler with frightened eyes and knew they were trapped.

15

'Rashid Khayar,' said Prescott softly. He had met Soames in the funereal atmosphere of his club and they were having an indifferent lunch in a secluded corner.

Soames knew why Prescott was standing him lunch. The Towler affair was taking up so much time that other, important work was being neglected. And there was too much 'coming and going' between the two men. It must have been noticed – which did not matter too much unless Sir Malcolm Read picked up the vibrations.

'Doesn't mean a thing,' said Soames who was stinging Prescott for a fillet steak. 'I'll do a check. Is he anything to do with the other business?'

'Rashid Khayar is Abdul.'

'Oh, dear.' Soames lowered his knife and fork. 'Where did you find this out?'

'Not by looking. It seems the department has lost the art of searching.' Prescott finished chewing. 'I was approached by another party. There is the possibility that the original game might start all over again but with different players.'

'This party wants him?'

'As did the others. This is more difficult because Middle East relations could be severely affected. This cock-up grows bigger by the day.' Prescott continued to eat but Soames was now right off his food.

Soames did not know what to say, so he said nothing and toyed with his steak thinking it would choke him if he tried to chew it.

It was Prescott who re-opened the exchange. He gazed very pointedly at Soames, winced as he moved his leg, and said, 'I gather you let Rashid Khayar go. A reasonable thing to do bearing in mind you did not know him by that name and we had nothing on him.'

At times like these Soames felt an odd sympathy with Towler, feeling a little of the same persecution. 'Is that what I did?'

'Your memory is going, Soames. Have you considered early retirement?'

'It would certainly give me time to write my memoirs.'

Prescott sipped his wine, his eyes chilling over the rim of the glass. 'Don't try a Peter Wright on me, old boy. This stuff is too contemporary. You're too old for a long spell in prison.'

'I'm getting rather tired of taking the can back for something of which I'm largely in the dark. I wouldn't mind so much if I knew what the bloody hell was going on. Just who are we protecting at my expense?'

'You're out of order, Soames. And being rather childish. You know the name of the game better than most. And it was you who started this off. Just remember that. We now have a name. Someone must know something about him. Try Joe Lingfield and some of his pals. Or that dreadful DIA fellow Matt Steiner; he has his fingers in some strange pies. Meanwhile, as before, I have to supply some answers to somebody who almost certainly will not believe me. I just pray that he does.'

Kate Parker used a stick. She had arranged a taxi from the apartment and the hall porter helped her down the steps to the cab. She was taken to a coffee shop off Bond Street where Sandra Dawson, wife of the Home Secretary, was already seated at a table. It was a favourite place for Sandra to meet her friends but the older woman was unmistakably frosty as she bade Kate sit down. 'Why the stick?'

'I've hurt my foot,' said Kate as she laid the stick beside her chair. 'Nothing serious.'

'Espresso, I seem to remember.' Sandra looked round for the waiter.

'You have a good memory,' Kate said sweetly. The two women had not met for over a year and then it had been by accident.

When the coffee arrived Sandra said, 'What is it you want

to speak to me about? It must be important for you to ring me like that.'

Kate was already thinking that she had made a bad mistake. But she had become desperate with nobody to turn to. Her model friend, in whose apartment she was living, was staying abroad for another week, happy that someone she knew was looking after the place, and Kate had become increasingly lonely.

She dropped a sweetener in her coffee. 'It's about James.' She was faltering already.

'You do surprise me.' Eyebrows lifted disdainfully. 'As if it could be anything else.'

'Could you please stop sniping at me? It's not my damned fault how things turned out. I'm worried about him.'

Sandra lost a little of her tension. She did not feel compassion, she was beyond that, but she saw how vulnerable Kate appeared to be. Kate was young and strong and had set up a business, probably with the help of James's money, but she had worked hard at it. Now she was unsure of herself and that was something new to her. 'What's he done this time that I don't know about?' Resentment was still strong.

'I was hoping you might know. Haven't you noticed anything? Any change in him?'

Sandra looked into her cup as if the answer lay there. 'He's been more secretive and more preoccupied. But I've seen that happen before. It's the nature of the job. I'm surprised that you ask; you're the one he turns to. Is he keeping something from you? He's been doing that to me for years.'

'I'm sorry. I shouldn't have come. I thought you might have noticed something, some change. Or he might have said something to you.'

'No, Kate, I have not.' And then, with a quizzical look, 'You really are worried about this, aren't you?'

'I think something is happening that he doesn't know about.'

'You mean behind his back? What's new? Politicians are doing that all the time.'

'Has he ever mentioned a man called Towler?'

'Not that I recall. Should I be concerned about this? Is there anything I can raise with him? Provided he's willing to say something he hasn't already told you.' Sandra Dawson was pointedly pulling on her gloves. 'Why don't you have a word with his secretary, the great Miss Megson. Between the pair of you, you probably know far more about my husband than anyone, including myself.'

It was not only a mistake to meet but a ghastly experience. And it would get back to James in a vindictive way. Yet Kate felt that she had to strike out in some way. She had sent Towler away, another mistake, but she dearly wanted to find him now and did not know how to start.

Towler and Cathy crouched behind the door. At any moment the lock would break. From the front room it sounded as if the window had been forced and someone was still trying to break in at the rear.

'Up the stairs, quick.' Towler pushed Cathy before him and she swore all the way. Spurred by the sound of the front door splintering they ran along the landing towards the front rooms.

Towler went straight to the windows and opened one to look down on to a white-coated garden. There was nothing to be seen of the stake-out; they were probably all trying to break into the house. There was a twenty-foot drop below them but he saw it as the only way out. The drop meant little to him; he had done more on training but he had to convince Cathy.

'Quick,' he said. 'Drop into the snow. Piece of cake. Here, give me the gun.'

Cathy looked down, wilting at the blast of freezing air cutting into the room. 'I'm not jumping down there. I'd break my neck.'

'For chrissake, would you rather have a bullet in the head? Climb out. I'll hold you until you jump.' He had pushed her gun into his waistband but still kept hold of his own.

'I can't do it, Sam.' She was trying to hold her hat in place.

'They'll be up here in seconds. Now get on that sill.' He tore her hat from her head and stuffed it into the top of her coat.

Still she hesitated in spite of the shouts below.

'O.K.,' he snapped. 'Take your chances. I'm not waiting to get a bullet up my arse.' He climbed on to the sill with both legs over and she panicked and grabbed at him. He caught her by both arms and dragged her on to the sill, flicking her legs over until she was hanging feet first while he held her arms. She looked up pleadingly and opened her mouth just as he whispered fiercely, 'For God's sake, don't scream. They're on their way up. It's snow down there.' He released her arms and before she had time to scream she hit the ground. He jumped off immediately.

He hit the ground and rolled. The snow was hard-packed but there was no time for niceties. Cathy was struggling in the snow and he grabbed her under the armpits uncaring of anything she might have broken; this was life or death. He somehow bundled her into the passenger seat of Wilshaw's Porsche, and threw himself across the bonnet to land near the driver's door. He opened up, fumbled for the key just as heads poked out of the window above them.

He could not see what was happening but neither could the men above him. Even so, Towler knew he had only seconds. The shapeless lump beside him was alive because he could hear Cathy groaning. He switched on; the engine should be warm enough to fire at once and it did. He did not hear the shots but felt the impact on the body work and accelerated away round the curve of the drive in a wide skid that sent powdered snow and gravel flying over the hedgerow. As he headed towards the open gates another car came straight towards them. Towler opened up and held his course. Cathy screamed, a terrified, lingering sound in the confines of the car. The on-coming car, headlights blazing, swerved at the last moment and crashed through the shrubs. The Porsche caught the tail end of it, ripped off its fender, and spun it round towards a tree.

Towler did not hear the crash but he could not miss Cathy bawling out repeatedly, 'You mad bastard. You mad, mad bastard.' She was striking him unremittingly on the shoulder but he held firm, skidded round the gates and on to the open road. 'Who dares wins,' he shouted to her but it was lost in her shrieking fear.

He was driving too fast. The tail end of the Porsche was swinging from side to side in a sickening motion that, for a while, quietened Cathy's screams as she tried to adjust to a new danger. Towler glanced at the fuel gauge and then at the central mirror; they must have more than one car and he expected to see headlights behind them at any moment. He was forced to slow for fear of going off the road.

It was the signal for Cathy to start on him again and she pounded his shoulder and head while he tried to contend with the road conditions. 'Guns,' she screamed, 'you never told me there'd be guns. You limey bastard. You wait until I tell Lew.'

The situation was too crucial for an answer, his concentration on keeping the car on the road. He felt a trickle of blood down his face where she had caught him with her nails. But she railed at him so much that finally he was forced to shout back. 'Keep quiet, you stupid bitch, or you'll have us off the road.' Glancing in his mirror he saw the four bouncing orbs behind them and he added more quietly, 'Calm down, Cathy, they're here. We're far from out of this.'

She looked back and saw the headlights and sat back panting heavily. 'You should have warned me.'

'I did. I gave you the chance to go home.'

'About the guns. You should have told me.'

He noticed the change in her tone. She was scared of course, but her invective was a result of deep anger. He had held out on her, and that suggested she might have opted out. Neither would ever know the answer.

'And another thing,' said Cathy, 'you've ruined my goddam tights and my shoes. You can buy me some more.'

'Sure,' said Towler. 'It will be with Lew's money.'

She did not reply to that but he thought she was quietly laughing. Cathy was breathing more steadily now but Towler was battling with the conditions.

'Give me back the gun.'

Towler did not know whether to laugh or cry. She was unpredictable. 'Why?'

'So that I can lean out and shoot at the bastards. Isn't that how you do it? They've made a bloody big hole on my side; I can feel the draught.'

The car suddenly swerved and they almost went off the road as they struck an ice patch. Towler did all the right things instinctively, but it was touch and go before he was able to pull out of the skid. 'It's like driving in a bloody tunnel on these country roads. The lights are bouncing back at us.' He had spoken calmly but was shaken by the near-miss.

They lapsed into silence after that. The rear was still slewing and he could understand how Cathy might be feeling. They reached the Amersham road and he turned left and reduced speed. Now they were in light traffic and there was always a chance of a police patrol car passing by. He was certain, though, that the stolen Porsche would not be reported as missing.

The car behind had closed up quite a lot and was now on dimmed lights. Towler knew he could not open the gap until they were on the approaches to the motorway.

Cathy, occasionally looking over her shoulder, said, 'I'm sorry, Sam. You probably saved our lives.' She saw his faint smile in the dim lights of the dashboard.

'I bloody nearly lost them, too. Sorry about the gun. Of course I should have told you. You're a great trouper, Cathy. I thought you would be. Lew would be proud of you.'

'What is it with you?' She sounded exasperated. 'Do I have to tote a gun to satisfy you? It's not what I do best.'

Towler glanced once more into the rear-view mirror. The headlights were still there. But Cathy was back to normal. He felt better about everything and that he could cope with the present problems. He would get them back to Lew's place and would shake off the opposition once they reached the London outskirts. It was not a complacent thought, but at this stage he considered Soames' men had probably missed their opportunity. This time. The next time he hoped Cathy would not be with him for they could not miss forever and he could feel the ropes tightening round him as the car behind sat relentlessly on their tail.

Soames was more disturbed than ever when he left Joe Lingfield. They met at the American's usual haunt near the United States Embassy and Soames asked outright the interest Lingfield might have in the Hereford shootings. When the answer came up nil and Lingfield revealed that he had been doing a favour for Matt Steiner, Soames saw increasing complication to an already complicated matter.

Nobody liked Steiner for one reason or another. Some of his colleagues maintained that he never looked into, nor could be seen in, mirrors. Some of the dislike arose from professional jealousy; Steiner had achieved some remarkable results but at what cost in human suffering was a subject nobody liked to raise. It was on one of his many successes that that particular issue had come under close scrutiny from his superiors in Washington. His results were accepted gladly but his methods, on that occasion, had to be disciplined. He had been posted to London as a sideways shift to get him out of the sight of those he annoyed most. Steiner accepted the hypocrisy of it, crossed the Atlantic, and carried on as usual.

Soames knew a fair amount about Steiner. He knew for example that he held Soames himself in considerable contempt, a fact which did not worry Soames unduly as he saw Steiner as a throwback to the dark ages, and in return held a question mark over those who were willing to employ him on his terms. What did annoy Soames was Steiner's sometimes open contempt of the Security Service. It made working on a friendly basis with the Company more difficult.

That Lingfield had been so open about Steiner's interest came as no surprise to Soames. The two men had worked together often enough and there had to be some show of co-operation however superficial. And Lingfield did not like Steiner either. It was difficult to find anyone who did.

Soames decided to go through official channels in order to make an appointment with Steiner appear more like a summons than an invitation. It was, after all, his territory.

The two men met in Soames' office and shook hands like old friends with a conviction that would have satisfied most auditioning actors. There was no point in beating around the bush with someone like Steiner so Soames addressed himself to the square-cut hulk on the other side of his desk and asked, 'What's your interest in the Hereford business, Matt?'

'Is that what you're offering me weak tea for? You're wasting my time. I haven't got an interest.'

'Joe Lingfield thinks you have.'

Steiner had not opened his topcoat but had removed his hat to place it on Soames' desk simply to annoy him. 'Has Joe crossed over? I could have sworn he was working for us.'

'Cut it out. There was nothing sinister about it. Exchange of ideas, nothing more. Joe was simply trying to tap me on your behalf. You should have come to me direct.'

'Would it have made a difference?'

'I don't know. It depends what you're looking for. What *are* you looking for, Matt?'

'It was no more than a routine interest. Strange business, though. Ever find out what was behind it?'

'There's not enough in it to interest us. Really a job for the anti-terrorist squad, D11, but I believe SB are handling it.'

'Two dead Arabs just the same. There must have been a time when you were interested.'

Soames accepted the opportunity Steiner had just presented. 'The only whisper I picked up which held my attention for more than five minutes was the suggestion from the SB that an ex-SAS man had been involved. Gone rotten. But what exactly his part was in it is difficult to define.'

'You mean he killed the Arabs?'

'I don't know. He might have set them up.'

'Who for? From what I read, before a D-notice was slammed down on this apparently unimportant caper, a Uzi SMG was found on the scene.'

'A magazine from one, actually. I thought you weren't interested?'

Steiner sat back with a wide grin. 'You're such a good story-teller, you intrigued me, Soames.' It was strange, reflected Steiner, that nobody seemed to know Soames' first name. Perhaps he did not have one or it was too horrific to reveal. He was known to everyone as Soames. 'Anyway, you found it important enough to invite me here.'

'I don't like foreigners, even friendly ones, asking questions about incidents that happen on our patch. It's bugger all to do with you.' The right rebuke, thought Soames, to a man like Steiner. He knew it would make no difference if Steiner was really interested, and it was a way of finding out.

'Whatever gave you the impression I'm a friendly foreigner? I'm here to do a job. If you don't like what I'm doing tell Washington I'm unacceptable here. It would suit me. Some of the people I have to deal with in London are a pain in the ass.'

Soames could not help a fleeting smile. Steiner was a fox. 'Well, I've made my point. There's nothing more to say.'

As if he had not heard, or the quick exchange of insults was merely a friendly game, Steiner said, 'Do you think Mossad was behind it?'

'Are you still on about the Hereford business?' It *was* a game, thought Soames, but a deadly serious one; at the moment the points were even. 'We thought it might have been but we had a visit from Sigi Grief who is most anxious to deny any connection. He was convincing but I still don't rule them out. I passed on his claim to Special Branch.'

'So you think this SAS guy was working for Mossad?'

'I have no idea. Anything's possible. The two Arabs killed were too minor for us to worry about. There was nothing to connect them with terrorism but there was obviously something going on. Perhaps one faction was taking care of another.'

'Not if an SAS man was involved. Now that's really weird.'

Soames was satisfied that he had directed Steiner's chain of thought the way he wanted. In a more conciliatory tone he said, 'If it really interests you, and I can only imagine that your interest is in what Mossad might be up to and not some renegade SAS man, I can let you know of any development, provided it doesn't turn out to be more serious than it looks.'

'Don't worry about it.' Steiner waved a hand in dismissal of the offer. 'One thing intrigues me, though; who is this sergeant?'

'Did I say sergeant?' So Steiner already knew about Towler. 'You know I can't tell you that. A pity you let your tea get cold.'

Steiner glanced at the cup. 'It saves me drinking it. Have you heard of an assassination squad arriving in this country?'

Soames' feeling of satisfaction left him. Was this the real game? 'Rumours. We've no hard information. Have you?'

Steiner screwed his face with the pain of recollection. 'It would seem to be no more than you have. Vague rumours.'

'If they exist who do they intend to assassinate, do you think?'

'I shouldn't think they'd be fussy. Charles, Diana, the Queen. Our President is due over in three weeks' time. Anyone big enough to shock the world and draw attention to their nit-picking ideals.'

'We're keeping our eye on the possibility. As we always do.'

Steiner got up and rammed his hat on his head. 'We should meet more often.' It was the most sarcastic comment made so far and Soames made no attempt to top it. He was satisfied with the seeds he had planted until Steiner said, 'Ever heard of a guy called Rashid Khayar?'

With the greatest effort, Soames somehow managed to keep fiddling with his pen. 'Not off-hand. Why?'

'I'm looking for him. If you hear anything, will you let me know?'

They left the Porsche in the Bayswater Road with the keys in the ignition. Cathy's boots were scratched but the heels were still intact and her laddered tights were merely a blow to her ego. She linked her arm through Towler's, but this time only for support. Towler reckoned that he had shaken off their tail but Cathy was suffering delayed shock and was shivering. Towler was fairly satisfied with the way they had come through and his nerves were the steadiest they had been for a long time.

They walked along the Bayswater Road and found a cab before they reached Marble Arch. They sank on to the back seat and relaxed for the first time in hours. Neither said much but as they neared home, Cathy ventured, 'I couldn't go through it again, Sam. I'm not cut out for it.'

'You were terrific.' He turned to face her. 'Do you think you can play it down to Lew? If he gets the full story, he'll kick me out.'

'We don't want that, do we?' she said with a touch of her old bravado. 'Sam, I did this for you so that Lew gets a story. Don't hold out on him.'

'I know that, Cathy. If I don't come through this, Lew can print what he likes. But if I do get to the bottom of it he'll have a cracking exclusive.'

'Did you get what you wanted down there? Or did we risk our necks for nothing?'

'I got some of it. The caper wasn't wasted.'

They left the cab a couple of blocks from the apartments as a matter of precaution. There were few pedestrians and even fewer as they rounded the corner. Towler picked up the sound of a kerb-crawling car before Cathy and was quick to see the shadows coming from the walls.

'Run,' he whispered urgently to her. 'Get back to the pad.'

She let go of him just as they were surrounded by about half a dozen men. He jumped for the wall to get his back against it as Cathy fled, but someone was already there and brought a cosh down hard on his back. As he fell he saw Cathy flung to the ground and kicked aside as she lay there.

Towler fought for his life. He was expert and tough but could not combat the number of men against him. They were all Arabs and they worked quite silently as they bludgeoned him to his knees while he tried to protect his head. The last he recalled was Cathy lying prone, legs curled up to her body, her hat in the gutter. A car door slammed nearby, then someone found the right spot to hammer his head and he was out.

It was over in no more than three minutes. Towler was bundled into a car which drove off with two of the men who had assaulted him, and the others went back to the shadows. The only person left in sight was Cathy, still lying huddled on the edge of the pavement.

After a while a young couple saw her and hurried forward to help. She was alive and there was a gash across her forehead.

'We'd better get the police,' said the man. 'Where's the nearest phone?'

'No cops,' murmured Cathy in great pain. 'Get me to my feet.'

'She's American,' exclaimed the girl.

With Cathy helping as much as she could they managed to prop her up against the wall and held her there while she tried to recover.

'What happened?' asked the man.

Cathy tried to smile at the obvious question. 'I was mugged.' She groaned as she straightened her back. 'My head's cold, where's my hat?'

The girl found it in the gutter and placed it on Cathy's head. 'Look, we really should call an ambulance or the police or somebody.'

'I'm O.K. Just get me to my door. It's the second along.'

As they helped her cover the short distance she mumbled, 'Twenty years in New York and I have to get mugged in London. Jesus, ain't life a gas?'

They reached the door and Cathy leaned against it. She

gazed at the hazy shapes in front of her and said, 'You kids have been great. Give me your address.'

'It's O.K. It's nothing. Anyone would have done the same.'

'Anyone else would have pissed off and left me there. Thanks, kids. Have a nice day.'

But half-way up the stairs she was violently sick and had to stop for a while. Her ribs ached where she had been kicked and her nerves were shattered. She managed to reach the apartment door and rang the bell, praying that Lew was in because she did not think she could find the key in a handbag still miraculously over her arm.

The door opened and she fell into Lew's arms and said, 'They've got Sam,' before she fainted.

He dragged her inside and lowered her on the settee, keeping her head well down. He managed to get the heavy fur coat off her, then her boots and tattered tights. He cleaned and dressed her forehead, relieved to find the cut was superficial. She opened her eyes and said, 'Just run the shower, Honey, I'm not as damaged as I look.'

'The hell you're not. I'll call the doctor.'

'Wait until you've heard what I have to say first. Get me a slug of brandy.'

When she had showered and was into her second brandy, she sat down carefully, clad in a dressing-gown with a towel wrapped round her head and a new dressing over the cut. Lew stood over her, worried and scared and waited for her story.

Cathy gave him a clipped account of what had happened in Buckinghamshire, but a fuller account of the attack outside their own home.

'They must have got word to accomplices in London. They let you get away then another team waited for you.'

'No. They weren't the same people. It was another crowd.'

'Jesus, just how many people are after him? I'll kill him when I see him. He shouldn't have dragged you into it.'

Cathy held out her glass for another drink. 'You're forgetting he asked you to ask me. I've no beefs. He didn't expect the second attack. He thought he was home and dry. As for killing him, Honey, I guess you'll have to join the queue. Maybe it's already been done.'

Quinn knelt down in front of Cathy and took her hands. 'I

hope not. But right now I've got to think of you. I still think you need a doctor but if you say no, I'll go along with it. What about the police?'

'I think Sam believes they can be manipulated. There's a higher power he's afraid of. I don't know the status of the person he saw but I can put two and two together. There seems to be some conspiracy against him. There's no doubt they're out to kill him. Why? I don't believe he's the kind of guy to deserve it.'

'Neither do I. I wouldn't have had him stay here if I thought that.' He saw her questioning look and added, 'O.K., I sensed a story. But he wouldn't be here if I didn't trust him. And that included with you.'

'Whoops!' She leaned forward and kissed him lightly on the lips. 'You were right about that, Lew.'

He rose, satisfied that Cathy was feeling better. 'Arabs, you say?'

'It's dark out there, but that's what they seemed like. Young and agile and badly dressed. I couldn't identify any of them again. I didn't see them long enough and they all look the same.'

'If they didn't wear hoods it means they don't care whether Sam can identify them or not. He's not coming back, Honey.'

Cathy covered her face and shuddered. Lew sat down beside her and put his arms round her. 'It's no use kidding ourselves. But who knew he was living here?' He believed he could guess but that only made everything much worse.

16

Kate Parker was increasingly feeling the frustration of being cut off from real information. Having bitterly regretted sending Towler away in order to protect Dawson, she belatedly realised there was nothing she could do to set the matter right. Even given the same circumstances she supposed she would do the same thing again but this time make sure she had a way of contacting Towler. But Towler was trusting no-one, not even her after her refusal to implicate Dawson.

There was something increasingly sinister about the whole affair; and no doubt that Towler was a wanted man. But for what? She rang Dawson at the Home Office, something she did very rarely, and refused to leave a message when told he was unavailable. She did not know which way to turn and her concern for Towler grew until she had to face the fact that it was not just the uncertainty about him but an increasing yearning. She *needed* him and everybody was trying to make sure that she made no contact, or if she did she was expected to pass on his whereabouts which was something she could not do.

She wished she had someone to talk to, but there was nobody. Her partner, after their first early meeting when she had returned from Hereford, was too busy running the health club on her own, and, anyway, unknown to Kate, had been advised to make no contact for a while, at least.

She was on the verge of going out, anywhere to get away from four walls, when the bell rang. It was Dawson. She gave him a quick kiss on the cheek and told him she had tried to contact him at the Home Office.

Dawson did not reply at once. He took off his gloves and coat and placed them carefully over the arm of a chair and sat down. He shook his head at her offer of a drink. He looked weary, unsure of himself, an image the public never saw.

'Kate,' he said without preamble, 'you've been a naughty girl. What on earth made you see Sandra?'

'She told you?'

'Of course she told me.' He was exasperated, running his hands over his lank hair. 'What on earth made you do it? You know how she resents you.'

'I was worried about you. I wondered if she was, too. If she had noticed changes.'

'Changes? Kate, what on earth are you on about?'

'Like now. You look exhausted.'

'It's the nature of the job. I'm always exhausted. You wouldn't have seen Sandra for something like that. You like her no more than she likes you. What was the real reason?'

Kate saw she could not win. 'All right,' she burst out. 'I've had it up to here with secrecy. Yes, and lies too. Something's going on I don't much care for and I just wonder if you know everything you should. Why should Nigel Prescott take such pains to come and see me? I'm hardly in his league.'

'Prescott? Came here?' Dawson did not hide his concern. 'What about?'

'The usual thing. To warn me off Sam Towler. To trot out innuendos about Sam that I'm convinced are rubbish. To ask me to betray Sam if he gets in touch with me. It all sounds so trivial until you realise that they are trying to kill Sam and are so worried about him that a man in Prescott's position comes to see someone like me. What the hell is he hiding? And probably hiding from you?'

Dawson rose uncertainly. He crossed to Kate and cupped her face in his hand. 'Oh, Kate. Don't carry a flag for Towler. He's not worthy of you. Prescott should have told me he was coming here but perhaps he found it embarrassing to do. He wants to protect you as I do. Get Towler out of your mind. You're still carrying an image of a knight on a white charger. Believe me he's not one.'

'And who told you he's not? Prescott?'

Dawson took his hand away. 'You're stepping into something you really don't understand, my darling. I can't discuss affairs of state with you, and particularly security matters.

Prescott is a loyalist to his finger tips. You don't have to worry about him. He's extremely experienced; not a man to jump to hasty conclusions.'

'How many would he sacrifice to protect his loyalty?'

Dawson was startled, then he smiled. 'Dear, oh dear. Oh, Kate. You think he's sacrificing Towler?'

'Yes.'

'For what reason?'

Kate faltered. 'I don't know. But something really stinks and I think you should see Prescott and have it out with him. There's something he's not telling you.'

There was an acute silence and then Dawson crossed the room to pick up his coat and gloves. He appeared hurt and a little bewildered.

Kate suddenly felt desperately sorry for him. 'I'm out of order, aren't I?'

He nodded almost imperceptibly. 'I suppose it's unfair of me to expect you to understand. But men like Prescott have immense resources; they don't make blind decisions.'

'Isn't it true, though,' she said very carefully, 'that, because of the nature of the job they sometimes have to make some very dirty decisions in the name of expediency?'

Dawson shrugged. 'You're showing your naïveté, Kate. The first consideration is always the safety of the State. Injustice comes from all directions, even to sinners.'

'What is Sam Towler's sin, James? I bet you're not even sure. And I bet Prescott isn't either; unless he's made one up.'

Dawson put on his coat. 'Why would he do that? But for him you wouldn't be here now. And that is much more than I should tell you.'

'And Sam wouldn't be on the run. I still say there is something about this business that hasn't been right from the beginning. I mean, who was the poor Arab I was being exchanged for? What had he done wrong?'

'I can't tell you that. And you know I can't. He was important enough for them to kidnap you in order to get him back. I wouldn't waste too much sympathy on him. Someone wanted him dead and that can only mean that he had been up to some pretty nasty business.' He looked at the mantelpiece clock. 'I must be off. Please don't get in touch with Sandra again. It causes too many problems all round.'

As he left the apartment, Dawson reflected that every time he came here he left in a sombre, uncertain mood and it used not to be like that at all. Kate had not spoken like a young woman besotted, but one with a personal conviction. There was nothing Prescott could be hiding from him. What could there be on this particular issue? It was true that security chiefs did all sorts of things unknown to their Ministers. Half the time the Minister would prefer not to know. Yet Dawson was aware of an increasing unease that was not solely due to Kate's concern. There did seem to be parts missing, irregularities that made little sense.

As he sat in the back of his official car, while the chauffeur turned up the heating and headed back towards the House of Commons, Dawson reflected on some of the earlier incidents, such as the delay over the exchange which Prescott had never explained, and the manner in which he avoided Dawson's repeated telephone calls. He sat wondering how to tackle the problem. And he was furious that Prescott had taken it on himself to visit Kate without informing him. It was one area which worried him above all others for it seemed to support at least part of what Kate believed.

It felt like a dentist's chair. His feet were raised clear of the ground and there was a head support. His body was leaning back at an angle and where he would have expected an arc-lamp to be there was a small ceiling rose, a wire with an empty light socket hanging from its centre at a slight angle. His head felt as if there was a tight band round it and when he tried to turn it he realised there actually was one and, but for the limited movement of his eyes, he could see neither right nor left.

Sensation returned in instalments, working from his head down to his feet. His wrists were bound to the padded chair arms, his ankles too were tied to something to prevent his moving legs. But above all it was the position of his body he found so compromising. The angle was all wrong. Nothing was real.

It was impossible to judge the size of the room he was in. The ceiling was fairly low and the cracked plaster was stained as if a heavy smoker had spent years down here. Down here? Why had he thought that? A basement? He had the general feeling that the room was small, although he was so positioned that he could not see any of the walls.

He had opened his eyes very slowly to see if anyone was standing over him to be on hand when he awoke. Where his head met the curved leather rest, it felt as though it had been cracked open, it was so painful. There was also pain behind his eyes and he had a massive headache. After the silent initial struggle against his bonds he accepted he had been trussed by an expert and spent the next few minutes in trying to detect whether there was anyone else in the room with him.

There was no sound anywhere. He searched the ceiling as far as he could and detected no television scanners. Apart from the chair the place had an empty feel about it and the air was far from fresh. By now he was convinced that he was strapped to an old dentist's chair. Growing awareness produced a nasty feeling in the pit of his stomach to convince him that he was in a crude, makeshift, torture chamber.

Towler had been trained to resist conditioning and many forms of psychological torture, but this was the first time it had become a reality and the difference was chilling. He could not move, vision was extremely limited and of no practical use, and the position of his body put him at a great psychological disadvantage. He forced his mind away from himself and reflected on Cathy. He did not know whether she was alive or dead and he could not forgive himself for that. He had used her, albeit she was willing, but he knew the name of the game and had not passed on as much as he should have done.

He let his mind wander in any direction it would take away from his present discomfort. He got to thinking about Kate. In the situation he was now in he could let his mind roam freely without responsibility. He had no need to hold back because he had no illusions about what was to happen to him here.

Isolated as he was, he could still compare the feeling he had had for the girl in Ireland with the attachment he found he had developed for Kate. It was different. Ireland now seemed to be decades ago although it was impossible to forget, and his feeling for the girl there had been spawned three years ago; he had not seen her for eighteen months. She was still there, though; still inside him. Perhaps it was the hopelessness from the beginning that had made it worse. Had he gone with her it might have turned out differently. Frustration had kindled his already strong feelings for her. Loneliness, too, had played its part. She had been a dream which would always be out of reach; perhaps that is what she always was, and would always be. It was now easier to face.

Kate, on the other hand, was growing more slowly on him. It had started out with concern for her, then puzzlement and worry, and the last time they had met he had been deeply hurt by her attitude and had immediately switched off, afraid of running into the same problems he seemed to have with women whenever he appeared to get close.

It was safe to think like this for he would never see either again. He could romance as much as he liked without fear of it ever hurting him. He could still feel the pain of Kate lying to him yet, now he could do nothing about it, he realised that it was not so easy to switch her off as he had thought. She was still there too, slowly nudging the other girl aside and creating a more realistic figure in his mind.

'Hi! Trying to dream up a way out?'

Towler jerked, annoyed with himself. He had not heard a door open and wondered whether the man had been there all the time. American. He could not see him until he moved to the side of the chair and then could only get a blurred figure on his peripheral vision.

'Hello, mate. Do you think you could push this chair upright? And the straps are a bit too tight.'

'You won't be so jaunty by the time I've finished with you.'

'I don't suppose I will. Shits like you can only operate when someone else does the dirty work.' Towler was straining to get a better view. He decided to take a chance. 'You're Steiner, aren't you? DIA? I hope your crowd find out about you one day, Steiner.'

Steiner kept tantalisingly out of view. There was a vicious edge to his voice as he said, 'Whatever chance you stood before, you stand none after that. You're Towler, aren't you?'

'You mean you have me trussed like a turkey and you're not

sure who you've got? You're a sloppy operator, Steiner.'

'I can always squeeze it out of that nympho Cathy Quinn or her dumb husband. It's up to you.'

Towler was silent. Had they brought Cathy here, too? At least she was alive then. Steiner would get the name one way or the other, so save the Quinns some aggro; anyway, he was already convinced and was merely making sure. 'Towler. Sergeant. 7014508.'

'You're not going to make sergeant-major, Towler, but I can make it painless for you. It's up to you.'

'Why should I want to make it easy for you? You're crap, Steiner.'

Towler did not feel the blow at first. He was aware of a tremendous jarring to one side of his face but the actual pain came later. He thought that whatever Steiner had smashed into his face had also smashed his cheek bone. It was made worse because he could not ride the blow by turning his head. He passed out momentarily and took his time coming round. If he did not know it before he now knew that he was dealing with a psycho.

'I thought you guys were supposed to be tough. That was just a friendly greeting and you passed out like one of your own rejections. Now let's get down to it. You were on that Hereford caper. Who were you escorting?'

Towler could hardly move his jaw. The pain had started and his face felt shattered. He kept his eyes closed. Because he was unable to move his head he still faced the ceiling and could feel Steiner's eyes riveting through him. He gave no sign that he was conscious.

Steiner was not impressed. Other people's pain did not touch him. 'How would you like your fingers removed one by one?'

Towler now knew who had taken off Kate Parker's toe with bolt-cutters and he fought back his anger so that he did not give himself away. Steiner had seen it all, and done it all, before.

Steiner picked up a bucket of ice-cold water and poured it over Towler's head. Unprepared, Towler gasped painfully for breath.

'That's better,' said Steiner. He repeated the question while Towler was still gasping.

'A young Arab.' Towler was drenched through from head to waist and the water was freezing cold.

'Did this guy have a name?'

The youngster was dead, what harm could there be in giving it? 'Yasser Azmin,' he spluttered.

It was clearly not the answer Steiner expected. After a while he asked, 'Describe him.'

Towler did his best, barely able to move his jaw and the wet was seeping further down his body.

'Was he one of the two Arabs killed?'

'Yes.'

'Have you ever heard of a guy called Rashid Khayar?'

'No.'

'That was too quick. Think again before I start on your fingers.'

'I can delay as much as you like but the name doesn't mean anything to me. It's difficult to remember names like that.'

'Don't bullshit me; you remembered Azmin's.'

'I had reason to. And we're talking of only a few days ago.'

'So am I. Think.'

Towler thought hard. A few days ago? Rashid Khayar? He stirred uneasily. Something stank, but it had all along. 'It's no use. I really don't know the name.' He borrowed one of Steiner's questions. 'Describe him.'

Steiner came in to view; just his head, and Towler had to strain his eyes to see him. Their gazes met and Towler could not miss the cold-bloodedness of the American.

Steiner ignored the request and went on. 'What was the name of the guy you picked up who was staying at the Hotel Florida in Paddington?'

'I didn't pick anyone up.'

Towler felt his hand being grasped and, although he could not see what was happening, he knew that the cold metal touch around his little finger was caused by bolt-cutters. Steiner seemed to be obsessed by small toes and little fingers.

'I *know* you did, a whole team from Five. Who was it you picked up, Towler?'

'If you're going to cut off my fingers with those bloody things you're going to have a bloody long wait for answers. I don't know who it was. Nobody did. We called him Abdul.

184

We couldn't get a word out of him.' The pressure on his finger eased while Steiner thought it over.

'What happened to him?'

'I think he was released.'

'Come again?'

'After a couple of nights in pokey we didn't keep him any more.'

'You let him go?'

Towler realised Steiner was at a dangerous point; his voice had changed and was full of seething anger and disbelief.

'Look,' said Towler. 'I'm the errand boy. I was on trial, that's all. I had been seconded and it was not a popular move. I was not privy to decision-making.'

Some steam left Steiner's voice as he instructed, 'Tell me all you know about Abdul'.

'He was picked up because I thought I recognised him from Middle East days. He was just a vaguely familiar face. But he kept moving hotels and that made him suspect. We tucked him away. A couple of days later he had gone and I assumed that because nobody got a bloody thing from him there was nothing to hold him on, and he was let go. Is he Rashid Khayar?'

'Who would know what happened to him?'

'Your contacts with Five will be better than mine. They did not exactly keep me in their confidence.'

'Don't be too clever, Towler. Why are you on the run?'

Towler took a deep breath. His face felt as if a red-hot iron was being held against it and now he was shivering from damp. 'I was hoping you could tell me. If I knew the answers I wouldn't be on the run.'

'I heard you are working for Mossad, that Hereford was a setup led by you.'

'Mossad? Whatever answer I give to that, you won't believe, anyway. But it was a setup all right. And I was the one set up. I'm looking for answers.'

'You don't have to look anymore.' Steiner spoke quietly with an unfeeling finality. 'You've been helpful but I'm left with the feeling that you've got more from me than I have from you.'

'I can only answer your questions.'

'Of course you can. And to remind you that during the next

185

session we have I want straight answers. Here's a taste of what you can expect if I don't get them.'

The sharp, terrible pain Towler then felt overrode the one in his face. He heard himself gasp and the sweat ran down him. But he did not lose consciousness, and clearly heard Steiner's grating laughter and the jibe that followed:

'What's wrong, tough guy? I've only taken it off at the first joint. When the water freezes on you you won't feel a thing.'

A door closed behind him and Towler wished that Steiner had finished him off then, instead of leaving him like this.

17

Lew Quinn had to get clearance to see Joe Lingfield in his embassy office. He wore a lapel tag and was escorted up in the elevator where Lingfield was waiting to take him to the office.

'You sounded disturbed on the telephone,' observed Lingfield as he went round to the other side of the desk. 'Coffee?'

'No thanks, Joe. Is Steiner around?'

Lingfield reached for a coffee jug. 'You want me to ring through?'

'If you would.'

Lingfield pressed a switch. 'Why don't you approach him direct?'

'Because I wouldn't have gotten this far.'

Lingfield stirred his coffee thoughtfully. 'Has Steiner upset you in some way?' He suddenly held up a restraining hand and spoke into the box. 'Will you put me through to Mr Steiner, Janie.' He glanced over at Quinn while he waited.

'You could say that. He called on me. What's his actual authority here?'

'Hold on. Yes, Janie?' Her voice came through, 'He's away for a few days. He didn't say where or for how long. I guess nothing's changed.' Lingfield looked up at Quinn. 'You heard that? I can't tell you his position.'

'For God's sake, Joe, I've done plenty of work for the Company. What's the problem? I only want to know what his authority is.'

'I know you do. He's over me. Not directly but that's what it comes to if the chips are down. What's bugging you?'

Quinn had to feel his way on how much to tell and what might be believed. 'Steiner came to see me two days ago.

Wanted to know my interest in the Hereford shootings. He picked it up from you.'

Lingfield was not put out and he knew that neither was Quinn. 'I know it's bugging him in some way but I don't know why. I've nothing to tell you.'

'Last night, a friend of mine was coming home with Cathy, no funny business between them, when Cathy was mugged by a bunch of young Arabs and my friend was kidnapped right outside our own place.'

'Isn't that for the police?'

'If that's what you advise. But I tie Steiner in with the kidnapping. I would have to tell the police that.'

'Steiner? Kidnapping? You're crazy, Lew.'

'I would have thought that was a minor misdemeanour for someone like Steiner. Don't try the whitewash, Joe.'

'But you said Arabs.'

'I did. Are you telling me that you have no Arabs on your payroll? Bullshit. You'll have roped in as many anti-Iranian government students as you could. America's the great Satan, Joe. You need all the Arab friends you can get.'

'Spare me the sermon.' Lingfield tasted his coffee, pulled a face and put the cup down. 'Who was it he was supposed to have snatched?'

This was more difficult although Quinn had been expecting it. 'A guy called Sam Towler. A sergeant in the SAS attached to Five. He was in on the Hereford caper which interests Steiner so much.'

'Shit. Are you sure about this?'

'I can't prove it. But I'm not far out. It's my guess that Towler was set up, probably by Five, for reasons he was trying to find out. I wouldn't be telling you any of this, because I need the story, but Towler's in trouble. He might already be dead.'

Lingfield pushed his cup away in disgust. 'And you've come to me for help?'

'Who else?'

'If Steiner's done this, and it's a big if, he will have his reasons. He may be the biggest bastard on earth but there is no doubt where his loyalties lie. Whatever he's doing, he's doing it for Uncle Sam.'

Lew Quinn sat back as if he could not believe his ears. 'What a trite load of crap. We are probably talking about murder here. What do you want, another international scandal? I would testify against you, Joe. I'll make note of this conversation and I'll file it.'

'So will I. I guess it will be your word against mine. Your past would come trotting out, Lew. Your reliability.'

'There's nothing wrong with my reliability, and you goddam know it.'

'It won't look that way, though, and you know that.' Lingfield had gone tight-faced, all friendliness suspended.

Quinn was exasperated. He rubbed his face as if to get some life back into it. 'Well, I guess I now know where I stand. Backs to the wall, guys. Close ranks at all costs, no matter who's being crucified and which shit is doing it.' He pushed his chair back. 'Don't ever ask me for favours again. Not ever.'

'I'm sorry you feel like that. Just what the hell do you think I can do? You've given me nothing positive. It's all in your mind. Five take a very different view of Towler. They're after him, Lew. Perhaps Steiner is doing them a favour. I'm not willing to destroy the friendly links I've built up with the Security Service here because of some kind of hunch you have. You admit yourself you're looking for a story.'

Quinn rose slowly. He felt drained but realised he should have expected nothing different. He had let emotions take over and was dealing with people who could not afford them. 'I've never manufactured a story in my life and I resent the implication that I might. You're the fiction department, Joe.' He put on his coat. 'I'll ask one last favour. Do you know of anywhere Steiner might hole up? Has he some secret place?'

Lingfield came round the desk looking unhappy. 'If I knew I wouldn't tell you. But in truth, I have no idea. Steiner is a secretive bastard, but then he's in a secretive game. I would help if I could, Lew.'

'Sure. How's it feel to be an accessory after the fact?'

Although it was mainly his upper half that was wet, the real cold started in his feet and gradually worked its way up his body. As the night progressed, the room became an ice box, his soaked clothes hardening to near freezing. He began to shiver very slightly, then as time went by, to shudder in spasms. The dreadful thing was not the pain in his face or his finger, where the blood had congealed unaided, but the fact that he could not move at all. The frustration of that was worse than all the rest.

Towler tried desperately to turn his head but achieved nothing more than grazing his forehead from friction against the strap. He could move his elbows a little, and his fingers. But he belatedly realised that he was also strapped at the knees. At odd times the facial pain came through the increasing numbness of the cold, and his finger was throbbing as if it would burst.

Towler was fighting to stay alive. In spite of Steiner's indication that he would be back for more questions, Towler was certain that it mattered very little if, when Steiner returned, he found Towler alive or dead.

To calm down required an enormous effort of will. He could face death, had faced it many times before, but not in so cruel a fashion. He had nothing to fight with but his mind and that was not enough to ward off hypothermia. He could not will his blood temperature to stop falling, and the further it fell the less he would be able to cope with it.

He concentrated on the pain itself, trying to bring it to the fore above all other sensations. He wanted to feel the damage to his face, and the swelling pain in his little finger. If he could continue to feel the pain then he might hold on. Feeling was life; when it finally went his life would go with it. There was no room in his mind now for Kate, and the girl in Ireland had faded forever. His sole concentration was on survival but there were many times when he was tempted to let go, to fade away as the cold took over body and all feeling ceased for all time.

Joe Lingfield sat thoughtfully at his desk for some time after Quinn had gone. What Steiner did was none of his business. What happened to the public image of the CIA was of interest to him. The irony here was that Steiner, as chief representative of the DIA in London, should be protecting that image, monitoring what the ostensibly subservient CIA was doing. Lingfield had no authority at all over the likes of Steiner. If he suspected anything rotten in the barrel, Steiner was the man he should go to. If he went through the more tedious accepted channels, it was still likely to finish up with Steiner.

Steiner was really doing work which should be left to the CIA. He had always acted like that and but for his success would surely have been disciplined. He was a bad appointment, here in London. The Brits did not like him, but, in Washington, somebody of high authority liked him even less, which was why he was here.

Lingfield was sorry he had upset Lew Quinn. He knew that Quinn was straight or he would never have used his occasional services. But when it came down to it why should he protect someone like Towler who had attracted a packet of trouble all round? He had enough on his plate without delving into other people's problems.

The argument was sound but the conviction less so. Lingfield went along the corridor to Janie's office. Janie Basto was plain, forty-five years of age, overweight and dressed indifferently, all of which was overshadowed by a tremendous personality. When Janie smiled everything around her came alive. She was the only PA who could handle Steiner, accept his brusqueness and bad manners, and occasionally put him in his place. He always complained about her but would never let her go.

Lingfield sat down uninvited and made sure he had closed the door behind him. He folded his arms and crossed his legs and geared himself up to what he was about to say.

Janie took off her glasses and viewed him seriously. She knew what he was going to ask but let him do it just the same.

'I think Matt might be in trouble, Janie. It's important that I contact him. Can you help?'

'I told you on the intercom; I really don't know where he is. He's always doing things like this. It drives me crazy.'

'Would you have a list of places where he might be?'

'There's no such list. He is not a creature of habit. I'm sorry.'

Lingfield expected her to protect Steiner but he thought she had spoken truthfully. He wondered how far it was safe to probe before Janie started to protect her boss more obviously. 'Do you know if he's running a cell of young Arabs over here?'

Janie's attentive interest changed; she appeared unusually severe. 'That question is out of order, Mr Lingfield. I did not hear it.'

She always called him Joe. He had gone over the top but what other way was there except to ignore the whole thing? 'Supposing there is a danger of him being brought into disrepute? Would you shield him then?'

'That's happened before now. I worked with him in Washington.'

'This isn't Washington, Janie. We're on friendly foreign soil. If what I hear is true, there's a likelihood of it not being so friendly. None of us wants that. Do we?'

'Of course we don't. But you should take this up with Mr Steiner direct.'

'Then tell me where he is before it's too late.'

'I *don't know*!'

Lingfield pointed to some of her paper work. 'You must know where payments go to. You must keep a record. Everything is accountable.'

'You've crossed the line again, Joe. I will have to report this and I find that sad.'

Lingfield sighed. 'You're a good secretary, Janie. I commend your loyalty. But in this case I think you're misguided. You must do whatever you feel is right, which is exactly what I'm doing asking these questions.'

'Is this all about the Hereford business?'

'What on earth made you say that?'

'Please answer me, Joe.'

'I think it's tied up with it, yes. What made you ask?'

'He's preoccupied with it. Even for him, he seems uptight about the whole thing.'

'Tell me what you can. It's obviously worrying you.'

Janie shook her head. 'He doesn't confide in me. He never does; not on anything he's handling outside. I know no details and if I did I could not give them to you. But he is in a strange mood.' She sat back. 'I don't like any of this, Joe. I really will have to report it. It's more than my job is worth to go any further.'

'I understand.' Lingfield raised his lanky form. 'I shall have to report it myself. As that means it will inevitably finish on Matt's desk, I shall have to go direct to Washington.'

Janie stared at him in such surprise he thought she was about to add something but all she said was, 'That bad?'

'I think it's life or death.'

Again he thought she was about to tell him something. Her lips opened and then she suddenly closed them again. But he was convinced that she knew something which might be useful to him.

When Lew Quinn entered his apartment, Cathy at once knew that he had failed to get anywhere. She had been drinking because she could not occupy herself without the sustenance of liquor. She was not an alcoholic but would fast become one unless she could control the habit.

Something was happening to Cathy Quinn which she did not really understand. Since Sam Towler's arrival everything had changed, but she was not sure exactly how. She had thrown herself at him and he had rejected her, not because he did not want her but because he valued and respected friendship much more than the limited pleasure she could give him. And above all, Sam Towler was loyal. It was a commodity she had lacked and it had made her face herself.

She was reasonably well off in her own right and Lew would not sponge on her, yet he had let her down in New York with his boss's wife. That had stung. She had always considered that she could lick the opposition, and she had not. It was her vanity that had been hurt, for she had never been strong on morality although she was now beginning to face its implications.

She saw Towler as almost too good to be true, yet at the same time she had seen his uncertainties, little give-aways he would prefer to hide; even fears. There were cracks in Towler but he was sufficiently strong to cope with them. She was grateful to him in many ways and in spite of her near terror at the house in Buckinghamshire, in retrospect she had enjoyed it and was glad she had not missed it. But when they had taken Towler and left her lying on the sidewalk, a whole new world had opened up and she saw that, from time to time, Lew had been part of that world.

She was now more worried about Towler than she could really explain to herself. It no longer had anything to do with getting him into bed. And she could think of no way to help him. Perversely, the arrival of Sam Towler had made her think more of her husband and when he entered the flat that evening she was more happy to see him than she had been for some considerable time. Cathy saw the news on his face and threw her arms round his neck and held him close.

Quinn smelled the liquor on her breath and said nothing. She was not drunk and he was happy that she was in his arms. 'I didn't get anywhere,' he whispered in her ear. 'Joe Lingfield's as bad as the rest of them. Hear nothing, say nothing and see nothing. You'd think they'd had enough scandals in the Company to make them stop and think, but they never learn. I don't know what we can do, Cath.'

They went into the drawing-room and Cathy poured two large drinks. Quinn made no attempt to stop her; he felt closer to her than for a long time and the feeling was good between them. Was it necessary to have a friend in dire danger to achieve this? He said nothing but had the uncomfortable feeling that was how it had happened. Towler might not return but he had left his mark.

'Do we give up?' Cathy raised her glass in a silent salute.

'I don't see what else we can do except report it to the police and it would look odd to have left it for so long.'

'But you think they're corrupt?'

'No. I never said that. I think Sam thinks that if they start enquiries they would somehow be stopped or side-tracked by the Security Service. I don't think it would achieve anything. I think we've just got to hope that Sam had a back-up.'

'So we do nothing?'

'There's nothing we can do unless we can find out where he was taken. If he doesn't show up in a couple of days it will be too late anyway. One thing has emerged, though. If his own people are after Sam, then, if Steiner pulled off this stunt, so are ours.'

Cathy was unusually quiet, and then she said, 'If Steiner gets no satisfaction from Sam he might think we can help.'

Quinn had been secretly thinking the same, yet he felt that they must stay put for at least two days just in case Towler managed to make contact. But he was well aware of the dangers; and he did not suggest to Cathy that she should go away for a while because he knew full well she would not and it would only confirm her own fears if he mentioned it.

*   *   *

James Dawson went to Bluie Prescott's home in Park Lane. He had telephoned his coming to avoid Prescott being out. But he was sorry he had had to announce his arrival in such a way. It removed the advantage of surprise.

Prescott opened the door himself and led the way into the drawing-room where he produced charged brandy balloons and Havana cigars. For the sake of good manners and in order to collect himself, Dawson allowed the niceties of polite conversation to continue until he felt they had done enough. Then he said, 'I don't think I've heard the complete truth about this exchange affair. I want to know what you haven't told me, Bluie.'

Prescott appeared not to be put out, though he showed some surprise. His troublesome leg was stretched out but otherwise he seemed quite relaxed. 'You mean the nitty gritty? The actual detail?'

'I mean exactly what you've been bloody well hiding from me.'

'I'm sorry, Minister, but you must enlighten me. You have something on your mind? Some aspect you are not quite happy about?'

'Bluie, if you continue like a schoolboy, I'll start an official enquiry. That could be embarrassing for you.'

'For you too. I don't think we should lose sight of how the whole business started.'

Dawson put down his goblet very carefully and formed an arch with the tips of his fingers. 'You're covering up something and there is no way I will leave this room until I know what. I'm well aware that I started it. I know that the PM would go berserk if this came out. I'm fully aware of the dangers of the press finding something; I'm sure they'll be scratching right now. All this does is to show the importance of my knowing exactly what happened and what has gone wrong. There's something I've not been told and I need to know, so just get on with it and tell me.'

Prescott gave no sign of being intimidated. He rubbed his knee slowly, the only sign that he was thinking furiously. He deliberately sipped his cognac and then cupped the balloon delicately in his big, strong hands. At last he lowered his head slightly as if conceding. Then he said, 'We have been trying to protect you, you know.' If he expected to draw some sympathetic comment from Dawson, he failed. He gazed up at the ceiling as if trying to correlate events. 'There have been some problems,' he admitted, 'but we saw no reason to tell you. We achieved what we set out to do and reasoned that was that.'

'But it's not, is it? Two men are dead and another is on the run. Tell me about it.'

'I was not involved with the actual detail. The man we were holding turned out to be a Rashid Khayar. At the time, we believed that, because of the secrecy of the operation, there was a communication problem and he was released before the exchange was set up. What's happened to him since, nobody knows. So we had to find someone else to exchange. No big deal in itself except that the poor blighter was unfortunately killed.'

Dawson hid his rising despair; this was the man the Sheikh had mentioned. 'If Khayar was released then why wasn't Kate?'

'Quite.' Prescott acknowledged the point. 'We think that what went wrong was that Khayar simply went to ground instead of going back to where he should have gone. Perhaps he was afraid of something. After all we never found out why his exchange was wanted in the first place. Nobody has ever heard of him. That is why there was such a delay. We realised that his release would not be believed if he could not be found. So we set up a ringer. It was dark, of course, and by the time the exchange was made it would have been too late for them to do anything about it. I must add that all this was done in order to ensure the safety of Kate Parker. Had we not done as we did she would probably be dead by now.'

Dawson was very still, his gaze penetratingly hard. He was still not satisfied that he was hearing the complete truth. 'So why should it go so disastrously wrong and why was Khayar released?'

Prescott shrugged. 'Until we find Towler I doubt that we shall ever know. Nobody knows precisely what game he was playing or for whom. He was the last man to be on duty while Khayar was still being held. Something might have gone on between them. After all it was at Towler's insistence that

Khayar was first brought in; nobody else was interested. It was true that we got nothing out of Khayar and it could be argued that there was no reason why he should not have been released. The whole matter was confusing.'

'So why was Towler used as an escort for the exchange if he was so suspect?'

'Oh, he wasn't at that time. It was after the event that we became suspicious. When selected he seemed to be the ideal type to handle such an exchange; particularly if things went wrong.'

'Things did go wrong.' Dawson's comment was stony.

'Indeed. And Towler went missing and is still missing. He's deeply involved in some way. But it took us all by surprise. He had been with us for so short a time that nobody really knew him. His handling officer wasn't keen on having him from the beginning, and it would seem that his judgment was right.'

Dawson sat quietly for several minutes. He was a little pale and his features rigid. It was some time before he said, 'Why wasn't I told this from the outset?'

'We did warn you about Towler. We were worried about Kate Parker's attitude to him. The shootings had nothing to do with the exchange as such. There is a much deeper reason behind those. As Towler had released Khayar, he was made to find a substitute and we feel that he went out to pick a man he deliberately intended to set up for reasons of his own or of those who operate him. It worked didn't it? And with a little less perception on our part he might have got away with the whole thing and been cosily taken back into our fold. Minister, we really saw no point in worrying you with these matters. The exchange worked from your point of view and the rest is our problem. We are not exactly untrained in these matters. I would still have preferred that you did not know. But I'm desperately sorry that you have found it all so worrying. That was never our intention.'

Dawson did not finish his cognac. He felt uneasier now than when he first arrived and he was not convinced by Prescott's explanation. 'Is there anything else you are hiding from me?'

Prescott appeared slightly pained. 'I would prefer to see it as protecting you, Minister. Isn't that what we've been doing all along?'

'You haven't answered my question.'

'There's nothing that we know about. When we catch up with Towler we might have something else for you. We simply must find that man and those who are pulling his strings. There could be far more to this than we can see.'

Dawson inwardly agreed but made no comment. In many ways he wished he had not come. He was unsettled and deeply worried by what he had heard. In spite of Prescott's easy assurances the whole business reeked of uncertainty and danger and he was far from satisfied. Short of calling Prescott a liar there was little else he could do at the moment. But he was convinced that moment would come and he dreaded it. As things stood he had to be careful but equally he could not allow Prescott to mislead him for too long. When they parted it was in a mood of hidden distrust.

Towler was slipping away and found comfort in it. It was no longer so cold; his whole body was numb and he could barely feel the bruising on his face and the swelling of his finger. It was dark now. Pitch black. It was a tomb of ice in which he could hear nothing but his own shallow breathing and the minute movements he had been able to make. There was nothing he could do to restore his circulation which seemed to have stopped pumping hours ago. He had no idea of how long he had been in the cellar and all he craved was the dignity of being able to die in modest comfort and away from the terrible chair to which he was strapped.

His body had set in one position, his spine welded to the shape of the chair. He could no longer see the ceiling but he knew its dirty pattern by heart, the only sight he'd had of anything since being here except the hazy shape of Steiner who seemed to have gone years ago and would never come back.

There were still odd moments when he roused himself to mumble unintelligible words but he had no control over his body and these tiny episodes of resistance were becoming far less frequent.

At some point he heard a sound he knew was not his own. It was somewhere behind him and immediately he called on his diminishing reserves to listen. There was a draught behind his back and he assumed that the door had opened. The draught disappeared and the complete silence returned. And then there was a blinding light as a beam flashed round the room finally to cast his own massive shadow against the wall and partially on the ceiling where his fractional image wavered.

'Bugger me!' a voice called out in astonishment.

Towler almost cried. 'You useless bastard!' he bawled. 'You were always bloody late on parade. Where the hell have you been?' As the last word faded to an inaudible whisper, he passed out.

18

Jacko Jackson had seen many a corpse in his time and had even created them. In the flashlight beam he could see that Towler was almost gone; he must have held on by sheer will-power. He noticed the face wound and the missing tip of the little finger of the left hand and the nasty swelling above it; he took all these things in almost at a glance. He found the battery operated light near the door, switched it on and then set about freeing Towler from the chair.

The wounds did not worry Jacko; he had seen worse on training exercises. It was the cold and the near completion of hypothermia that worried him. His fingers were too cold to cope with buckles so he cut through the leather bonds. He heaved Towler out of the chair and tried to support him but found his weight too much. He laid him on the concrete flooring and started slapping him very hard across the face. He rubbed arms and legs, ripped off the shoes and massaged the feet, all the time bellowing and cajoling Towler into trying to help himself.

His Browning was rammed into his waistband and he was prepared to shoot the first sign of life coming through the door which he faced. It was some time before he could get Towler to stir and when he did he was merciless in his treatment. He shouted at Towler to pull himself up by the chair arms, anything to get him moving.

Towler loathed the chair more than anything else and it had a remarkable effect in pulling him round. But he could not touch it once he was upright. Jacko helped him walk round the room time and again, and started to abuse him again.

'You stink, you bastard, worse than after three days in a

foxhole. God, I can't stand the stench of you. Let's get out of here and get you changed.'

Once his circulation improved so, too, did Towler's movements. He was weak and had to find support from Jacko but he slowly came round.

'Come on. Let's go,' said Jacko impatiently.

'No. I'm going to wait for him. Give me a pistol.'

'Don't be stupid. You couldn't hit a target if I held it in front of you.'

'If the target is Steiner I can't miss.'

'O.K.,' Jacko stepped back and pulled a spare Browning from a waistband holster. 'I thought we might need an extra piece. Catch.' He tossed the gun across the room towards Towler.

Normally, Towler would have caught it with ease but now he dropped it and when he tried to pick it up stumbled and dropped it again.

Jacko made no attempt to help him as Towler fumbled. 'Satisfied? Got any more tricks? You're still frozen through, you silly bugger. You need warming up and it can't be done here. Now come on.'

Towler finally managed to tuck the gun into his pocket and tried to reach the door unaided. He involuntarily grabbed the chair to steady himself and felt a wave of revulsion at the contact. After that he allowed Jacko to help him up a dog-leg of chipped concrete steps until they reached a door which Jacko pushed open.

They were in a large hall which smelled of dust. Jacko shone his flashlight and Towler saw uncarpeted stairs leading up to a deserted landing. The house felt empty and was in such a bad state of repair that it was probably condemned. Jacko helped Towler to the front door, opened it, and a blast of iced air came through to make them shiver.

'Watch the steps,' warned Jacko as they walked down together. He helped Towler round the corner to where he had left his car. They climbed in after Jacko had used a lock defreezer and Towler sat shivering, his teeth chattering.

'Where are we?' asked Towler with difficulty.

'Lambeth. Definitely not the Palace end. Don't worry, I've made note of it.' Jacko drove carefully through the deserted streets. It was 2am and the wheels crackled on the freezing surface. 'Steiner, you called him? Once he finds you gone he won't come again. Maybe he didn't intend to return anyway.'

'I'm going to kill him,' said Towler flatly. 'Just what the bloody hell happened to you? You were supposed to be waiting at Quinn's place where they snatched me.'

'I was. And for longer than you deserve. I was there for over two hours in this sodding weather.' Jacko took a turn and felt the slight swish of the tail. 'I saw it happen but there was no way I was going to take on half a dozen fanatical Arabs. They were all scared and that makes them worse. There were too many to fire at and it would have woken the neighbourhood. So I followed and that had to be done very carefully. The car you were bundled into was driven by a European. I've got the number if it's any help. He was a tough-looking sod. Would that be your Steiner?'

'Probably.' Towler was trying to stop shivering in spite of the car heater being on full blast.

'The car pulled in at one stage and I had to continue on past and then dowse my lights and wait round the next corner. My guess is that you were trussed at that stage and the two Arabs who had gone with you were dropped off. When the car went past again I could only see one shape. I thought they might have ditched you but I followed on. Are you O.K., Sam?' Jacko did not like the look of Towler.

Towler nodded. 'I can cope. I thought you wouldn't be coming. I had given you up long ago.'

'You should have more bloody faith. When has any of the regiment let any member down? I had to keep a gap so I didn't see the actual house you were dragged into. It took time to find it. Several are condemned round there, some of them full of squatters. I knew you had to be in one of them. I couldn't get too close and I didn't see Steiner come out but I saw the car leave.' Jacko glanced quickly at Towler. 'You should have known I would stick it out. What other way is there between old mates?'

Towler managed a feeble smile. 'You're right, Jacko. You've had plenty of practice sussing out houses. I'd forgotten you're into crime. Where are you taking me?'

'My place where you can thaw out. You're still in a dodgy

state. And I'll see if I can get a bent quack to look at that finger.' And then sarcastically, 'Thanks, Jacko. Thanks a lot.'

Towler echoed with conviction, 'Thanks, Jacko. Thanks a lot. If ever you need a character reference in court let me know. Well, at least I know one bastard who has some answers, and believe me he's going to talk.'

For a while they drove in silence and then Towler gripped Jacko's arm making the car swerve.

'What the hell are you playing at? You nearly had us off the road.'

'I must get to a phone quickly.'

'Then use the car phone, for chrissake. Don't do that again or you'll finish the job Steiner started. Apart from attracting the fuzz.'

Towler was trying desperately to pull himself together but was in a far worse state than he would admit. 'I hope I can remember the number.' He dialled and the number rang out for so long he was about to re-dial when a bleary, but irritated voice answered.

'Lew? This is Sam.' Towler was aware that his voice sounded strange. 'Yes, *Sam*. I'm sorry about the time but I've just got free. Is Cathy O.K.? Thank God. It was Steiner. You'd better get out of there quick. Never mind the time. When he finds I've gone he'll come searching for any clues he can get. I can put the finger on him and he'll try to stop me any way he can and that will include through friends.'

Towler listened for a while then turned to Jacko, 'Give me a number where Lew can make contact with me.'

Jacko gave his own number and Towler passed it on. 'Go to the Franklin Hotel in Bayswater. I'll contact you there and give you what I've got so far. You deserve at least that much. Give my love to Cathy; she'll know which way to take it. But get out of there.' He hung up.

Jacko grinned. 'You're beginning to find out who your friends are, mate.'

'I always knew my friends. It's my enemies I'm doubtful about.'

At 5am that same morning Matt Steiner returned to the house in Lambeth. He left his car a block away and walked round

203

the corner into an empty and still dark street and let himself in with a key. One of the young Arabs he used had told him about this place a long time ago. He rarely used it and fully recognised the dangers of doing so, which was one of the reasons he kept to hours when few were about.

The intense cold did not worry him. He seemed to be impervious to all weather conditions. In the dark hall he pulled out a pencil flashlight and beamed it around to see if anything had changed. There were footprints in the dust of the floor but he thought they were probably his own and the heel marks of Towler when he had dragged him inside.

He went down slowly to the basement. He was a cautious man who often gave the impression of being reckless. He pulled his gun out at the basement door and produced one of the keys to the locks he had had fitted. When he found the door ajar he did not burst in but first inspected around the lock. There were no marks and he received the first jolt to his confidence. The door had been opened by a professional with the right equipment. It made him ponder his next move.

Standing back to the wall he dowsed his flashlight and slowly pushed the door open. Two minutes later, when there was no reaction, he believed the room was empty. He rushed in at a crouch so that he was facing the chair. Still crouched he switched on and now knew for certain that the room was empty. He switched on the battery light he had rigged some time ago.

For a rare moment in his life, Steiner had been reduced to defensive action and it rattled him. He closed the door and locked it to avoid being surprised, and inspected the chair. The smell of Towler was still there and that was all. Most of the straps had been cut by a heavy duty knife but the chair was still reclining in the same position as when he had first strapped Towler to it.

Steiner broke into a cold fury of obscene language. There was nobody to hear and nobody to see how vulnerable he could be when outsmarted. It was this more than Towler's escape that got to him. Towler had arranged a back-up and what disturbed Steiner was that he had not noticed. Just who was he up against?

His only satisfaction was that Towler must have been in no

condition to wait for him. Perhaps Towler had died? But he could no longer afford that kind of wishful thinking. He had slipped up and it was not due to carelessness. He should have got more out of Towler while he had him. Perhaps he had concentrated on the wrong questions. One thing, though, was absolutely certain: they would meet again. Neither man was the type to leave matters as they were. And he would start looking at once. There was an obvious starting point.

He left the cellar and did not bother to close the door but put out the light; it would be too risky to use the place again.

Towler felt more alive after a hot bath, a shave, and a bowl of soup. The house was in Notting Hill and reeked of money and bad taste but to Jacko it was the home he had always dreamed of. And he had achieved it in remarkably quick time. Towler had no intention of arguing how the money was obtained; Jacko was an old mate and only those who had suffered the deprivations which that very special force had suffered in the field, conditions which no average person could possibly stand, would know what that meant.

Jacko was also a crack shot, as were all of them, but he was one of those used for demonstration purposes when top politicians visited the Northern Ireland Province and had to be impressed. A colleague would sit in a chair facing him with a big board behind and Jacko would stand with his Heckler and Koch and scare the wits out of everyone watching by firing at his friend in short bursts. When he had finished, his friend would rise unharmed from the chair so that everyone could see the ring of shots outlining the body on the board. It was not merely a demonstration of incredible marksmanship but of the complete confidence the men had in each other. They had experienced some of that close bond during the last few hours.

Jacko provided Towler with a change of clothing and put those that had been bought with Quinn's money in an outside incinerator. The topcoat had been kept and was drying out with the shoes. Later that morning a slightly effeminate and badly dressed doctor called to cauterise and dress Towler's finger, and to check on his anti-tetanus jabs. He asked no questions but did a thorough job for which Jacko paid.

'I'm building up debts I might not be able to pay back,' commented Towler after the doctor had gone. 'And not just to you.'

Jacko grinned. 'If I was the bloody Mafia I'd call in your debts at a later date. You don't see yourself as becoming a judge do you, Sam? Anyway it's been like old times. What happens next?'

'I'm being attacked on two fronts. By both on the same night as it happened. I've got to try to fight my way out. Is there a call box near here?'

'Use my phone.' And when Towler shook his head, Jacko added, 'You going to try a number that might be tapped? There's a box on the corner. You'll need some change.'

He rang Kate. By now it was just after 11am. 'Are you still speaking to me?' he asked cautiously.

'I've been trying to trace you. I'm sorry about the other day. I'm glad you've phoned, Sam. I've been worried about you.'

'Why?'

'Damn it, you are the one who told me that someone is trying to kill you. Of course, I've been worried.'

'What makes you now believe me?'

'Are you trying to start a row? I believed you then and still do. It's others who don't. I've tried to convince them, though.'

'Thanks, Kate. But I hope you realise what you're saying. Someone must have called on you.'

'Yes, and they put up plausible arguments against you. They claim that they only want to speak to you.'

'Why would they visit you? Did they think you might know where I am?'

'Yes. They disapprove of my feelings for you.'

Towler found his hand shaking. 'What feelings, Kate?'

There was a long silence but he could just hear her breathing, and then she said, 'That was unfair. It's difficult over the phone. But I'm increasingly worried about you. You matter to me, Sam. Is it possible to meet?'

'There's nothing I'd like better but there are a few things to sort out. Do you think this call is being monitored?'

'They wouldn't dare.'

'Because of James Dawson?'

'So you're back to that again. Oh, Sam don't spoil it. One day I'll explain. When we're alone together.'

He wondered if there really was anything to explain. 'They could go behind his back.'

'It's possible. But it would be a very dangerous thing for them to do.'

'Well, we can find out one way or the other. I'm in a call box and that takes time to trace and I'm going to hang up soon. I'm going to ask you to do something for me. If it works we'll both know the answer to a phone tap. But we will have found out something more important than that and it will take any doubts from your mind about me.'

'I haven't got any doubts.'

'Yes, you have. And they'll work on them. Now listen, Kate, because I'm beginning to push my luck. But do what I ask only if you want to. Really want to.'

On the way back to Jacko's place he reflected that Kate had made no attempt to disclaim any knowledge of Dawson as she had done the last time they met. He was not sure of his feelings about that but it at least showed the beginning of an open-mindedness on her part. He fervently hoped she would come to no harm doing what he had asked. Cathy, Lew, Jacko, and now Kate; they were all taking risks for him and it both deeply touched and worried him.

Lew Quinn and Cathy left their home twenty-five minutes before a dangerously moody Steiner arrived at 5.50am. He rang the bell and, on getting no answer, opened the door with a pick-lock. He made no pretence about what he was doing. With gun in hand he went from room to room and saw all the signs of a hasty departure. So Towler had survived and had warned them.

He spent some time in Quinn's den foraging through papers, searching for any clue that might point to where they had gone or to whom they could make contact. Quinn had taken with him his book of phone numbers but there were several scribbled notes on the desk and a message pad. Using one of the pencils on the desk Steiner shaded over the impressions left on the top sheet and came up with three different telephone numbers which were just about legible. He copied them out on a blank sheet of paper, went round the apartment once more, and then left.

At midday Kate rang the number Prescott had left with her should there be any development over Towler. She gave her name and was put through to Prescott immediately. When she heard Prescott's voice she suddenly had a fit of nerves and put the phone down. She stood against the wall trembling. It was one thing agreeing to do something for someone who was becoming dear to her, and sincerely to intend to help, but quite another actually to do it.

Prescott was no fool. He was clearly a leading figure in British Security and she was suddenly afraid of making a mess of things. It had to be done, though. For Sam's sake, it must be done. She reached for the phone again and recoiled as it suddenly rang. She grabbed it and breathlessly answered. The shock of Prescott being on the other end produced the right nervous attitude for her to cope. Keeping her voice down and unable to control the quiver she said, 'I'm sorry I had to hang up quickly.'

'Is it all right now?' Prescott sensed that something important might have happened and her nervousness was quite clear.

Almost in a whisper Kate said, 'I thought he was coming into the room but he's still in the bath.'

'Towler?'

'Yes. He came this morning, in quite a state.'

There was no time to ask why she had changed her attitude about Towler. Prescott said with an urgency she could not mistake, 'Keep him there. Any pretext. We'll be round. Someone will mention the electrics. And thank you, Miss Parker, you've done the right thing.'

Kate put down the phone again and stared at it as if it had become electrified. She stood against the wall, her legs weak, and she knew that, by sheer chance, she had handled it well. But she was scared of the prospect of handling the next stage with the same conviction. It was some time before she unwound enough to make herself a strong coffee and could not keep the cup still when she tried to drink.

208

Afterwards she ran both bath taps and wet the soap so that the bath would appear to have been recently used. Then she sank to a chair and wondered what she had started. She fastened her mind on Towler and it helped, but she was on her own and needed his direct support. She still could not phone him because she had no number and she realised he was right not to give it.

The door-bell rang and she jerked from her reverie. Fifteen minutes? Surely it could not be Prescott's men in that time? She rose shakily, almost knocking the cup off the small table by the chair. She steadied herself and went to the door. When she peered through the spy hole she could only see one man and he looked innocuous enough. She called out to ask his business and he held up some sort of identity card for her to see.

'The name's Hastings, ma'am. I've come about the electrics.'

Kate slipped off the chain and released the lock. She opened the door and before she could say a word three men rushed past her, one closing the door to stand with his back to it while the others went straight into the drawing-room.

Kate walked slowly away from the man guarding the door feeling strange and weak. When she reached the drawing-room neither of the other men were in sight but all the doors leading off were open. As Hastings came charging out of the bathroom, Kate saw him hastily put a gun away under his coat.

He snapped, 'Where the hell is he?'

'He's gone.'

Hastings stared frostily at Kate. He was middle height, under forty and slightly arrogant. His brown eyes were far from warm and he was trying to control a rising anger. 'Why the blazes didn't you say so?'

His demanding attitude was the right medicine for Kate; it infuriated her. She said brusquely, 'You didn't give me a chance to say anything. You barged past me as I was about to tell you so I let you get on with it. Anyone would think you were looking for a dangerous criminal instead of someone you just wanted to speak to.'

It pulled Hastings up. He glanced sheepishly at a colleague who emerged from one of the other rooms and gave a slight shake of the head. With a little more politeness he said, 'Well he left damned quick after your phone call. We broke records getting here. What went wrong?'

'I think he must have got suspicious. Perhaps he heard me on the phone. I don't know. He was in a highly nervous state from the moment he arrived. Perhaps I didn't convince him he was safe here. There was nothing I could do. It was a miracle you didn't bump into him on the way up.' She heard the second man speaking behind her and when she turned saw that he was talking into a two-way radio transmitter to ask someone outside whether he had seen Towler.

Kate said angrily to Hastings, 'It does nothing for my confidence to see you with a gun. Just what do you think you're doing?'

Hastings was still looking around the room as if there was some spot he had missed. 'Well you are right, actually ma'am. He is dangerous. The gun is merely a safeguard. Well there's nothing more we can do. Will you advise us if he returns?'

'If I get the chance. But I don't think he's likely to come again. It looks as if I gave the game away.' Kate was both horrified and satisfied. She did not have to act being shaken as she led the way back to the door. But it was obvious that none of the men was satisfied.

When they had left she went back into the drawing-room and stared out of the window at the hard wintry scene. Sam had been right all along. And the Security Service had lied to her. But it did show that Prescott, so far, had not dared to put a tap on her phone.

'Put a tail on the girl.'

Soames' moon face showed no reaction to the instruction. He was thoroughly tired of the whole affair. So far as he was concerned, Prescott, the Deputy Director, was holding too much back. They all accepted the 'need to know' basis but he felt that this went beyond that and was operating on the lines of MI6 rather than the defensive mechanism of Five. Prescott was covering for someone and that must be someone very high up the tree. His inclination was to put out a background check on Kate Parker but knew that such a course would get back to Prescott. He tried the direct approach.

'What do we know about this girl? Has she some meaning that has not come my way?'

'So far as I'm concerned she's just a young girl who co-partners a health club and who was snatched to effect an exchange for a minion. She was probably taken at random.'

'But someone must have been sufficiently concerned about her to agree to an exchange. After all, this "minion" has caused havoc one way and another.'

'That was your fault, Soames. It was I who sanctioned the exchange. We didn't want an attractive young lady carved up for someone who did not matter to us. It wasn't necessary. It blew up because we blew it up ourselves and I suggest that you don't lose sight of that. It should never have happened. Keep an eye on the girl and she may lead us to Towler. Once Towler is out of the way the affair is closed.'

'All right. But wouldn't it be sensible to put a tap on her phone?'

'I've considered that. It means getting a Home Office sanction and that requires explanation. We don't want that to happen, do we?'

Soames nodded agreement but was thinking that Prescott had conveniently forgotten his earlier mention that he was answerable to someone else. The continuing insistence of the business would suggest someone of Cabinet rank. It had not mattered before but as Soames increasingly saw himself as the fall guy, he could be aligned with the antics of Towler, so now it mattered very much who Prescott might be protecting at his expense.

'Don't let the girl know she's being followed. That is paramount. She probably won't know but if she makes contact with Towler he'll be alert to anything. Get A4 to use a full fourteen-man team round the clock.'

There could be no better indication of Prescott's concern. To tie up fourteen men in this way when they were urgently needed elsewhere was proof enough of someone of high rank behind Prescott. Soames supposed he had really known that all along, but it was now taking on a new significance and he was beginning to see why the girl was so important and why she must never find out she was under surveillance. All he needed was a name. Soames was satisfied that, beneath his urbanity, Prescott was sweating enough to take some dangerous risks. Soames decided that, in order to protect his own back, he must really make an effort to see beyond Towler to the deeper issue Prescott was guarding.

Their gaze met once more as Soames departed and each man quietly raised concern in the other.

19

Joe Lingfield received Quinn's telephone call and left his office without telling his secretary where he was going or how long he would be. He went up to the third floor room of the small Bayswater hotel where Quinn was waiting for him outside the door.

When Lingfield showed his surprise at seeing Cathy in the room, Quinn said, 'Cathy's in up to her neck and has the bruises to prove it.'

Lingfield noticed the open suitcase and the clothes strewn on the bed which stood between the two men as something more than a physical barrier. He saw that Quinn had not shaved and his tie was hanging loose round his neck. The grubby little room was chilly but nobody seemed to notice. The atmosphere was grim.

'I've taken a big risk in telling you where we are. You've got to do something about Steiner,' said Quinn. 'He's dangerous, if not crazy, and he's on the loose.' He explained what had happened.

When he had finished Lingfield sank on to the edge of the bed and the springs squeaked. He stretched his long legs and said, 'We've been through it already, Lew. I can't accept this about Steiner. Anyway, nobody knows where the bastard is. Meanwhile all I have from you is that Cathy was mugged by Arabs and you have only Towler's word for the rest. Is this what you called me over for?'

'I trust Towler. He was kidnapped, for chrissake, what more do you want?'

'I accept that. It's Steiner's tie-in I need convincing about. There's nothing there. Where is Towler?'

'I don't know. I have a phone number where I can leave a

message but I can't let you have that when I haven't got your full confidence. You might be working with Steiner.'

'Then why call me? Don't give me that shit. It seems to me that the only person who can definitely tie in Steiner with what you say happened to Cathy and Towler, is Towler himself. If I can't get to him there's nothing I can do. I'd be laughed down if I tried presenting what you've given me.' Lingfield stood up. 'We've really gotten no further. I'd like to help. But I don't see how I can as things stand.'

Quinn and Cathy exchanged worried glances. 'Don't let Steiner know where we are,' pleaded Quinn.

'That much I can promise you. But bear in mind that you've run away on Towler's advice. And nobody can find him except you. That could make you vulnerable too, if what you say is true.'

'What the hell do you think we're doing here? You're making a mistake, Joe. And if we all get out of this, as I warned you before, I won't protect you, not after what has happened to Cathy.'

'I can't deal with this officially until I have more to go on. If you can arrange a meet with Towler then fix it.' He smiled wrily. 'Perhaps there is one thing I can do. Trust me. O.K.? Hang in there.'

Jacko drove Towler to Edwardes Square and parked his Ferrari in a reserved but vacant slot. He slapped a doctor's sticker on the windscreen before helping Towler out of the car.

Towler was dressed as a Lieutenant-Colonel and was wearing a false moustache. His gloves covered the damage to his finger and he had discarded the sling the doctor had provided. Amongst other enterprises, some serving as useful fronts, Jacko had a small warehouse in the East End of London which was stocked with a collection of second-hand and stage clothes, which he hired out to television, film companies and photographic studios. He sometimes found it useful to use them himself. At the moment he was dressed as a sergeant in the Royal Irish Rangers. Neither he nor Towler had any problem in presenting a military image.

Towler was impressed with the way Jacko was coming through for him. It was the kind of comradeship he had missed during his brief spell at MI5. Jacko acted as escort and the two men walked briskly to the entrance of the apartment block. When they stood on top of the steps, Jacko spoke out of the side of his mouth to say, 'There's nothing obvious. I think you might be right; it's too early for a team to start surveillance. I'll stay here, though, just in case.'

Towler marched across the foyer, ignoring the porter's enquiring look, and continued on to the lift. There was nobody else in the foyer. He rode up to get out on the floor below Kate's apartment, and walked slowly up the remaining stairs. He felt groggy and rested at the dog-leg to peer up at the landing above.

The corridor was empty when he reached it. He continued on towards Kate's door and rang the bell. He removed his military cap and faced the spy hole squarely. The door was opened in a rush and they were holding each other tightly and Kate began to cry.

Neither wanted to let go. They entered the drawing-room with their arms around each other as if they were long-separated lovers. Towler swung Kate round to face him and put a finger to his lips. He leaned forward to whisper in her ear. 'They may have planted bugs.'

It hadn't occurred to her and she looked startled. 'I don't think they had time,' she whispered back. 'They wouldn't have seen a need to.'

He went round the apartment and searched the obvious places. Prescott's men had had less chance in the drawing-room because Kate had been there most of the time but Towler checked just the same. Reasonably satisfied he kept his voice low and advised Kate to do the same.

He took off his gloves and coat and at once she saw the bandaged finger. It was no time for hedging. 'Steiner did it,' he said. 'Just the tip of the finger. Yours was far worse and I reckon he did that too. He has a fetish for bolt-cutters.'

'The American? He got hold of you? Sam, what does it all mean?'

'It means that there is a bloody big cover-up as I said all along, and that somehow, the Americans, or at least, Steiner, is wrapped up in it.' Towler took the plunge he knew he must make. 'And so is James Dawson in some way.'

Kate looked steadily at him and suddenly broke into a slow smile.

It was far from the reaction he expected. 'What's so funny?'

'It's your uniform. An officer. You look so splendid in it. And it suits you.'

'It's stage stuff. It was the only way I was going to make colonel! And a good way to slip a tail. Stop hedging, Kate. We've got to face it, whatever it is. Just what is Dawson to you? Is it so difficult to give him up?'

They were sitting side by side on the settee and lightly holding hands. Her grip tightened and he saw that she was both surprised and shocked. Then she snatched her hand away. Incredulously, she said, 'You think I am his mistress?!'

He caught the denial in her inflection. 'What else could I think? You were so secretive about him. You even lied about him.'

'Sam, how could you? He's old enough to be my father.'

'There would be nothing new in . . .' Towler stopped, nerves strumming. 'Your father?'

'I was born on the wrong side of the blanket, Sam.'

'Oh, Christ. Forgive me. But why the hell didn't you tell me?'

'I didn't know I was going to feel this way about you. I had to protect him not only from scandal, but from the press, and his political opposition. And particularly from the Prime Minister.'

Towler was tremendously relieved but shaken. A good many things began to fall into place; but far from all. 'So that's why you were snatched. It was an under-the-counter deal. But it all went wrong, didn't it? And we still don't know why.' He tried to get his mind back to what Kate had actually admitted. 'He's a bit careless about keeping you a secret.'

'It's an open secret, Sam. It always has been. I was a love child but his family had other plans for him. He was, and still is, politically ambitious, and the family he married into had connections that could help him. O.K., he sacrificed love for ambition and that was unforgivable. I can imagine the dreadful effect it had on my mother who was carrying me at the time he got married. My mother died after a long illness when I was six. But he never, ever, forgot her. He really did love her.

His close friends all knew about it but he had to continue on the path he had taken. I was fostered but he made sure I went to a good home and he paid for my education. He kept a distant eye on me until I was on my own feet. Is this shocking you?'

Towler took her hand again. 'Hell, no. I'm stunned, though. And I'm angry at what he did. He's a selfish bastard. But if it's any help – you know, I was fostered too. So we have a bond, although I'd like to think of it as more than that.' Relief was still flooding through him. 'If you want to talk about it, then get it off your chest and we won't raise it again.'

'He's made up for a lot. I remind him of my mother so he can never escape a sense of guilt. From my late teens on we became closer and talked things out and had a meal from time to time. His wife Sandra doesn't like me for obvious reasons but I've never intruded into their family life. It all happened so long ago that almost everybody has lost sight of our relationship.'

'Not everybody, Kate. Far from everybody. Someone had eyes on you from the moment they wanted an exchange. People like the KGB would have you on file.'

'But he can't be blackmailed over me. He wouldn't stand for that. He hasn't tried to hide me.' She suddenly stopped, and her expression clouded. 'I remember James – I always call him that so as not to embarrass him in front of people by calling him Daddy – once told me that his father-in-law went to Cambridge with Kim Philby; he would have known. But James would let it be made public rather than submit to blackmail. Damn it, these days politicians have illegitimate children while in office and still survive.'

'Sure. But would they let one of their kids be tortured and killed?' Towler added begrudgingly, 'At least he's shown a real love for you. But does he know what's really going on, Kate, or is he in the dark?'

'What *is* going on?'

'That's what I'm trying to find out. Something went wrong over the exchange and it's becoming clearer what. The bloke we exchanged was not the one he should have been and he was cynically murdered. Who set it up and why? And does Dawson know what's going on behind the scenes in his name?'

'You want me to tell him all this?'

'Yes. As long as you can convince him that Five are trying to top me, he might listen.' He squeezed her hand. 'But, Kate, you've got to brace yourself for two possibilities: first, Dawson might already know, for he entered into a clandestine arrangement to have you released. He went against the declared policy of the Government. The PM has very strong views on that sort of thing and won't deal with terrorists at any price. It's political dynamite. I don't need to spell it out to you, do I?'

'The other possibility is that he knows no more than I do about what is actually being covered up or of the American involvement. If he finds out, what will his reaction be? What steps is he willing to take to protect his position? He's an ambitious man. Five see me as a fall-guy. Get rid of me and there's nothing more to worry about. Will he see me in the same light?'

Kate could not answer. She had a deep feeling for Dawson but, as Towler laid out the possibilities, she was more concerned about how she herself would react. She saw the dreadful prospect of having to take sides. Could she betray her own father, or the man who had saved her life? She could now see clearly why they wanted Towler out of the way. He was meant to die that night at Hereford. Without quite realising what she was doing, she raised Towler's injured hand to her lips and kissed it.

'What will you do?' asked Towler softly, knowing what was going through her mind. 'If he didn't care about his position and his future in politics, he wouldn't have done it this way in the first place. It's well recorded that his ambition is to be Prime Minister.'

'He wouldn't do anything to harm you once he knows the truth.'

'Have you thought out the alternative? He'd be finished. They'd crucify him. His friends couldn't afford to stand by him.'

'Sam, I wouldn't allow you to be hurt. I love you too much.'

'Does that go for him too? You've been protecting him so far.'

Kate did not know how to answer. She stood up and limped over to the window. 'It won't come to that,' she said at last.

Towler joined her and put an arm round her, drawing her to him. 'I'm not trying to confuse you, Kate. But you can't run away from it. You might find yourself having to take sides. He is your father after all. There can be no compromise. I'm sorry to be so brutal about it but it's no longer an issue of trying to help me but of who survives.' He turned to cradle her and they stood there together for a long time.

Neither wanted to raise the subject again but it had to be done. 'Speak to him,' said Towler. 'You might be able to make a judgment on whether or not he knows what is actually going on.' Towler thought for a moment. 'Don't tell him about Steiner and me. It might confuse the real issue of whether Five are playing some game of their own behind his back. You'll have to take it from there. We've proved that there's no tap on your phone. But that could change, so be careful.'

'James would never consent to it.'

He touched her lips with a finger. 'Don't be naïve. The gloves are off. Everyone is out to protect themselves. I'll keep in touch in any way I can. Give me an old boyfriend's name. We'll work out a simple code.'

Towler left Kate with mixed feelings of elation and sorrow. Events had created a dilemma which he had made her face. She loved two men in different ways and that love was going to be put to the test in a most unpleasant form. He wished he had not had to tell her.

He walked down the stairs for exercise and to give himself longer to think things over. When he reached the foyer he saw Jacko speaking to another man. Both turned as he approached and Jacko sprang to attention and saluted. Towler realised with horror that the man with Jacko was Dawson's police bodyguard. He returned the salute and said crisply, 'Let's get moving, Sergeant.' Above him he heard the elevator doors open and close and he realised what a near thing it had been. He felt sick at the thought of what Kate had to face so soon.

There was still no sign of a thaw as Joe Lingfield crossed Trafalgar Square to be circled by hungry pigeons. He was surprised at the number of people feeding the birds in the atrocious weather. Perhaps that was why!

He crossed the square and then the Mall at Admiralty Arch and made his way into a bleak, snow-covered, and largely deserted St James's Park to follow the path running roughly parallel with the Mall. He took the turning towards the bridge and bore left the other side. The benches opposite the pond were, not surprisingly, deserted, although they had been swept clear of snow. Ducks skidded on the ice around the perimeter of the pond and called noisily for food.

Soames joined him some five minutes later and the two men walked along slowly, the American almost towering above the shorter and stouter Englishman. They presented an odd couple but had a great deal in common.

'It's not like you to meet like this,' Soames said half complainingly. 'What's wrong with your place or mine?'

'I needed to clear my head. And to get away from my own environment. And I didn't want to be seen at Curzon Street.' Lingfield pulled his coat collar up against a sharpening wind. 'Are you still after this Towler guy?'

'With the number of people who know about him it's a wonder the press haven't started a "find the sergeant" campaign. I've heard you've made an enquiry or two. What's your interest?'

'Personally, none.' Lingfield looked around him. The traffic in the Mall passed in the distance like 'dinky' toys. The trees were stark and stripped and birds puffed themselves out on leafless branches. 'Steiner found him. That was more than you could manage.'

Soames stopped to cover his chagrin. 'I knew he was interested,' he countered mildly. 'He called on me and made a clumsy attempt to pump me. Where is Towler now? And what is Steiner's interest?'

'Towler underwent the Steiner treatment. Towler escaped but it was obvious he had help. He's free again. And, before you ask, Steiner has split. We don't know where he is.'

They continued to walk again. Soames had his head down which made him appear even shorter against the rangy Lingfield. He rammed his hat on tighter as the wind almost snatched it off. He said, 'I'll put in an official request that Steiner must see us. Let's avoid unpleasantness. We could kick him out, but we'd rather have some answers.'

'That's why I'm here,' reminded Lingfield. 'I'm anxious to keep things on a friendly basis. This is becoming a little embarrassing for us. What I've told you is hearsay, but my source is very reliable. I don't like what Steiner's doing, either.'

'How did he find Towler?'

'You'd have to ask him. Steiner always had secret little cabals. He runs a secret organisation within a secret organisation. Steiner trusts nobody.'

'Why do you tolerate him?'

'Nobody is willing to take the responsibility of firing him. He gets results so his methods are not looked at too closely and if they are, and they are found to be unacceptable, he gets a sideways shift because his record is so good. He ruffled feathers in Washington which is why he is here.'

'Did he ever mention anything to you about an assassination squad?'

'Here in London?'

'That is my impression.'

'There was talk of one of the old terrorist groups, long out of favour, who were re-forming to make their impact on the world and to make the other groups realise that they were still in business. It was not taken too seriously. Why?'

'Steiner asked me if I knew of one. The group you're talking about was a splinter group of Black September. We looked into it with little result. But Steiner does not ask idle questions.'

They walked on for a while then, in silent consent, turned round and began to walk back towards Admiralty Arch.

'There's nothing I can do officially about Steiner. It's all too sketchy.'

'Which is why you have passed it on to me. Thanks, Joe.'

'You don't want it?'

'I didn't say that. I'm intrigued by the connection and not a little worried. So should you be.'

'I am. There's something very nasty about this business. Why do you want Towler so badly?'

'I told Steiner. Let him tell you.'

'Did he believe you?'

Soames looked up at the taller man. 'Does he believe anyone? Will you let me know the moment he pitches up?'

When the two men separated, Soames more readily showed

his feelings. He was very disturbed and considered that he must tell Prescott at once that Steiner was behind the kidnapping of the girl. It came as an immense shock. Steiner clearly had some tame Arabs running round for him. He wondered what Towler might have told him. And by now he might well have guessed what had actually happened to the man called Rashid Khayar. Steiner suddenly presented an unexpected new danger; he had become the wild card in the pack.

A shaken James Dawson called on Bluie Prescott after leaving Kate. He had been convinced by Kate's stand for Towler, particularly when she told him about the armed visit of Prescott's men. At first he was furious with her for taking such dangerous action against the Security Service in order to prove a point. But as she stood her ground, sometimes with great emotional strain, he began to see she was right.

He did not like the increasing influence Towler seemed to have on her; he told her the man was not good enough for her. It was the first real quarrel they had had and, in the end, Kate reminded him that he had not married her mother for the same snob-ridden reasons.

It shook Dawson to see his young, pretty daughter, who was so much like her mother, confront him like this. It brought back the past and left a nasty taste in his mouth.

The meeting with Prescott was intermittently stormy. Dawson accused him of lying but could get little from him. Prescott held out because he had meanwhile received Soames' report on his meeting with Lingfield and was now deeply unsettled about Steiner's part. At all costs the Home Secretary must be shielded from the American involvement, particularly now that the odds were that it was Steiner who cut off Kate Parker's toe.

Prescott had never seen Dawson so angry. In an attempt to give something extra he said, 'It is now clear that the man we held was Rashid Khayar but he is a nobody, as I've already told you. The only thing I can think of is that Towler told him he would be released and sent back to his friends. Perhaps that was the last thing he wanted; perhaps they weren't so friendly. So, once out, he went to ground.'

'Don't side-track me, Bluie. Your job is on the line. You

told me you wanted to interview Towler. Interrogate, if you like. You bloody well sent armed men after him, for God's sake. You lied to me.'

'Misled you perhaps, but only to protect you. It's quite common for our men to be armed when after someone as battle-hardened as Towler. The man's an arms and explosive expert. He's been trained to kill with his bare hands. He wouldn't come peacefully. And with respect, Minister, if my job is on the line, then so too is yours.'

There was a deathly silence. Of the two men, Prescott was the more controlled. He was still clinging to lies and knew he had to hold out.

'Are you trying to threaten me, Bluie?'

'No more than you are threatening me, Minister. We did our best for you. Some things went wrong. If you would only leave it to us to straighten out, everything will be resolved. I have to say that your emotional involvement is not helping us; I understand it, but you must let us get on with our work or arrange for our dismissal.'

Somehow that last, almost contrite statement, created more threat than anything else. Dawson saw that he had made an elementary mistake in calling here. He should have summoned Prescott to his own office. He had given way to his own emotions and that could be fatal when making important decisions. It was too late now to take another line. He stood up angrily but his voice was quite steady as he said, 'You had better not let anything happen to Towler. I want to be informed the moment you have him.'

'Would that still apply if his safe passage meant that you would drown, Minister? I do believe that you have not really thought this thing through.' Prescott stared unflinchingly back at his superior and he could see that he was shaken. Prescott inwardly smiled; Dawson had reached his moment of truth.

'Why should he be so dangerous?'

'For the reasons we have given you all along. The only possibilities are that he was involved in the shoot-out, which we believe, or smelled a rat that we don't know about. Apart from anything else he must be getting near to the truth concerning you. It might be his whole object. He's had too much time to think things over and he knows we are after him.

He already knows too much for all our comfort and the question is, just what will he do if he wriggles off the hook? The Home Secretary is not a man to take kindly to persecution and that's the way he will see it. Why did he run away in the first place? With the greatest respect, we don't know what Kate Parker might have told him. If he knows you're her father, it would certainly point Towler in your direction. That could be disastrous, Minister.'

Dawson slowly sat down again. He appeared drained but the crisis he now faced had a calming effect on him. He observed without heat, 'So I am right. You've been lying through your teeth. You do intend to kill him.'

'I would have preferred that you did not know, but you are clearly not satisfied. Wouldn't it be better all round?' Prescott moved his leg painfully, almost the only emotion he had shown throughout.

Dawson sat back and realised how little he knew about this big, beguiling man who faced him as if they were talking about a commodity instead of a human life. Perhaps it was this same brand of ruthlessness that had made him so successful a sportsman in his youth. He sat there like a highly polished Mafia Godfather issuing a contract against one of his family and not being touched by the human tragedy of it. 'What am I supposed to say to that?'

Prescott shrugged almost indifferently. 'I'm still trying to protect you. If Towler blabs then you are finished in politics and you could bring the Government down with you. You must admit that it will make an enormous scandal. You hold one of the highest ministerial posts in the realm. It would be the main topic of the media for weeks: the double standards of HM Ministers. It would be unanswerable. People won't be interested in the saving of an illegitimate daughter. You'll be branded a dirty old man. One rule for you and another for the rest of us. The whole manner of the thing won't stand up in Parliament or anywhere else. Do you want all this to happen to you and your friends, Minister? Do you really want a change of Government?'

Dawson felt the blood draining from him but he remained dignified for it seemed that demeanour was all he had left. 'You're not just thinking of me, Bluie. You're thinking of your own skin. And you are thinking of the Service you represent and see yourself as its next Director. I can understand that you don't want it disgraced; we've had too much of that over the years. But you are far from solving what went wrong at Hereford. I'm personally not convinced that Towler is the answer. Nor am I satisfied that I've heard the whole story from you.'

Prescott sighed softly. 'It's true that I did this favour for you because you assured me I would take Sir Malcolm's place when he retired. But in protecting my own ambitions I am most certainly protecting you at the same time. I'm bound to safe-guard us both, and the Service. But none of that alters a thing. Have I your agreement, Minister?'

'My authority for you to kill Towler? You've been trying to do that all along. You're putting it to me now only because I've found you out.'

'I am convinced we would be destroying a traitor.'

'I'm not going to do your job for you, Bluie. You make the decisions here. And you are answerable for them. You are not going to point the finger at me if things go wrong. And it would seem that there is a habit of that happening on this affair.'

'But you don't say no?'

'I've made it clear that I don't want Towler killed.'

Prescott made a gesture of resignation. 'Then the result of that will be on your own head, Minister. I do implore you to think over all the probabilities and what they may lead to. Do let me know if you change your mind.'

Dawson smiled bitterly. He stood up again but remained by the chair. 'We both know that you will still go ahead with what you think is best. And I cannot deny you the right of responsibility. Good day, Bluie.'

When the door had closed, and after Dawson had been escorted down, Prescott told his secretary to hold all calls. He remained seated and gazed at the door with faint cynicism. 'Pontius Pilate,' he murmured to himself. 'But God help us if we make any more cock-ups.'

They changed back into civilian clothes at Jacko's house and put the uniforms in the trunk of the car. Jacko went upstairs just as the telephone rang. He called out, 'Answer that, Sam.'

Towler picked up the phone, gave the number, and a man with an American accent he would never forget asked if he could speak to Mrs Whelan.

Towler gripped the phone as if he would crush it. He had the first attack of nerves in days. He could only stare at the instrument waving before his eyes. He got a grip on himself and put the receiver back on the cradle. Even as he did it he knew he was making a mistake. He was virtually telling Steiner that he had recognised his voice. And Steiner now knew where he was.

20

'You sure it was him?'

'You don't forget a voice like that in the situation I was in. It was Steiner. I'd better ring Lew Quinn. Steiner must have got the number through him one way or another.'

There was no reply from Quinn's room and Towler said, 'I'd better get round there. Steiner might have found him.'

Jacko said drily, 'How do you know that Steiner didn't call from the box on the corner? He might be waiting out there for you.'

'I can't just hang around. I'll ring for a cab.'

'I'll come with you. Let's strap up.' Jacko produced two shoulder holsters and they each had a Browning pistol.

By the time they left the house it was already dusk and visibility bad. Jacko kept the hall light off so that it would be difficult for anybody to see them leaving. Once they were in the Ferrari the whole neighbourhood knew it would take an expert to catch them.

They reached the small Bayswater hotel fifty minutes later, having taken a circuitous route. Jacko waited in the foyer having pushed his pistol up the sleeve of his topcoat, ready to drop it into his waiting hand. He had not met Steiner but Towler's description had been graphic.

Towler took the stairs rather than be trapped in an elevator and knocked on Quinn's third floor door.

'Who is it?' It was Cathy's voice.

'It's Sam, Cathy.'

Cathy opened the door and as Towler went in he knew that there was someone standing behind the door. He swung round, going for his gun, only to see Lew standing there with a raised baseball bat.

Quinn lowered the bat. 'Steiner has that effect on people, doesn't he? We feel like prisoners here, Sam. How much longer do you think?'

Towler gave Cathy a quick hug and a peck on the cheek. 'Not much longer. I rang you but there was no reply so here I am. Steiner's running wild. A bit like myself. He's found out where I'm staying and I wondered if he'd got at you. It's a relief that he hasn't.'

Cathy was pouring drinks at the dressing-table when Quinn replied.

'We were tired of being cooped up so we went for a short walk. I've been thinking about what we left behind in the apartment. He might have picked up impressions of telephone messages from my note pad. It hit me too late to do anything about it. It's all I can come up with.'

'I promised you a story and I'm going to give you what I know so far. I can't take the chance of it dying with me.'

'Don't talk like that, Sam.' Cathy handed out the drinks.

'It's the way it is. I want your word that you won't release anything until I say so or until I'm dead.'

'You've got it.' Quinn reached for pen and paper.

On the way back to Jacko's place Towler said, 'Steiner probably picked up some impressions of numbers from a note pad Lew left behind. He'll have dug up the addresses and rung round to narrow the possibilities. I've brought him to your own doorstep, Jacko. I'm sorry.'

Jacko was grinning. 'That's his bloody bad luck.'

When Towler looked again he saw that Jacko was actually enjoying himself; he had always been reckless, and Towler wondered how he ever got into the SAS. In a brief, unwelcome flash of insight, he saw a similarity between Steiner and Jacko, but Jacko had a great sense of humour, had openly joined the bad guys and was strong on loyalty. Perhaps, too, was Steiner.

'How long do you think we have before he's on the spot?' Jacko asked.

'Let's assume that he's already there. He has his own private army. They seem to do what he wants, but I don't think idealism has anything to do with it, although he may use it on them; it's money, pure and simple. I wonder if Uncle Sam knows exactly what he's financing?'

'We'd better come in from opposite ends of the street,' said Jacko.

'Not yet. How many villains can you dig up in a hurry?'

Jacko glanced across. 'Are you crazy? You can't start a war.'

'How many?'

Jacko pulled in. 'Three, maybe four. It depends what you want them for.'

'I want them to lift somebody. Put the frighteners on for a little persuasion.'

'In that case I'd be lucky to get two at short notice. They will want paying and they don't come cheap.'

'It's not safe to get at my own money until this is over. I can dish out IOUs in case I don't come through. I owe Lew Quinn a fair whack but I've got a bit put by.'

'Are you asking me to be banker? You've got a bloody nerve.'

'You're right, Jacko. It's too much to ask. You've already done more than enough.' Towler suddenly heard Jacko laughing quietly to himself.

'You should have been a con man,' said Jacko. 'You'd have pulled off some good scams. I'll do it for old times' sake, O.K.? And because at present I'm loaded. You've saved my bacon more than once. But I want it back. Now, what's on your mind?'

'I'll tell you as we go. Don't go back to your place now. Can we put up in your warehouse for the night?'

'Sure. When do you want the men?'

'Now. Tell them to be at the corner of Half Moon and Curzon Street by 1800 hours.'

Jacko, who had raised the phone, now put it down. 'Don't be stupid. I might not be able to get hold of them. Don't push your luck because Steiner rattled you.'

'It doesn't need rehearsing. All they have to do is to snatch the guy I finger. Can you get a couple of walkie-talkies?'

'You're giving me not much more than an hour. Forget it. Tomorrow or not at all. You're ignoring all basic training.'

Towler gazed at Jacko in surprise. 'Of all the reckless bastards to say a thing like that. What's happened to you?'

'Be careful, Sam, or you'll be on your own, mate. There are

other men to think of and I might need them again. Get the bit out of your teeth.'

Towler seemed to come out of a daze. 'O.K., I'm out of order. It's not Steiner, though. I know exactly where I stand with him. Can you get things started now? They'll need to be fitted out.'

Jacko was already dialling. 'Harry? Look . . .'

When Jacko had finished the first call, Towler said quickly, 'Who's Harry?'

'Harry Bateman. Just the bloke for this sort of job. Good organiser. Does outside contract work for anyone willing to pay well. Reliable. Been away for a few days. I was surprised to find him in.'

Towler said drily, 'If he's who I think he is, I know where he's been. You'd better make sure he's been pulled off the last job.'

Jacko turned in his seat to gaze at Towler. 'You can't be serious?'

'I was attacked outside my own pad. The only name that cropped up was Harry, the boss man. O.K., he might be some other Harry, but in this business the odds shorten.'

'If he works for me he won't work for anyone else at the same time. I'll get back to him to check.'

Towler nodded. 'Sure. If it is the same bloke and Five have dropped him for their own men, I just hope he does a better job organising for me than he did *against* me. I don't rate him.'

Soames saw there was something wrong with Prescott the moment he stepped into his office. The big man was broody and unusually quiet until he snapped, 'I want a progress report.'

He did not have to say about what, or on which of the many issues with which Soames was at present involved. There was only one case at the moment which threatened them. Towler. He hated that name, yet was developing a sneaking admiration for it.

'We've been checking on his friends. Not an easy task. The SAS closed ranks and it was like opening a tin can with a tooth pick. The Regiment looks after its own and nobody knew anything until I did the only thing they seem to understand and pulled rank on them.'

Soames raised a computer disc. 'It's all on there. I can get a print-out if you want. But I know most of it by heart. Most of his friends are still serving soldiers. There are one or two who are now civilians. We've concentrated on those as the most likely to give Towler shelter, or to find it for him. He was close to three in particular while they served. A Sergeant McLean who is now a successful business man.' Soames smiled smugly. 'Making a fortune out of security. Another is a William Jackson. Answers to Jacko or Glasshouse Willie. Kicked out of the SAS and served time in the glasshouse. Had an exemplary record until he went wild after a brother died. Nobody knew why. The Met say he's up to his eyeballs in crime. The third man, James Willis, is somewhere in South America, probably helping the CIA.'

'Have you contacted any of them?' Prescott was already bored with the breakdown of the search.

'We've interviewed McLean who deigned to give us five minutes of his valuable time. Says he hasn't seen Towler since he left the mob. The answer was too pat but he really doesn't give a damn whether we believe him or not. We have him under surveillance. We've only just managed to locate Jackson who covered his tracks quite well. We've mounted a surveillance on a café he owns in Soho, a clothes warehouse in the East End, and his private house in Notting Hill, as from this evening.'

'And the girl?'

'There's been no contact with Towler. We've now put a tap on her phone.'

When Soames eventually dug out the significance of Kate Parker his blood ran cold. No wonder Prescott was edgy; the phone tap was a desperate decision and had not been done with Dawson's consent. They were all sitting on an unexploded bomb. He faced the big man on the other side of the desk and added, 'If Towler contacts any of these people we'll have him.'

The traffic was chaotic on the way through the City, but it thinned considerably as they approached the unfashionable part of the Docklands. Towler was lost in thought as the Ferrari purred like a cheetah through the approaches to the Thames. On the other hand, Jacko, who had finished his calls before joining the rush-hour traffic, was very much alert.

Jacko had exchanged one risky business for another and the need to survive was imbued, aided by the most rigorous of training. Whenever he approached any of his properties he did so with open eyes and suspicion, and, as with Towler, was well versed in picking out the various shades of shadow in darkness.

Beyond the maze through which Jacko now drove, was a long line of high-powered street lamps. By instinct he kept to the lesser-known routes. Here the light was poor, a condition he preferred. He was driving on dimmed lights but suddenly flooded the narrow approach to his warehouse, just one of many jostling buildings on a fairly long stretch, to light up the whole area.

The sudden action instantly brought Towler to full alert as he sensed that Jacko was disturbed. When the accelerator was pressed down and the car shot over the ice he saw something of what Jacko had picked out. The place was staked out.

Jacko touched the brake as he reached the first corner and the Ferrari skidded round. Two cars were parked in this intersection and one set of lights came on at once. Jacko remained on full beam until he hit a smattering of other traffic and was forced to dim.

As they raced on it was clear to Towler that Jacko was familiar with the whole area and kept to the back streets; although they were difficult to negotiate there was far less risk of heavy traffic and he was driving down narrow alleys and little-used streets, as if he had practised the route many times. Towler looked behind to see the waving mist of distant head-lights falling behind.

Jacko took the next turning and the next to find the approaches to the nearest main street. It was still the rush hour and they were heading for the nearest snarl-up. Five minutes later they were reduced to a crawl as Jacko headed for St Paul's. He sat back and curbed his impatience. With the mass of dimmed lights behind them it was impossible to know whether or not they had shaken off their tail.

Both men knew that the Ferrari would stand out but on the other hand, with Jacko's skill, it had put considerable distance between them and the following car. Once down Ludgate Hill and across the Circus, Jacko used the taxi drivers' routes to head for Soho and then down to Trafalgar Square; a long and misleading way round.

'They've linked us, Jacko. All your places will be covered. We'd better get out of town for the night.'

They went sedately across Westminster Bridge and into Lambeth. Towler began to get worried. 'You're not thinking of the cellar?'

'No, too dodgy. Further than that.' He said no more but, before reaching the Brixton Road, turned off into a short street lined with the usual rows of parked cars, turned again and they were now tucked away from the main arterials. He drove on until he found a gap and pulled in. He dowsed the lights and switched off. Towler climbed out and walked back to the nearest corner.

The district was what estate agents call a decaying area. In daylight the Ferrari would stand out like a beacon but the street lights were poor here as if time had left it alone and the world passed by just a few blocks away. As he stood at the corner, Towler's finger was throbbing and he used the top of his coat as a sling to rest his hand. His right hand gripped the Browning which he had removed from its holster and slipped into his topcoat pocket. The sound of traffic on the main roads reached him as a constant, low-pitched hum. The lights hovered above the roof tops in a canopied orange haze.

Little stirred in the street itself. Workers occasionally came home to disappear into indistinct terraced houses and sometimes a car went by. There was a sadness and lack-lustre about the place which, coupled with the bad weather, made an unhappy picture.

After twenty minutes Towler decided there was no point in hanging on. He walked slowly back to the Ferrari and climbed in beside Jacko who said, 'Looks as if we slipped them.'

'You did well to spot them.'

'One of the dozy buggers was taking a drag on a cigarette behind cupped hands. The number of times we've hammered that into recruits. Standards ain't the same, Sam. Not even with gunmen. If that's the best they can do we've nothing to worry about.'

Towler knew it was only talk. Jacko's way of showing relief. He meant quite the opposite and had hung around for that

233

very reason. 'You'll have to ditch the car, Jacko. It's been marked.'

'No problem. Watch me.'

Jacko pulled out and went further into the heartland of the back streets. He turned into a minuscule drive at the end of a short street with main intersections at both ends, and pulled up before a garage. He climbed out, opened the garage, and then drove the Ferrari inside. He pulled down the door from inside and entered the house by a side door with Towler following.

'If this is yours they'll have it listed too, Jacko.'

They went down a small passage and entered a tiny sitting-room. Jacko felt his way across the room, pulled the heavy curtains and asked Towler to switch on the lights by the door. The room was run down and the few pieces of shoddy furniture were a depressing brown.

'It's not mine,' answered Jacko. 'I have an understanding with the guy who owns it. He has a few more like this. Makes a fortune out of them. We'll kip here tonight, and go to war tomorrow.'

'It's better you know that the odds are stacked against us.'

Jacko flung himself into a chair and the springs twanged. 'Tell me when they've ever been in our favour. You've gone soft, Sam.'

'That's better than saying I've lost my nerve.'

Jacko gripped his hands behind his head. 'I heard about that. I've seen no sign of it, mate.'

'I seem to be coping. Maybe the change did the trick.'

'I suppose it was over Taffy?'

'He died in my arms. I should have spotted the danger.'

'You were out there too long. You were so bloody good they wouldn't let you go. I know what it's like to lose someone you care for.'

Towler knew that Jacko was talking about his own brother. He was about to raise it but saw something in Jacko's reflective pose that forbade him. It was difficult to imagine the kind of relationship that could so readily send Jacko off the rails. So far as he knew, Jacko had never discussed it with anybody. Perhaps he had felt responsible for his younger brother, but who could tell? 'I'm looking forward to tomorrow,' Jacko said to the stained ceiling.

As Towler studied him he wondered if Jacko had developed a death wish. He seemed not to be troubled by any danger and it was not just because he could hide his feelings so well. Right at this moment he was not hiding them at all and there was something frightening about his expression.

James Dawson was morose to a degree where he heard little of what his wife Sandra was saying to him. They had a delayed dinner because he had been late back from the Commons. There was nothing new about that but rarely had she seen him so preoccupied that he was completely ignoring her. She waited until they were alone together in the drawing-room then said angrily, 'What the hell's the matter with you? It's that damned girl, isn't it?'

Even the sharpness of her tone did not at first get through to him, but belatedly he gazed across at her and said acidly, 'That damned girl is my daughter. Don't ever speak about her like that again.'

Sandra put down her coffee with unsteady hands. 'Well she's not *my* daughter. And I won't have her intruding in *my* house. What on earth has happened to make you like this? Is she in trouble? It wouldn't surprise me. She must stand on her own feet and you must get rid of that ridiculous cross you carry for her. Damn it, James, it's a quarter of a century ago.'

'I'm sorry.' Dawson looked at his wife with some affection. 'I'm not blind to how it affects you. You're quite right, darling, she is in trouble but it's not of her making and I don't know what to do about it. I was hoping for your help.'

'She's always been your particular problem; how can I possibly help?'

'I want to bring her over here to have a talk with her.'

Sandra bridled. 'She's not entering this house. I'll meet her outside but not here.'

'There's no reason for you to meet her at all. You must have known she was desperate to ask to see you the other day.'

'She was worried about you. You seem to spend your lives worrying about each other. It's just too much to ask of me.'

'It could be a matter of life or death.'

He never used that ultra-quiet tone unless he was deadly serious. His bland expression told her nothing, but his tone said it all. 'Why can't you tell me about it?'

'I will, once it's over. Be patient. I'll give her a call.' Dawson rose and walked towards the door.

Sandra called after him, 'Is she being used against you? Is someone blackmailing you?'

He shook his head. 'Not blackmail. That couldn't possibly work. I may not have advertised Kate's existence but I haven't hidden it either. There are ways other than blackmail. There's nothing for you to worry about. But I must sort it out and I don't want to be seen in public with Kate.'

'You've been seeing a lot of her lately?'

'Yes. Of necessity. I want to get her into my own environment for what I have to say. Anyway she needs a break from where she is; she has an injured foot.'

'I noticed. Is that a mystery, too?'

Dawson hesitated for a long time before saying, 'Her little toe was amputated with bolt-cutters.' And he left Sandra with a look of horror on her usually urbane features.

'Thanks for sending the car. It must be serious.' Kate pecked Dawson on the cheek as she entered the wide hall. She gazed around her; it was the first time she had been allowed into the house.

Dawson had let her in himself and now led her by the arm to his book-lined study. Once inside he locked the heavy door and signalled her to a chair by the huge desk.

As Kate sat down she was full of fear. Sandra must have sanctioned this visit and for that to happen must mean that this meeting was of the most serious nature. When Dawson sat behind the desk, for the first time in her life she viewed him as a Cabinet Minister instead of her father. It was a strange, even terrible feeling because she was so naturally warm-hearted. He appeared so grave that she felt she was about to be lectured rather than talked to. She was being confronted with a whole set of new, uneasy feelings and suddenly wanted to leave, though she continued to sit.

'You're not limping so much,' he said as he watched her across the desk. She was so pretty, her hair darkened to copper in the artificial light. She was so much like the mother she never got to know, and the woman he had loved. Her face, so usually alive, was grim and he knew that she expected something bad. It did not help him to tell her.

'I'm getting used to it. I can put more weight on it now. What is it, Daddy? What have you got to tell me?'

He almost broke down. He could not remember when she had last called him that for they had made their agreement quite early on. He was as near to revoking his decision, so painfully arrived at after hours of agonising, as he would ever get. For a second or two he suffered a mental blockage and almost conceded defeat. Then it was too late and he knew he must plough on.

'Would you like a drink, Kate?'

'I don't need a drink to listen. Do you find you need one to say what you have to say?' Her voice faltered.

'All right. It's not easy for me and I know that it will be worse for you. I've been in touch with our Intelligence people and it would seem that they have been trying to protect me from certain truths. Our relationship is not unknown to them, of course, which is why we managed to get you freed.' He noticed Kate was sitting very upright and was clenching her hands tightly together. Her expression was grim.

'They've been holding back about Towler. They have information about him that they have kept to themselves out of deference to you and me, but which would have saved a lot of grief had they told us at the outset. He's a bad lot, Kate. He was kicked out of the SAS for reasons which even I cannot disclose.'

'How strange.'

It was a voice he did not recognise; cold and disbelieving, and worst of all, distant. She had suspended her relationship to him. 'Why strange?'

'MI5 took him in, this man who was kicked out of the SAS.'

'MI5 never wanted him. And that's the truth. They were forced to take him by the head of our Intelligence Services because he happens to think the SAS can do no wrong. He also used the excuse that if Towler was so bad what better opportunity would there be to monitor him. Of course nobody knew at that time that Towler was knee-deep in treachery with a foreign agency.'

'You're lying.'

Dawson felt sick. 'I expected you to take it badly. But we can't get away from the facts. Don't use that expression again, Kate. Do you think I'm enjoying this? I did what you asked of me. I went for the throat and only succeeded in forcing the hand of the Deputy Director of MI5. It was far from pleasant for me, I tell you. Please try to understand. I know it's not easy but face it. For me.'

Kate was quite pale but she had adopted a dignified pose. 'I suppose that if my exchange was publicly known it would put you in a very difficult position?'

'Naturally. I put myself out on a limb for you. What I did is not allowed. As a government we profoundly disagree with any dealings with terrorists. I ignored that because I love you.'

'I know that, Father. Is what you are now doing because you love me?'

He was listening to an emotionless stranger; a pretty young girl with no outward sign of distress, whom he did not know. It was uncanny. For a dreadful moment he wondered what she was doing there. 'What I'm saying to you now is a separate issue. It has nothing to do with the original concept of the exchange.'

'If I went to a newspaper and told them what had happened to me and why you had acted as you did, what effect would it have?'

'I don't see the point of this line of questioning. I would have to resign, of course. I would have no other course. And because of the seriousness of my breach, and of my position, there is every possibility that I'd pull the Government down with me. It would be very difficult for them to survive.'

'Is that why you are doing this to Sam? Because he's close to knowing what you're up to and what really happened at Hereford? You're willing to sacrifice him so you and the Government can survive?'

Dawson shifted uncomfortably. 'That's wild talk, Kate. That's a dreadful thing to say. Do you think I'd do that to you?'

She was close to tears now. 'Don't worry. I won't betray you. You did save my life after all. Tell everybody concerned that they are quite safe.' It was difficult to hold on but she managed. 'I now know what happened to my mother. You betrayed her in exactly the same way. You put your own career before your love. Your ambition *is* your love. Part of you loved mother and me, and you were genuine in what you did for me. But we have never been able to compete with your career; your need for power. But you've compromised yourself with your own Intelligence Service. They won't let you forget.'

Kate rose a little unsteadily but she wouldn't let herself down now. 'We won't meet again. Thank you for what you've done for me in the past. I'll see myself out.'

'Kate! For God's sake don't be like this. Calm down and think about it. Don't be obsessed by this man.'

As she moved towards the door he said, 'Let me get the car round. I'll call you tomorrow.'

Kate wheeled round eyes blazing behind the build-up of tears. 'I'd rather walk. And don't dare contact me tomorrow or any other time.' She was about to turn towards the door again when she added, 'I almost forgot. I think I am being watched. It's not easy to keep an eye on the apartments without being noticed. I've no doubt your Intelligence people know I am here. And they seem to have disobeyed your instructions not to put a tap on my phone. Or did you change your mind about that too?'

Dawson moved towards her, then stopped, seeing that it would be disastrous if he did. He watched her go, a slight, dignified figure, hurt deeply yet holding her head high. As she closed the door behind her he collapsed on to his chair. He had only felt as wretched as this once before in his life. It was like history repeating itself. There was no way back. He could make all the excuses he could find but Kate had made him face himself as her mother never had and he did not like what he saw. Equally, he knew it would make no difference whatever the pain; and that was considerable.

Outside the house Kate held on until she was inside a cab and on her way back to the apartment. She would move back into her own home; just what did it matter now what happened to her? And then she realised that she must stay put in case Sam tried to contact her. More than ever she realised he needed help. And love. And so did she. She leaned against the side of the cab and the tears gushed out uncontrollably.

21

There was nothing about Harry Bateman to suggest he was a hired killer. He was tall, dark and fit, quite well dressed, with twinkling eyes and a sense of humour. Whatever induced him to choose his deadly occupation was well hidden beneath a general ordinariness. He gave no indication that he knew about, or had ever heard of, Sam Towler. They did not shake hands by natural consent but Bateman was professional enough to hide any sign of recognition. All he did observe, when Jacko introduced them, was that the men he had hired were taken off a recent case against a hard bastard who knew a trick or two. There was no further mention.

Jacko provided two-way radios similar to those used by the police and Towler went over the detail of the plan which was simple and operable provided the time factor was favourable. They broke up after lunch and reassembled mid-afternoon to go over the ground twice more.

At 5pm that evening, Towler positioned himself on the corner of Piccadilly and Half Moon Street. The traffic was heavy and crawling. At various intervals along Half Moon Street were Jacko, Harry Bateman, and two of his men. Towler had a scarf above his chin line and wore a hat. Inside his topcoat was a radio transmitter which he had tested several times with Jacko, who had the other one. Fiddling with a frequency had taken a little time but villains were well aware of police frequencies.

Towler stood gazing up Half Moon Street wishing that the light was a little better. But provided he knew the physical aspects of whoever he was looking for, he could detect a person by walk or stance or just general appearance.

It was 5.20 when he picked out Soames, whose gait he would

recognise anywhere. He turned to the wall and spoke into the top of his coat; 'On the east side, coming towards me. Medium height, trilby hat, dark coat with red scarf hanging out.' The red scarf was Soames' way of cocking-a-snook at the enemy.

Jacko, who was half-way up Half Moon Street, immediately scanned the area, picked out Soames, crossed the road towards him and tried to listen to Towler's reaction.

'You're on target. Close in and walk just behind him.'

Jacko quickened his pace until he was directly behind Soames but was sufficiently lost among the many other hurrying commuters.

When they were nearer to Piccadilly, Towler said, 'O.K., finger him.'

Jacko brushed past Soames, knocking him slightly, and turned to apologise before hurrying on. Harry Bateman, who had been keeping an eye on Jacko, crossed over and rapidly caught up with Soames, slowing his pace as he came up behind him. He waited until they were closer to Piccadilly, then almost leaned over Soames' shoulder as he said, 'Excuse me, sir.' Soames turned irritably to see a man whom he did not recognise but, ironically, had indirectly hired.

'Detective-Sergeant Squires, sir.' Bateman held out a warrant card and offered an apologetic smile. 'It is Mr Soames, isn't it, sir?'

'Yes. What do you want? I'm in a hurry.' Soames had slowed but was still moving.

'Could you just hang on a minute, sir. I'm new to SB but was told to get an urgent message to you about a Mr Towler.'

Only now was Soames suspicious. He turned to talk to Bateman who had kept slightly behind him, then swung round to head for Piccadilly. He immediately bumped into another man who made no effort to move aside, and then suddenly realised that he had been blocked off by a third. He was edged against the wall while he was still wondering what best to do. It was no use yelling unless there was a policeman in sight. People had a habit of disappearing when they saw other people in trouble.

Even as the thought crossed Soames' mind, Bateman said in quite a friendly way, 'The message is, sir, that if you shout or scream or cause any problems at all, we're to blow your guts out right here and now.'

Soames quickly saw that all three men had their hands in their pockets and he accepted that the bulges pointing at him were silenced guns. He, more than most people, was only too aware of what one could get away with on the open streets. And particularly in this atrocious weather.

'What do you want?'

'There's a car parked just round the corner of Piccadilly. It has a disabled driver's badge on it. Just get in. We'll be with you all the way. Don't try to run because you'll be topped and tailed. You know the form.'

'You're being rather foolish. There is no way you will get away with this.'

'The story of my life, sir.' Bateman smiled as he motioned Soames forward.

One of the men opened the door of a Ford Granada for Soames to get in just as Towler got in on the opposite side. Bateman sat in front and the driver climbed out for Jacko to take over. Once they were on the move everybody relaxed except Soames who was very aware of the Browning Towler held loosely on his lap.

'Well you've found me,' said Towler. 'I thought I'd make it easy for you.'

'You have some strange friends,' commented Soames. 'All crooks by the look of them.'

'You used some of them to try to top me. They got a conscience about it and are trying to make up.'

Bateman half-turned when he heard that. In his game he never really knew who he was working for, only who hired him.

'We can sort this out quite amicably,' Soames said smoothly. 'Had you made contact before there would have been no problem. Where are we going?'

'It's a mystery tour. I'll give you some words of comfort, though. I don't intend to do to you any more than you would have done to me. That's fair, isn't it?'

It took some time to break out of constant traffic jams, but nobody seemed to be in a hurry. There was no chatter, which did nothing for Soames' nerves which were beginning to strum.

He knew that Towler had nothing to lose whatever he did.

Bateman was dropped off the south side of Westminster Bridge. As he climbed out Towler said, 'We might need you again.' He winked. 'You did a better job on him than you did on me.'

Bateman grinned and held up two fingers; Jacko laughed as he pulled out and headed for Lambeth.

They made sure the street was empty before moving. Jacko climbed out and went round the corner to see if the coast was clear, came back to the corner and gave a signal to Towler.

'Out,' ordered Towler. 'You know better than to try anything. Anyway, you haven't got the speed. Walk just in front of me.'

Soames slipped as he climbed out but Towler caught him by the arm and steadied him. They went round the corner where Jacko had returned to wait outside the door of the house Steiner had used. As they entered Soames showed the first signs of nervousness. Towler helped him down the steps to the cellar.

Jacko closed the door and switched on the lamp and he and Towler forced Soames' chunky figure into the old dentist's chair. Jacko produced some nylon cord to replace the straps he had cut and bound Soames exactly as Towler had been with the chair at the same uncomfortable angle. They then strapped his head back so that his overall view was restricted as Towler remembered so bitterly.

Soames said scathingly, 'You are fools, both of you. You know you can't win, there's too much stacked against you. Whatever you do to me will make no difference.'

'So what have we to lose?' Towler peered over Soames and knew exactly how he was feeling. 'Let's get straight down to it. What happened to Abdul the night I was on duty at the Mayfair Suite?'

'You don't have to treat me like this for that. There's no mystery; we let him go. Quite simply we had nothing on him except your suspicions.'

Towler looked across to the door where Jacko was standing, then turned back to Soames. 'You must know Steiner, or at least, of him. He strapped me to this chair in exactly the same way as we've done to you, and asked me the same question as

I've just asked you. Except, he called Abdul, Rashid Khayar, who seemed to be quite important to him. Of course, I didn't know what had happened but I told him what I knew, just as you're going to when you've stopped lying.'

Towler stood back a little, as Steiner had done, so that Soames could barely see him. He saw Soames trying to move his head and was aware of the agonies he was beginning to suffer. 'Did you know Rashid Khayar was one of Steiner's men? If Steiner was merely out to finish him, he'd have settled for you or anyone else taking him out of circulation. But he must have been someone very special to Steiner for him to take the steps he did to retrieve him. But he didn't get him, did he? You fitted me up to provide a ringer. And I was supposed to be wiped out with the rest of them so that it looked like an outside job and it would be believed that Khayar was dead. It took Steiner no time at all to discover the corpse wasn't his man. So what happened to Khayar?'

'I told you. We let him go and he went to earth. We couldn't find him again. We had to find a ringer to save the girl.'

'You mean the Home Secretary's daughter?' Towler moved forward so that Soames could see just a little more of him. 'Behind this chair are some bolt-cutters. Steiner used them to snap off Kate Parker's toe and he used them on me to sever the tip of my finger.' Towler held his bandaged finger in front of Soames' eyes. 'That was after he threw a bucket of water over me. Then he left me to die in the freezing cold. I almost did. You, in your condition, won't last half the night. Now that's exactly what I'm going to do to you if I don't get the right answer.'

Towler stepped out of Soames' sight and said, 'Pass those bolt-cutters, matey.'

The cutters were missing but Jacko scraped his gun against the door and said, 'Mind, they're heavy.'

Towler watched Soames try to struggle just as he had done and the movement was minimal. He moved forward and took Soames' left hand and said, 'You dirty bugger, you've wet yourself.' He separated the little finger and added, 'I haven't Steiner's expertise so I'll have to cut off the whole finger.' Knowing that Soames could not see what he was doing he touched the finger with the cold metal of his Browning.

244

Soames jerked as much as his bonds allowed and he yelled out, 'For God's sake, Sam, I have a heart condition. All right. I'll tell you.' Sweat was pouring down him in spite of the icy cold. 'What can it matter now?' He closed his eyes as he tried to collect himself. In a slightly wavering voice he said, 'Rashid Khayar is dead. He committed suicide during the night you were on. It must have been after you left. Jerry Cutter fell asleep on duty and I found the mess myself. He hacked his wrists with a plastic knife which he had sharpened against the wall. I sent Cutter home and put out a call for the "clean-up squad".'

'That ties in with what Tony Wilshaw told me, but he didn't know who the corpse was.'

'You bastard. You knew already.'

'Not what actually happened. What made him do it? Was he afraid to go back to Steiner?'

'Only Steiner can answer that. My guess is that when I told him he was being released and would be returned to his friends, he put the wrong interpretation on it and thought we were sending him back to his *Arab* friends. He must have been terrified at the prospect, and, with hindsight, would guess that they were out searching for him. If he were tied in with one of the groups and was actually working for Steiner, they would make him die very slowly if they caught him. He might even have been playing a dangerous treble game and was working for a high-ranking Arab interest.' Soames was like a wet rag, his breathing heavy as he lay in the restricted position.

'Well, that at least accounts for why you wanted the ringer dead and buried. Did you know Steiner was involved?'

'His name has only cropped up recently. I don't know to what extent he's involved or what his connection is with Khayar. He must have wanted him very badly indeed. It was a great shock to us; we all thought we were dealing with Arabs, not with Steiner's private circus.'

'Where does Steiner hang out?'

'He's missing. Nobody knows where he is.'

'Is he in the Company? Or is he working for one of the Arab factions?'

'DIA, rather than CIA. He's a law unto himself.'

'He must have a contact at the Embassy.'

245

'He usually works with a crony called Tony Bellardi. Neither is in touch with the Embassy at the moment.'

'There must be someone at the Embassy who knows what he's up to.'

'Joe Lingfield is the only one who has some sort of interest in him. Nobody else wants to know. But Lingfield really has no idea what Steiner is up to. I doubt that even Bellardi knows much.'

'Do I assume that Lingfield wants to know?'

'Joe Lingfield is a Company man through and through. He cares about its reputation, so people like Steiner worry him. But Steiner is over Lingfield so it's not much help.'

Towler stepped back again and edged over to Jacko. 'We can't release him.'

Soames suddenly started to yell at the top of his voice. Towler moved back and rammed a handkerchief into Soames' mouth. 'The place is empty. I knew that when Steiner walked off without gagging me. We've got to leave you here, Soames. At least you haven't got a bucket of water over you and you still have all your fingers. We'll be back as soon as we can.'

Jacko unlocked the door but did not open it. Soames began to moan. Towler called out, 'You'd better pray that your boys don't knock us off. And if they don't, then that neither do Steiner's. If we get through that lot we'll be back to release you. Meanwhile nobody but us knows where you are.' Towler looked back at the ungainly figure. 'You set it in operation. You've only yourself to blame.'

'I can stop it but not from here.'

'Balls, Soames. We've made the position worse. Besides you've got the Home Secretary to protect. You'd better wish us luck.'

Soames was silent as the light went out and the door was locked.

They stopped at the nearest pay phone and Towler called Kate. From the moment she answered he knew she was distressed. 'It's all right, Kate. I know the line is bugged but they'll have a team on you by now so meeting would be dicey. Just follow my lead and speak freely. Your talk with Aunt Jane seems to have done no good. We both hoped she could use a little influence. Never mind, you did your best.'

Thus guided Kate hesitated at first then answered, 'I have seen her again. She's less helpful than before, unfortunately.'

Towler picked up the fearful inflection. 'Don't worry. We have one of them. He has been helpful. If they don't pull off the bulldogs as from now, I'm afraid he will die of exposure. He was quite informative.' Then, 'That was for the tape recorder and not for you, Kate. You bearing up?'

'I'm worried sick for you, Sam.'

Towler guardedly let his emotions loose. 'I love you like that, Kate.' It was a declaration he never expected to make and it felt good. 'I don't intend to lose you so hang on there. We'll be lucky if Aunt Jane approves, though.'

'I won't be seeing her again so it really doesn't matter.'

'I'd better go now, Kate. They'll be working overtime to trace the call. I've got good friends helping me, so don't worry. I'll be back.' He hung up and went back to Jacko in the Ford Granada. It was Jacko's stand-in for the Ferrari.

One of the very few friends Matt Steiner had, and perhaps the only person he really trusted, was Tony Bellardi. They had always worked as a team with Bellardi usually doing most of the leg work, although recently that had been reversed and, to Bellardi's annoyance, Steiner had become not only more active but more secretive.

Bellardi was sitting in a car at an angle to Jacko's terraced house, his knees high in front of him as he tried to get his long legs into a more comfortable position. Bellardi had been moved to London with Steiner some ten months ago. They operated like a football manager and coach: where one was transferred, the other usually followed. It was Bellardi who had set up much of the anti-Khomeini network, amongst others, to form a buffer against anti-American groups in Britain. He and Steiner had collected some valuable information stemming from the Middle East, and that was how they had first recruited Rashid Khayar.

The problem now was that, even with the grossly inflated sums they were paying many of the young Arabs, it was difficult to find reliable men to stake out Jacko's house in this sort of weather. A car was cold and windscreens iced up. To run the engine was to invite curiosity. Accordingly they had been provided with portable heaters at their feet but this did little other than knock the edge off the cold. What it did do, though, was to keep the windows misted up instead of iced. It meant wiping over the insides every now and again, and that in itself could be a give-away.

Also, Bellardi had the feeling this caper was getting out of hand. But it had been started and had to be completed so as to leave no untidy ends. He was thinking thus while still watching Jacko's house when the nearside door opened and Steiner climbed in beside him.

'Anything?' asked Steiner.

'Two plumbers called about an hour ago. They're still in there. Their van is that blue one further along. Our guy the other end of the street checked the name on the van.'

'How did they get in if nobody is in the house?'

'We don't know for sure that there was nobody in. There may have been someone there all the time.'

'You think the plumbers belong to Five?'

'Sure as hell. They knew how to get in without ringing the bell. They had A1(A) written all over them. They weren't plumbers' tools they were carrying in their bags, either.'

'So we're all waiting like dummies for the same guy?'

'Looks like it. I think Five have also got themselves a room almost opposite the house. Is this all worth while?'

Steiner showed no expression in the poor light of the car interior. 'I thought Towler would croak overnight. And if he didn't he would be more likely to cough up anything he forgot to tell me the first time. I was then going to leave him with all fingers pointing to Five. He must have had help. I slipped up on that.'

'Is that the only thing you slipped up on?' No one else could get away with such a question to Steiner.

'What's on your mind?' There was a hint of warning in Steiner's tone.

'We seem to be in a peculiar position. Is it really necessary to kill Towler? I mean, why not let Five do it for us?'

'I want to get there first. Towler can finger me. He will have worked out that I snatched the girl and took her toe off.'

'*You did what?*' Bellardi sounded alarmed. 'You didn't tell me that.'

'I had to do something quick. It took a long time and a lot of patience to get Khayar infiltrated. Our President is due over next month and Khayar reckoned he was going to be targeted. And so was Prince Charles. It wasn't bullshit. This bunch of hot-headed has-beens are bouncing back into business just to let everyone know they are still a force to be reckoned with. Even the PLO disowned them. But Khayar had a lot of tentacles; information just seemed to come to him, perhaps because he could slide into any background and not be noticed. And then Five stuck their goddam nose in just as Khayar was on the point of getting some red-hot information; he was so scared that he wouldn't stay anywhere for long and I was meeting him almost nightly so that he could make a quick break if he had to.'

Steiner was sitting quite still. 'I think Khayar was also reporting back to a group of sheikhs who are trying to bring some sense into the Middle East. He probably thought I didn't know. I guess they paid him even more than we did.'

Bellardi did not want to be side-tracked. He came back to the point that worried him most. 'But it was the daughter of a British Cabinet Minister whose toe you cut off. For chrissake, there will be hell to pay if that little gem crosses the pond.'

'Stop worrying. Dawson has compromised himself. Nobody will learn from him and he would have warned the girl. Anyway, she's on file. I should think that almost every foreign agency has her on record. She used to carry a red card, Tony. She's a red activist.'

'How far back are you going?'

'It doesn't matter. Fanatics never change. She must have been a goddammed embarrassment to her father while he was climbing the ladder.'

'It hasn't stopped him helping her. You're going back too far, Matt. She was only a kid at the time.' He added bitingly, 'You're beginning to sound like McCarthy. This whole caper has got out of hand. When was the last time we had to get rid of a guy? I don't like it, Matt. And I don't like crossing Five in their own backyard.'

'Those assholes started the whole goddam shebang. They

should have kept out of it. Anyway, it would have been over long since. Most guys with the odds stacked against them hightail it as far away as they can get. This guy Towler keeps coming back at us. I guess I should have looked into his background more thoroughly. It sticks in my throat, but he's a tough bastard and now he seems to have a pal. Even so, he can't win in the end, and the sooner he's dead the happier we'll all be.'

'That's great. How much longer do we have to wait here?'

Steiner turned to look at his friend. 'You've not gone chicken, have you, Tony?'

'Certainly I have. I don't like what's happening and we're getting in deeper.'

'I'm not spending time and money to penetrate a bunch of highly toxic maggots to see it destroyed by some interfering limeys. Don't put me in a position where I have to add you to the list.'

The cold Bellardi felt then had no connection with the weather. He had known Steiner to go wild, to step outside the realms of acceptability while the hypocrites in Washington wrung their hands in protest as they derived smug satisfaction from the results, but this was different. Steiner was so obsessed that he was no longer thinking and far less was he caring. 'Is that a real threat?'

'To you?' Steiner grinned in the darkness. 'Come on, we've been together a long time. But I can't afford for this to go wrong. And neither can you. You're not thinking straight. The issue is quite clear. Besides we'll have Dawson over a barrel once this is cleared up. It'll be useful to have a stooge in the British Government. And we'll be able to nail that big, plum-in-mouth bastard Prescott as well; he must have sanctioned what's gone on. He must have agreed to the plumbers going in. We'll have a useful couple of puppets, won't we?'

Bellardi put his hand on the door-catch. Steiner had gone mad. He had done crazy things often enough but he had reached a point where he did not know the difference between knowing them to be crazy and accepting them as normal practice. Somewhere along the line, and quite recently, he had crossed the borderline between the reality of knowing he was doing something wrong and hoping to get away with it, and of thinking everything he did was right. Bellardi had been scared before at some of Steiner's antics but had always gone along with them. But he had never before been as scared as this.

Bellardi very carefully took his hand away from the door-catch. Steiner was unstable. And at the root of it Bellardi guessed that Steiner did not like losing. It had to be put right at any cost. In an attempt to get matters on a more normal level he asked, 'Did you ever find out what actually happened to Khayar?'

Steiner replied quite rationally. 'Soames said he let him go. Five had no further use for him. I don't buy it. Khayar would have come straight to us if he was released. They killed him.'

'Who? Five?'

'They probably went too far in torturing him for information. So they provided a ringer. As if I wouldn't know. Look out, there's a car coming.'

Headlights swept blindingly from the other end of the street and slowed right down as they neared Jacko's house, when they suddenly dipped. Both Steiner and Bellardi leaned forward to wipe the mist from the windscreen as they heard the screech of brakes. Just as they thought the car was about to stop, it surged forward again, plum in the middle of the street. It was a Ferrari. Steiner and Bellardi craned sideways to see who it was just as their nearside door was wrenched open and Steiner felt a hard gun barrel boring painfully into his ear.

22

Steiner's reaction was fast for such a solidly built man. He snatched at the gun, but was not quick enough. Towler withdrew it just that fraction sooner and then whipped it round Steiner's face and pulled him from the car. As Steiner came out, head low, Towler hit him hard again at the back of the ear. He levelled his gun at Bellardi who was slower to move.

'You know how to do it,' Towler said quietly. 'Just toss it out of the car.' He made space for Bellardi to throw his gun out. 'Now push off,' said Towler. He slammed the door aware that Bellardi had seen the silencer. He then fired a shot into the front tyre so that it would deflate slowly. Bellardi pulled out and disappeared in a cloud of exhaust fumes which lay heavily on the cold air.

At the far end of the street, well behind Bellardi, there was a tremendous squeal of brakes as the Ferrari spun on its axis and raced back towards the spot where Towler stood over Steiner. The rear door was already swinging open as it drew level with Towler who whipped out Steiner's gun and then heaved him into the back with Jacko's help. He scooped up Bellardi's gun, threw it over the nearest railings before climbing in beside the crumpled Steiner as Jacko raced back to the driver's seat. There was a wild skid as Jacko drew out. In the rear, Towler made sure the hard-headed Steiner was really out, and then started the awkward job of tying his wrists and ankles.

By the time Jacko was half-way up the street, the two plumbers were racing towards their van, a radio transmitter waving in the hands of one of them, and across the street, four men burst from a house and ran for two separate cars while one of them radioed instructions to another team elsewhere.

Car doors opened and slammed shut and in spite of the freezing cold, windows in the nearby houses crashed open and shouts of protest at the noise echoed down the street. Someone called out for the police and others telephoned for them. Car engines spluttered to uncertain life and two cars pulled out with blazing headlights and the plumbers' blue van was close behind.

By the time the Ferrari had turned the first corner in a wild skid, another car, engine already running, pulled out behind it. Both cars veered round Bellardi, who, realising that his front tyre had been blown, was trying to swing in to get out of the way.

Behind the Ferrari, at irregular intervals, were three cars and the van. On the narrower side streets the Ferrari held little advantage. The smaller, more street-wise saloon cars coped better with the conditions.

Jacko took another turning, glanced into his mirror, saw several sets of lights behind him, checked his position, and then briefly flashed full beams. Another set of lights came on ahead of him from a stationary car with its engine running. As the Ferrari flashed by, the car pulled out with its lights now dowsed. It stopped in the middle of the street and Harry Bateman jumped out to run back behind a row of parked cars.

The first of the chasing cars hit the abandoned car head-on and carried it along for some distance with the terrible, agonising shriek of ruptured metal. The front of the pursuing car caved in and the driver crashed half-way through the windscreen to remain suspended there as the second car, with slightly more warning, swerved but could not avoid the snared, steaming heap of torn vinyl and crushed metal swinging round in front of it.

The driver managed to avoid the full tragedy of the first car by hitting the tangled, still moving heap at its fringe. The car was swung round in a wild, terrifying arc to crash sideways into the line of parked cars, punctured its fuel tank and burst into flame. The driver and his passenger were able to fling themselves free just before the car blew up and the whole neighbourhood awoke from deep sleep to scream murder out of shock and anger.

Those in the last car, followed by the van, saw what was

happening but had little time to avoid the spreading fireball. With tremendous presence of mind the driver swung to the other side of the street, scraped along the row of stationary cars with a dreadful tearing of metal and torn off wing mirrors, bounced between them and the flaming mass on the other side, got through and continued on with its own side mirrors ripped off and huge dents in its bodywork.

The van was the most unscathed as it benefited from the car in front, and literally bulldozed a gap just wide enough to take it, and by the skill of a driver who had no time to think but had good reflexes.

The succession of crashes happened at speed and, although knocking out two of the opposition vehicles, had not given Jacko as much extra distance as he would have liked. Nor could he head for the main streets, for the whole area would soon be swamped by police. He edged obliquely away from the scene to keep to the lesser streets in order to give the police more room.

The wail of sirens was already penetrating the night air, and, at one point, Jacko saw the reflection of a blue flasher before it changed direction, away from them. He took another turn quickly, knowing that those in the car and the van behind them would be no more anxious to run into the police than he and Towler. By now he was driving by a villain's instinct to escape and he let that instinct dictate the route.

Everything had happened so quickly, and Jacko's driving was so erratic, that Towler had to suspend tying up Steiner until the car followed a more stable course. When he'd finished he bawled out, 'Are you sure you've got a bloody licence?'

Jacko grinned; he was enjoying himself. He left concern about the dead and injured to Towler who had seen it all happen through the rear window. He now concentrated on keeping out of the way of the police, which was more important, at the moment, than shaking off the remaining tail. He took a very long route to Lambeth and touched main streets only when he had to cross them.

Towler pushed Steiner to the floor and placed his feet on top of him. He peered back through the window but could see no following lights until just before they took a corner. 'We might still have them,' he called out.

'Can you stop them?'

'Is there a small square around here? One you can quickly loop back to where you started?'

Jacko thought for a while. 'Sure. About half a mile away. What about matey?'

Towler moved Steiner with his feet. 'He should cause no trouble. Give me good warning.'

A short time later Jacko took a corner and immediately braked. 'Now.'

Towler jumped out, closed the door, backed into a doorway and crouched with Browning ready.

The car had closed the gap more than he had first believed. The hit team had chosen its drivers well. The light was very poor but he recognised the car as soon as it came into view; one door was almost hanging off. He could barely detect two passengers. Towler waited until it had just passed him before he fired two careful shots low down. In the darkness it was impossible to take proper aim, and he hated silencers: they threw a gun off balance. It was almost impossible to tell whether or not he had scored. That tyres exploded on receiving a shot was fallacy; they lost air slowly depending on the size of the hole. As the car neared the next corner he thought he saw it sway.

Where was the van? It should have been close to the car. What worried him now was the possibility of being caught between the two and the longer he waited the bigger was the chance of that happening.

The world suddenly went dead. Nothing stirred nor was there any kind of sound. The cutting wind had dropped and the snow was visible only in feeble pools at the foot of the widely spaced lamp posts. The car had disappeared, there was no sign of the van, and what had happened to Jacko? It verged on the uncanny after the hyper-action.

He heard voices. They were muted before a man started to curse loudly and he wondered if the car driver had discovered the flat and found it to be the final straw. Someone was trying to placate the angry man and then quite suddenly there were running footsteps coming his way. The Ferrari must have been lurking, for there was a sudden roar from its engine and there it was at the corner and Towler raced towards it aware of being chased.

Jacko leaned across to open the door and Towler hurled himself in the back, curling flat on the seat. 'Keep your head down.'

Towler had barely finished the warning when the window above his head shattered and he was covered in splinters of glass. Jacko swore, pulled away as fast as he could and swung the wheel to double back on the route. Shots ripped into the car. The rear window shattered and the windscreen spider-webbed around a small dark hole slightly to Jacko's left.

'Jesus Christ! That went straight through the car. The bastards just missed me.' Jacko fought with the wheel and a long, sickening skid, and yelled out again, 'Get ready. I'll come back at them.' As he spoke more shots thudded lower down into the Ferrari and Towler lay partially on top of Steiner.

Towler bawled at the top of his voice, 'They're trying for the tyres. Take the next bloody turning, you stupid bastard. I can't steady a shot from here.'

Jacko saw the sense of it and swung round the next corner, then another which he took on two wheels. The firing stopped and the near-panic subsided into a wild, sometimes reckless drive.

'Who's going to pay for the damage?' yelled a furious Jacko, who was sorting out the route again.

'Your insurance.'

'With cannon holes all over it? You're crazy.' At the moment, Jacko was more concerned about the state of the car than the danger to themselves. When common sense returned he said, 'Where's the van?'

Towler was suffering the same doubts. Where was the van? He heaved himself back on to the seat as Steiner groaned. 'He's coming round.'

Steiner had moved and was lying awkwardly. Towler reached down to adjust his position and felt blood. Steiner had been hit. The American started to speak unintelligibly, his voice slurred as if he had been drinking; Towler did not like the sound of it. He peered back through the cracked window. The second shot had smashed a wider opening because the glass had already been weakened by the first. A gale seemed to be blowing through the many cracks. Towler could see no lights behind them and believed that the immediate danger had receded. He knelt on the seat to feel glass segments pricking into his knees, and groped for Steiner. His exploring hands became increasingly tacky.

'Untie me, you dumb bastard. I've been hit at least twice.' There was nothing wrong with that delivery although the voice was weak and Steiner was obviously in pain.

Towler raised his head and said to Jacko, 'Did you hear that?'

'Don't untie him until he's croaked.'

Steiner said nothing to that; he would have been surprised had they taken any other view. After a few seconds he said, 'Who was firing?'

'Not your lot,' Towler responded. 'That was good shooting.'

'Then why was I hit instead of you bastards? Just drop me off at the nearest hospital.' The amount of blood suggested that the pain in his voice was genuine, but Steiner had his pride and he would admit nothing to a man he should have killed.

There was nothing Towler could do. There was insufficient light and Steiner was too heavily clad to enable him to pinpoint his wounds. It was impossible to judge whether he needed a tourniquet or where to apply one. All he knew was that Steiner had been hit somewhere on the body.

'I need a doctor,' Steiner rasped.

'So did I when you left me to freeze to death. So did Kate Parker when you hacked off her toe. Don't worry, we'll take you somewhere where you'll feel at home.'

Jacko was within a five-minute drive of the cellar but he was not satisfied he had shaken the tail and was still puzzled about the blue van. Twenty minutes later he pulled up directly outside the derelict house. It was about 1.30am, the place was completely deserted and the extreme weather was freezing everything hard and dangerously before a new day began.

Towler untied Steiner's ankles and, with Jacko's help, half-carried him across the pavement and into the empty hall. It was increasingly clear that the American was badly wounded but he was still dangerous so they issued the customary warning, although he was far too experienced not to know when the odds were against him. They threatened to throw him down the cellar steps if he did not help them get him down; they unlocked the door and heaved him in.

257

Towler lit the lamp while Jacko went back to move the car. Towler re-bound Steiner's ankles, and dragged him to a corner. There was no sound from the trussed Soames and when the lamp had settled Towler went over to have a look at him.

Soames' pulse was barely detectable and there was an almost imperceptible, spasmodic tremor running through him like a mild electric current. Soames did not look too good, and Towler judged that he needed treatment; he must have been telling the truth when he claimed he had a heart condition.

Towler waited until Jacko was back before doing anything to help either of them. They dealt with Soames first and released him from the chair, but not before tying his hands behind his back and binding his ankles. Steiner then took Soames' place in the chair. It was then that Steiner put up his fight, and he was a powerful and determined man. But his wounds had weakened him and he was up against two experts. They finally got him tied down.

Towler stood by his side so Steiner could get a reasonably clear view of him. 'I haven't time for your subtle little tortures, Steiner. The sooner I get the truth from you, then the sooner we send for medical help. As far as we can make out you've been shot once in your guts and seem to have a flesh wound in your thigh. Nothing frantic, given treatment, but until that happens you're slowly bleeding to death. It's up to you.'

Steiner said, 'It makes no odds what you do to me, you and your buddy are dead, Towler. There's no way out for you. If we don't get you, Five will.'

'That's what Soames said. Neither of you will be around to know the final answer, though. I'm not asking a lot. All you have to do is to spill what's left of your guts and let me know your position in this business. The sooner you talk, the sooner you get out of here.'

Still Steiner said nothing so Towler added, 'Stop trying to show how tough you are. We all know you're granite, particularly in the head. Are you afraid that Soames might hear? He's beyond it.'

Steiner's eyes moved painfully and Towler found no satisfaction in knowing what he was suffering. 'O.K.,' said Towler when it was again clear that Steiner would not speak. He turned to Jacko. 'Ring up the United States Embassy on your

258

car phone and ask for the Duty Officer. Tell him you want to be put through to Joe Lingfield. It concerns the life and death of Matt Steiner. Tell him we know where he is, that he's been wounded by MI5 men, and that a head of department of MI5 is at present keeping him company and that both will croak if he doesn't pull his finger out. Give him instructions on how to get here.'

'There is no need for that,' said Steiner in an agitated voice. 'There's no big deal here. What do you want to know?'

Steiner could only relate his side of the affair, but with what Towler had already found out, the final penny dropped. MI5 had snatched one of Steiner's men at a crucial moment. Rashid Khayar was no ordinary agent and things were getting hot so far as Steiner was concerned, and he wanted his man back at once without revealing his own involvement. He had made his move in typical fashion and would have succeeded if Khayar had not panicked. Khayar's nerve had probably broken down because of the increasing importance of the information he was collecting, and the immense danger that went with it. That he had been under surveillance by anyone had come as an immense shock and had vastly weakened the remaining tatters of his confidence. From then on Five were guilty of a series of moves to cover themselves and had succeeded only in creating blunders. Steiner himself had made some bad moves but when it came down to it, both he and Soames were guilty of underestimating first Towler's, then Jacko's, ability. Soames had allowed personal dislike and a supercilious contempt to obscure clear sight of what he was up against, and Steiner had considered himself impregnable.

Towler and Jacko left the cellar knowing that, personally, they were no better off. Quite simply they knew too much.

Once in the Ferrari, Towler rang the United States Embassy and relayed an urgent message for Joe Lingfield.

From the corner across the street Tony Bellardi waited until he was sure they had left, then walked back to where his car, now with changed wheel, was waiting. He pulled up directly outside the cellar. Obviously the location was known to him.

23

'Cut the goddamm things. You're fumbling like a middle-aged virgin.'

'How would you like me to leave you here?' Bellardi snapped back, 'I've had a bellyful of your bullshit. I'm not even supposed to know about this place, you've become so damned secretive.' Bellardi had never spoken to Steiner like that before in their long association. His fingers were frozen from working at the wheel change and the cords were difficult to shift.

Bellardi had come to the cellar because he had found out about it by accident. Steiner had uncharacteristically jotted down the address and dropped the slip of paper in his office, which Bellardi had then retrieved for him, after taking mental note of it as he handed it back. He had been trying to get odd tabs on his chief ever since he started to worry more about some of his increasingly wild antics. He had come here one day on his own to check it out. It was reasonable to assume that Steiner would have brought Towler here and that Towler might want sweet revenge.

Steiner was eventually free and he sat on the end of the chair, doubled up in pain, but even then he was not finished with Bellardi. 'You should have plugged Towler while we were in the car.'

'You were nearer, why didn't you?' Bellardi dare not add that once he had seen the Ferrari close to the cellar and realised that Towler and Jacko were inside, he had decided against taking them on. His job was to save the life of his boss, not to lose his own.

'Get me to a doctor. One we know.'

'O.K. But you need a hospital.'

'The doc can fix it with the American Hospital. Just get moving.'

'I'll get you in the car first and come back for Soames.'

'Soames can take his chances. Leave him here.'

'Give it to me in writing or he comes with us.'

Steiner tried to straighten, his face screwed up. 'You're getting brave, Tony, while I'm like this.'

'I should have done it a long time ago. You've gone too far on this one and I'm not carrying the can for you.'

When Steiner was in the car, Bellardi took the keys with him when he returned for Soames. He did not trust Steiner's judgment any more and would not put it past him to drive off in spite of his condition. Getting Soames to the car was difficult and Bellardi wondered if it was already too late.

As Bellardi heaved Soames on to the seat, a dark limousine drifted out of the shadows and pulled up in front of his car. About to go for his gun, he stopped as he saw Joe Lingfield climb out with two companions.

Lingfield said, 'Don't act dumb, Tony. You've gone too far this time.' He walked over to peer inside the car to see Steiner and Soames. 'We'd better get these two to hospital.' He peered into the car again. 'This is your last jaunt, Matt. Washington now knows about it. You're through.'

Steiner shouted a profanity.

It was 7.30 in the morning when Towler and Jacko pulled up outside the town residence of the Right Honourable James Dawson, MP. The light was poor but the milkman had been and the streets were already fairly active. In this small, exclusive cul-de-sac, the only visible sign of human life was the uniformed policeman on the steps of Dawson's Georgian house with its splendid shell hook above the magnificent door.

Jacko had stolen a Jaguar XJ12; the Ferrari was inappropriate for this visit and, in any event, was badly shot up. The two men had stayed the rest of the night in Jacko's borrowed bolthole, and now wore the two uniforms they had used before.

Jacko climbed out and opened the door for Towler, giving the policeman a quick, friendly wink. Towler glanced up at the house as he climbed out, straightened his jacket, and crossed the pavement. He mounted the steps and the policeman moved discreetly with practised politeness.

The policeman touched his helmet; 'Morning, sir. Can I help?'

Towler gave a perfunctory salute. He seemed to be about to reply when Jacko, who had come round on the flank, stuck his Browning in the policeman's back and said, 'Touch the button and I'll shatter your spine.'

The policeman's hand had gone instinctively towards the panic button on his radio which would transmit an alarm straight to security HQ. Towler relieved him of his dilemma by reaching out and carefully detaching the transmitter from the policeman's uniform. He moved to block off view of what was happening from the street. 'Ring the bell.'

'You won't get away with it. The place will be surrounded in no time.'

'Ring it just the same.'

The policeman remained cool but, seeing no immediate solution, rang the bell. The door was opened by a young housekeeper who scarcely had time to absorb what was happening. The policeman was pushed forward with force and took the girl with him as he staggered into the hall. Towler and Jacko entered quickly and closed the door behind them. The girl was about to scream when she caught Jacko's warning expression and froze.

'Lie flat, both of you. Don't make it worse than it is. We don't want to shoot you, O.K.?' Towler kept his voice down. While the policeman and the girl became prostrate, Jacko disappeared into the bowels of the house and Towler remained as guard in the wide hall. Minutes later there was a commotion upstairs and a woman screamed but Towler did not move. A door slammed and then footsteps scuffed on the stairs and Jacko reappeared behind Dawson who was still holding a towel in his hand and was naked to the waist. He was white and flustered, and seeing the policeman and the maid stretched out in the hall made him realise the worst.

'Get down with the others,' ordered Jacko. 'Have a little chat together.'

'You must be mad.' Dawson had difficulty taking in what he saw. Then he faced Towler, saw the bleak expression above the gun that was pointing at him, and slowly lowered himself to his knees in fear and disbelief. 'You don't stand a chance,' he said to impress the other two lying prone. But he joined them just the same.

Jacko disappeared again and came back with string and kitchen scissors. He tied the girl and the policeman and then gagged them both with tea towels. He disappeared once more.

When Jacko returned he was more relaxed and wore a slight grin as he reported, 'His wife is locked in the main bedroom. She's been warned that if she screams or tries to get out, chummy, here, will be shot. All telephone extensions have been disconnected. The study phone has been left.'

Towler gave a nod and Jacko dragged the policeman to a utility room at the rear of the house and roped him to two sets of cupboard handles to restrict his movement. He carried the terrified girl to the breakfast room and tied her to a chair. 'Don't worry, love,' he said as he left her. 'It's all a big game.' He winked as he closed the door.

Dawson was allowed to walk unaided to his study with Towler and Jacko just behind him. They made him sit in front of the desk where they could see his every movement. He was shivering, wearing only pyjama trousers. Jacko left once more and returned with a bath towel which Dawson wrapped round him.

In his own study and away from the others Dawson was slightly more at ease. 'You're fools,' he said. 'The police officer reports by radio at intervals. Once a call is missed the alarm goes up. My personal bodyguard is due on duty quite soon and when he can't get in the same thing will happen. Whatever you do to me you won't be able to get out. You've trapped yourselves.'

'My name is Towler. Does that explain anything?'

'I thought it might be. I can't help you.'

Towler sat on the edge of the desk dangling the Browning. 'We haven't a lot of time so let's get straight down to it. You're in deep, deep trouble, Minister.'

'I think you'll find that it is the other way round.'

'O.K. Will you accept that we have nothing to lose? Whether we croak you, maim you, what's the odds? There have already been several attempts on our lives. Sanctioned by you. Nothing worse can happen to us.'

'That is a lie. I've sanctioned no such thing.' The edge of confidence had left Dawson's voice. Towler was right; they had absolutely nothing to lose whatever they did to him and the fact was sinking in.

'The people you control sanctioned it. The responsibility is therefore yours. You are already responsible for several deaths. Two up at Hereford and probably a few after the pile-up last night. I wonder what view the Prime Minister will take after listening to your little capers to protect yourself?'

Dawson just sat there, the towel pulled close to his body, occasionally shivering; the central heating was not yet up to full blast. He was thinking that the best thing that could happen was for these two men to be shot while leaving the premises which they would have to try some time.

'I'll get to the point,' said Towler coldly. 'The one decent thing you did was to try to save your daughter, Kate. You've since negated that by putting her on the scrap-heap as you did with her mother. But maybe there are some things that even you don't know about. What happened to Rashid Khayar? The guy who was supposed to be exchanged for Kate?'

'I understand someone, probably you, let him go before the exchange took place.'

'Is that what your loyal subordinates told you?'

Dawson could not miss the note of scorn. 'I believe that was what happened, yes.'

'Khayar topped himself. Suicide. Soames so badly handled the news that he was to be exchanged, that Khayar thought he was being handed over to a fanatical section of an already extremist terrorist group who, he believed, must have caught up with him. Suicide was the least painful way to go.'

Dawson was ashen. 'This can't be true.'

'Ring the Deputy Director, Prescott. Nail him with it. Soames executed it but Prescott knew what was going on. It was Soames' idea to have a ringer but one who must die to make it appear Khayar had been killed. It had to look like an outside job so one or two others had to go at the same time, including me. It was a cock-up and has been ever since. Your bunch of patriots haven't been protecting you, Minister,

264

they've been protecting themselves. And, of course, the Service. We mustn't forget that.'

Dawson was sitting with eyes dulled, wanting to disbelieve Towler yet suspecting he was at last hearing the truth. All he could see ahead was disaster.

'They've pulled the wool over your eyes all along the line and I've been the scapegoat. What makes it worse is the fact that you believed them.' Towler stared hard at the shivering Dawson and could feel no pity. 'And you believed because you wanted to believe. It was your way out. Well, this is ours, Minister.'

'Why on earth should I take your word? You are probably lying through your teeth.'

Towler grimaced. 'You'd know all abut that. Khayar was Steiner's man. Steiner, as you must know, is the head of DIA in London. It was he who cut off Kate's toe in order to get his man back. He also came nearer to getting me than Soames' raggle-taggle army did.' He held up his bandaged finger. 'He has a passion for bolt-cutters. He's a nutter, but he's tough and has guts. He should be in the hands of the CIA by now as we told them where to find him. He was wounded by Soames' men after a street shoot-out. He's difficult, but he'll confirm every bloody word I've told you if only to get back at Prescott and Soames who destroyed an agent it took him a long time and a lot of planning to plant.' Towler added slowly, 'I feel I must also tell you that Soames is not too well, but the chances are that the CIA will have picked him up with Steiner.'

Dawson gripped his jaw as if he suddenly had toothache. The towel dropped from one shoulder exposing pale, flaccid flesh which was slightly freckled. He appeared incongruous, so scantily clad, but there was nothing humorous about the tragic expression and the deep staring eyes that seemed to have withdrawn in a matter of seconds.

He shook his head very slowly as if the movement hurt him. 'It makes no difference now. If what you say is true there is still nothing I can do. You can shoot me but that would be better for me than the final indignity of bringing down the Government with me. If I die, you die.'

'We take your point. We're dead the moment we stick our heads out of the door. You are willing to sacrifice us for the sake of a cover-up as you have been all along. We might just as well shoot you.'

Dawson shrugged; he was shattered. 'I can't survive after this anyway. If I can't explain what happened I can at least save my colleagues some embarrassment.'

'No you can't, Dawson.' Towler abruptly brought Dawson to the same level. 'I have given this story to a journalist. The moment we are killed the story will be published. The whole shebang will come tumbling down.'

Dawson covered his shoulder again. 'No newspaper would dare publish it. A "D" notice would go out immediately.'

'I'm talking about the American press. You control them too? And their television networks?'

Dawson rose shakily. 'If you've already given the story to an American journalist he'll publish anyway. If he can. What is your point?'

Dawson, convinced now that he was close to dying, was showing more dignity. He gazed over to where Jacko was standing at the side of the huge windows. 'We can all squeeze out from under but it will cost you,' Towler said.

Before Dawson could answer Jacko observed:

'They're beginning to arrive. The D11 Blue Berets have a marksman on the opposite roof. A van has just parked down the street; they're unloading some gear. Probably the Anti-Terrorist Squad, C13.' He turned to give a brief smile to Towler. 'Similar stuff to that we used in Ulster. I'd better draw the curtains, make it more difficult for the guys with binoculars and it'll muffle our voices a bit.' He pulled the heavy drapes as Towler switched on the lights.

'We haven't got much time, Dawson, so listen carefully. My journalist friend will want paying for not publishing. It's the story of a lifetime and I'll have the devil's own job to dissuade him. I have to convince him that if he publishes then we are dead. But I don't see why he should be out of pocket.'

Dawson moved towards the desk but Towler stopped him. Dawson said, 'So we've arrived at blackmail.'

Towler gripped Dawson by the throat and shook him until Jacko jumped forward to intervene. Dawson fell back on to the chair gasping for breath.

'Take it easy, Sam. I'm supposed to be the mad one.'

Towler tried to calm down. 'It was too much to take from a bastard who would let us die to save his own lousy skin.'

Dawson rubbed his throat and the words came out hoarsely, 'How much will he need?'

'Two hundred thousand. Pounds. Petty cash to you. And then there's Jacko here. He's had a lot of expenses and has had his Ferrari shot up by Soames' bunch. How much do you reckon, Jacko?'

'The car can be fixed. It will cost, though.' He pondered the point. 'Ninety-five grand including expenses. A give-away.'

Dawson looked up wearily as if it was all a game of which he was tiring. 'And what is your asking price, Towler?'

'I wouldn't touch anything from you, Dawson. But I want compensation for loss of office from Curzon Street.'

Dawson was still rubbing his throat. He gazed at Towler for a long time, bewildered and totally uncertain. 'There is no way this will hold together. The money is no problem. That could all be paid into Swiss or Austrian banks. But I would only have your word. And that is not enough.'

'If we broke our word we'd be back to square one. You think we want to be on the run for the rest of our lives? It will be an uneasy alliance but neither you nor we would want to break it. And the passing of time would make it impossible to resurrect. Ultimately the very idea would become a joke. It would keep you and your Government where you want to be. All we want is out, and fair compensation. All you want is things to be as they were before anyone ever heard of Rashid Khayar. Steiner is totally discredited with his own people and will be *persona non grata* here. Prescott can cover up as he sees fit. If I were you I'd sack him but I suppose he's holding one over you.'

It was clear that Dawson could not see it working, yet the alternative was more horrifying. 'What about Kate? She might well feel the urge to get back to me. Perhaps I can talk to her again.'

'She won't let you near her. Don't worry about her. She's your best guarantee that I'll keep my mouth shut. You will never harm her, and I'll be part of her.'

Dawson wondered how many more shocks he could absorb this winter's morning, but this he could not accept. 'She'd

267

never live with you, Towler. If the rest of your premise is as shakily founded, you have nothing to offer.'

Towler moved to the telephone. He dialled Kate's number and when she answered he said, 'Just listen, Kate. I'm with your father. We're trying to hack out a deal. There is a sticking point. He doesn't believe that you and I have a future together. Do you think we might have?'

'You've taken your time raising it. I think we can work something out. But I'd like a formal proposal, Sam.'

Towler said, 'Will you tell your father that?' He held the phone out but Dawson waved it away and rose like a defeated man. Towler spoke into the telephone again. 'Thanks, Kate, I think he accepts it. I'll be back soon.' He put down the phone.

Dawson could still not accept that the mess he had originally created could disappear. 'And just how do we explain all this? You have me at gun point. You've attacked and trussed a policeman and our housekeeper. You locked up my wife. The street is filling with police, and I'm sure your own SAS have been called in. None of it can be explained away. It's all a pipe dream.'

'Sit down again,' instructed Towler. 'It needs nerve and a modicum of acting. You ring Prescott and tell him to have the dogs called off. You tell him to advise only those who need to know that it was his idea to test the security surrounding Her Majesty's Government Ministers following the latest round of IRA threats. But it had to be done secretly and convincingly for it to be of any value at all. You tell him that his idea was a good one because the security has been tested and found to be wanting. Prescott is not going to argue but if he does you can shove Rashid Khayar down his throat.

'Nobody has been hurt. The copper will have his leg pulled by his colleagues and will eventually laugh with them. You explain to the girl and give her a rise and have a good laugh with her too. When Prescott has done his part you escort us to the door. We stand there chatting and shaking hands and you congratulate us and pat us on the back. You'll provide us with a chauffeur-driven car because the one outside is stolen which was all part of the credibility of the exercise. The police can return the car. If it helps you, had this been an exercise we might well have tackled it this way. Now, do we go for it or not? Think of the alternative.'

Dawson took his time. Everything hinged on his thinking it through. He saw an escape route and gave it the closest mental scrutiny. After a while he said, 'You believe we can get away with it?'

Towler said, 'It will be the easiest part of the whole balls-up. As Jacko will tell you, the apparently toughest jobs are often a piece of cake. It will be tomorrow's news, unless you slap on your "D" notice, and the next day it will be forgotten. The SAS never confirm or deny anything. And it will have served to provide a realistic exercise for the Security Service. You'll probably be congratulated.'

Dawson took his time, examining the possible weaknesses, but in the end, what had provoked most of his reactions, his own welfare, prevailed. He picked up the telephone and rang Prescott.

When Dawson had finished, Towler said, 'O.K., we wait. While we do we can sort out the financial arrangements.'

'You must leave your arms here.'

Towler sensed a trap. 'Why?'

'We can't risk a shoot out on the doorstep. If you have no weapons there is no possibility of that happening.'

'You think we're trigger-happy?'

'I think your reflexes might respond to the slightest sign, however innocuous. We cannot take that risk.'

'Reflexes? Are you aware that we haven't fired a single shot at anybody during this whole caper? The furthest we've gone is to blow out some tyres. You think we're reckless? You'd better speak to the bastards who have been trying to get us if you want to know about recklessness. We keep our arms. We don't trust you. If you've set up something with Prescott in some way, we go out firing.'

Half an hour later there had been no return call from Prescott and all three men were uneasy. Their fate, at the moment, lay in the hands of someone whom none of them trusted. Dawson asked if he could change and Jacko went upstairs with him. When they returned some ten minutes later

Dawson was dressed in a heavyweight, charcoal, wool lounge suit.

They all knew that the activity outside would be settling as men took up positions and movements were made for audio surveillance. Yet nobody had tried to communicate. The police had not phoned in to make contact, to discover the demands or whether anyone was hurt.

The strain was beginning to show on all three faces for quite different reasons but with disaster of one kind or another facing each one of them. To break the increasing agony of the silence Dawson said, 'I'll arrange for a small leak to the *Daily Telegraph* to explain away the street scenes and to satisfy the neighbours.'

Yet even as he spoke none of them really believed it was going to happen; the delay was too long.

When the telephone did ring they all started and nobody moved until Towler stood aside for Dawson to lift the receiver. It was Prescott. The stand-down had been arranged. Dawson asked a few pertinent questions but, now that the crucial moment had arrived, Towler saw a secret instruction in every one of them, and Dawson himself was nervy.

'Do you trust him?' asked Towler uneasily.

'In this I have to.'

'We'll keep as close to you as we can. But we'd better not overdo the camaraderie.' Towler added quietly, 'If he's arranged to pick us off as we leave we'll try to take you with us.'

'I understand.'

Nobody seemed to want to move until Towler said, 'We'd better go.'

Towler and Jacko slipped their guns inside their topcoats and moved towards the door with Dawson preceding them. They entered the large empty hall and slowed down as they reached the front door.

'Open it.'

Dawson straightened, gave a quick nervous smile and pulled back the catch. He pulled the door wide open and moved on to the deep top step to switch on his professional smile. Towler and Jacko went with him, scanning the area as they emerged into the cold daylight. A police car was opposite, two policemen with pistols hanging down, standing by it. Towler immediately detected a marksman on the roof opposite, a lone figure caught against the grey light dangling a rifle with a telescopic sight. Further along other men were standing behind cars and the tip of a rifle could be seen above the roof of one of them. The tension in the street spread right along it; nobody really knew what was happening and everyone was highly nervous. Towler gave a nod to an armed policeman opposite the house and the man acknowledged.

The three men stood quietly on the top step, then Dawson shook hands with Towler and Jacko and the words, 'Congratulations, Colonel,' reached those nearest to the house as they were intended to do. The act was not overplayed and Towler and Jacko descended to the waiting car; the XJ12 had already been removed.

This was the worst moment. The two friends were alone and an easy target, yet they had to see out the charade and could not draw the guns they were itching to hold. Even when they were in the rear of the car and the chauffeur took his seat behind the wheel, they did not feel safe. It was all so silent, so unnatural, as staring faces peered at them as the car drew out and reached the end of the street. They had perhaps travelled a hundred yards when the driver called out, 'Where to, gentlemen?' It was the Cockney accent which gave them the first real taste of reassurance, but even then they did not go all the way.

'Drop us round the next corner,' instructed Towler. 'We'll find our own way from there.'

When they were on the street, traffic now at its densest, and a slight flurry of snow swirling round them, Towler said, 'Thanks, Jacko, for everything. There's no way I could have handled it alone.'

'You mean it's all over?' Jacko feigned disappointment. 'Let's have a coffee somewhere. That's if colonels drink with sergeants.'

'No, it's not all over. Dawson has probabaly learned his lesson but we don't know which way Prescott will play it. Watch your back for some time to come. Maybe, after a couple of years we can relax again. I'd disappear for a bit, if I were you.'

They turned into a Forte's and ordered coffee and

271

beefburgers. They stood at the bar, grateful for the hot food.

'What do you intend to do?' asked Jacko, before taking a mouthful.

'I've got to straighten things out with Lew Quinn and Cathy, first. Lew wanted the break but he won't do anything to harm us. He'll have enough to return to the States if that's what he wants to do. I think their marriage has taken a turn for the better. I hope so.'

Towler took a long swig of coffee as if it was an elixir; as it was a drink he had not expected to be able to take, its taste would have been wonderful whatever was in the cup. 'Then I'm going to book some tickets to the French Riviera for Kate and myself, after another loan from you until my money is through.'

'You'll like it there,' said Jacko, munching away. 'The loan's no problem.'

'And then we're going to head in the opposite direction, without booking anything in advance.'

Jacko looked up and stopped chewing, suddenly losing taste for the food. 'You bastard! You really don't think it's over, do you?'

'Not until we see the colour of their money.'